ORIGIN IN DEATH

Titles by J. D. Robb

ORIGIN IN DEATH

J. D. ROBB

G. P. Putnam's Sons

New York

G. P. PUTNAM'S SONS
Publishers Since 1838
Published by the Penguin Group
Penguin Group (USA) Inc., 375 Hudson Street, New York, New York 10014, USA •
Penguin Group (Canada), 10 Alcorn Avenue, Toronto, Ontario M4V 3B2, Canada
(a division of Pearson Penguin Canada Inc.) • Penguin Books Ltd, 80 Strand, London
WC2R 0RL, England • Penguin Ireland, 25 St Stephen's Green, Dublin 2, Ireland
(a division of Penguin Books Ltd) • Penguin Group (Australia), 250 Camberwell Road,
Camberwell, Victoria 3124, Australia (a division of Pearson Australia Group Pty Ltd) •
Penguin Books India Pvt Ltd, 11 Community Centre, Panchsheel Park, New Delhi–110
017, India • Penguin Group (NZ), Cnr Airborne and Rosedale Roads, Albany, Auckland
1310, New Zealand (a division of Pearson New Zealand Ltd) • Penguin Books (South
Africa) (Pty) Ltd, 24 Sturdee Avenue, Rosebank, Johannesburg 2196, South Africa

Penguin Books Ltd, Registered Offices: 80 Strand, London WC2R 0RL, England

ISBN 0-399-15289-X

Printed in the United States of America

This is a work of fiction. Names, characters, places, and incidents either are
the product of the author's imagination or are used fictitiously, and any
resemblance to actual persons, living or dead, businesses, companies,
events, or locales is entirely coincidental.

While the author has made every effort to provide accurate telephone numbers and
Internet addresses at the time of publication, neither the publisher nor the author
assumes any responsibility for errors, or for changes that occur after publication.
Further, the publisher does not have any control over and does not assume any
responsibility for author or third-party websites or their content.

Blood is thicker than water.

—JOHN RAY

There will be time to murder and create.

—T. S. ELIOT

ORIGIN IN DEATH

PROLOGUE

DEATH SMILED AT HER, AND KISSED HER GENTLY ON THE cheek. He had nice eyes. She knew they were blue, but not like the blue in her box of crayons. She was allowed to draw with them for one hour every day. She liked coloring best of all.

She could speak three languages, but she was having trouble with the Cantonese. She could draw the figures, and loved to make the lines and shapes. But it was hard for her to *see* them as words.

She couldn't read very well in any of the languages, and knew the man she and her sisters called Father was concerned.

She forgot things she was supposed to remember, but he never punished her—not like others did when he wasn't there. She thought of them as The Others, who helped the father teach her and care for her. But when he wasn't there, and she made a mistake, they did something that hurt her, and made her body jump.

She wasn't allowed to tell the father.

The father was always nice, just like he was now, when he sat beside her, holding her hand.

It was time for another test. She and her sisters took a lot of tests, and sometimes the man she called Father got wrinkles in his forehead, or a sad look in his eyes when she couldn't do all the steps. In some of the tests he had to stick her with a needle, or hook machines to her head. She didn't like those tests very much, but she pretended she was drawing with her crayons until they were over.

She was happy, but sometimes she wished they could go outside instead of *pretending* to go outside. The hologram programs were fun, and she liked the picnic with the puppy best of all. But whenever she asked if she could have a real puppy, the man she called Father just smiled and said, "Some day."

She had to study a lot. It was important to learn all that could be learned, and to know how to speak and dress and play music, and discuss everything she'd learned or read or seen on-screen during her lessons.

She knew her sisters were smarter, faster, but they never teased her. They were allowed to play together for an hour in the morning and an hour before bed, every day.

That was even better than the picnic with the puppy.

She didn't understand loneliness, or might have known she was lonely.

When Death took her hand, she lay quietly and prepared to do her best.

"This will make you feel sleepy," he told her in his kind voice.

He'd brought the boy today. She liked when he brought the boy, though it made her feel shy. He was older, and had eyes the same color blue as the man she called Father. He never played with her or her sisters, but she always hoped he would.

"Are you comfortable, sweetheart?"

"Yes, Father." She smiled shyly at the boy who stood beside her bed. Sometimes she pretended the little room where she slept was a chamber, like the ones in the castles she sometimes read about or saw on-screen. And she was the princess of the castle, under a spell. The boy would be the prince who came to save her.

But from what, she wasn't sure.

She hardly felt the needle stick. He was so gentle.

There was a screen in the ceiling over her bed, and today the man she called Father had programmed it with famous paintings. Hoping to please him, she began to name them as they slid on, then off.

"*Garden at Giverny 1902,* Claude Monet. *Fleurs et Mains,* Pablo Picasso. *Figure at a Window,* Salvador Da . . . Salvador . . ."

"Dalí," he prompted.

"Dalí. *Olive Trees,* Victor van Gogh."

"Vincent."

"I'm sorry." Her voice began to slur. "Vincent van Gogh. My eyes are tired, Father. My head feels heavy."

"That's all right, sweetheart. You can close your eyes, you can rest."

He took her hand while she drifted off. He held it tenderly in his while she died.

She left the world five years, three months, twelve days, and six hours after she'd come into it.

I WHEN ONE OF THE MOST FAMOUS FACES ON or off planet was beaten to a bloody, splintered pulp, it was news. Even in New York City. When the owner of that famous face punctured several vital organs of the batterer with a fillet knife, it was not only news, it was work.

Getting an interview with the woman who owned the face that had launched a thousand consumer products was a goddamn battle.

Cooling her heels in the plush-to-the-point-of-squishy waiting area of the Wilfred B. Icove Center for Reconstructive and Cosmetic Surgery, Lieutenant Eve Dallas was fully prepared to go to war.

She'd had just about enough.

"If they think they can turn me out a third time, they're ignorant of the greatness of my wrath."

"She was unconscious the first time." Content to lounge in one of the luxurious, overstuffed chairs and sip some complimentary tea, Detective Delia Peabody crossed her legs. "And heading into surgery."

"She wasn't unconscious the second time."

"Recovery and Observation. It's been less than forty-eight, Dallas." Peabody sipped more tea and fantasized what she would have done if she were here for face or body sculpting.

Maybe she'd just start with hair extensions. No pain, some gain, she decided, combing her fingers through her dark, bowl-cut 'do.

"And self-defense looks pretty clear."

"She put eight holes in him."

"Okay, maybe a little excessive, but we both know her lawyer's going to claim self-defense, fear of bodily harm, diminished capacity—all of which any jury's going to buy." Maybe blonde hair extensions, Peabody thought. "Lee-Lee Ten is an icon. Perfection of female beauty, and the guy played a mighty tune on her face."

Broken nose, shattered cheekbone, broken jaw, detached retina. Eve ran through the list in her head. She wasn't looking to hang a homicide on the woman, for God's sake. She'd interviewed the medical tech who'd treated Ten on-scene, and she'd investigated and documented the scene itself.

But if she didn't close this case down today, she was going to be dealing with the drooling hounds of the media yet again.

If it came to that, she'd be tempted to play a tune on Ten's face herself.

"She talks to us today, and we shut this down. Or I'm slapping her bevy of attorneys and reps with obstruction of justice."

"When's Roarke due home?"

With a frown, Eve stopped pacing long enough to look at her partner. "Why?"

"Because you're getting a little edgy . . . edgier than usual. I think you have Roarke-withdrawal." Peabody let out a wistful sigh. "Who could blame you?"

"I'm not having anything-withdrawal." She muttered it, and began pacing again. She had long legs on a long body, and felt a little confined in the overly decorated space. Her hair was shorter than her partner's, a deer-hide brown worn carelessly choppy around a lean face with large brown eyes.

Unlike many of the patients and clients of the Wilfred B. Icove Center, physical beauty wasn't one of her priorities.

Death was.

Maybe she missed her husband, she admitted. It wasn't a crime. In fact, it was probably one of those marriage rules she was still trying to learn after more than a year in the game.

It was rare for Roarke to take a business trip that lasted more than a day or two now, and this one had stretched to a week.

She'd pushed for it, hadn't she? she reminded herself. She was very aware he'd set a lot of his work aside in the past months to help with hers, or just to be there when she needed him.

And when a man owned or had interest in nearly every area of business, art, entertainment, and development in the known universe, he had to keep a lot of balls in the air.

She could handle not being juggled in for a week. She wasn't a moron.

But neither was she sleeping very well.

She started to sit, but the chair was so big, and so *pink*. It gave her an image of being swallowed whole by a big, shiny mouth.

"What's Lee-Lee Ten doing in the kitchen of her three-level penthouse at two in the morning?"

"Late-night snack?"

"AutoChef in her bedroom, another in the living area, one in each guest room, one in her home office, one in her home gym."

Eve wandered to one of the banks of windows. She preferred the dull, rainy day outside to the perky pink of the waiting area. Fall of 2059 had, so far, proved cold and mean.

"Everyone we've managed to interview stated that Ten had dumped Bryhern Speegal."

"They were completely *the* couple over the summer," Peabody put in. "You couldn't watch a celeb report on-screen or pick up a gossip mag without . . . not that I spend all my time on celebrity watch or anything."

"Right. She dumps Speegal last week, according to informed sources. But she's entertaining him in her kitchen at two in the morning. Both of them are wearing robes, and there is evidence of intimate behavior in the bedroom."

"Reconciliation that didn't work?"

"According to the doorman, her security discs, and her domestic droid, Speegal arrived at twenty-three fourteen. He was admitted, and the household droid was dismissed to its quarters—but left on-call."

Wineglasses in the living area, she thought. Shoes—his, hers. Shirt, hers. His was on the wide curve of the stairs leading to the second level. Her bra had been draped over the rail at the top.

It hadn't taken a bloodhound to follow the trail, or to sniff out the activity.

"He comes over, he comes in, they have a couple of drinks downstairs, sex comes into it. No evidence it wasn't consensual. No signs of struggle, and if the guy was going to rape her, he wouldn't bother to drag her up a flight of steps and take off her clothes."

She forgot her image of the chair long enough to sit. "So they go up, slap the mattress. They end up downstairs, bloody in the kitchen. Droid hears a disturbance, comes out, finds her unconscious, him dead, calls for medical and police assistance."

The kitchen had looked like a war zone. Everything white and silver, acres of room, and most of it splashed and splattered with blood. Speegal, the hunk of the year, had been facedown, swimming in it.

Maybe it had reminded her, just a little too horribly, of the way her father had looked. Of course, the room in Dallas hadn't been so shiny, but the blood, the rivers of blood, had been just as thick, just as wet after she'd finished hacking the little knife into him.

"Sometimes there's no other way," Peabody said quietly. "There's no other way to stay alive."

"No." Edgy? Eve thought. More like losing her edge if her partner could see into her head that easily. "Sometimes there's not."

She rose, relieved when the doctor stepped into the room.

She'd done her homework on Wilfred B. Icove, Jr. He'd stepped competently into his father's footsteps, oversaw the myriad arms of the Icove Center. And was known as the sculptor to the stars.

He was reputed to be discreet as a priest, skilled as a magician, and rich as Roarke—or nearly. At forty-four, he was handsome as a vid star with eyes of light, crystalline blue in a face of high, slashing cheekbones, square jaw, carved lips, narrow nose. His hair was full, swept back from his forehead in gilded wings.

He had maybe an inch on Eve's five-ten, and his body looked trim and fit, even elegant in a slate gray suit with pearly chalk stripes. He wore a shirt the color of the stripes, and a silver medallion on a hair-thin chain.

He offered Eve his hand, and an apologetic smile that showed perfect teeth. "I'm so sorry. I know you've been waiting. I'm Dr. Icove. Lee-Lee—Ms. Ten," he corrected, "is under my care."

"Lieutenant Dallas, NYPSD. Detective Peabody. We need to speak with her."

"Yes, I know. I know you've tried to speak with her before, and again, my apologies." His voice and manner were as groomed as the rest of him. "Her attorney's with her now. She's awake and stable. She's a strong woman, Lieutenant, but she's suffered severe trauma, physically and emotionally. I hope you can keep this brief."

"That'd be nice for all of us, wouldn't it?"

He smiled again, just a twinkle of humor, then gestured. "She's on medication," he continued as they walked down a wide corridor accented with art that highlighted the female form and face. "But she's coherent. She wants this interview as much as you do. I'd prefer it wait at least another day, and her attorney . . . Well, as I said, she's a strong woman."

Icove passed the uniform stationed at his patient's door as if he were invisible. "I'd like to attend, monitor her during your interview."

"No problem." Eve nodded to the uniform, stepped inside.

It was luxurious as a suite in a five-star hotel, strewn with enough flowers to fill an acre of Central Park.

The walls were a pale pink, sheened with silver, accented with paintings of goddesses. Wide chairs and glossy tables comprised a sitting area where visitors could gather to chat or pass the time with whatever was on-screen.

Privacy screens on a sea of windows ensured the media copters or commuter trams that buzzed the sky were blinded to the room inside, while the view of the great park filled the windows.

In a bed of petal pink sheets edged with snow-white lace, the famous face looked as if it had encountered a battering ram.

Blackened skin, white bandages, the left eye covered with a protective patch. The lush lips that had sold millions in lip plumper, lip dye, lip ice, were swollen and coated with some sort of pale green cream. The luxurious hair, responsible for the production of bottomless vats of shampoo, conditioner, enhancements, was scraped back, a dull red mop.

The single visible eye, green as an emerald, tracked over to Eve. A sunburst of color surrounded it.

"My client is in severe pain," the lawyer began. "She is under medication and stress. I—"

"Shut up, Charlie." The voice from the bed was hoarse and hissy, but the lawyer thinned his lips and shut up.

"Take a good look," she invited Eve. "The son of a bitch did a number on me. On my face!"

"Ms. Ten—"

"I know you. Don't I know you?" The voice, Eve realized, was hissy and hoarse because Lee-Lee was speaking through clamped teeth. Broken jaw—had to hurt like a mother. "Faces are my business, and yours . . . Roarke. Roarke's cop. Ain't that a kick in the ass."

"Dallas, Lieutenant Eve. Detective Peabody, my partner."

"Bumped hips with him four—no five years ago. Rainy weekend in Rome. Holy God, that man's got stamina." The green eye sparked a moment with bawdy humor. "That bother you?"

"You bump hips with him in the last couple years?"

"Regretfully, no. Just that one memorable weekend in Rome."

"Then no, it doesn't. Why don't we talk about what happened between you and Bryhern Speegal in your apartment night before last?"

"Cocksucking bastard."

"Lee-Lee." This gentle admonishment came from her doctor.

"Sorry, sorry. Will doesn't approve of strong language. He hurt me." She closed her eyes, breathed slowly in and out. "God, he really hurt me. Can I have some water?"

Her lawyer grabbed the silver cup with its silver straw and held it to her lips.

She sucked, breathed, sucked again, then patted his hand. "Sorry, Charlie. Sorry I told you to shut up. Not at my best here."

"You don't have to talk to the police now, Lee-Lee."

"You've got my screen blocked so I can't hear what they're saying about me. I don't need a screen to know what the media monkeys and gossip hyenas are saying about all this. I want to clear it up. I want to have my goddamn say."

Her eye watered, and she blinked furiously to stem a tide of tears. And in doing so earned points of respect from Eve.

"You and Mr. Speegal had a relationship. An intimate relationship."

"We fucked like rabbits all summer."

"Lee-Lee," Charlie began, and she pushed her hand at him. A quick, impatient gesture Eve understood perfectly.

"I told you what happened, Charlie. Do you believe me?"

"Of course I do."

"Then let me tell it to Roarke's cop. I met Bry when I got a part in a vid he was shooting here in New York last May. We were in the sack about twelve hours after the how-do-you-dos. He's—he was," she corrected, "gorgeous. Toss-your-skirt-over-your-head gorgeous. Dumb as a toad, and—as I found out night before last—vicious as a . . . I can't think of anything that vicious."

She sucked on the straw again, took three slow breaths. "We had some laughs, we had great sex, we got a lot of play on the gossip circuit. He started to get a little too full of himself. I want this, you're not doing that, we're going here, where have you been, and so on. I decided to break it off. Which I did, last week. Just let's chill this awhile, it's been fun, but let's not push it. Pissed him off some, I could tell, but he handled it. I thought he handled it. We're not kids, for God's sake, and we weren't starry-eyed."

"Did he make any threats at that time, was he physical in any way?"

"No." She lifted a hand to her face, and though her voice was steady, Eve saw her fingers trembled lightly. "He played it like, 'Oh yeah, I was trying to figure out how to say the same thing—we've about wrung this dry.' He was flying out to New L.A. to do some promos for the vid. So when he called, said he was back in New York, wanted to come up and talk, I said sure."

"He contacted you just before eleven P.M."

"Can't say for sure." Lee-Lee managed a crooked smile. "I'd had dinner out, at The Meadow, with friends. Carly Jo, Presty Bing, Apple Grand."

"We spoke with them," Peabody told her. "They confirm your

dinner engagement, and stated that you left the restaurant about ten that evening."

"Yeah, they were going on to a club, but I wasn't in the mood. Bad call on my part, as it turns out." She touched her face again, then let her hand fall to the bed.

"I went home, started reading this script for a new vid my agent sent me. Bored the shit—sorry, Will—out of me, so when Bry called, I was up for some company. We had some wine, talked the talk, and he made a couple moves. He has some good ones," she said with a hint of a smile. "So we took it upstairs, had ourselves an intense round of sex. After, he says something like, 'Women don't tell me when to chill,' and he'll let me know when he's finished with me. Son of a bitch."

Eve watched Lee-Lee's face. "Pissed you off."

"Big-time. He'd come over there, got me into bed just so he could say that." Color joined the bruising on her cheeks. "And I let him, so I'm as pissed at myself as I am at him. I didn't say anything. I got up, grabbed a robe, went downstairs to settle down. It pays— and it can pay damn well—not to make enemies in this business. So I go in the kitchen, going to smooth out my temper, figure out how to handle this. I'm thinking maybe I'll make an egg-white omelette."

"Excuse me," Eve interrupted. "You get out of bed, you're angry, so you're going to cook eggs?"

"Sure. I like to cook. Helps me think."

"You have no less than ten AutoChefs in your penthouse."

"I like to cook," she said again. "Haven't you seen any of my culinary vids? I really do that stuff, you can ask anybody on production. So I'm in the kitchen, pacing back and forth until I can calm down enough to break some eggs, and he waltzes in, all puffed up."

Lee-Lee looked over at Icove now, and he walked to her bedside, took her hand.

"Thanks, Will. He strutted around, said when he paid for a whore, he told her when to clock out, and this was the same thing. Hadn't he bought me jewelry, gifts?" She managed to shrug a shoulder. "He wasn't going to let me spread it around that I'd tossed him over. He'd do the tossing when he was damn good and ready. I told him to get out, get the hell out. He pushed me, I pushed back. We were yelling at each other, and . . . Jesus, I didn't see it coming. The next thing I know I'm on the floor and my face is screaming. I can taste blood in my mouth. Nobody's ever hit me before."

Her voice trembled now, and thickened. "Nobody ever . . . I don't know how many times he hit me. I think I got up once, tried to run. I don't know, I swear. I tried to crawl, I screamed—tried. He pulled me up. I could hardly see, there was so much blood in my eyes, and so much pain. I thought he was killing me. He shoved me back against the counter—the island counter, and I grabbed it so I didn't fall. If I fell, he'd kill me."

She paused, closed her eyes for a moment. "I don't know if I thought that then, or later, and I don't know if it's true. I think—"

"Lee-Lee, that's enough."

"No, Charlie. I'm going to have my say. I think . . ." she continued. "When I look back now, I think maybe he was done. Maybe he was finished hitting me, maybe he realized he'd hurt me more than he'd meant to. Maybe he just meant to mess up my face some. But at that moment, when my own blood was choking me, and I could hardly see, and my face felt like someone had set it on fire, I was afraid for my life. I swear it. He stepped toward me, and I . . . the knife block was right there. I grabbed one. If I'd been able to see better, I'd have grabbed a bigger one. I swear that, too. I meant to kill him, so he didn't kill me. He laughed. He laughed and he reared back with his arm, like he was going to backhand me."

She'd steadied again, and that emerald eye stayed level on Eve's face. "I ran that knife into him. It slid right into him, and I pulled it out and stabbed him again. I kept doing it until I passed out. I'm not sorry I did it."

And now a tear escaped, ran down her bruised cheek. "I'm not sorry I did it. But I'm sorry I ever let him put his hands on me. He broke my face to pieces. Will."

"You'll be more beautiful than ever," he assured her.

"Maybe." She brushed carefully at the tear. "But I'll never be the same. Have you ever killed someone?" she asked Eve. "Have you ever killed someone and not been sorry?"

"Yes."

"Then you know. You're never the same."

When they were finished, Lawyer Charlie followed them into the hall.

"Lieutenant—"

"Reverse your thrusters, Charlie," Eve said wearily. "We're not charging her. Her statement is consistent with the evidence and other statements we've documented. She was physically assaulted, in fear of her life, and defended herself."

He nodded, and looked slightly disappointed that he wouldn't be required to jump on his expensive white horse and ride to his client's rescue. "I'd like to see the official statement before it's released to the media."

Eve made a sound that might have passed for a laugh as she turned and walked away. "Bet you would."

"You okay?" Peabody asked as they headed for the elevators.

"Don't I look okay?"

"Yeah, you look fine. And speaking of looks, if you were going to go for Dr. Icove's services, what would you pick?"

"I'd pick a good psychiatrist to help me figure out why I'd let somebody carve on my face and/or body."

The security to get down was as stringent as it had been to get up. They were scanned to ensure they'd taken no souvenirs, and most important, any images of patients who were promised absolute confidentiality.

As the scans were completed, Eve watched Icove rush by, then key into what she saw was a private elevator camouflaged in the rosy wall.

"In a hurry," Eve noted. "Somebody must need emergency fat sucking."

"Okay." Peabody exited the scanner. "Back on topic. I mean, if you could change anything about your face, what would it be?"

"Why would I change anything? I'm not looking at it most of the time anyway."

"I'd like more lips."

"Two aren't enough for you?"

"No, jeez, Dallas, I mean plumper, sexier lips." She pursed them as they got on the elevator. "Maybe a thinner nose." Peabody ran her thumb and forefinger down it, measuring. "Do you think my nose is fat?"

"Yes, especially when you're poking it into my business."

"See hers." Peabody tapped a finger on one of the automated posters lining the elevator walls. Perfect faces, perfect bodies, modeled for passengers. "I could get that one. It's chiseled. Yours is chiseled."

"It's a nose. It sits on your face and allows you to get air through two handy holes."

"Yeah, easy for you to say, Chiseled Nose."

"You're right. In fact, I'm starting to agree with you. You need plumper lips." Eve balled a hand into a fist. "Let me help you with that."

Peabody only grinned and watched the posters. "This place is like the palace of physical perfection. I may come back and go for one of their free morphing programs, just to see how I'd look with more lips, or a skinny nose. I think I'm going to talk to Trina about a hair change."

"Why, why, why, does everybody have to change their hair? It covers your scalp, keeps it from getting wet or cold."

"You're just scared that when I talk to Trina she's going to corner you and give you a treatment."

"I am not." She was, too.

It was a surprise to hear her name paged through the elevator's communication system. Frowning, Eve cocked her head.

"This is Dallas."

"Please, Lieutenant, Dr. Icove asks that you come, right away, to the forty-fifth floor. It's an emergency."

"Sure." She glanced at Peabody, shrugged. "Reroute to forty-five," she ordered, and felt the elevator slow, shift, ascend. "Something's up," she commented. "Maybe one of his beauty-at-any-price clients croaked."

"People hardly ever croak from face and body work." Peabody ran a considering finger down her nose again. "Hardly ever."

"We could all admire your skinny nose at your memorial. Damn shame about Peabody, we'd say, and dash the tears from our eyes. But that is one mag nose she's got in the middle of her dead face."

"Cut it out." Peabody hunched her shoulders, folded her arms over her chest. "Besides, you couldn't dash the tears away. You'd cry buckets. You'd be blinded by your copious tears and wouldn't even be able to see my nose."

"Which makes dying for it really stupid." Satisfied she'd won that round, Eve stepped off the elevator.

"Lieutenant Dallas. Detective Peabody." A woman with a— hmmm—chiseled nose and skin the color of good rich caramel rushed forward. Her eyes were black as onyx, and currently pour-ing tears. "Dr. Icove. Dr. Icove. Something terrible."

"Is he hurt?"

"He's dead. He's dead. You need to come, right away. Please, hurry."

"Jesus, we saw him five minutes ago." Peabody fell in beside Eve, moving quickly to keep up with the woman who all but sprinted through a hushed and lofty office area. The glass walls showed the storm still blowing outside, but here, it was warm, with subdued lighting, islands of lush green plants, sinuous sculptures, and ro-mantic paintings—all nudes.

"You want to slow down?" Eve suggested. "Tell us what hap-pened?"

"I can't. I don't know."

How the woman managed to stand much less sprint on whip-thin heels Eve would never understand, but she bolted through a pair of double doors of frosted sea green and into another waiting area.

Icove, pale as death but apparently still breathing, stepped out of an open doorway.

"Glad to see the rumors of your death are exaggerated," Eve be-gan.

"Not me, not . . . My father. Someone's murdered my father."

The woman who'd escorted them burst into fresh and very noisy tears. "Pia, I want you to sit down now." Icove laid a hand on her shaking shoulder. "I need you to sit down and compose yourself. I can't get through this without you."

"Yes. All right. Yes. Oh, Dr. Will."

"Where is he?" Eve demanded.

"In here. At his desk, in here. You can . . ." Icove shook his head, gestured.

The office was spacious yet gave the feeling of intimacy. Warm colors here, cozy chairs. The view of the city came through tall, narrow windows in this room, and was filtered by pale gold screens. Wall niches held art or personal photographs.

Eve saw a chaise in buttery leather, a tray of tea or coffee that looked untouched on a low table.

The desk was genuine wood—good old wood by her estimate, in a masculine, streamlined style. The data and communication equipment on it was small and unobtrusive.

In the desk chair, high-backed and buttery leather like the chaise, Wilfred B. Icove sat.

His hair was a thick, snowy cloud crowning a strong, square face. He wore a dark blue suit, and a white shirt with thin red pencil stripes.

A silver handle protruded from the breast of the jacket, just under a triangle of red that accented the pocket.

The small amount of blood told Eve it had been a very accurate heart shot.

2 "PEABODY."

"I'll go get the field kits, and call it in."

"Who found him?" Eve asked Icove.

"Pia. His assistant." He looked, Eve thought, like a man who'd just taken an airjack in the gut. "She . . . she contacted me immediately, and I rushed up. I . . ."

"Did she touch the body? Did you?"

"I don't know. I mean to say, I don't know if she did. I . . . I did. I wanted to . . . I had to see if there was anything I could do."

"Dr. Icove, I'm going to ask you to sit down over there. I'm very sorry about your father. Right now, I need information. I need to know the last person who was in this room with him. I want to know when he had his last appointment."

"Yes, yes. Pia can look it up on his schedule."

"I don't have to." Pia had conquered the tears, but her voice was rusty from them. "It was Dolores Nocho-Alverez. She had an eleven-thirty. I . . . I brought her in myself."

"How long was she here?"

"I'm not sure. I went to lunch at noon, as always. She needed the eleven-thirty, and Dr. Icove told me to go ahead to lunch, as usual, and he'd show her out himself."

"She'd have to go out through security."

"Yes." Pia got to her feet. "I can find out when she left. I'll check the logs now. Oh, Dr. Will, I'm so sorry."

"I know. I know."

"Do you know this patient, Dr. Icove?"

"No." He rubbed his fingers over his eyes. "I don't. My father didn't take many patients. He's semiretired. He'd consult when a case interested him, and sometimes assist. He remains chairman of the board of this facility, and is active on several others. But he rarely did surgery, not for the last four years."

"Who wanted to hurt him?"

"No one." Icove turned to Eve. His eyes were swimming, and his voice uneven, but he held on. "Absolutely no one. My father was beloved. His patients, through over five decades, loved him, were grateful to him. The medical and scientific communities respected and honored him. He changed people's lives, Lieutenant. He not only saved them, he improved them."

"Sometimes people have unreal expectations. A person comes to him, wants something impossible, doesn't get it, blames him."

"No. We're very careful with whom we take into this facility. And, to be frank, there was little my father would consider unrealistic in expectations. And he proved, time and again, he could do what others considered impossible."

"Personal problems. Your mother?"

"My mother died when I was a boy. During the Urban Wars. He never remarried. He has had relationships, of course. But he's been, by and large, married to his art, his science, his vision."

"Are you an only child?"

He smiled a little. "Yes. My wife and I gave him two grandchildren. We're a very close family. I don't know how I'm going to tell Avril and the kids. Who would do this to him? Who would kill a man who's devoted his life to helping others?"

"That's what I'm going to find out."

Pia came back in, a few strides ahead of Peabody. "We have her going through exit security at twelve-nineteen."

"Are there images?"

"Yes, I've already asked security to send up the discs—I hope that was the right thing," she said to Icove.

"Yes, thank you. If you want to go home for—"

"No," Eve interrupted. "I need both of you to stay. I don't want either of you to make or receive any transmissions or speak with anyone—or each other—for the time being. Detective Peabody is going to set you both up in separate areas."

"Uniforms coming up," Peabody stated. "It's routine," she added. "There are things we need to do, then we'll need to talk to you both, get statements."

"Of course." Icove looked around, like a man lost in the woods. "I don't . . ."

"Why don't you both show me where you'd be most comfortable while we're taking care of your father?"

She glanced back at Eve, got the nod while Eve opened her field kit.

Alone, Eve sealed up, switched on her recorder, and for the first time moved over to examine the body.

"Victim is identified as Wilfred B. Icove, Doctor. Reconstructive and cosmetic surgery." Still, she took out her Identi-pad, checked his prints and his data. "Victim is eighty-two, widowed, one son— Wilfred B. Icove, Jr., also a doctor. There is no sign of trauma other than the death wound, no sign of struggle, no defensive wounds."

She took out tools, gauges. "Time of death, noon. Cause of death, insult to the heart—went right through this really nice suit and shirt with a small instrument."

She measured the handle, took images. "It appears to be a medical scalpel."

Manicured fingernails, she noted. Expensive, yet subtle, wrist unit. Obviously a proponent of his own medical area as he looked more a fit and toned sixty than eighty-plus.

"Run Dolores Nocho-Alverez," she ordered when she heard Peabody come back. "Either she stuck our friendly doctor, or she knows who did."

She stepped back, heard Peabody open a can of Seal-It. "One wound, only takes one when you know what you're doing. She had to get close, had to be steady. Controlled, too. No rage. Real rage doesn't let you just pop a blade in and walk away. Maybe pro. Maybe a hit. Woman's pissed off, she'd mess him up."

"No blood on her with that kind of wound," Peabody pointed out.

"Careful. Well thought out. In at eleven-thirty, out by, what, twelve-oh-five, max. She's through security at twelve-nineteen. It takes that long to get downstairs, through the scanners. Just long enough to make sure he's dead."

"Nocho-Alverez, Dolores, age twenty-nine. Citizen of Barcelona, Spain, with an address in that city, another in Cancún, Mexico. Nice-looking woman—exceptionally nice." Peabody looked up from the screen of her hand unit. "Don't know why she'd need a consult for a face job."

"Gotta get a consult to get close enough to kill him. Check on her passport, Peabody. Let's see where Dolores has been staying in our fair city."

Eve circled the room. "Cups are clean. She doesn't sit and drink . . ." She lifted the top of the silver pot, wrinkled her nose. "Flower petal tea—and who can blame her? I bet she doesn't touch anything she doesn't need to touch, and deals with that when she's done. Sweepers won't find her prints. Sits there." She gestured to one of the visitor chairs facing the desk. "Has to go through the consult, talk. Has to fill thirty minutes until the assistant goes to lunch. How'd she know when the assistant goes to lunch?"

"Could have heard the vic and the admin talk about it," Peabody put in.

"No. She already knew. She's scoped it out, or had inside data. She knew the routine. Admin's at lunch till one, giving the killer plenty of time to do the job, get out of the building, before the body's discovered. Moved in close."

Eve walked around the desk. "Flirting with him, maybe, or giving him some sad tale of having one nostril a millimeter smaller than the other. Look, look at my face, Doctor. Can you help me? And slide that blade right into his aorta. Body's dead before his brain can catch up."

"There's no passport issued in the name of Dolores Nocho-Alverez, Dallas. Or any combination of those names."

"Smelling like pro," Eve murmured. "We'll run her face through

IRCCA when we get back to Central, see if we get lucky. Who'd put out a hit on nice old Dr. Wilfred?"

"Will Jr.?"

"That's where we start."

Icove's office was bigger and bolder than his father's. He went for a sheer glass wall with wide terrace beyond, a silver console rather than a traditional desk. His seating area boasted two long, low sofas, a mood screen, and a fully stocked bar—health bar, Eve noted. No alcohol, at least visible.

There was art here as well, with one portrait dominating. She was a tall, curvy blonde with skin like polished marble and eyes the color of lilacs. She wore a long dress of the same hue that seemed to float around her, and carried a wide-brimmed hat with purple ribbons trailing. She was surrounded by flowers, and the astonishing beauty of her face was luminous with laughter.

"My wife." Icove cleared his throat, gestured with his chin toward the portrait Eve studied. "My father had it done for me as a wedding gift. He was like a father to Avril, too. I don't know how we'll get through this."

"Was she a patient—client?"

"Avril." Icove smiled up at the portrait. "No. Just blessed."

"Big-time. Dr. Icove, do you know this woman?" Eve handed him a hard copy of the image Peabody had printed out from her hand unit.

"No. I don't recognize her. This woman killed my father? Why? For God's sake, why?"

"We don't know that she killed anyone, but we do believe she was, at least, the last person to see him alive. Her information indicates she's a citizen of Spain. Resides in Barcelona. Have you or your father connections to that country?"

"We have clients all over the world, and off planet as well. We don't have formal facilities in Barcelona, but I—and my father—have traveled extensively to consult when the case warrants."

"Dr. Icove, a facility like this, with its various arms and endorsements, its consultations, generates a powerful amount of income."

"Yes."

"Your father was a very wealthy man."

"Without question."

"And you're his only son. His heir, I assume."

There was a beat of silence. Slowly, with great care, Icove lowered himself into a chair. "You think I'd kill my own father, for *money*?"

"It would be helpful if we could eliminate that area of investigation."

"I'm already a very wealthy man myself." He bit off the words as his color rose. "Yes, I'll inherit a great deal more, as will my wife and my children. Other substantial sums will go to various charities, and to the Wilfred B. Icove Foundation. I want to request another investigator on this matter immediately."

"You can," Eve said easily. "You won't get one. And you'll be asked exactly the same questions. If you want your father's murderer brought to justice, Dr. Icove, you'll cooperate."

"I want you to find this woman, this Alverez woman. I want to see her face, to look into her eyes. To know why—"

He broke off, shook his head. "I loved my father. Everything I have, everything I am, began with him. Someone took him from me, from his grandchildren. From the world."

"Does it bother you to be known as Dr. Will rather than your full title?"

"Oh, for God's sake." This time he put his head in his hands. "No. Only the staff call me that. It's convenient, less confusing."

Won't be any confusion anymore, Eve thought. But if Dr. Will had plotted and planned and paid for his father's death, he was wasting his time in the medical field. He'd double his fortune in vids.

"Your field is competitive," Eve began. "Can you think of a reason why someone might want to eliminate some of the competition?"

"I can't." He left his head in his hands. "I can hardly think at all. I want my wife, and my children. But this facility will continue without my father. He built it to last, he built toward the future. He always looked ahead. There was nothing to be gained by his death. Nothing."

There's always something, Eve thought as they headed back to Central. Spite, financial gain, thrills, emotional satisfaction. Murder always offered a reward. Why else would it remain so popular?

"Round us up, Peabody."

"Respected, even revered physician, one of the fathers of reconstructive surgery as we know it in this century, is killed, efficiently and in a controlled manner in his office. An office in a facility that has strong security. Our primary suspect for this crime is a woman who walked into that office, by appointment, and left again in a timely fashion. While reputedly a citizen and resident of Spain, she has no passport on record. The address given on her official documentation does not exist."

"Conclusions?"

"Our primary suspect is a professional, or a talented amateur, who used a false name and information to gain entry to the victim's office. Motive, as yet, murky."

"Murky?"

"Well, yeah. It sounds chillier than unknown, and like we're going to clear the air and see it."

"How'd she get the weapon through security?"

"Well." Peabody looked out the window, through the rain to an animated billboard celebrating vacation packages for sun-washed beaches. "There's always a way around security—but why risk it? Place like that has to have scalpels around. Could've got an assist on the inside, had one planted. Or she might've gotten in at another time, copped one, planted it herself. They've got tight security, yeah, but they've also got privacy issues. So no security cams in patient rooms or in the hallways in patient areas."

"They've got patient areas, waiting areas, gift shop areas, office areas, operating and exam areas. And that's not counting the attached hospital and emergency areas. Place is a fricking maze. You're cool enough to walk in, stab a guy in the heart, and walk out again, you do your recon. She knew the layout. She's been in there before, or done a hell of a lot of sims."

Eve threaded through the sluggish traffic and into the garage at Cop Central. "I want to review the security discs. We'll run our suspect through IRCCA and imaging. Maybe we'll pop a name or an alias. I want full background on the vic, and a financial from the son. Let's eliminate him from the field. Or not. Maybe we'll find unexplained and large sums of money transferred recently."

"He didn't do it, Dallas."

"No." She parked, slid out of the car. "He didn't do it, but we run it anyway. We'll talk to professional associates, lovers, ex-lovers, social acquaintances. Let's get the why of this."

She leaned back against the wall of the elevator as they started up. "People like suing doctors, or bitching about them—especially over elective stuff. Nobody gets out clean. Somewhere along the line, he's botched a job, or had a patient pissed at him. He's lost one, and had the grieving family blaming him. Payback seems the most likely here. Killing the guy with a medical instrument. Symbolism, maybe. Heart wound, same deal."

"Seems to me heavier symbolism would have been to cut up his face, or whatever body part was involved if it was payback on a procedure."

"Wish I didn't agree with you."

Cops and techs and Christ knew who else started piling on when they reached the second level, main. By the time they hit five, Eve had had enough, muscled her way off, and switched to a glide.

"Hold on. I need a boost." Peabody hopped off, arrowed toward a vending area. Thoughtfully, Eve trailed after her.

"Get me a thing."

"A what thing?"

"I don't know, something." Brow knitted, Eve scanned her choices. How come they put so much health crap in a cop shop? Cops didn't want health crap. Nobody knew better that they weren't going to live forever.

"Maybe that cookie thing with the stuff inside."

"Gooey Goo?"

"Why do they give this stuff such stupid names? Makes me embarrassed to eat it. Yeah, the cookie thing."

"Are you still not interacting with Vending?"

Eve kept her hands in her pockets as Peabody plugged in her credits and choices. "I work with a mediator, nobody gets hurt. If I interact with one of these bastards again, someone will be destroyed."

"That's a lot of venom for an inanimate object that dispenses Gooey Gos."

"Oh, they live, Peabody. They live and they think their evil thoughts. Don't believe otherwise."

You have selected two Gooey Goos, the scrumptious crispy treat with the gooey center. Go with the Goo!

"See," Eve said darkly as the machine began to list the ingredients and caloric content.

"Yeah, I wish they'd shut the hell up, too, especially about the calories." She passed one of the bars to Eve. "But it's programmed in, Dallas. They don't live or think."

"They want you to believe that. They talk to each other through their little chips and boards, and are probably plotting to destroy all humankind. One day, it'll be them or us."

"You're creeping me out, sir."

"Just remember, I warned you." Eve bit into the cookie as they turned toward Homicide.

They split the duties, with Peabody veering off to her desk in the bull pen and Eve heading into her office.

She stood in the doorway a moment, studying it as she chewed. There was room for her desk and chair, one unsteady visitor's chair, a filing cabinet. She had a single window that wasn't much bigger than one of the drawers in the filing cabinet.

Personal items? Well, there was her current candy stashed, where it had—to date—gone undetected by the nefarious candy thief who plagued her. There was a yo-yo—which she might play with occasionally while thinking her thoughts. With her door locked.

It was good enough for her. In fact, it suited her fine. What the hell would she do with an office even half the size of either of the doctors Icove? More people could come in and bother her if there was actually room for that. How would she get anything done?

Space, she decided, was another symbol. I'm successful so I have all this room. The Icoves obviously believed in that route. Roarke, too, she admitted. The man loved to have his space, and lots of toys and goodies to fill it up.

He'd come from nothing, and so had she. She supposed they just had different ways of compensating for it. He'd bring gifts back from this business trip. He always managed to find time to buy things, and seemed amused with her discomfort at the constant shower of gifts.

What about Wilfred B. Icove? she wondered. What had he come from? How did he compensate? What were his symbols?

She sat at her desk, turned to her computer, and began the process of learning about the dead.

While she gathered data on her computer, she tagged Feeney, Captain of the Electronic Detectives Division.

He came on-screen, hangdog face, wiry ginger hair. His shirt looked as if he'd slept in it—which was, always, oddly comforting to Eve.

"Need a run through IRCCA," she told him. "Big-deal face and body sculptor went out in his office this morning. Last appointment looks like our winner. Female, late twenties, name and address—which is Barcelona, Spain—"

"*Olé,*" he said dourly, and made her smile.

"Gee, Feeney, I didn't know you spoke Spanish."

"Had that vacation at your place in Mexico, picked up a few things."

"Okay, how do you say 'bull's-eye in the heart with a small-bladed instrument'?"

"*Olé.*"

"Good to know. No passport under the listed name of Nocho-Alverez, Dolores. Addy in sunny Spain is bogus. She got in and out clean through heavy security."

"You smelling pro?"

"I've got a whiff, but no motive on my horizon. Maybe one of your boys can match her through the system, or through imaging."

"Shoot me a picture, see what we can do."

"Appreciate it. Sending now."

She clicked off, sent the ID image, then, crossing fingers that her unit could handle another simultaneous task, fed the security disc from the Center into a slot to review.

Eve hit her AutoChef up for coffee, sipped as she scanned. "There you are," she murmured, and watched the woman currently known as Dolores walk to a security station at the main level. She wore slim pants, a snug jacket, both in flashy red. Mile-high heels in the same shade.

Not afraid to be noticed, are you, Dolores, Eve mused.

Her hair was glossy black, wore long and loosely curled around a face with cut-glass cheekbones, lush lips—also boldly red—and heavy-lidded eyes nearly as dark as her hair.

She passed through security—bag scan, body scan—without a hitch, then strolled at an easy, hip-swaying pace toward the bank of elevators that would take her to Icove's level.

No hesitation, Eve noted, no hurry. No attempt to evade the cameras. No sweat. She was cool as a margarita sipped under a pretty umbrella on a tropical beach.

Eve switched to the elevator disc and watched the woman ascend—serenely. She made no stops, made no moves, until she exited on Icove's floor.

She approached reception, spoke to the person on duty, signed in, then walked a short distance down the corridor to the ladies' room.

Where there were no cameras, Eve thought. Where she either retrieved the weapon where it had been planted for her, or removed it from her bag or person where it had been disguised well enough to beat security.

Planted, most likely, Eve decided. Got somebody on the inside. Maybe the one who wanted him dead.

Nearly three minutes passed, then Dolores stepped out, went directly to the waiting area. She sat, crossed her legs, and flipped through the selection of book and magazine discs on the menu.

Before she could pick one, Pia came through the double doors to lead her back to Icove's office.

Eve watched the doors close, watched the assistant sit at her own desk. She zipped through, while the stamp flashed the passage of time until noon, when the assistant removed a purse from her desk drawer, slipped on a jacket, and left for lunch.

Six minutes later, Dolores came out as casually as she'd gone in. Her face showed no excitement, no satisfaction, no guilt, no fear.

She passed the reception area without a word, descended, crossed to exit security, passed through, and walked out of the building. And into the wind, Eve thought.

If she wasn't a pro, she should be.

No one else went in or out of Icove's office until the assistant returned from lunch.

With a second cup of coffee, she read through the extensive data on Wilfred B. Icove.

G uy was a fricking saint," she said to Peabody. The rain had slowed to an irritating drizzle, gray as fog. "Came from little, did much. His parents were doctors, running clinics in depressed areas and countries. His mother was severely burned attempting to save children from a building under attack. She lived, but was disfigured."

"So he goes into reconstructive surgery," Peabody finished.

"Inspired, one assumes. He ran a portable clinic himself during the Urban Wars. Traveled to Europe to help with their urban strife. Was there when the wife got hit while volunteering. Son was a kid but already on his way to becoming a doctor, and would later on graduate from Harvard Medical at the age of twenty-one."

"Fast track."

"Betcha. Senior worked with his parents, but wasn't with them when his mother was hurt, thereby escaping death or injury. He was also in another part of London working when the wife got hit."

"Either really lucky or really unlucky."

"Yeah. He'd already moved into reconstructive surgery by the time he was widowed, his mother's case pushing him into making it his mission. Mom was, reputedly, a wowzer. I pulled out a file photo, and she looked pretty hot to me. There's also file photos of what she looked like after the explosion, and we could say grim.

They were able to keep her alive, and do considerable work on her, but they weren't able to put her back the way she was."

"Humpty Dumpty."

"What?"

"All the king's horses?" Peabody saw Eve's blank look. "Never mind."

"She self-terminated three years later. Icove dedicates himself to reconstructive, and continuing his parents' good works, volunteers his services during the Urbans. Lost his wife and raised his son, devoted his life to medicine, founded clinics, created foundations, took on what were assumed to be hopeless cases—often waiving his fee—taught, lectured, sponsored, performed miracles and fed the hungry from a bottomless basket of bread and fish."

"You made that last part up, right?"

"Doesn't feel like it. No doctor's going to practice for sixty years, more or less, without dealing with malpractice suits, but his are well below the average, less than you'd expect, especially considering his field of practice."

"I think you have sculpting prejudice, Dallas."

"I'm not prejudiced about it. I just think it's dumbass. Regardless, it's the kind of field that draws suits, and his record for them is dead low. I can't find a single stain on his record, no political ties that might prompt a hit, no history of gambling, whoring, illegals, diddling patients. Nothing."

"Some people are really just good."

"Anybody this good has a halo and wings." She tapped the generated files. "There's something in there. Everybody's got a deep and dark somewhere."

"You wear your cynicism well, sir."

"Interestingly, he was the legal guardian of the girl who grew up to become his daughter-in-law. Her mother, also a doctor, was killed during an uprising in Africa. Her father, an artist, ditched his little family shortly after Avril Hannson Icove was born. And was, subsequently, killed by a jealous husband in Paris."

"Lot of tragedy for one family."

"Isn't it just." She pulled up in front of the Upper West Side townhouse where Dr. Icove, the surviving one, lived with his family. "Makes you think."

"Sometimes tragedy haunts families. It's like a karma thing."

"Do Free-Agers believe in karma?"

"Sure." Peabody stepped out on the curb. "We just call it cosmic balancing." She walked up a short flight of steps to what she assumed was the original door, or a hell of a reproduction. "Some place," she said, running her fingers over the wood as the security system asked their purpose.

"Lieutenant Dallas, Detective Peabody." Eve held her badge up to be scanned. "NYPSD, to speak with Dr. Icove."

One moment, please.

"They've got a weekend place in the Hamptons," Peabody continued. "A villa in Tuscany, a pied-à-terre in London, and a little grass shack on Maui. They'll add two other prime properties to their personal geography with Icove Sr.'s death. Why couldn't McNab be a rich doctor?"

Ian McNab, EDD hotshot, was Peabody's cohab and apparently the love of her young life.

"You could ditch him for one," Eve suggested.

"Nah. Too crazy about his bony butt. Look what he gave me." She dug under her shirt, drew out a four-leaf-clover pendant.

"What for?"

"To celebrate the completion of my physical therapy and complete recovery from being injured in the line. He says it's to keep me from being hurt again."

"Riot gear might work better." She saw Peabody's pout form, and remembered partnership—and friendship—had certain requirements. "It's pretty," she added, taking the little charm in her palm for a closer look. "Nice of him."

"He comes through when it counts." Peabody tucked it back under her shirt. "Makes me feel, I don't know, warm knowing I'm wearing it."

Eve thought of the diamond—big as a baby's fist—she wore under her shirt. It made her feel silly, and awkward, but warm, too, she supposed. At least since she'd gotten used to its weight.

Not its physical weight, she admitted, but the emotional. It took time, at least in her experience, to grow accustomed to carrying love.

The door opened. The woman from the portrait stood framed in the entrance with a shower of gold light behind her. Even eyes swollen from weeping couldn't diminish her outrageous beauty.

 "I'M SORRY TO HAVE KEPT YOU WAITING, AND in the rain." Her voice matched her, a lovely and rich tone, thickened by grief. "I'm Avril Icove. Please come in."

She stepped back into a foyer accented by a chandelier—each teardrop crystal was illuminated with soft gold light. "My husband is upstairs, finally resting. I hate to disturb him."

"We're sorry to intrude at this time," Eve said.

"But . . ." Avril managed a sad smile. "I understand. My children are home. We took them out of school, brought them home. I was upstairs with them. This is so hard for them, so hard for all of us. Ah . . ." She pressed a hand to her heart. "If you'd come up to the second floor. We entertain on the main level, and it doesn't seem appropriate for this."

"No problem."

"The family living areas are on the second floor," she began as she turned to the stairs. "Can you tell me, is it all right to ask? Do you have any more information on the person who killed Wilfred?"

"The investigation is in its early stages, and very active."

Avril glanced over her shoulder as she reached the top of the stairs. "You really do say things like that. I enjoy crime drama," she explained. "The police really do say things like that. Please, make yourselves comfortable."

She gestured them into a living room done in lavenders and forest greens. "Can I get you some tea or coffee? Anything at all."

"No, thanks. If you'd come back with Dr. Icove," Eve told her. "We'd like to speak to both of you."

"All right. This may take a few minutes."

"Nice," Peabody commented when they were alone. "You expect elegant, like the main level, but this is nice and homey." She looked around, taking in the sofas, the sink-into-me chairs, shelves holding family photographs and memorabilia. One wall was dominated by a nearly life-size family portrait. Icove, his wife, and two pretty children smiled out at the room.

Eve stepped up to it, read the signature on the bottom right corner. "Her work."

"Beautiful and talented—I could hate her."

Eve wandered the room, studying, accessing, dissecting. Family-oriented look, she decided, with feminine touches. Actual books rather than disc copies, entertainment screen concealed behind a decorative panel.

And all tidy and ordered, like a stage set.

"She studied art at some fancy school, according to her records." Eve slid her hands into her pockets. "Icove was named her legal guardian through parental stipulation in her mother's will. She was six. After she graduated from college, she married Junior. They lived, primarily, in Paris for the first six months, during which she painted professionally, and had a successful showing."

"Before or after her father's unfortunate demise?"

"After. They came back to New York, to this residence, had two kids—she took professional-mom status after number one. She continues to paint, portraits being her primary interest, but rarely takes commissions, and donates the proceeds to the Icove Foundation, thereby keeping her professional mother status."

"You got a lot of data in a short amount of time."

"Straightforward," Eve said with a shrug. "No criminal on her, not even minor brushes. No previous marriage or cohab, no other children on record."

"If you factor out the dead parents, dead in-laws, it's a pretty perfect life."

Eve glanced around the room again. "Sure looks that way."

When Icove stepped in she was facing the doorway. Otherwise, she wouldn't have heard him. The carpet was thick, and his shoes made no sound over it. He wore loose pants and a pullover rather than his suit. And still managed to look as if he were wearing one, Eve noticed.

Roarke could do that, too, Eve thought. No matter how casually attired, he could radiate authority in a finger snap.

"Lieutenant, Detective. My wife will be here in another moment. She's checking on the children. We deactivated the domestics for the day."

He moved to a floor cabinet, opening it to reveal a mini AutoChef. "Avril said she offered you refreshment but you declined. I'm having coffee, if you'd like to change your minds."

"Coffee'd be good, thanks. Just black."

"Sweet and light for me," Peabody added. "We appreciate you seeing us, Dr. Icove. We know this is difficult."

"Unreal, more like." He programmed the unit. "It was horrible at the Center, there in his office. Seeing him like that, knowing nothing could be done to bring him back. But here, at home . . ."

He shook his head, drew out cups. "It's like a strange, sick dream. I keep thinking my 'link will buzz and it'll be Dad, wondering why we don't all have dinner on Sunday."

"Did you often?" Eve asked. "Have dinner together."

"Yes." He passed the coffee to her, to Peabody. "Once a week, sometimes twice. He might just drop by to see the kids. The woman? Have you found the woman who . . ."

"We're looking. Dr. Icove, records indicate everyone on your father's personal staff at the Center has been with him three years or longer. Is there anyone else, anyone he had cause to dismiss or who left unhappily?"

"No, none that I know of."

"He'd work with other doctors and medical staff on cases."

"Certainly, a surgical team, psychiatrists, family services, and so on."

"Can you think of anyone in that area of his work he may have had issue with, or who may have had issue with him?"

"I can't. He worked with the best because he insisted on doing superior work, and giving his patients the very finest resources."

"Still he had unhappy patients and clients in his practice."

Icove smiled a little, humorlessly. "It's impossible to please everyone, and certainly to please everyone's lawyer. But my father and I, in turn, vet our patients very carefully, in order to weed out those who want more than can be given, or who are psychologically inclined to litigate. Even so, as I told you before, my father was semiretired."

"He was consulting with the woman who called herself Dolores Nocho-Alverez. I need his case notes."

"Yes." He sighed, heavily. "Our lawyers aren't happy, want me to wait until they do some motions and so on. But Avril convinced me it's foolish to think of legalities. I've ordered them turned over to you. I have to ask, Lieutenant, that the contents be considered highly confidential."

"Unless it pertains to the murder, I'm not interested in who had their face retrofitted."

"I'm sorry I was so long." Avril hurried into the room. "The children needed me. Oh, you're having coffee after all. Good." She sat beside her husband, took his hand in hers.

"Mrs. Icove, you spent a lot of time in your father-in-law's company, for many years."

"Yes. He was my guardian, and a father to me." She pressed her lips together. "He was an extraordinary man."

"Can you think of anyone who would want to kill him?"

"How could I? Who would kill a man so devoted to life?"

"Did he seem worried about anything recently? Concerned? Upset?"

Avril shook her head, looked over at her husband. "We had dinner together here two nights ago. He was in great spirits."

"Mrs. Icove, do you recognize this woman?" Eve took the print out from her file bag, offered it.

"She . . ." Avril's hand trembled, had Eve poised on alert. "She killed him? This is the woman who killed Wilfred." Tears swam into her eyes. "She's beautiful, young. She doesn't look like someone who could . . . I'm sorry."

She handed the photo back, wiped at the tears on her cheeks. "I wish I could help. I hope when you find her you ask her why. I hope—"

She stopped again, pressed a hand to her lips, made a visible effort to steady herself. "I hope you ask her why she did this thing. We deserve to know. The world deserves to know."

Wilfred Icove's apartment was on the sixty-fifth floor, three blocks from his son's home and a brisk five from the center he had built.

They were admitted by the building concierge, who identified herself as Donatella.

"I couldn't believe it when I heard it, simply couldn't." She was a toned and polished forty, at Eve's gauge, in a sharp black suit. "Dr. Icove was the best of men, considerate, friendly. I've worked here ten years, the last three as concierge. I've never heard a single bad word said about him."

"Somebody did more than say it. Did he have a lot of visitors?"

The woman hesitated. "It's not gossip, I suppose, under the circumstances. He socialized, yes. His family, naturally, visited here regularly. Individually and in a group. He might have small dinner parties for friends or associates here, though more often, he used his son's home for that. He did enjoy the company of women."

Eve nodded to Peabody, who pulled out the photo.

"How about this one?" Peabody asked, and the concierge took it, studied it carefully.

"No, sorry. This would be the type, if you understand. He enjoyed beauty, and youth. It was his profession, in a way. Beautifying people, helping them keep their youth. I mean to say, he did amazing work with accident victims. Amazing."

"Do you log in guests?" Eve asked her.

"No, I'm sorry. We clear visitors, of course, with a tenant. But we don't require sign-ins. Except for deliveries."

"He get many?"

"No more than his share."

"We could use a copy of the log, for the last sixty days, and the security discs for the last two weeks."

Donatella winced. "I could get them for you more quickly, and with less complication, if you'd make a formal request from building management. I can contact them for you now. It's Management New York."

A dim bell rang in Eve's head. "Who owns the building?"

"Actually, it's owned by Roarke Enterprises, and—"

"Never mind," she said when Peabody snorted softly behind her. "I'll take care of it. Who cleans the place?"

"Dr. Icove didn't keep domestics, droids or humans. He used the building maid service—droid model. Daily. He preferred droid in domestic areas."

"Okay. We'll need to look around. You've been given clearance for that from the next of kin."

"Yes. I'll just leave you to it."

"It's a really nice building," Peabody said when the door closed behind the concierge. "You know, maybe you can get Roarke to make like a chart or something so you'd know before you asked what he owns."

"Yeah, that would work, seeing as he's buying shit up every ten minutes, or selling it at an obscene profit. And no snorting in front of witnesses."

"Sorry."

The space, Eve thought, was what they called open living. Living, dining, recreational areas all in one big room. No doors, except on what she assumed was a bathroom. Above was another open area that would be the master bedroom, guest room, office space. Walls could be formed by drawing panels out from pockets, to add privacy.

The idea made her twitchy.

"Let's go through it, level one then two," she decided. "Check all 'links for transmissions, in or out, last seventy-two hours. Take a look at e-mail, voice mail, any personal notes. We'll let the boys in EDD dig deeper, if necessary."

Space, Eve thought as she got to work, and height. The rich seemed to prize both. She wasn't thrilled to be working on the sixty-fifth floor with a wall of windows the only thing separating her from the crowded sidewalk a very long drop down.

She turned her back on it and took a closet while Peabody took drawers. Eve found three expensive topcoats, several jackets, six scarves—silk or cashmere—three black umbrellas, and four pairs of gloves—two pairs black, one brown, one gray.

The first-floor 'link offered a call from his granddaughter asking for his support in campaigning for a puppy, and a transmission from him to his daughter-in-law, doing just that.

Upstairs, Eve found that what she had assumed to be a sitting room or second guest room behind pebbled glass walls was in actuality the master bedroom closet.

"Jeez." She and Peabody stood, staring at the huge space organized with shelves, cupboards, racks, revolving rods. "It's almost bigger than Roarke's."

"Is that a sexual euphemism?" Peabody cocked her head, and this time it was Eve who snorted. "This guy really liked clothes. I bet there are a hundred suits in here."

"And look how they're all organized. Color, material, accessories. I bet Mira'd have a field day with somebody this compulsive about wardrobe."

In fact, Eve thought, she might consult the psychiatrist and profiler on just that. Know the victim, know the killer, she decided.

She turned, saw that the back of the glass wall was mirrored, with an elegant grooming station fit into it.

"Appearance," she said. "That was a priority with him. Personal, professional. And look at his living space. Nothing out of place. Everything color coordinated."

"It's a beautiful space. Perfect urban living—upper-class urban living."

"Yeah, beauty and perfection, that's our guy." Eve walked back into the bedroom area, opened the drawer on one of the nightstands. She found a disc reader and three book discs, several unused memo cubes. The second nightstand was empty.

"No sex toys," she commented.

"Well, gee," Peabody said, and looked slightly mortified.

"Healthy male, attractive, with another forty on his average life span." She walked into the master bath. It held a large jet tub, a generous shower stall tiled in pristine white with a detached drying tube, and slate gray counters with a little garden of bright red flowers in shiny black pots.

There were two sculptures, each of tall, slender nudes, fair of face.

One entire wall was mirrored. "Guy liked to look at himself, check himself out, make sure everything was thumbs-up." She went through cupboards, drawers. "Upscale enhancements, lotions, potions, standard meds and pricey ones for youth extension. He's concerned with his own appearance. We might even say obsessed."

"*You* might," Peabody commented. "You figure anybody who spends more than five minutes primping's obsessed."

"The word 'primping' says it all. In any case, we'll say he was highly aware of himself—his health and his appearance. And he enjoys having naked women around—artfully. But it's not sexual, or not anymore. No porn vids, no sex toys, no dirty mag discs. Kept it clean."

"Some people set sex on the back burner at a certain period of their life."

"Too bad for them."

Eve wandered out, noted that there was another area devoted to exercise, which flowed into office space. She tried the computer. "Passcoded. Figures. We'll let EDD play with this, and take all the discs back to Central for review.

"Not a thing out of place," she mumbled. "Everything in its slot. Neat, ordered, coordinated, stylish. It's like a holo program."

"Yeah, sort of. Like those ones you play with when you're fantasizing about your dream house." She slanted a glance toward Eve. "Well, I do sometimes. You just happen to live in Dream House."

"You can look at this." Eve stepped to the glass rail. "And you can see how he lived. Up in the morning—early, I'd say. Thirty minutes on his equipment—keep it toned—shower, groom, do a three-sixty in the mirror just to make sure nothing's pudging or sagging, take daily meds, head on down for a healthy breakfast, read the paper or some medical journal crap. Maybe catch the morning reports on-screen, keep that on while you come back up to select today's wardrobe. Dress, primp, check appointment book. Depending on that, maybe do a little paperwork here, or head out to the office. Walk most days, unless the weather's ugly."

"Or pack a bag, a briefcase, cab it to a transpo station," Peabody put in. "He lectured, consulted. Some travel in there."

"Yeah, have a nice meal, see the sights. Take a few appointments here and there, some board meetings, whatever. See the fam, hang out a couple times a week. Dinner or drinks with a lady friend occasionally, or a business associate. Come back to your perfect apartment, do a little reading in bed, then nighty-night."

"He had a good life."

"Yeah, looks like. But what does he do?"

"You just said—"

"It's not enough, Peabody. Guy's a big wheel, big brain, creates centers, foundations, all but single-handedly advances his field of expertise. Now he what, takes the occasional case, or consults, bops off to lecture or consult out of town. Plays with his grandkids a couple days a week. It's not enough," she repeated, shaking her head. "Where's the kick? No sign he's sexually active, at least not regularly. No sport or hobby equipment in here. Nothing in his data to indicate interests in those areas. He doesn't golf, play retired-guy games. Basically, he's pushing paper and buying suits. He'd need more than this."

"Such as?"

"I don't know." She turned, frowned into the office space. "Something. Contact EDD. I want to know what's on that computer."

More out of habit than necessity, Eve slated the morgue as next on her list. She found Morris, chief medical examiner, loitering in the tiled hallway at Vending—and if she wasn't mistaken, flirting with a stupendously endowed blonde.

Big breasts and batting lashes aside, Eve made the blonde as a cop. They broke off as she approached, and each turned eyes sparking with lust in her direction.

It was more than a little disconcerting.

"Hey, Morris."

"Dallas. Looking for your dead?"

"No, I just like the party atmosphere around here."

He smiled. "Lieutenant Dallas, Detective Coltraine, recently transplanted to our fair city from Savannah."

"Detective."

"I've only been with the four-two for a couple of weeks, but I've already heard of you, Lieutenant."

She had a voice like melted butter and eyes of drowning blue. "Nice meeting you."

"Sure. My partner, Detective Peabody."

"Welcome to New York."

"Sure is different from home. Well, I've got to get along. Appreciate the time, Dr. Morris, and the Coke." She held up the tube from Vending, batted those lashes again, then sort of glided down the hall of death.

"Magnolia blossom." Morris sighed. "In full bloom."

"You must be full up, sucking all that nectar."

"Just a little taste. Usually I steer clear of cops, in that area. But I may have to make an exception."

"Just because I'm not going to bat my lashes at you doesn't mean you can't buy me a drink."

He grinned at her. "Coffee?"

"I want to live, and the coffee here's poison. Pepsi, and the same for my pal, who will also not be batting lashes at you. Only the I'm-forever-on-a-diet variety for Peabody."

He ordered two tubes. "Her first name's Amaryllis."

"Oh, Christ."

"Ammy for short."

"You're making me sick, Morris."

He tossed her a tube, passed the second to Peabody. "Let's go see your dead guy. That'll make you feel better."

He led the way. He wore a suit the color of walnuts, with a dull gold shirt. His dark hair was pulled back into two queues, one stacked on the other and twined with gold cord.

Snappy was Morris's style of dress, and it suited his sharp face and avid eyes.

They passed through the doors into Holding, where Morris walked to the bank of drawers. There was a puff of vapor as he unlocked one.

"Dr. Wilfred B. Icove, aka Icon. He was a brilliant man."

"You knew him?"

"Reputation only. I attended some of his lectures over the years. Fascinating. As you can see, we have a male, approximately eighty years of age. Excellent muscle tone. The single wound punctured the aorta. Common surgical scalpel."

He moved over to Imaging and flipped on a screen to show her the wound and surrounding area magnified. "One jab, bull's-eye. No defensive wounds. Tox screen clear of illegals. Basic vitamins and health meds. Last meal, consumed approximately five hours before death, consisted of a whole-wheat muffin, four ounces of orange juice—the real deal—rose hip tea, some banana, and some raspberries. Your vic was a fan of his field of practice and has had superlative work done, face and body. Muscle tone indicates he believed in working for his health and youthful appearance."

"How long did it take him to die?"

"A minute or two, though essentially he was dead instantly."

"Even with something as sharp as the scalpel, it would take a good solid jab to pierce through the suit, the shirt, flesh, and into the heart—not to mention accuracy."

"Correct. Whoever did this was up close and personal, and knew what they were doing."

"Okay. Sweepers got nothing on-scene. Frigging place is hydrocleaned nightly. No prints on the weapon. It was coated." Idly, Eve drummed her fingers on her thighs while she studied the body. "I watched her walk through the building—security discs. She never touched a thing. They don't do audio, so no shot at a voice print. Her ID's bogus. Feeney's running her image through IRCCA, but since I haven't heard from him, I'd say he's not having any luck so far."

"Smooth operator."

"She's that. Thanks for the drink, Morris." To make him laugh, she batted her eyes.

"What kind of name is Amaryllis?" Eve demanded when she and Peabody were back in the car.

"Floral. You're jealous."

"I'm what?"

"You and Morris have a thing. Most of us have a little thing for Morris, who is oddly sexy. But the two of you have a special thing, and here comes Southern Belle Barbie getting him worked up."

"I don't have a thing for Morris. We're friendly associates. And her name was Amaryllis, not Barbie."

"The doll, Dallas. You know, Barbie doll. Jeez, didn't you ever have dollies?"

"Dolls are like small dead people. I have enough dead people, thanks. But yeah, now I get you. Ammy for short? How can you be a cop with a name like that? Hello, my name is Ammy, and I'll be arresting you today. Please."

"It's a nice little thing you've got with Morris."

"There is no thing, Peabody."

"Right, like you never thought of doing him on one of the slabs in there." When Eve choked on her Pepsi, Peabody shrugged. "Okay, that's just me, then. Hey look, it stopped raining, which is a big change of subject before I further humiliate myself."

Eve caught her breath, stared straight ahead. "We'll never speak of this again."

"That'd be best."

When Eve walked back into her office carrying her share of the victim's office discs, Dr. Mira was standing by her desk.

Must be the day for sharp-dressing doctors, Eve thought.

Mira was elegant in one of her trademark suits, this one a rosy pink with a short, nipped-in jacket that buttoned to the throat. Her mink-colored hair was swept back and sort of rolled at the nape of her neck. Small triangles of gold glinted at her ears.

"Eve. I was just about to leave you a memo."

Sorrow, Eve noted, in those soft blue eyes, in that smooth, pretty face. "What is it?"

"Do you have a moment?"

"Sure. Sure. You want—" She started to offer coffee, remembered Mira favored herbal tea. And her AutoChef didn't stock any. "Anything?"

"No, thanks. No. You're primary on Wilfred Icove's murder."

"Yeah, caught it this afternoon. I was already on-scene on another matter. I was thinking of running what I've got on the suspect by you, and . . . And you knew him," Eve realized.

"Yes, I did. I'm . . . staggered," she decided, and sat in the visitor's chair. "Can't get my head around it. You and I should be used to it, shouldn't we? Death every day, and it doesn't always pass by those we know, those we love or respect."

"Which was it? Love or respect."

"Respect, a great deal of it. We were never romantically involved."

"He was too old for you anyway."

A smile wisped around Mira's mouth. "Thank you. I met him years ago. Years, when I was just starting my practice. A friend of mine was involved with an abuser. She finally broke things off, began to get her life back together. He abducted her, then he raped her, sodomized her. He beat her unconscious and threw her out of his car near Grand Central. She was lucky to live through it. Her face was shattered, her teeth broken, broken eardrum, crushed larynx, a medley of pain and potential disfigurement. I went to Wilfred, to ask him to take her as a patient. I knew he was reputed to be the best in the city, if not the country."

"And he did."

"Yes, he did. More, he was so kind, and so endlessly patient with a woman who'd had her spirit and her courage shattered as much as her body. Wilfred and I spent considerable time together over my friend, and became friends ourselves. His death, like this—it's very hard to accept. I understand a personal connection like this might influence you to keep me a step back. I'm asking you not to."

Eve considered a minute. "You ever drink coffee?"

"Now and again."

She went to the AutoChef, programmed two cups. "I could use some help understanding the vic and getting a profile on the killer.

If you tell me you're able to work the case, then you're able to work the case."

"Thank you."

"Did you see the victim much in the last few years?"

"Not really." Mira accepted the coffee. "A few times a year socially. Dinner, or a dinner party, cocktails, the occasional medical conference. He had offered me the position of head of psychiatric at his center, and was disappointed, perhaps a little annoyed, when I declined. So we haven't consulted professionally in some time, but maintained a social relationship."

"You know the family."

"Yes, his son's another brilliant mind, and seems the perfect choice to carry on his father's work. His daughter-in-law is a talented artist."

"Doesn't do much with it now."

"No, I suppose not. I have one of her early works. Two grandchildren, about nine and six, I believe. Girl and boy. Wilfred doted on them. He always had new holos or photographs to show off. He adores children. The center here has the finest pediatric reconstructive department in the world, in my opinion."

"He have enemies?"

Mira sat back. She looked tired, Eve noted. Grief, she knew, could sap the system, or energize it.

"There are some who envy him—his talent, his vision—and some who've questioned it along the way. But no, I don't know of any in our community who would have wished him harm. No one in the social circle I shared with him either."

"Okay. I might need some help going through his medical files. Interpreting the lingo."

"I'm happy to give you as much time as you need. It certainly isn't my area of expertise, but I can help you understand his notes, I'd think, and his case files."

"It looks professional. Looks like a hit."

"Professional?" Mira set the untouched coffee aside. "That seems impossible. Even ludicrous."

"Maybe not. Doctors who build medical empires, financially lucrative empires, generate not only a lot of money, but a lot of politics, power, a lot of influence. Somebody may have wanted him taken out. The suspect used a bogus ID, claimed to be a citizen of Spain. That mean anything?"

"Spain." Mira ran a hand over her hair, over her face. "No, not immediately."

"Late twenties, an eye-popper." She dug in her bag to give Mira a copy of the photo. "Never flicked an eyelash going through security. Stabbed him through the heart with a medical scalpel, timing it so his admin was at lunch, giving her time to exit the building—which she did, again without a flick. I'd consider droid, but that would've popped on the body scan. But that's how cool she was—before, apparently during, and certainly after."

"Well planned, organized, and controlled. No reaction." Mira nodded, and seemed steadier with work to balance her. "Possible sociopathic tendencies. The single wound would also indicate control, efficiency, and lack of emotion."

"It's likely the weapon was planted. Ladies' room. Which means someone inside, or with access inside, was an accessory or the driving force. They do a sweep of the building every week, and the cleaning system all but sterilizes the place every night. That weapon hadn't been there long."

"You have the log?"

"Yeah. I'm checking it out. A couple of patients, his staff. But other departmental staff or employees don't log in if they pop up there. Then there's the cleaning crew, maintenance. I'll be running the security discs for the forty-eight hours prior to the murder, see what I see. I doubt the weapon was there longer than that. If it was there at all. Maybe she just had to pee." Eve shrugged. "I'm sorry about your friend, Dr. Mira."

"So am I. If there's anyone I'd want standing for a friend under these circumstances, it would be you." She rose. "Anything you need from me, you have only to ask."

"Your other friend, the one who got smashed up back a ways, how'd she do?"

"He gave her her face back, and that—along with several years of therapy—helped her get her life back. She moved to Santa Fe and opened a little art gallery. Married a watercolorist and had a daughter."

"How about the guy who smashed her?"

"Apprehended, tried, and convicted. Wilfred testified regarding her injuries. The bastard's still in Rikers."

Eve smiled. "I like happy endings."

4

EVE SWUNG INTO EDD, WHERE, IN HER MIND, the cops dressed more like club patrons and vid stars than civil servants. Clothes were painfully trendy, hair was colorful, and gadgets were everywhere.

Several detectives swaggered, swayed, or shimmied around the room, talking into headsets or reciting incomprehensible codes into their handhelds. The few who worked at desks or cubes seemed oblivious to the constant chatter of voices and clicks and hums of equipment.

Like a hive of overactive bees, Eve thought, and knew she'd go crazy before the end of a single shift with the e-squad.

Feeney, however—whom she considered the most sensible and stable of cops—seemed to thrive there. He sat at his desk in his wrinkled shirt, sucking on coffee as he worked.

Some things you could count on, Eve thought, and walked in. So intent was his concentration that she'd skirted around his desk to take a look at his desk screen before he registered her presence.

"That's not work," she said.

"Yes, it is. End—"

Without mercy, she slapped a hand over his mouth to stop him from ordering the program to end. "That's not a sim or scene re-construct."

He made some sound against her palm.

"That's a game. It's a cops and robbers game. Roarke has this."

He shoved her hand off his face and struggled for dignity. "Technically it's a game. But it exercises hand-eye coordination, tests reflexes and cognitive skills. It keeps me tuned."

"If you're going to spread all this bullshit around, you could at least offer me boots first."

"End program." He sulked at her. "Ought to remember whose office this is, and who outranks who."

"Ought to remember some of us are trying to find real bad guys."

He jabbed a finger toward his wall screen. "See that? There's your image match running right now. I ran your girl through IRCCA—name, MO, image. Nothing. McNab ran a standard image match, nada. So I'm running a secondary myself. Got boys going over the equipment from the crime scene, and a pickup unit heading out to bring in the personal from the vic's apartment. Any other little thing I can do for you today?"

"Don't get pissy." She sat on the corner of his desk, helped herself to some of the sugared nuts he kept in a bowl. "Who the hell is she? Somebody who kills like that and doesn't blip on the radar anywhere?"

"Maybe a spook." He scooped up a handful of nuts himself. "Maybe your vic was a sanctioned hit."

"Doesn't play. Not off the data I have on Icove, not with this method. If you're a deep underground government spook, why do you walk through heavy security? Flash your face around? Easier, cleaner, to take him out on the street somewhere. Or his apartment. Security there's a hell of a lot lighter than it is at the Icove Center."

"Rogue?"

"If she'd gone rogue, all the more reason to keep your face off the radar screen."

He shrugged, crunched. "Just tossing them at you, kid."

"She makes an appointment, goes through security, uses ID that passes their system. She knows when the admin's going to be out for an hour, giving her a clear road out before the body's discovered. The weapon was previously planted—had to be. It's all slick as spit. But . . ."

Feeney rolled his shoulders, waited for her to finish.

"Why there? No matter how you slice and serve it, taking him out in his office was more complicated than doing him at home. Plus the guy walks to work, barring inclement. You're that good, you stick him on the street and keep walking. He took his car today. Underground lot in his building. You could get to him there—security, sure, but still easier than his office."

"She had a reason to take him there."

"Yeah. And maybe she had something to say to him before she killed him. Or something she wanted him to tell her. Anyway, if this was her first time, she had some major beginner's luck. No missteps, Feeney, not one. Not a single bead of sweat on her delicate brow after she stabs a guy through the heart. Dead through, too. Like he had a fucking target over it. Insert blade here."

"Practiced."

"Bet your ass. But jabbing a droid or a dummy or a sim, doing it in a holo, whatever. . . . It's not the same as flesh and blood. You know that. We *know* that."

She munched, considered. "And the vic? He's nearly as unreal as she is. Not a smudge, not a smear in eighty years of living, more than a half century of medical practice. Sure he's got a few suits filed against him along the way, but they're outweighed by good works and professional kudos. His apartment? It's like a stage set. Nothing out of place, and I'm pretty sure the guy's got more suits than Roarke."

"Not possible."

"Pretty sure. Of course, he's got close to fifty years on Roarke, so that could be the difference. He doesn't gamble, he doesn't cheat, he doesn't screw his neighbor's wife—at least not so it shows. His son will benefit somewhat financially by his death, but it doesn't fit. He's solid in that area, and was at this point basically running the show at the Center. Center staff so far interviewed sings the vic's praises to the point of hallelujahs."

"Okay. There's a skeleton in his closet, some dirt under his rug."

She absolutely beamed as she punched Feeney's arm. "Thank you! That's what I say. Nobody's that clean. No fricking body. Not in my world. The kind of money this guy generated, he could've greased the right palms to get something expunged from his data. Plus, he's got too much downtime, the way I see it. Can't figure what he did with it. Nothing shows in his office or his apartment. His appointment book shows at least two days and three evenings a week where he's got nothing going. What does he do, where does he go?"

She checked her wrist unit. "I've got to go fill in the commander. Then I'm taking my toys and going home to play with them. Anything pops for you, I'm ready to hear it."

She traveled the maze of Central to Commander Whitney's office and was shown right in. He was at his desk, a big man with big shoulders that bore the weight of his authority. Over time, that authority had carved lines into his dark face and threaded some gray through his hair.

He gestured to a chair, and Eve had to control a frown. After more than ten years as her commander, he knew she preferred giving her orals standing.

She sat.

"Before you begin," he said, "there's a somewhat delicate matter I need to address."

"Sir?"

"During the course of your investigation you will likely be required to review the patient list for the Icove Center, cross-referencing names with the victim, and with his son."

Oh-oh. "Yes, sir, that's my intention."

"During this process, you will find that the younger Dr. Icove . . ."

Oh shit.

"The younger Dr. Icove, with the victim as consultant, executed some minor cosmetic procedures on Mrs. Whitney."

Mrs. Whitney. Thank God, Eve thought, and felt her stomach unclench. She'd been terrified her commander had been about to tell her he'd used the Center's services himself.

"Okay. Excuse me. Yes, sir."

"My wife, as you may suspect, would prefer to keep this matter private. I'm going to ask you, as a personal favor, Lieutenant, that unless you see a connection between Mrs. Whitney's . . . what she calls her tune-ups," he said with obvious embarrassment, "and your investigation, you keep this matter, and this conversation, to yourself."

"Absolutely, Commander. Certainly I see no relation between, um, the aforesaid tune-ups and the murder of Wilfred Icove, Sr. If it would be helpful, please assure Mrs. Whitney of my discretion in this matter."

"Damn right I will." He pressed his fingers to his eyes. "She's hounded me via 'link since she heard about it on the media report. Vanity, Dallas, comes at considerable price. So who killed Dr. Perfect?"

"Sir?"

"Anna mentioned that some of the nurses called him that— affectionately. He's known for being a perfectionist, and expecting the same from those who work with him."

"Interesting. And it fits what I've learned about him so far." Deciding the personal aspect of the report was over, she got to her feet, gave her report.

It was well past end of shift when she headed home. Not that it was unusual, she decided. And with Roarke out of town, she had less motivation to go home. Nobody there but the pain in her ass, in the form of Roarke's majordomo, Summerset.

He'd make some crack when she walked in, she thought. About her being late, not *informing* him—as if she'd voluntarily speak to him. He'd probably sneer, and congratulate her on making it home without getting blood on her shirt.

She had a comeback for that one ready. Oh yeah. She'd say there was still time, fuckhead. No, no, fuckface. Still time, fuckface. Planting my fist through your needle-dick nose ought to get some blood on my shirt.

Then she'd start up the stairs, stop like she'd just thought of something, and say: Oh wait, you don't run on blood, do you? I'd just end up with viscous green goo all over me.

She entertained herself all the way uptown with varieties of the same theme, and alternate intonations.

The gates opened for her, and lights bloomed on to illuminate the curving drive that wound through the grounds toward the house.

Part fortress, part castle, part fantasy, it was home now. Its peaks and towers, its juts and terraces silhouetted against the broody night sky. Windows, countless windows, glowed against the gloom of the evening in a kind of welcome she'd never known before he'd come into her life.

Had never expected to know.

Seeing it, the house, the lights, the strength and beauty of what he'd built, what he'd made, what he'd given to her, she missed him outrageously. She very nearly drove around the loop, headed out again.

She could go see Mavis. Wasn't her friend and music disc star in town? She was pregnant—a lot pregnant now, Eve calculated. If she went to see Mavis, she'd have to run the gauntlet first—touch the scary belly, listen to knocked-up talk, be shown strange little clothes and weird equipment.

After that, it would be fine, it would be good.

But she was too damn tired to go through the hoops first. Besides, she had work to do.

She grabbed the loaded disc and file bag, left her car at the steps—mainly because it annoyed Summerset—and headed inside, somewhat cheered she'd be able to use her stored insults.

She stepped inside, into the warmth of the grand foyer, into light and fragrance. Deliberately she stripped off her jacket, tossed it over the newel post—another little poke at Summerset.

But he didn't ooze like evil fog out of the walls or woodwork. He *always* oozed like evil fog out of the walls or woodwork. She had a moment to be puzzled, then irritated, then mildly concerned he'd dropped dead during the day.

Then her heart picked up a beat, something shivered along her skin. She looked up, and saw Roarke at the top of the stairs.

He couldn't have become more beautiful than he'd been a week before, but it seemed to her, in that shimmering light, that he had.

His face—the strength, power, and yes, the beauty of a fallen angel with no regrets—was framed by the thick black of his hair. His mouth—full, carved, irresistible—smiled as he came toward her. And those eyes—impossibly, brilliantly blue—dazzled her where she stood.

He made her weak in the knees. Foolish, foolish, she thought. He was her husband, and she knew him as she knew no other. Yet her knees were weak, and her heart was tumbling in her chest. She only had to look at him.

"You're not supposed to be here," she said.

He stopped at the base of the stairs, lifted a brow. "Did we move while I was out of town?"

She shook her head, dropped her bag. And jumped into his arms.

The taste of him—that was home, that was true welcome. The feel of his body—lean muscle, smooth flesh—that was both thrill and comfort.

She sniffed at him like a puppy, scented him, caught the whiff of soap. He'd just showered, she thought, while her mouth met his again. Changed out of business clothes and into jeans and a pullover.

It meant they were going nowhere, expecting no one. It meant it was the two of them.

"I missed you." She caught his face in her hands. "I really, really missed you."

"Darling Eve." Ireland drifted through his voice, as he took her wrist, turned his face so his lips pressed to her palm. "I'm sorry it all took longer than I'd hoped."

She shook her head. "You're back now, and a hell of a better welcoming committee than the one I was expecting. Where is the walking dead?"

He tapped a finger on the shallow dent in her chin. "If you mean Summerset, I encouraged him to go out for the evening."

"Oh, so you didn't kill him."

"No."

"Can I kill him when he comes back?"

"It's comforting to see nothing's changed in my absence." He glanced down to look at the enormous cat that wound between his legs, then Eve's. "Apparently Galahad missed me as well, and he's already hit me up for some salmon."

"Well, if the cat's fed and the butler from hell's away, let's go upstairs and flip a coin."

"Actually, I had another activity in mind." When she bent to pick up the bag, he took it from her, winced at the weight. "Work?"

Once, it had always been work. Only been work. But now . . . "It can wait a bit."

"I'm hoping this takes longer than a bit. I've been saving up." He slid his free arm around her waist so they walked upstairs hip-to-hip. "What's the coin toss for?"

"Heads I jump you, tails you jump me."

He laughed, leaned down to nip her ear. "Screw the coin. Let's jump each other."

He dumped her bag at the top of the steps, spun her back to the wall. Even as his lips crushed down on hers, she was boosting herself up to clamp her legs around his waist.

Her hands fisted in his hair, and everything inside her went hot and needy.

"Bed's too far, too many clothes." She dragged her mouth from his to bite his neck. "You smell so good."

He found and hit the release for her harness, just a flick of fast hands. "I'm about to disarm you, Lieutenant."

"I'm about to let you."

He turned, nearly stumbled over the cat. When he cursed, Eve laughed so hard her ribs ached.

"Wouldn't be so bloody funny if I'd dropped you on your ass."

Laughter still dancing in her eyes, she linked her arms around his neck as he navigated toward the bedroom. "I love you, a week's worth more since the last time I touched you."

"Now you've done it. How can I drop you on your ass after that?"

Instead he carried her up the steps of the platform where the wide bed stood, then laid her on sheets soft as rose petals.

"You already turned down the bed?"

He brushed her lips with his. "I favored my chances."

She yanked his shirt over his head. "So do I."

She pulled him down to her, steeped herself in the heat of it, the sizzle of blood, the fever of lips. So good to touch him, to feel the shape of him, to have his weight pressing on her. Lust and love were a glorious tangle in her system, and all of it was coated with simple happiness.

He was with her again.

He nipped his way down her throat, filling himself on the flavor of her skin. Of all of his appetites, his for her was the only one never quite sated. He could have her and still want her. And those days and nights without her, jammed with work and obligations, had still been empty.

Drawing her up, he dragged off her harness, shoving it aside, opening her shirt while her teeth, her lips, her hands wrought havoc on him, in him. He cupped her breasts through the thin tank she wore, watched her face as his thumbs teased her nipples.

He loved her eyes, the shape of them, the rich brandy color, and the way they stayed on his even when she began to tremble.

She lifted her arms, and he tugged the tank up, off. Then took her—warm, soft, firm—into his mouth. She gathered him closer, purring in her throat, arching her back to offer more. He took, she took, peeling and pulling away clothes so flesh could find flesh. As he worked his way down her, exploring, it was his name that purred in her throat.

Need gathered in her, a fist of excited pleasure that seemed to punch through her so that she moaned and shuddered on the release. Only to gather again, harder and tighter, until her fingers dug into him urging him up, drawing him back to her. Into her.

Her hips lifted and fell, a silky rhythm that bound them together, that quickened even as hearts quickened.

Deeper, he sank deeper into her, losing himself as he only could with her. And the sweetness of it followed him over.

When his lips pressed to her shoulder, she stroked his hair. It was good to drift on this quiet, this contentment. She often thought of these as stolen moments, a kind of perfection that helped her—

maybe helped them both—survive the ugliness the world shoved at them day after day.

"Did you get everything done?" she asked him.

Lifting his head, he grinned down at her. "You tell me."

"I meant with work." Amused, she gave him a little poke.

"Enough to keep us in fish and chips for a bit. Speaking of which, I'm starving. And by the heft of that data bag you hauled in, I'd say the chances of our eating in bed and having another round for dessert are slim."

"Sorry."

"No need." He bent his head to kiss her, light and easy. "Why don't we have a meal in your office, and you can tell me about what's in that bag."

She could count on him for that, Eve thought as she pulled on loose pants and an ancient NYPSD sweatshirt. Not just to tolerate her work, the horrible hours, the mental distraction of it, but to *get* it. And to help whenever she asked.

Well, whenever she didn't ask, too.

There'd been a time—most of the first year of their marriage, actually—when she'd struggled to keep him out of it a great deal of the time. Unsuccessfully. But it wasn't simply the lack of success that had eased her toward using him on cases.

The man thought like a cop. Must be the flip side of the criminal mind, she decided. The fact was, she often thought like the criminal. How else did you get into their heads and stop them?

She'd married a man with a dark past, a clever mind, and more resources than the International Security Council. Why waste what was under your nose?

So they set up in her home office, one Roarke had outfitted for her to resemble the apartment where she'd once lived. It was just that sort of thinking—of knowing what would make her most comfortable—that had made her a goner almost from the moment they'd met.

"What'll it be, Lieutenant? Does the case you're working on call for red meat?"

"I'm thinking fish and chips." She shrugged when he laughed. "You put it in my head."

"Fish and chips it is, then." He moved into her kitchen while she organized the data discs and files out of her bag. "Who's dead?"

"Wilfred B. Icove—doctor and saint."

"I heard that on the way home. I wondered if he'd be yours." He came back with a couple of plates, steam rising from the fried cod and chipped potatoes, fresh from the AutoChef. "I knew him a bit."

"I thought you might. He lived in one of your buildings."

"Can't say I knew that." He'd walked back into the kitchen as they spoke. "I'd met him, and his son—son's wife—at charity functions. Media report said he'd been killed in his office, at his landmark center here in New York."

"They got that right."

He brought back vinegar for the chips, salt—his woman used bloody blizzards of salt on damn near everything—and a couple of cold bottles of Harp.

"Stabbed, was he?"

"Once. Through the heart. No lucky jab." She sat with him, ate with him, and filled him in, using nearly the same straight, efficient reporting style she had with her commander.

"Can't see the son for it," Roarke said, forking up some fish— and memories of his own youth in Dublin with it. "If you want an outside opinion."

"I'll take it. Why?"

"Both devoted to their field of medicine—a lot of pride in that, and each other. Money wouldn't be a factor. And power?" He gestured with his fork, then stabbed more fish. "From what I know the father's been ceding that to the son, more as time went on. The woman looks professional to you?"

"The hit looked pro. Clean, quick, simple, well planned. But . . ."

He smiled a little, picked up his beer—as comfortable, Eve knew, with the brew and fried fish as he would have been with a two-thousand-dollar bottle of wine and rare filet.

"But," Roarke continued for her, "the symbolism—the heart wound, death in his office in the center he founded, the sheer *cojones,* to borrow the Spanish she purported to be—of the murder in a place so well secured. A point proven."

Yeah, Eve thought, she'd be wasting a valuable resource if she shut Roarke out of her work. "Maybe she's a pro, maybe not. We've got no hits on her, not through IRCCA, not through Feeney's imaging. But if she was hired, the motive was personal. Personal in a way, I think, that relates to his work. He could've been taken out quick and easy elsewhere."

"You've run his immediate staff by now."

"Whistle clean, every one. And nobody has a bad word to say about him. His apartment looks like a holo-room."

"I'm sorry?"

"You know, one of those programs used to fabricate a home for realtors. Perfect urban living. It was clean and coordinated to fricking death. You'd hate it."

Intrigued, he angled his head. "Would I?"

"You got the high life, same as he did. Got it different ways, but you're both drowning in money."

"Oh," he said easily, "I can tread water quite well, and for quite a while."

"While you're doing the backstroke, he's got a two-level apartment, where everything's squared off, the bathroom towels match the bathroom walls, sort of thing. No creativity, I guess I'm saying. You've got this place, which may be big enough to hold a small city itself, but it's got—well, it's got style and life. It reflects you."

"I think that's a compliment." He raised his beer to her.

"It's an observation. You're both perfectionists in your ways, but his ran toward obsession—everything just so. You like to mix it up. So maybe his need for perfection caused him to bruise somebody, or fire them, or refuse to take them as a patient. I can't make this just so, so forget about it."

"I'd say it was a big bruise to warrant murder."

"People kill for a chipped fingernail, but you're right there. This was big enough to do something showy. Because under the efficiency, the tidiness, this was showing off."

Eve snagged another fry. "Take a look at her. Computer," she ordered, "display ID image, Nocho-Alverez, Dolores, on wall screen one."

When it flashed on, Roarke lifted his eyebrows. "Beauty is often deadly."

"So why would somebody who looks like that consult with a face and body sculptor? Why would he take her?"

"Beauty's often irrational as well. She may have convinced him she wanted something more, something else. Being a man, and one who obviously appreciates beauty and perfection, he might have been curious enough to take the appointment. You said he was all but retired. Time enough to spend an hour with a woman who looks like that one."

"That's one of the things. Too much time. A guy who's spent all of his life working, dedicated, striving, making history—in his field—what does he do when he's not working? I can't find play-time for this guy. What would you do?"

"Make love with my wife, steal her away for long, indulgent holidays. Show her the world."

"He doesn't have a wife, or a specific lover. Not that I can find. Long blocks of time blank on his appointment calendar. He did something with it. Something on those discs. Somewhere."

"We'll have a look then." He polished off his beer. "How did you sleep while I was gone?"

"Fine. Okay." She rose, figuring since he got the meal, she had to clear it away.

"Eve." He laid a hand over hers to stop her, bring her eyes to his.

"I bunked in here some nights, in the sleep chair. You can't worry about that. You've got business out of town, you've got to go. I can handle it."

He brought her hand to his lips. "You had nightmares. I'm sorry."

She was plagued with them, but they were worse when he wasn't with her. "I can deal." She hesitated. She'd sworn she would go to her grave telling no one. But he'd be weighed down with guilt, she knew. "I slept in your shirt." She tugged her hand free, gathered up dishes to keep the confession light. "It smelled like you, so I slept better."

He rose, took her face in his hands and said, softly, "Darling Eve."

"Don't get sloppy. It's just a shirt." She stepped back, walked around him. Then stopped at the entrance to the kitchen. "But I'm glad you're home."

He smiled at her back. "So am I."

THEY SPLIT THE DISCS, ROARKE IN HIS AD-
joining office, Eve at her desk. Where Eve spent a
frustrated ten minutes trying to cajole her unit into
reading what turned out to be encoded data.

"He's got a block on the discs," she called out. "Some sort of privacy protection thing. My unit won't accept or override."

"Of course it will," Roarke said and had her frowning up at him.
He'd come back into her office without her hearing him move. He
only smiled, and laying a hand on her shoulder, rubbing a bit,
scanned the screen. "Here you are, then." With a few keystrokes he
bypassed the privacy mode and something resembling text popped
onto her screen.

"It's still coded," she pointed out.

"Patience, Lieutenant. Computer, run deciphering and transla-
tion program. Display results."

Working . . .

"I guess you already did yours," Eve complained.

"This unit's equipped to handle code, my technologically challenged cop. You've only to tell it what to do. And . . ."

Task complete. Text displayed.

"Fine. I've got it now. Or would if I was a frigging doctor. It's medical crap."

He kissed the top of her head. "Good luck," he added, and strolled back to his own office.

"Passcoded the unit," she muttered. "Privacy protected the discs, and coded them. Reasons for that." She sat back a moment, drummed her fingers. Could be just his perfectionist nature. Obsessive. Compulsive. Doctor-patient confidentiality. But it seemed like more.

Even the text was secretive. No names, she noted. The patient was referred to throughout as Patient A-1.

Eighteen-year-old female, she read. Height: five feet, seven inches. Weight: one hundred fifteen pounds.

He listed her vitals, blood pressure, pulse rate, blood work, heart and brain patterns—all within normal range, as far as she could tell.

The disc seemed to be a medical history, detailing tests, results, examinations. And grades, she realized. Patient A-1 had excellent physical stamina, intelligence quotient, cognitive abilities. Why would he care about those things? she wondered. Eyesight corrected to 20/20.

She read quick details on hearing tests, stress tests, more exams. Respiration, bone density.

Then was thrown again by notes on mathematic abilities, language skills, artistic and/or musical talents, and puzzle-solving ability.

She spent an hour with A-1, spanning three years of similar tests, notes, results.

The text ended with a final note.

A-1 treatment complete. Placement successful.

She rapidly scanned another five discs, finding the same sorts of tests, notes, with occasional additions of surgical corrections. Nose planing, dental corrections, breast enhancements.

Then she sat back, propped her feet on the desk, and stared up at the ceiling to think.

Anonymous patients, all referred to by numbers and letters. No names. All females—at least in her stash. Treatment was either complete or terminated.

There had to be more. More notes, more complete case files. If so, there had to be another place. Office, lab, something. Most of the face or body sculpting, which was supposed to be his specialty, was minor on these cases.

Tune-ups, she mused.

The records were more an ongoing evaluation: physical, mental, creative, cognitive.

Placement. Where were they *placed* after treatment was complete? Where did they go if and when it was terminated?

And what the hell had the good doctor been up to with more than fifty female patients?

"Experiments," she said when Roarke came through the door. "These are like experiments, right? Is that how it reads to you?"

"Lab rats," he agreed. "Nameless. And these notes strike me as being his quick reference guide, not his official charts."

"Right. Just something he could flip through to check a detail or jog his memory. A lot of shields for something this vague, which is telling me it springs out of something more detailed. Still they fit my gauge of him. In each of the cases I reviewed, he's aiming for perfection. Body type, facial structure—which would be his deal. Then he veers off to stuff like cognitive skills and whether they can play the tuba."

"You got a tuba?"

"Just a for-instance," she said with a wave of her hand. "What does he care? What does it matter if the patient can do calculus or speak Ukrainian or whatever? I've got nothing that indicates he worked on brain sectors. Oh, and they're all right-handed. Every one, which goes against the law of averages. They're all female—interesting—and all between the ages of seventeen and twenty-two when the notes end. With either 'placement' or 'treatment terminated.'"

"*Placement*'s an interesting word, isn't it?" Roarke eased a hip onto the corner of her desk. "One might assume employment. If one weren't of a cynical bent."

"Which you are, which makes you a good match for me. Some people would pay a lot of money for a perfect woman. Maybe running a slavery ring was Icove's little hobby."

"Possibly. Where does he get the goods?"

"I'm going to do a search. Coordinate the dates of the case notes with missing persons and kidnappings."

"There's a start. Eve? It'd be a hell of an operation to keep this many people under control, and to keep such a thing concealed. Can you consider it might be voluntary?"

"I'm going to volunteer to be sold to the highest bidder?"

He shook his head. "Consider. A young girl, for whatever reason unhappy with her appearance or her lot, or simply looking for more. He might pay them as well. Earn money while we make you beautiful. Then we'll match you up with a partner. One with enough money to afford the service, one who selects you out of all the others. Heady stuff for the impressionable."

"So he's creating, basically, licensed companions, with their consent?"

"Or spouses, for all we know. Both, either. Or—a thought that hit my perhaps overactive brain—hybrids."

Her eyes rounded. "What, half-LC, half-spouse? A guy's wet dream."

He laughed, shook his head. "You're tired. I was thinking more along the lines of an old, classic plotline. Frankenstein."

"The monster guy?"

"Frankenstein was the mad doctor guy who created the monster."

She swung her feet off the desk. "Hybrids. Part droid, part human? And way, way illegal? You thinking he might dabble in hybridizing humans? That's out there, Roarke."

"Agreed, but there were experiments a few decades ago. Military, primarily. And we see it every day on another level. Artificial hearts, limbs, organs. He made his name with his reconstructive surgery techniques. Man-made is often used in that area."

"So maybe he's making women?" She thought of Dolores, absolutely calm before and after a murder. "And one of them turns on him. One of them isn't happy with her placement, and comes back to off the creator. He agrees to see her because she's his work. It's not bad," she decided. "Out there, but not altogether bad."

She slept on it, and woke so early Roarke was just out of bed and pulling on sweats.

"You're awake. Well then, let's have a workout and a swim."

"A what?" She blinked groggy eyes at him. "It's not morning."

"It's after five." He stepped back up to the bed, hauled her out. "It'll clear your mind."

"Why isn't there coffee?"

"There will be." He bundled her into the elevator and had it heading for the home gym before her brain woke fully.

"Why am I working out at five in the morning?"

"Five-fifteen, actually, and because it's good for you." He tossed her a pair of shorts. "Suit up, Lieutenant."

"When do you leave town again?"

He tossed a top into her face.

She dragged on the clothes, then set her equipment for a beach run. If she was going to work out before the sun came up, at least she could pretend she was at the beach. She liked the feel of sand under her feet, and the sounds and scents and sights of surf.

Roarke set up next to her with the same program. "We could make this a reality after the holidays."

"What holidays?"

Amused when she picked up her pace, he matched her. "We're nearly to Thanksgiving. Which is actually something I wanted to discuss with you."

"It's on a Thursday. You eat turkey whether you like it or not. I know about Thanksgiving."

"It's also an American holiday. A . . . family holiday, traditionally. I thought it might be appropriate to invite my Irish relations here for dinner."

"Bring them to New York to eat turkey?"

"Essentially."

She watched him out of the corner of her eye, noted he was

slightly embarrassed. A rarity for him. "How many of them are there, anyway?"

"About thirty or so."

Her breath wheezed in. "Thirty?"

"More or less. I'm not entirely sure, though I doubt all of them could get away, with a farm to run and other work. All those children. But I thought Sinead, at least, with her family, might be able to take a day or two here, and the holiday seemed the right time. We might invite Mavis and Leonardo, Peabody and so on. Whoever you'd like. Make a right bash of it."

"Gonna need one big-ass turkey."

"I think the food will be the simplest of the details. How would you feel about having them here?"

"A little weird, but okay. How about you?"

He relaxed. "A little weird, but okay. I appreciate it."

"As long as I don't have to bake a pie."

"God forbid."

The workout did indeed clear her mind, and she added a stint with weights, polished it off with twenty laps in the pool.

She'd intended to do twenty-five, but Roarke caught her on the twenty-first turn. And she ended the workout with a different sort of water exercise.

She was alert and ravenous by the time she'd showered and grabbed her first cup of coffee.

She went for waffles, exchanged beady eyes with Galahad when the cat tried to slink up to her plate.

"He's got to have space."

"Cat's got the run of the bloody house."

"Not the cat. Icove," Eve said and got an absentminded mmm-hmm from Roarke as he scanned the morning stock reports on-screen in the sitting area of their bedroom. "Not in the apartment," she continued. "Too many *patients* coming in and out. Lab. Maybe in the Center, maybe someplace else entirely. He'd need privacy. Even if it's not anything illegal, it's strange. He didn't go through all the trouble to private the discs and his unit, then conduct all these exams or experiments or case studies in the open."

"It's a big facility, the Center," Roarke began, and switched to the media bulletins. "But there are a lot of people through there. Patients, staff, visitors, stockholders. Very possible, if he was careful enough, to have a private area. But wiser, I'd think, to do this other work—particularly if it skirts the law—off-site."

"The son would know. If they were as close, personally and professionally, as I think they were, the father and the son would both be involved with this . . . project. We'll call it a project. Peabody and I'll pay him another visit, see if we can go at this the direct way. We'll take a deeper look at the financials. If this is a by-fee project, it would have generated big bucks. And I'll look at property in his name, the son's, the daughter-in-law, grandchildren, under the Center or his other arms. If he's got a place, we'll find it."

"You'll want to save them. The girls," he continued when she said nothing. "You'll want to stop them from being arranged, let's say, if that's the case." He turned from the screen to look at her. "If this is some sort of training ground, some kind of preparation area, you'll see them as victims."

"Aren't they?"

"Not like you were." He took her hand. "I doubt very much it's anything like that, or that you'll be able to stop yourself from seeing it that way regardless. It'll hurt you."

"They all hurt me. Even when they have nothing to do with what happened to me. They all take a toll."

"I know." He kissed her hand. "Some more than others."

"You'll ask your family here for Thanksgiving, and it'll hurt you. Because your mother can't be here, and you'll think of that. Won't be able to stop yourself from remembering what happened to her when you were only a baby. It'll hurt you, but it won't stop you from asking them here. We do what we have to do, Roarke. Both of us."

"So we do."

She rose, reached for her weapon harness. "You're off, then?" he asked her.

"Might as well get an early start, since I'm up."

"Then I'd best give you your present." He watched her face—the surprise, the chagrin, the resignation. And burst out laughing. "Thought you'd gotten away clean, did you?"

"Hand it over, get it done."

"Gracious to the last." To her surprise he went to his closet, opened it, and pulled out a large box. He set it on the sofa. "Open it, then."

Another fancy dress, she supposed. As if she didn't already have enough of them to clothe an army of fashion plates. Of which she was the chipped one, hidden on the top shelf. But buying glam made him happy.

She pulled off the top, stared. "Oh. Oh wow."

"An atypical reaction for you, Lieutenant," he said with a grin, but she was already yanking the long black leather coat out of the box, burying her nose in it to sniff.

"Oh boy, oh boy." She whirled it around, swirled it on while he watched. It hit her an inch above the ankles, carried deep pockets, and was smooth as butter.

"You make a picture," he complimented, pleased that she'd already spun toward the mirror to see for herself. It was masculine— a deliberate choice on his part. No frills, no feminine touches. In it she looked sexy and dangerous, and just a little aloof.

"Now *this* is what it is. This is a goddamn coat. I'll bung it up before the end of shift, but it'll look even better with a few scars." She spun around, and the coat swirled around her legs. "Nice job. Thanks."

"My pleasure." He tapped his lips so that she walked over to plant hers on them. Then he slid his arms under the coat and around her.

My God, he thought, it was good to be home.

"There are a number of inside pockets, if someone needed to secret a weapon of some sort."

"Frosty. Man, Baxter's going to crap himself when I walk in wearing this."

"Lovely image, thanks."

"It's really great." She kissed him again. "I really love it. I gotta go."

"See you tonight."

He watched her walk away, and thought she looked like a warrior.

Since she had nearly an hour before the start of her shift, Eve took a chance and headed to Mira's office first. As she had expected, the doctor was in, and her dragon of an admin wasn't.

Eve knocked on Mira's open office door.

"Sorry."

"Eve. Did we have an early appointment?"

"No." Mira looked tired, Eve noted. And sad. "I know you usually try to get in before hours, catch up on paperwork or whatever. Sorry to get in the way of that."

"It's all right. Come in. Is this about Wilfred?"

"Wanted to run something by you." And she felt lousy for doing it. "Doctor-patient relation sort of deal. You keep case files."

"Of course."

"And in addition to the consult position with the department, you do some private work. Counseling, therapy, and the like. You sometimes treat patients on an ongoing basis. Over the course of years, say."

"Certainly."

"How do you keep the files, the data?"

"I'm not sure what you mean."

"You passcode your unit, for security?"

"Absolutely. All files are confidential. The private cases. And the consults for the department are on a need-to-know basis."

"The discs themselves? Those protected, too?"

"I would add a layer onto the more sensitive material, if I felt it necessary."

"You encode the data?"

"Codes?" This time Mira smiled. "That would be a bit paranoid of me, wouldn't it? Are you worried about leaks on my end, Eve?"

"No. Other than paranoia, why would a doctor passcode unit, discs, then encode the data on the discs?"

The smile had faded. "I would have to assume the structure in which the doctor worked required such precautions, or the data itself was hypersensitive. There is the possibility the doctor had reason to suspect someone might attempt to access the data. Or the work being documented was highly experimental."

"Illegal."

"I didn't say illegal."

"Would you if you weren't aware I was asking about Icove?"

"There are a lot of reasons, as I've just told you, why such data might be particularly protected."

Eve sat without invitation, kept her eyes level with Mira's. "He gave the patients labels rather than names. They were all female, all between the ages of seventeen and twenty-two. There was little surgery of the type he's known for. They were all tested and graded in areas such as cognitive skills, language, artistic talents, physical prowess. Depending on their progress and level, treatment—which was never clearly detailed—was either continued or terminated. If continued, it ended in what was termed 'placement,' at which time the file was ended. What does it mean?"

"I can't say."

"Best guess."

"Don't do this to me, Eve." Mira's voice trembled. "Please."

"Okay." Eve pushed to her feet. "Okay, I'm sorry."

Mira only shook her head. Eve stepped back out of the office, and left her alone.

On the way to Homicide, Eve pulled her 'link out of her pocket. It was still early, but as far as she was concerned, doctors and cops had no schedule. She had no problem waking Dr. Louise Dimatto.

Louise looked dewy, her gray eyes blurry with sleep, her blond hair tousled. She said. "Ugh."

"Got some questions. When can you meet me?"

"Morning off. Sleepy. Go far, far away."

"I'll come to you." Eve checked the time. "Thirty minutes."

"I hate you, Dallas."

The screen wavered a moment, then a handsome and sleepy male face joined Louise's. "So do I."

"Hey, Charles." Charles Monroe was a professional LC, and the other half of the couple who were Charles and Louise. "Thirty minutes," she repeated, and ended the transmission before anyone could argue.

She backtracked, deciding it would be simpler to pick up Peabody at her home and head straight out. When Peabody came on screen her hair was wet and she had a towel clutched to her breasts.

"I'm picking you up in fifteen," Eve told her.

"Somebody dead?"

"No. I'll fill you in. Just—" McNab stepped out of what she saw now was the shower, and she thanked God the video cut off at his sternum. "In fifteen. And for the sake of all that's decent and holy, learn to block video."

Peabody managed to pull it together in fifteen, Eve noted with satisfaction. She came quickly out of the door hustling on those airskids she favored. Dark green today, to go with a green-and-white-striped jacket that fell just past her hips.

She jumped in the car, then her eyes went wide and glassy. "The coat! The coat!" Her hand shot out to rub leather, and Eve slapped it away.

"No touching the coat."

"Can I sniff it? Please, please? *Please!*"

"Nose one full inch from sleeve. One sniff."

Peabody complied, dramatically rolled her eyes. "Roarke got home early, right?"

"Maybe I bought it for myself."

"Yeah, right. Maybe little pink piggies fly on gossamer wings. Okay, if nobody else is dead, why are we on the clock early?"

"Need to consult a medical. It's touchy with Mira—personal relationship with vic—so I've got Louise as backup. We're heading there."

Out of her bag, Peabody dug lip dye. "Didn't have time to finish," she said when Eve slanted her a look. "And if we're going to see Louise and Charles?"

"Probably."

"I want to be spruced."

"Do you have any interest whatsoever in the progress of the investigation?"

"Sure. I can listen, access, deduce while I spruce. Deduce while I spruce," Peabody repeated in a jaunty rhythm.

Eve ignored the lip dying, the hair brushing, the scent spritzing while she relayed the information and fought with traffic.

"Off-the-record and potentially illegal experimentation," Peabody mused. "His son would know."

"Agreed."

"Admin?"

"She's straight office drone. No medical training on her record, but we'll interview her with this angle. What I want first is a medical opinion. I want a doctor's eyes to see the data. Mira was too close to this guy."

"You said fifty or so patients. Seems like too many for him to handle alone."

"What I've got covers more than five years. Various stages of testing or prep, or whatever the hell it is. There were some groupings—A-one, -two, -three. Like that. But no, even with that schedule, he most likely had help. His son, certainly. Possibly lab techs, other doctors. If this placement business is fee-based, there have to be records of income, and somebody who handled that end."

"Daughter-in-law? She was his ward first."

"We'll give that a push, but no medical training on record there, either. No business experience, no tech skills. Why is there never any parking around here?"

"A question for the ages."

Eve considered double-parking. Considered further the probability that her fairly new ride would get bashed by a pissed-off commuter, and circled around until she found a second-level street slot two blocks from Louise's building.

She didn't mind the walk, especially in her icy new coat.

6 THEY LOOKED LIKE A COUPLE OF SLEEPY cats, Eve thought. All limber and loose, like they were ready to curl up together for a little morning nap in a block of sunlight.

Louise wore some sort of long white tunic that struck Eve as a bit goddessy—but it suited her. Her feet were bare, the toes painted a shimmery pink. Charles hadn't bothered with shoes either, but at least he didn't go for pink toes. He'd chosen white as well, in roomy white pants and a generously sized shirt.

They looked so rosy, Eve wondered if they'd managed to sneak in a quickie since her call. Then immediately wished her brain hadn't delved in that area.

She liked them both, had even started to get used to the idea of them as a couple. But she didn't want to think about the coupling part.

"Bright and early, Lieutenant Sugar." Charles kissed Eve on the cheek before she could evade. "Look at you." He took Peabody by the arms and gave her a quick, warm buss on the lips. "Detective Delish."

Peabody pinked and fluttered until Eve jabbed a finger in her side. "Official business."

"We're having coffee." Louise walked back into the living area, plopped on the sofa, lifted a cup. "Don't ask me anything official until I've had my first jolt. Between the clinic and the shelter, I put in fourteen full ones yesterday. Today is for sloth."

"Did you know Wilfred Icove?"

Louise sighed. "At least sit down, have some coffee that my gorgeous lover so gallantly arranged. Have a bagel."

"I already had breakfast."

"Well, I didn't." Peabody sat, plucked up a bagel. "She got me out of the shower."

"You look great," Louise commented. "Cohabbing agrees with you. How are you feeling, physically?"

"Good. Finished the PT, got a thumbs-up."

"You did good." Louise patted Peabody's knee. "The injuries you sustained from the assault were damned serious, and it was only a few weeks ago. You worked hard to come back this fast."

"Sturdy constitution helps." Secretly, Peabody wished she were more delicate, more fine-boned, like Louise.

"If we're all caught up now?" Eve narrowed her eyes.

"Yes, I knew Dr. Icove, and know his son a little, professionally. What happened is a tragedy. He was a pioneer in his field, and very likely had decades left to work and enjoy life."

"You knew him personally?"

"Through my family somewhat." Louise's blood was wealthy blue. "I admired his work and his dedication. I hope you quickly find who killed him."

"I'm looking through some of his case files, particularly at this point the ones he kept in his home office. He had his unit passcoded, his discs sealed, and the text coded."

Louise pursed her lips. "Very cautious."

"In them, he refers to his patients by letter and number, never by name."

"Extremely cautious. He had many important people, political types, celebrities, business moguls, and so on as patients—or so one assumes as he never revealed names."

"Doubtful in this case. All female, all between the ages of seventeen and twenty-two."

Louise's elegant eyebrows drew together. "All?"

"More than fifty, all documented for treatment over the course of four to five years on these discs."

Her attention was caught now as Louise straightened. "What kind of treatment?"

"You tell me." Eve took out a hard copy of one of the discs, passed the several pages across the coffee table.

As she read, Louise's brow knitted. She began to murmur to herself, shake her head. "Experimental, certainly, and vague on the details. These can't be his actual case notes. It's an overview: physical, mental, emotional, intelligence. Treating the whole patient, as was his method. One I agree with. But . . . Young female subject, excellent physical condition, high intelligence quotient, small corrections to vision and facial structure. Four years of study and treatments wrapped in a few pages. There has to be more."

"Is the subject human?"

Louise's eyes flicked up, then back to the notes again. "The vitals and treatments all indicate a human female. One who was tested regularly, and thoroughly, not only for defects and disease but for mental and artistic progress and prowess. There were fifty of these?"

"That I've found, to date."

"Placement," Louise said softly. "Educational placement? Employment?"

"Dallas doesn't think so," Charles commented with his eyes on Eve's.

"Then what—" Louise broke off, reading the look that passed between her lover and Eve. "Oh God."

"You have to be tested to get an LC license," Eve began.

"That's right." Charles picked up his coffee. "You're tested physically to ensure against disease or condition. You undergo some psychiatric evals, to hopefully eliminate any sexual deviants or predators. And to keep your license current, you're required to have regular exams."

"And there are various levels, with various fee scales."

"Of course. The level of your license is determined not only by your preference, but your skills. Intelligence, knowledge of art and entertainment, your . . . style. A street level, for instance, isn't required to be able to discuss art history with a client, or know Puccini from pig Latin."

"The higher the level, the bigger the fee."

"Correct."

"And the higher the level placed, the bigger the placement fee for the agency that either trains or tests and certifies the LC."

"Also correct."

"It doesn't make sense," Louise interrupted. "First someone with Icove's resources, skills, and interests testing potential LCs? For what purpose? And it doesn't take years to train and certify. His fees would be nominal compared to his real work."

"Boy needs a hobby," Peabody added, and considered another bagel.

Charles played his fingers over the tips of Louise's hair. "She's not thinking traditional LCs, sweetie. Are you, Dallas? Not selling services, but the whole package."

"Selling . . ." Louise went pale. "Dallas, my God."

"It's a theory. I'm working on a couple of them. You'd agree, as a doctor, that the security on these discs is more than usual."

"Yes, but—"

"That the notes themselves are sketchy, and also unusual."

"I agree I'd have to see more to have an opinion to their purpose."

"Where are the images?" Eve asked. "If you, as a doctor, were documenting information such as this on a patient over the course of years, wouldn't you have images of that patient. At certain points? Certainly before and after procedures?"

Louise said nothing for a moment, then let out a long breath. "Yes. I'd also clearly document the steps of any procedure, who assisted, the duration of the procedure. I would've listed the names of the patient as well as the names of any medical or laystaff who assisted in tests. There would, most likely, be personal observations and comments added. But these aren't thorough notes, certainly not medical charts."

"Okay. Thanks." Eve held out her hand for the hard copies.

"You think he may have been involved in some sort of . . . human auction? That's why he was killed."

"It's a theory." Eve got to her feet. "A lot of doctors have God complexes."

"Some," Louise said, coolly now.

"Even God didn't create the perfect woman. Maybe Icove figured he could one-up God. Thanks for the coffee," Eve added, and let herself out.

"I think you pretty much ruined her day," Peabody commented as they walked to the elevator.

"Might as well go for a streak and ruin Dr. Will's day next."

A domestic droid opened the door of the Icoves' home. She'd been created to replicate a woman in her comfortable forties, with a pleasant face, a trim build.

She showed them directly into the main living area, offered them a seat, refreshment, then stepped out. Moments later, Icove came in.

There were shadows under his eyes and a weary pallor to his cheeks.

"You have news?" he asked immediately.

"I'm sorry, Dr. Icove, we don't have anything to tell you at this time. We do have some follow-up questions."

"Oh." He rubbed the center of his forehead in a firm up-and-down motion. "Of course."

As he crossed over to take a seat, Eve saw the young boy peek around the doorway. His hair was so blond it was nearly white and spiked up—as the current fashion demanded—from a youthful and pretty face. He had his mother's eyes, she noted. So blue they were nearly purple.

"I think we might want to discuss this in private," Eve told Icove.

"Yes. My wife and children are still at breakfast."

"Not all of them." Eve inclined her head, and Icove turned in time to catch a glimpse of his son before the boy scooted back out of sight.

"Ben!"

The sharp command had the boy sliding into view again, chin on chest. But those eyes, Eve saw, where bright and avid despite the shamed posture.

"Haven't we discussed eavesdropping on private conversations?"

"Yes, sir."

"Lieutenant Dallas, Detective Peabody," Icove said, "my son, Ben."

"Wilfred B. Icove the Third," the boy announced, straightening his shoulders. "Benjamin's my middle name. You're the police."

Because Peabody knew her partner, she took the front line with the boy. "That's right. We're very sorry about your grandfather, Ben, and we're here to talk to your father."

"Somebody killed my granddad. They stabbed him right in the heart."

"Ben—"

"They *know*." Ben's face was a study in frustration as he turned to his father. "Now they have to ask questions and follow leads and gather evidence. Do you have suspects?" he demanded.

"Ben." Icove spoke more gently and wrapped an arm around his son's shoulders. "My son doesn't want to follow family tradition and enter the medical field. He hopes to be a private investigator."

"Cops have to follow too many rules," the boy explained. "PIs get to break them and they get big, fat fees and hang out with shady characters."

"He enjoys detective book discs and games," Icove added with a light of amusement—and, Eve thought, pride—in his eyes.

"If you're a lieutenant, you get to boss people around, and yell at them and stuff."

"Yeah." Eve felt a smile twitch at her lips. "I like that part."

There was the sound of footsteps moving fast down the hall. Avril appeared, apology on her face. "Ben. Will, I'm sorry. He got away from me."

"No harm. Ben, go back into the breakfast room now with your mother."

"But I want—"

"No arguments."

"Ben." Avril's voice was a murmur, but it worked. Ben's head drooped again as he dragged his feet out of the room.

"Sorry for the interruption," Avril said, curved her lips in a smile that didn't quite reach her eyes, then retreated.

"We're keeping the children home for a few days," Icove explained. "The media doesn't always respect grief, or innocence."

"He's a great-looking kid, Dr. Icove," Peabody put in. "He favors your wife."

"Yes, he does. Both our children favor Avril." His smile warmed, became genuine. "Fortunate DNA. What do you need to know?"

"We have some questions regarding some information accessed from discs recovered from your father's home office."

"Oh?"

"The data they're on was coded."

There was a change—just a flicker—when puzzlement became shock, a shock masked by mild interest. "Medical notes often seem like code to the layman."

"True enough. Even when the text was accessed, the contents are puzzling. Your father appears to have taken notes on the treatment of some fifty patients, female patients from their late teens to early twenties."

Icove's expression remained neutral. "Yes?"

"What do you know about those patients, those . . . treatments, Dr. Icove?"

"I couldn't say." He spread his hands. "Certainly not without reading the notes. I wasn't privy to all my father's cases."

"These strike me as a special project, and one he took some care to keep secure. My impression was his field of interest was reconstructive surgery and sculpting."

"Yes. For more than fifty years, my father dedicated his skills to that field, and led the way to—"

"I'm aware of his accomplishments." Deliberately, Eve hardened her voice. "I'm asking about his interests, and his work, outside of that field, the field he's publically known for. I'm asking about his sidelines, Dr. Icove. Those that involve testing and training young women."

"I'm afraid I don't understand."

Eve took out the hard copies, passed them to him. "These give a glimmer?"

He cleared his throat, read through them. "I'm afraid not. You say you found these on disc in his home office?"

"That's right."

"Possibly copies from a colleague." He lifted his head, but his eyes didn't quite meet Eve's. "There's nothing on here to indicate to me that these are my father's notes. They're very incomplete. Case studies of some sort, of course. And honestly, I fail to see what these might have to do with your investigation."

"I determine what has to do with my investigation. What I found on discs in your father's possession deals with more than fifty unidentified young women who were subjected to tests and evaluations, some surgeries, over a course of years. Who are they, Dr. Icove? Where are they?"

"I don't care for your tone, Lieutenant."

"I get that a lot."

"I assume these women were part of a voluntary test group which interested my father. If you knew anything about reconstructive surgery, or sculpting, you'd be aware that the body isn't merely the box that holds the prize. When the body is seriously injured, it affects the brain, the emotions. The human condition must be treated as a whole. A patient who loses an arm in an accident loses more than a limb, and must be treated for that loss, must be treated and trained to adjust to it and live a contented and productive life. Quite possibly my father was interested in this particular case study as a means to observe individuals, over the course of a span of years, who were being tested and evaluated on every level."

"If this study took place in the Center, you'd be aware of it?"

"I'm sure that I would."

"You and your father were close," Peabody said.

"We were."

"It seems if he was interested enough in a project like this one, enough to keep records in his home office, he would have discussed it with you at some point. Father to son, colleague to colleague."

Icove started to speak, then stopped, seemed to rethink. "It's possible he intended to. I can't speculate on that. Nor can I ask him. He's dead."

"Killed," Eve pointed out, "by a woman. A strong physical specimen, like those documented on the discs."

She heard him suck in a shocked breath, watched that shock, and a hint of fear, widen his eyes. "You . . . You actually believe one of the patients documented on those discs killed my father?"

"Physically, the suspect fits the documented descriptions of most of the subjects. Height, weight, body type. One or more of these patients may have objected to what's termed 'placement.' Potential motive. It would also explain why your father agreed to the appointment."

"What you're suggesting is ludicrous, out of the question. My father helped people, he improved lives. He saved them. The president of the United States contacted me personally with condolences. My father was an icon, but more, he was a man who was loved and respected."

"Someone disrespected him enough to shove a scalpel into his heart. Think about that, Dr. Icove." Eve rose. "You know how to reach me."

"Knows something," Peabody commented when they were out on the sidewalk.

"Oh yeah. What do you figure our chances are of getting a search warrant for the surviving doctor's house?"

"With what we've got? Slim."

"Let's see if we can get more before we spin that wheel."

She hit Feeney next, back at Central, and got a frown on his mopey face.

"Got into the unit, no problem. What you got in there's medical mumbo. Can't see anything hinky about it. But it turns out Jasmina Free's tits didn't come from God, and neither did those pillow lips of hers, or her chin. Or her damn ass either."

"Who's Jasmina Free?"

"Jesus, Dallas. Vid goddess. Starred in last summer's biggest blockbuster, *Endgame*."

"I was a little busy over the summer."

"Took an Oscar last year for *Harm None*."

"I guess I was a little busy last year, too."

"Thing is, girl's an eyepopper. Now that I know most of it came from the sculpting knife, it spoils things."

"Sorry to rain on your prurient fantasies, Feeney, but I'm a little busy now, too, just trying to close a case."

"Giving you what I got, aren't I?" he grumbled. "A lot of other high-dollar names on his client list. Some just getting a couple of tweaks, others going the full-body and face route."

"Full names listed?"

"Yeah, sure. It's his patient list."

"Right." She nodded. "Interesting. Keep going."

"I took a look around, poking for some underlayment. See if the doc had any sideline in changing faces and whatnot for new ID purposes."

"That's a good thought."

"Didn't find any. Came up and up. You know what Jasmina paid for those tits? Twenty grand each." A faint smile ghosted around his mouth. "Guess I gotta say, money well spent."

"You're scaring me, Feeney."

He shrugged. "The wife thinks it's midlife crisis, but she doesn't mind. Man doesn't appreciate a good rack—God- or man-made— he might as well apply for a self-termination permit."

"You say. Lot of high-powered, famed names on his patient and consult lists. So it's interesting that he keeps coded files in his home office."

She filled him in, then gave him copies on the off chance he might see or find anything on them she'd missed.

When he left her office, Eve was curious enough to look up Jasmina Free on Icove's records.

Thoughtfully she studied the images. As Louise had verified, there were several, before and after, every procedure, various angles. She didn't see anything wrong with the breasts in the before, but was forced to admit they were a reckoning force in the after.

Now that she saw the image she recognized the vid star. She supposed people in Free's profession looked at tit jobs and lip fattening as job security.

A lot of young girls fantasized about being vid stars, she supposed. Or music stars like Mavis.

Placement.

Create perfect specimens then place them in their fantasy. But what teenager has the money for that?

Rich parents. The newest underground method of fulfilling your little darling's fondest wish.

Happy birthday, honey! We got you some rocking new breasts.

Not much more out there than Roarke's Frankenstein theory.

Following through, she brought up Free's official data.

Born twenty-six years ago in Louisville, Kentucky, one of three children. Father a retired city cop.

Forget that theory as applies to Free, Eve decided. Cops didn't make enough for big doctor's fees.

Of course, being a humanitarian, he could have taken some of them on for free. But she read through the data, found no gaps.

Still, it was a thought to go down on her list. Something else to fiddle with.

Curious, she brought up Lee-Lee Ten's data. She and Will Icove had seemed pretty damn chummy.

Born in Baltimore, no sibs. Raised by mother after termination of legal cohab with father. First professional modeling, age six months.

Six months? What the hell did a six-month-old model? she wondered.

Modeled, did screen ads, baby bits in vids.

Jesus, Eve thought, reading. The woman had worked her entire life. No placement possibilities there, she decided. None of Icove's records listed placements before the age of seventeen.

But she ran the name through the Center's records and noted Lee-Lee had had a number of "tune-ups" over the years.

Was no one satisfied with the package God put her in?

She ran probabilities on her computer, toying with various scenarios. Nothing rang for her. She got coffee, then settled in to wade through Icove's many properties, arms, connections, looking for locations that might provide him with privacy for side projects.

She found dozens: homes, hospitals, offices, treatment and health centers, research facilities, physical, mental, emotional rehabilitation centers, and combinations thereof. Some he owned outright, some were owned by his foundation, others he had interests in, or was affiliated with, or served in some capacity.

She separated them into her own priorities, concentrating first on locations where Icove had held full control.

Then she rose and paced. She couldn't discount the sites that were out of the country, even off planet. Nor could she positively state she wasn't chasing the wild goose by concentrating on this single angle.

But she wasn't, Eve thought as she stared out at the bleak November sky through her skinny window.

The doctor had kept a secret, and secrets were what haunted. Secrets were what hurt.

She should know.

He'd given them labels, she thought. Denying people a name dehumanized them.

They'd given her no name when she'd been born. Had given her none for the first eight years of her life while they had used and abused her. Dehumanizing her. Preparing her. Training her through rape and beatings and fear to make a whore of her. She'd been an investment, not a child.

And it was that not-quite-human thing that had broken, that had finally broken and killed what had tormented and imprisoned her.

Not the same. Roarke was right, it wasn't the same. There was no mention of rape in the notes. No physical abuse of any kind. On the contrary, care seemed to have been taken to keep them at the height of physical perfection.

But there were other kinds of abuse, and some of it looked so benign on the surface.

Somewhere in those notes was motive. Somewhere beyond them was more specific documentation. That's where she'd find Dolores.

"Eve."

She turned at Mira's voice. Mira stood in the open doorway, hollow-eyed. "I came to apologize for brushing you off this morning."

"Not a problem."

"Yes, it is. Mine. I'd like to come in. Close the door."

"Sure."

"I'd like to see what you wanted to show me this morning."

"I consulted another medical expert. It isn't necessary for you to—"

"Please." Mira sat, folded her hands in her lap. "May I see?"

Saying nothing, Eve got the papers, gave them to Mira.

"Cryptic," Mira said after a few moments of silence. "Incomplete. Wilfred was a meticulous man, in all areas of his life. Yet in their way these are meticulously cryptic."

"Why aren't they named?"

"To help him keep his distance, his objectivity. These are long-term treatments. I would say he didn't want to risk emotional attachment. They're being groomed."

"For?"

"I can't say. But they're being groomed, educated, tested, given the opportunity to explore their personal strengths and skills, improve their weaknesses. Those in the lower percentile are terminated as patients after it's deemed they're unlikely to improve. He sets the bar high. He would."

"What would he need to pull this off?"

"I'm not sure what *this* is. But he'd need medical and laboratory facilities, rooms or dormitories for the patients, food preparation areas, exercise areas, educational areas. He would want the best. He'd insist on it. If these girls were indeed his patients, he would want them comfortable, stimulated, well treated."

She looked up at Eve. "He would not abuse a child. He would not harm. I don't say this as his friend, Eve. I say this as a criminal profiler. He was a fiercely dedicated doctor."

"Would he conduct experiments outside the law?"

"Yes."

"You don't hesitate on that."

"He would consider the science, the medicine, the benefits and the possibilities more important than law. Often, they are. And on some level, he would consider himself above the law. There was no violence or cruelty in him, but there was arrogance."

"If he was spearheading, or even involved in a project that was grooming—as you said—young girls into what some might consider perfect women, would his son have known?"

"Without question. Their pride in each other—their affection for each other—was genuine and deep."

"The kind of facility you've described, long-term treatment as indicated by the data, the equipment, the security. All of that would cost big."

"I imagine it would."

Eve leaned forward. "Would he agree to meet with . . . let's call her a graduate of his project? She was a label to him, a subject— and still he worked with her for several years, watched her progress. If she contacted him at some point after she was placed, would he meet her?"

"His professional instinct would be to refuse, but both his ego and his curiosity would war with that. Medicine is risk, day after day. I think he would have risked this for the satisfaction of seeing one of his own. If indeed she was."

"Wasn't she? Isn't it more likely, given the method of the murder, that he knew her, and she him? She had to get close, had to want to. One stab wound, in the heart. No rage, but control. As he had control over her. A medical instrument as murder weapon, a clean cut. Objective, as he'd been objective."

"Yes." Mira closed her eyes. "Oh God, what has he done?"

7 EVE SNAGGED PEABODY AT HER DESK IN THE bull pen. "We're going to spin that wheel. Mira's writing up a vic profile to add weight to what we've got. Then we're pushing for a search warrant."

"I've got nothing that stands out on the financials," Peabody told her.

"Daughter-in-law, grandkids?"

"Nothing out of line."

"There's money somewhere. There always is. Guy has that many fingers in that many pies, he probably has some secret pies tucked away somewhere. For now, we're going back to the Center, talking to people—admin down."

"Can I wear your new coat?"

"Sure, Peabody."

Peabody's face beamed like the sun. "Really?"

"No." With a roll of her eyes and a sweep of leather, Eve started out.

Peabody sulked after her. "You didn't have to get my hopes up."

"If I don't get them up, how can I crush them? Where would I get my satisfaction?" She sidestepped for a pair of uniforms who were muscling a bruiser down the corridor. The bruiser sang obscenities at the top of his voice.

"Well, he can carry a tune," Eve remarked.

"A very pleasant baritone. Can I try on the coat sometime when you're not wearing it?"

"Sure, Peabody."

"You're getting my hopes up again, only to crush them, right?"

"Keep learning that fast, you may make Detective Second Grade one day." Eve sniffed the air as she hopped on a glide. "I smell chocolate. Do you have chocolate?"

"If I did, I wouldn't give it to you," Peabody muttered.

Eve sniffed again, then followed the aroma trail with her eyes. She spotted Nadine Furst crammed on the upcoming glide. The Channel 75 on-air reporter had her streaky hair swept up in some sort of twisty roll, wore a canary-yellow trench coat over a dark blue suit. And carried a hot-pink bakery box.

"If you're taking that bribe to my department," Eve called out, "there'd better be some left for me."

"Dallas?" Nadine squeezed through the jam of bodies. "Damn it. Wait. Wait at the bottom. Oh my God, the coat! Wait. I need five minutes."

"Heading out. Later."

"No, no, no." As they passed, nearly shoulder to shoulder, Nadine managed to shake the box. "Brownies. Triple chocolate."

"Bitch." Eve sighed. "Five minutes."

"Surprised you didn't just rip it out of her hands, then thumb your nose at her," Peabody commented.

"Considered, rejected. Too many witnesses." Besides, Eve thought, she might be able to use Nadine as much as she could use a triple chocolate brownie.

Nadine's shoes matched her coat, and both the heels and toes looked sharp enough to sever a jugular. Yet somehow she managed to stride along in them as if they were as comfy as Peabody's airskids.

"Show me the chocolate," Eve said without preamble. Obliging, Nadine lifted the lid of the box. Eve gave a brief nod. "Good bribe. Walk and talk."

"The coat." Nadine said it like a woman praying. "It's extreme."

"Keeps the rain off." Eve swiveled her shoulder when Nadine stroked a hand over the leather covering it.

"Don't pet it."

"It's like smooth black cream. I'd give an astounding sexual performance for a coat like this."

"Thanks, but you're not my type. Is my coat going to be the topic of discussion during your five minutes?"

"I could talk about that coat for days, but no. Icove."

"The dead one or the live one?"

"Dead. We've got bio data up the ying, and we'll be using it. Wilfred Benjamin Icove, medical pioneer, healer, and humanitarian. Philanthropist and philosopher. Loving father, doting granddad. Scientist and scholar, yaddah, blah. His life's going to be covered endlessly by every media outlet on and off planet. Tell me how he got dead."

"Stabbed through the heart. Give me a brownie."

"Forget it." And Nadine hooked both arms around the box to prevent a snatch-and-run. "A voice-cracking on-air for his high school data screen's got that much. Chocolate's not cheap. We've got the beautiful and mysterious female suspect angle. Security guards, medical and administrative staff don't have to be bribed to blab. What have you got on her?"

"Nothing."

"Come on." Nadine reopened the lid of the box, waved her hand over it as if to waft the scent into Eve's face.

Eve had to laugh. "It's believed the female individual who allegedly was the last person to see Icove alive used false ID. The investigating officers and the EDD section of the department are working with all diligence to identify this individual so that she can be questioned in regards to Icove's death."

"An unidentified woman, using false ID, slipped through the elaborate security at the WBI Center, strolled into his office, stabbed him in the heart, strolled out again. Got it."

"I'm not confirming that. We are very interested in identifying, locating, and questioning this individual. Give me a damn brownie."

When Nadine lifted the lid, Eve snatched two. Before a protest could be voiced, she passed one to Peabody. "Further," she said with a mouthful of chocolate so rich she all but heard her tonsils hum, "we are pursuing the theory that the victim knew his attacker."

"Knew her? That's fresh."

The brownie was worth fresh. "We have not yet identified the attacker as male or female. However, the death blow was inflicted at close range, and there is no evidence of struggle, duress, no defensive wounds. There is no indication of robbery or other assault. There is a strong likelihood that the victim knew his attacker. Certainly, evidence doesn't indicate he felt threatened."

"Motive?"

"Working on it." They'd made their way down to garage level. "Off the record."

"I hate that." Nadine hissed. "Off the record."

"I think the doctor was into something slippery on the side."

"Sex?"

"Possibly. If the trail we're following leads to that, it's going to be hot. The reporter who breaks it might get singed."

"I'll dig out my heat shields."

"Save me time. Dig info instead. I want all the data your researchers have on Icove, then I want more. Anything that has to do with medical or social areas of interest that are off-center."

Nadine pursed her lips. "In which direction?"

"Any. You get me something that helps me, when this is ready to go public, I'll give you the whole ball, a full media cycle ahead of the pack."

Nadine's eyes, a feline green, were vivid with interest. "You think he was dirty."

"I think anybody who looks that clean's got grime washed down some drain."

When they were in Eve's vehicle, the bakery box tucked in the back, Peabody produced finger wipes out of her bag. "You don't believe someone can live a blameless life?" she asked. "Be intrinsically good, even selfless."

"Not if they're made of blood and bone. Nobody's spotless, Peabody."

"My father's never hurt anyone. Just a for-instance."

"Your father doesn't pretend to be a saint, or have a PR firm spinning his halos. Got himself arrested a couple times, right?"

"Well, just minor charges. Protesting. Free-Agers mostly feel honor-bound to protest, and they don't believe in permits. But that's not—"

"It's a mark," Eve interrupted. "A little one, sure, but a mark. He doesn't try to erase it. A slate this squeaky clean? Somebody washed it."

The slate remained pristine as they worked their way through staff at the center. From his administrative assistant to lab techs, from doctors to orderlies. It was, Eve thought, more shrine than slate.

Eve tried the admin again, from a different angle.

"It seems, looking over Dr. Icove's schedule, his personal calendar, he had a lot of free time. How did he use it?"

"He spent a lot of time visiting patients, here and at other facilities where he was affiliated." Pia wore black, head to toe, and had a tissue balled in her hand. "Dr. Icove believed, strongly believed, in the personal touch."

"From his surgical and consulting schedule, it didn't appear he had a great many active patients."

"Oh, he also visited patients who weren't his own. That is, he considered every patient or client who came into one of his facilities to belong to him. He spent several hours every week doing what you'd call informal visits. Keeping his finger on the pulse, he liked to say. He also spent considerable time reading the medical journals, keeping current. And writing papers for them. And he was doing another book. He'd published five. He kept busy, even though he was semiretired."

"How often, per week, did you see him?"

"It varied. If he wasn't traveling, at least two, sometimes three days a week. He'd also check in holographically."

"You ever travel with him?"

"Occasionally, when he needed me."

"Did you ever . . . meet his needs in personal areas?"

It took her a moment to translate, and Eve knew there'd been no sexual relationship here. "No! No, of course not. Dr. Icove would never have . . . Never."

"But he had companions. He enjoyed the company of women."

"Well, yes. But there was no one specific, or serious. I'd have known." Pia sighed. "I wish there had been. He was such a lovely man. But he still loved his wife. He told me once there were some gifts, some relationships that could never be replaced or replicated. His work sustained him. His work, and his family."

"How about personal projects? Experimental projects he was working on that he wasn't ready to make public. Where did he keep his personal lab, his personal charts?"

Pia shook her head. "Experimental projects? No, Dr. Icove used the research facilities here. He considered them the best in the world. Anything he or the researchers worked on would have been logged. Dr. Icove was meticulous about recording data."

"I bet," Eve replied. "His last appointment. How did they greet each other?"

"He was at his desk when I brought her in. He stood up. I'm not sure . . ."

"Did they shake hands?"

"Um. No. No, I don't think . . . I remember he stood up, and smiled. She said something first, even before I made the introductions. I remember that now."

Pia continued. "Yes, I remember, she said something like it was good to meet him, and that she appreciated him taking his valuable time for her. Something along those lines. I think he said he was very pleased to see her. I think that's what he said. He gestured to the refreshments in the sitting area, maybe started to go around his desk, but she shook her head. She said thank you, but she didn't care for anything. Then Dr. Icove told me they'd be fine. 'We'll be fine, Pia, you go ahead to lunch at your usual time. Enjoy yourself.'

"It's the last thing he said to me." Now she began to cry. "'Enjoy yourself.'"

With Peabody, Eve closed herself into Icove's office. Crime Scene had been through, leaving their faint scent behind. She'd already run the probabilities and the reconstruction programs, but she wanted to see it on-site, with people.

"Be Icove. At his desk," she ordered Peabody.

As Peabody obliged, Eve crossed back to the door, turned. "What are you doing? With your face?"

"I'm trying for an avuncular smile. Like a kind doctor."

"Cut it out. It's creepy. Admin and Dolores enter. Icove stands. The women walk over. No handshake, because she's probably sealed, and he'd feel it. How does she get out of it?"

"Ah." Standing in Icove's place, Peabody considered. "Shy? Eyes downcast, maybe hands, both hands, on the handle of her bag. Nervous. Or—"

"Or she looks him right in the eye, because they know each other already. And her face, the look, signals him that they're going to skip the handshakes and how-are-yous. Think about what he said, according to his admin. He was happy to see her—Dolores. Not happy to meet her, or meet with her, but see her."

"Unspoken 'again'?"

"That's what I'm hearing. Refreshments offered, refused. Admin leaves, shuts the door. They sit."

Eve took the seat across from the desk. "She has to bide her time, wait for the admin to go to lunch. They talk. Maybe he suggests they move to the sitting area for tea, but she wants him at his desk, turns it down."

"Why at the desk?" Peabody asked. "It would've been easier for her to get close if they were on the sofa there."

"Symbolic. Behind the desk is in charge, is the power. She wants him dead on his seat of power. Taking it back from him. There you are, she might think, behind your beautiful desk in your big office high above the city, reigning over the center you built in your own name. Wearing your expensive suit. And you don't know you're dead."

"Cold," Peabody added.

"The woman who walked out of here had plenty of chill. Time passes, she gets up."

As Eve rose, so did Peabody. "He'd stand," Peabody stated. "He's old school. A woman stands, he stands. Like he did when she first came in."

"Good point. So she says: 'Sit, please.' Maybe gestures him down.

She has to keep talking, but nothing confrontational. No, she has to keep him at ease. She has to come around the desk to him."

Eve mimicked the move she saw in her head. Walking to the desk, unhurried, eyes calm. She saw the way Peabody instinctively swiveled in the desk chair to face her more truly.

"Then she has to . . ." Eve leaned over until her face and Peabody's were nearly on a level. And with the pen she'd palmed gave her partner a light jab at the heart.

"Jeez!" Peabody jerked back. "No poking. I thought, for a really weird minute, you were going to kiss me or something. Then you . . . Oh."

"Yeah. The angle of the wound. She standing, he's sitting, but with her height factored in, his seated height calculated, she leaned over him. She came from this angle, he turned in the chair—automatically—just like you did. Got the weapon palmed. He never saw it. He's watching her face.

"She shoves it in him, and it's done. He knew her, Peabody. One of his placements, I give you odds. Maybe he even helped her get the fake ID, maybe that's part of the service. She could still be a pro, but it feels less and less like a work for hire."

"The son didn't know her. I'd give you odds on that."

"Didn't recognize is different from didn't know."

Frowning now, Eve circled the room. "Why doesn't he have any data here? Here, where he works two or three days a week. Why doesn't he have any of those coded files in his office, in his power seat?"

"If it's a sideline, maybe he wanted to keep it on the side."

"Yeah." But Eve studied the desk, the file drawers in it had been locked. She had those files now, but that didn't mean they were complete.

The door opened. Will Icove strode in. "What are you doing here?" he demanded.

"Our job. This is a crime scene. What are you doing here?"

"This is my father's office. I don't know what you're looking for here, or why you seem more interested in smearing my father's good name than apprehending his killer, but—"

"Apprehending his killer is the goal," Eve countered. "To do that we have to look at and for things that may not please you. Was the woman who called herself Dolores Nocho-Alverez your father's patient?"

"You've looked through his records. Have you found her?"

"I don't believe we've seen all of his records." Eve opened Peabody's file case, removed the photo of Dolores. "Take another look."

"I've never seen her before." But he didn't look at the still Eve held out. "I don't know why she killed my father, or why you seem bent on blaming him for his own death."

"You're wrong. I blame the person who put the knife in him for his death." Eve replaced the picture. "It's the why I question, and if he and his killer had a history, that speaks to the why. What was he working on? What had he been working on, privately, for so long?"

"My father's work was revolutionary. And it's documented. Whoever this woman was she was unbalanced, obviously unbalanced. If you find her, which I've come to doubt you will, she'll be found to be mentally defective. In the meantime, my family and I are in mourning. My wife and children have gone to our home in the Hamptons, and I'll join them tomorrow. We need privacy, a time to retreat and finalize plans for my father's memorial."

He paused, seemed to struggle with his emotions. "I don't know anything about your sort of work. I'm told you're very competent. Trusting that, I'm going to wait until we come back to the city. If at that time, there's been no progress, and you've continued to investigate my father rather than his death, I intend to use whatever influence I have to have this matter transferred to another investigator."

"That's your privilege."

He nodded, moved back to the door. With his hand on the knob, he drew a breath. "He was a great man," he said, and left the room.

"He's nervous," Peabody observed. "Grieving—I don't think he's faking that—but nervous, too. We've pushed on a sensitive spot."

"Sent the wife and kiddies away," Eve mused. "Good time to clean out anything incriminating. We're not going to get that search order in time to stop him, not if he moves right away."

"He wipes data, EDD will dig it out."

"Spoken like an e-groupie." But Eve nodded. "We'll push for the warrant."

She was still waiting for it at end of shift, and as a last resort hauled Nadine's bakery box into the cell-like office of an assistant prosecuting attorney.

APAs, Eve noted, didn't fare much better than cops when it came to work environment.

Cher Reo had a rep for being hungry. Eve earmarked her because if the brownies didn't turn the tide, the prospect of having part in a scandal that would generate days of screen time should.

Despite the sunny sweep of silky hair, the baby-doll blue eyes and curvy pink lips, Cher was known to be a piranha. She was wearing a stone-gray skirt—demurely to her knees—and a simple white shirt. The matching jacket was draped neatly over the back of her chair.

Her desk was covered with files, discs, notes. She drank coffee out of a super-sized to-go cup.

Eve waltzed in, dropped the candy-pink box on the desk. And watched Cher's nostrils flare.

"What?" She had a little Southern in her voice, like a dusting of sugar. Eve had yet to decide if it was genuine.

"Brownies."

Cher leaned a little closer to the box, sniffed. Shut her eyes. "I'm on a diet."

"Triple chocolate."

"Whore." Lifting the box a fraction, Cher peeked, groaned. "Filthy whore. What do I have to do for them?"

"I'm still waiting for the warrant on Icove Jr.'s residence."

"You'll be lucky if you get it at all. You're poking pointy sticks in the eye of a saint, Dallas." Cher sat back, swiveled. Eve saw she had airskids on her feet. And dignified gray heels tucked into the corner of the room. "My boss doesn't want to give you the go to jam it in. He's going to want more."

Eve leaned a hip on the edge of the desk. "Convince him otherwise. The surviving son knows something, Reo. While your boss is playing politics instead of throwing his weight with mine—and Mira's—to a judge, data may very well be lost. Does the PA's office want to hinder the investigation into the murder of a man of Icove's stature?"

"Nope. And it sure doesn't want to toss shit into his grave either."

"Push for the warrant, Reo. If I get what I'm after, it's going to be big. And I'll remember who helped me get it."

"If you turn up nothing? Nobody's going to forget who helped you screw this up either."

"I'll turn up something." She pushed off the desk. "If you can't trust me, Reo, trust the brownies."

Reo blew out a breath. "It'll take a while. Even saying I can convince my boss—and that's going to take some doing—we've got to convince a judge to sign off."

"Then why don't you get started?"

This time when she got home, Summerset was where she expected him to be. Lurking in the foyer like some prune-faced gargoyle. She decided to let him take the first shot. She preferred retaliation, because it usually gave her the last word.

She stripped off her coat while they eyed each other. And decided it made even more of a statement draped over the newel post than her usual jacket did.

"Lieutenant. I need a moment of your time."

Her brow knit. He wasn't supposed to say that, and in a polite, inoffensive tone. "What for?"

"It regards Wilfred Icove."

"What about him?"

Summerset, a brittle stick of a man in a stiff black suit, kept his dark eyes on hers. His face, usually grim in Eve's mind, seemed even more strained than usual. "I'd like to offer any assistance I can in the matter of your investigation."

"Well, that'll be the day," she began, then narrowed her eyes. "You knew him. How's that?"

"I knew him, slightly. I served as a medic—somewhat unofficially—during the Urban Wars."

She glanced up as Roarke came down the steps. "Did you already know this?"

"Just shortly ago. Why don't we go sit down?" Before she could protest, Roarke took her arm, led her into the parlor. "Summerset tells me he met Icove in London, and worked with him at one of the clinics there during the wars."

"*For* him is more accurate," Summerset corrected. "He came to London to help establish more clinics, and the mobile medical units that eventually transformed into Unilab. He had been a part of the team that had established them here in New York, where the outbreaks started before they bled into Europe. Some forty years ago now," he added. "Before either of you were born. Before my daughter was born."

"How long was he in London?" Eve asked.

"Two months. Perhaps three." Summerset spread his bony hands. "It blurs. He saved countless lives during that period, worked tirelessly. Risked his own life more than once. He implemented some of his innovations in reconstructive surgery on that battlefield. That's what the cities were then. Battlefields. You've seen images from that period, but it was nothing compared to being there, living through it. Victims who would have lost limbs, or gone through their lives scarred, were spared that due to his work."

"Would you say he experimented?"

"He innovated. He created. The media reports that this might have been a professional assassination. I have contacts still, in certain circles."

"If you want to use them, fine. Poke around. Carefully. How well did you know him, personally?"

"Not well. People who come together in war often bond quickly, even intimately. But when they have nothing else in common that bond fades. And he was . . . aloof."

"Superior."

Disapproval covered Summerset's face, but he nodded. "That term wouldn't be inaccurate. We worked together, ate and drank together, but he maintained distance from those who worked under him."

"Give me a personality rundown, deleting the sainthood level."

"It's difficult to say with any accuracy. It was war. Personalities cope, or shine, or shatter during war."

"You had an opinion of him, as a man."

"He was brilliant." Summerset glanced over, with some surprise, as Roarke offered him a short glass of whiskey. "Thank you."

"Brilliant's on record," Eve said. "I'm not looking for brilliant."

"You want flaws." Summerset sipped the whiskey. "I don't consider them flaws when a young, brilliant doctor is impatient and frustrated with the circumstances, with the equipment and the poor facilities where we worked. He demanded a great deal, and because he gave a great deal, accomplished a great deal, he usually got it."

"You said aloof. Just to other doctors, medics, volunteers, or to patients, too?"

"Initially, he made a point of learning the names of every patient he tended, and I would say he suffered at each loss. And losses were . . . horrendous. He then implemented a system assigning numbers rather than names."

"Numbers," Eve murmured.

"Essential objectivity, I believe he called it. They were bodies that needed tending, or reconstruction. Bodies that needed to be kept breathing, or terminated. He was hard, but circumstances demanded it. Those who couldn't step back from the horror were useless to those who suffered from that horror."

"His wife was killed during that period."

"I was working in another part of the city at that time. As I remember, he left London immediately upon being notified of her death, and went to his son, who was being kept safe in the country."

"No contact since."

"No. I can't imagine he would have remembered me. I've followed his work, and was pleased that so much of what he'd hoped to do came to be."

"He talked about that? What he hoped to do."

"To me? No." What might have been a smile passed over Summerset's face. "But I heard him speak to other doctors. He wanted to heal, to help, to improve the quality of life."

"He was a perfectionist."

"There's no perfection during war."

"That must have frustrated him."

"It frustrated us all. People were dying all around us. No matter how many we saved, there were more we couldn't reach, couldn't help. A man might be shot down in the street because he had decent shoes. Another might have his throat cut because he had none at all. Frustration is a small word."

Eve chased through her mind. "So his kid's tucked away in the countryside, and his wife's working beside him."

"Not beside, no. She volunteered in a hospital that had been set up to treat injured children, and to house those lost or orphaned."

"He fool around?"

"Excuse me?"

"It's war, he's away from his family. His life's on the line. Did he sleep with anybody?"

"I don't see the purpose in so crude a question, but no, not that I was aware of. He was devoted to his family and his work."

"Okay. I'll get back to you." She got to her feet. "Roarke?"

She moved out of the room, heard Roarke murmur something before he followed her. She waited until they were upstairs before she spoke. "You didn't tell him anything about the data we found."

"No. And it's an uncomfortable position."

"Well, you're going to have to be uncomfortable for a while. I don't know if his murder had its roots back as far as the Urban Wars, but it's something I want to think about. Unless his killer was able to shed a good decade surgically or through enhancements, she wasn't born during that time either. But . . ."

"She had a mother, a father. And they would have been."

"Yeah. Another possibility. War orphans. Could've started experimenting, treating, placing." She paced the bedroom. "It isn't tidy, is it, just to leave kids scavenging around on the streets, during a war, after the madness of war? Some of them won't survive, and you're in the business of survival. You're interested in improving that quality of life. But also appearance. See a lot of carnage during a war. Maybe it twisted him up."

She checked her wrist unit. "Where the hell's my warrant?"

She dropped down on the sofa, studied Roarke thoughtfully. "How'd you feel back then, when Summerset took you in off the streets?"

"I got fed, got to sleep in a bed. And nobody was beating the bloody hell out of me on a daily basis." The man who'd seen to that, Roarke thought, had given him a great deal more than clean sheets and food for his belly. "I was half dead anyway when he took me in. By the time I was able to think clearly, get out of bed, I was over my shock at my luck. Considered that he might be a mark, which he disabused me of the first time I tried to pick his pocket. And I learned to be grateful, for the first time in my life."

"So when he told you what to do, when he educated you, housed you, set rules, you went along."

"He didn't put shackles on me. I'd've slipped the locks and run. But yes."

"Yeah." She leaned her head back, stared at the ceiling. "And then he becomes family. Father, mother, teacher, doctor, priest. The ball of it."

"In essence. Ah, speaking of family. Several members of mine will be coming over from Clare. Now that I've done the thing, I don't know quite what to expect."

She looked back at him. "Well, that makes a pair of us."

8

TICK-TOCK, EVE THOUGHT, AND SCOWLED AT the 'link she'd set on the dining room table. There was a cheery fire in the hearth and some sort of fancy pig meat on her plate.

"Don't you know a watched 'link never beeps." She shifted her gaze to Roarke as he stabbed some meat from her plate onto his fork and held it out to her. "Be a good girl and eat your dinner."

"I know how to feed myself." But because it was there, she took the offering. Damn good pig. "He'll have wiped documents by now."

"Anything you can do about that?"

"No."

"Then you might as well enjoy your dinner."

There were some sort of fancy potatoes to go with the fancy pig. She gave them a try. "They've got to have money hidden somewhere. You interested in finding it?"

Roarke sipped his wine, cocked his head. "Lieutenant, I'm always interested in finding money."

"Whether or not this warrant comes through, I'm going to want the money trail. Funding for whatever this project is, fees or profit generated from it."

"All right. Plans are to have the meal in here."

She frowned at him. "We are having the meal in here." She stabbed some pork, held it up. "See?"

"Thanksgiving, Eve." And he could admit he was a bit wound up about it as he was so completely unsure of his steps.

He knew how to handle people, parties, meetings, his very complicated wife. He knew how to run an interplanetary empire, and still carve out time to dabble in murder cases. But how the hell was he going to handle family?

"Oh, right. Turkey, sure." Eve looked vaguely around the room with its huge table, stunning art, glints of silver, and warm, glowing wood. "Well, this would be the place for it. So this assignment? It would be official. No slippery stuff."

"Well, you take the fun out of it, don't you?"

"I can get authorization for a full-level financial search. Icove's murder, the several working theories. Blackmail, whacked-out former patient, the possibility it was a professional and/or terrorist hit."

"None of which you subscribe to."

"I don't eliminate them," Eve said. "But they're bottom of my list. I've also got the secured and encoded discs to add weight to the authorization. I can argue that whatever this project was, it led to the murder. Push all that together, and I can get authorization without offending any sensibilities. Not saying Icove was dirty, but that something to do with his work—and income from same—led to his murder."

"Clever of you."

"I'm a clever gal. Until I have more, I don't make noises about possible human hybridization or sex slavery or companion training. Get me the money, so I can."

"Good as done, then."

He tried to relax into his dinner and not worry about the logistics of this event he'd started. The transportation was no problem. He'd already seen to that. And housing them, well, the place was big enough to tuck them in even if the whole lot of them hopped the shuttle.

But what the hell was he going to do with them once they got here? It wasn't like entertaining business associates or even friends.

He had relations, for God's sake. How was he supposed to get used to having them, dealing with them, when he'd lived nearly the whole of his life without them?

Now they were going to be under his roof, and he hadn't a clue what they would expect.

"Should we have something separate for the children, do you think?"

"What?" Eve frowned at him as she poked at the food on her plate. "Oh, that. Hell, I don't know. You're supposed to know how to do this stuff."

His face was a mirror of his frustration. "And how am I supposed to know how to do something I've never done before?" He scowled into his wine. "It's unnerving, that's what it is."

"You could contact them, say something's come up. Cancel."

"I'm not a bloody coward," he muttered in a way that made her think he'd considered doing just that. "And it would be rude as well."

"I can be rude." Shifting work to one side, she gave it some thought. "I like being rude."

"That's because you're so good at it."

"True. You could tell them that due to my obsessive involvement in a juicy murder case, Thanksgiving's been cancelled. No turkey for you. See, then it's all on me. Me bloody wife's driving me starkers," she said in an exaggerated Irish accent while she waved the water glass around. "The lieutenant, she's working all the day and half the night as well, and not giving me five minutes of her precious time. What's a man to do, then? Bugger it."

He sat silent a moment, just staring at her. "I don't sound a bit like that, nor does anyone of my acquaintance."

"You haven't heard yourself when you're drunk, which you would be out of frustration with my selfish behavior." She shrugged, drank some water. "Problem solved."

"Not nearly, but thanks for the strange and generous offer. Well, back to murder, which as it happens is a simpler matter for both of us to deal with."

"Got that right."

"Why do you suppose a man of Icove's stature would dabble, if your theory's correct, in gray medicine?"

"Because he could, that's one. And because he was hoping to build a—what do you call it?—better mousetrap. The human body's flawed, right. It breaks down, needs regular repair and maintenance. It's fragile. He grew up seeing its fragility with his parents' work. Then with his mother's accident and subsequent suicide. His wife's death, and the whole ugly nightmare of the Urbans. So how much of a rush would it be to try to make it perfect, to make it stronger, more durable, smarter? You've already done considerable work toward that goal, and gotten accolades for it. Gotten way rich for it. Why not take it up a level?"

"With only women?"

"I don't know." She shook her head. "Maybe he had a thing for women. His mother, his wife. Maybe he focused on women because his women had proven too fragile.

"And rich or not, he's got to have income to sustain the work. Probably, that's more your area than mine. It's still easier to sell a female than a male. There are still more female LCs than male. Sexual predators are most usually male. You guys equate sex with power or virility, even life. Punishment, if you're twisted. Women, mostly, equate it with emotion first. Or see it as a commodity or bargaining tool."

"Or weapon."

"Yeah, that, too. It's how the machine ticks. See ..." She ate without thinking about it now that the pieces of the case were shifting around in her mind. "You've got this big-deal doc—big brain, big name, big bucks. Big ego. You get that."

Roarke smiled. "Naturally."

"He's already got a lot under his belt. Lots of good, public work, lots of important slaps on the back. And a hell of a good lifestyle. But there's always more. More to do, more to want to do. More to just want. That Frankenstein guy, he must've been pretty smart."

He loved watching her wind her way through a case, he thought. The way her brain picked at details and knitted them together. "Well, creating life out of dead body parts."

"Okay, disgusting, but smart. Lots of medical, scientific, technological advances come through little bits of craziness, a lot of ego."

"Or happy accidents," Roarke pointed out.

She nodded toward the candles burning on the table. "Bet the first guy who made fire figured he was a god, and the other cave-men bowed down to him."

"Or bashed him in the head with a rock and stole his burning stick."

She had to laugh. "Yeah. Well, yeah, but you get me. So you make fire, then, hey, let's see what we can do with this. Wow, no more raw mastodon! Make mine medium-well. Oh shit, I set Joe on fire!"

Now Roarke's laugh rolled out, and made her grin. "Oops, sorry, Joe," she continued. "So now you have to figure out how to treat a burn. And how to deal with somebody who *likes* to set Joe on fire, and maybe torch the village. Next thing you know, you've got hospitals and cops and climate control and—" She forked up more meat. "Roast pig on demand."

"A fascinating capsule view of civilization."

"I think I got off my point somewhere around the mastodon. Anyway, what I'm saying is, you do something big—universal big, life-and-death big, and get known for it. What's next?"

"Bigger."

When her 'link beeped, she snatched it up. "Dallas."

"You'd better be right." Reo's Southern-comfort voice was all business. "Because our asses are sharing the same sling."

"Just shoot me the paper."

"No, I'm bringing the warrant personally. I'll meet you at Icove Jr.'s residence in twenty minutes. Oh, and Dallas, if that sling rips, I'm tossing you out and using you to break my fall."

"Fair enough." She clicked off, glanced at Roarke. "Well, here we go," she said, and beeped Peabody.

She beat Reo and Peabody, and used her waiting time to study Icove's home. There was a light on, third-floor window. Home office, bedroom? Another, giving a backwash of pale light, second floor. Probably a hall light left burning for convenience.

The main level was dark but for dim security lights, and the steady red blink at the entrance door indicating lockdown.

It meant the doctor was in, which would make the entry easier and the search itself messier. She'd just leave the diplomacy of that to Reo.

It was after nine now, full dark, with a cool, kicky breeze. A neighboring house had some sort of folk-arty decoration on its front door in the shape of a fat turkey.

It made her think about Thanksgiving and having numerous Irish strangers underfoot.

Roarke's family, she reminded herself. She'd have to figure out how to get on with them—or get around them. She'd liked Sinead, his aunt, the only one of the group she'd met. But that didn't mean she knew what to do with her, or the rest of them, when they were just hanging around.

Family relations were way out of her orbit.

He hadn't said for how long, and she could admit now she'd been afraid to ask. Maybe it was just for the day. Just an overnight thing.

What if it was longer? What if it was a week?

Maybe she'd get lucky, catch some vicious, violent homicide that would keep her out of the house for most of their stay.

And that, she thought with a sigh, was just sick.

Roarke was nervous about this deal, she reminded herself. And he had ice for blood most of the time. So that meant it was important to him. Really important. Which meant she had to be supportive and wifely.

God. It wouldn't actually be her fault if a vicious, violent homicide landed in her lap, would it? She couldn't control these things.

She caught sight of Peabody coming up from the west corner. And of the skinny form in neon-green skin-pants and purple duster strolling beside her.

"Mag coat," McNab said. "Do they make it in brights?"

"I wouldn't know. Did I tell you to bring your boy toy?"

"Figured we could use an e-man."

McNab smiled, his green eyes twinkling in his pretty face. "Not that I mind when she toys with me. Hey, Mavis says hi. We saw her as we were heading out. Getting large," he added, rounding his arms over his belly to indicate the extent of Mavis's pregnancy. "What size is the coat?"

"Lieutenant size. You assist on the search," Eve added. "No on-site e-duty unless so ordered. Since you're here, you can oversee any transfer, should we deem appropriate, of any units, data, and communication, to Central."

"Got it."

"Aw, look at the turkey." Peabody grinned over at the neighbor's holiday door art. "We used to do stuff like that when I was a kid. Not that we ate turkey on Thanksgiving, that being considered a commercial and/or political symbol of oppression and commercialization to us Free-Agers."

Where the hell was Reo, Eve wondered, and dug her hands into her pockets. "We're having a Thanksgiving thing, if you guys are interested."

"Really?" Surprise and sentiment covered Peabody's face. "Aw, that's so nice. I'd really like to, but we're going out to spend a couple days with my family. As long as we're not on active. It's the first sort of family deal as a couple."

McNab showed his teeth in a smile, and Eve saw the nerves in it. What was it about family that scared the brave and true?

"We're saving up to spend a couple days in Scotland with Mc-Nab's clan right after Christmas." And now Peabody got that same sick smile on her face. "Get it all done in one year if we can swing the fare."

"No big." But Eve was disappointed. It was going to cut into her I-actually-know-these-people portion of the party.

She put the problem aside when she saw the city car swing to the curb. Reo, in her lady suit and matching heels, stepped out.

Reo handed a paper warrant to Eve. "Let's go find something. Detective Peabody, right?" Reo's gaze skimmed over to McNab flirtatiously. "And?"

"Detective McNab." His skinny shoulders straightened. "E-unit."

"Cher Reo." She offered him her hand before she drifted toward the entrance.

And Peabody gave him an elbow when Reo's back was turned.

When Eve rang the bell, the security system blinked and responded.

We're sorry, the Icoves are neither expecting nor accepting visitors at this time. If you would care to leave a message, one of the family or household staff will get back to you if deemed appropriate.

Eve held up her badge, and the warrant. "Dallas, Lieutenant Eve, NYPSD, along with Peabody and McNab, Detectives, and Reo, Assistant Prosecuting Attorney. We have a warrant authorizing us to enter and to search these premises. Inform Dr. Icove or a member of the household staff. If we're not given entry voluntarily within five minutes, we will take other appropriate measures."

One moment, please, while your identification and documents are scanned and authenticated.

"Go ahead. Clock's ticking."

A pale green light washed over her badge and the seal of the warrant. A minute dribbled by while the security unit hummed.

Your identification and documents have been authenticated. One moment, please, while the main household droid is activated. Dr. Icove has not yet acknowledged this inquiry.

Interesting, Eve thought. "Record on, Peabody," she ordered, and engaged her own as well.

Three of the five minutes elapsed before the security light blinked to green. The door was opened by the same tidy female droid Eve had seen on her prior visit.

"Lieutenant Dallas, I'm sorry you were kept waiting. I was not on active service." She stepped back, politely. "Dr. Icove is upstairs in his office. I'm afraid I was ordered not to disturb him prior to being deactivated for the evening."

"That's okay. I wasn't."

"But . . ." As Eve turned toward the stairs, the droid clutched her hands together. "Dr. Icove is very particular about not being disturbed when he's in his office. If you must speak to him, I wonder if you might go through household communications first." She gestured toward a household scanner and 'link, similar to the ones Eve had at home.

"Reo, go that route. McNab, check security. Peabody, with me." Eve continued up the stairs

"Reo put the eye on him," Peabody muttered as they reached the second floor.

"What?"

"On McNab. She put the juicy eye on him. And she better make sure that's all she puts on him, or I'll have to kick her tiny Southern ass."

"Maybe you could make some pretense about actually being on duty," Eve suggested. "Just for the frigging record."

"Just saying." She glanced around as they turned toward the third-floor stairway. "Big place. Nice colors, pretty art. Quiet."

"Wife and kids are supposedly tucked into their summer house. I'd imagine his office is soundproofed. Deactivates his household droid for the night, puts a no-pass on his security. Yeah, he's serious about not being disturbed."

The third floor had been reconfigured into three rooms. She noted the play area—kid world—with high-end arcade games, entertainment screen, lounging chairs, snack bar. Beside it was an area more adult, and more female by Eve's gauge. A kind of woman's sitting room/office done in pastels with arches and curves.

Across from it, a door was closed. Assuming soundproofing, she didn't knock, but pressed the intercom button. "Dr. Icove, this is Lieutenant Dallas. I'm accompanied by two detectives and an assistant prosecuting attorney. We've entered the residence with a warrant to search. You are legally obligated to open this door and cooperate."

She waited a beat, heard no response. "Should you refuse to cooperate, we are authorized to bypass the locks and enter. You may contact your attorney or representative for verification. You may request that your attorney or representative be present to supervise said search."

"Silent treatment," Peabody commented after a moment.

"Let the record show that Dr. Icove has been informed and has refused to respond verbally. We are entering without his acknowl-edgment."

Eve dug out her master, slid it through the standard interior lock.

"Dr. Icove, this is the police. We're coming in."

She opened the door.

The first thing she heard was music, the soft, mindless mush of-ten played in elevators or on 'link holds. The desk stood in front of a trio of windows. If he'd been working there, there was no sign. A door to the left opened into what she could see was a bath. Beside the door was a mood screen, set on a soft, mindless mush of colors to match the music.

There was art, and books, family photographs, what she as-sumed were awards, diplomas.

The privacy screens were engaged on the glass, the lights were on low, and the room was comfortably warm.

A sitting area was stylishly arranged in the right front corner. On the table were a glossy black thermal pot, a plate of fruit and cheese, an oversized white cup and saucer, and a pale green cloth napkin.

On a long merlot-colored sofa, its leather as rich as her coat, lay Wilfred B. Icove, Jr. His feet were bare, and a pair of black slippers were neatly tucked at the end of the sofa. He wore dark gray loung-ing pants and a pullover in a lighter tone.

The heart blood stained the sweater, and the handle of the scalpel gleamed silver in the light.

"Field kits," Eve snapped out to Peabody. "Call it in. Have Mc-Nab seal up and hit the security discs right now. Seal the house."

"Yes, sir."

"Son of a bitch," Eve said softly when she was alone. "Son of a bitch. Victim visually identified by investigating officer is Icove Jr., Dr. Wilfred B. Victim is DOS, visual determination. Until investi-gators are sealed, the body will not be examined, nor will the room be entered to avoid contamination of scene. What appears to be a medical scalpel, of similar or same type used in the case of Icove Sr., has been inserted in victim's chest. It's heart blood. As seen on record, victim is in a reclining position on a sofa in his home office.

The door to the office was secured, lights were on low setting, privacy screens on all windows engaged."

She held up a hand as she heard footsteps—high heels. "APA Reo approaching scene. No entry, Reo. We seal up first."

"What's happened? Peabody said Icove's dead. I don't—"

She broke off, looking around Eve into the room. Her eyes tracked, from the bath, across the room, to the sofa.

Then they rolled back in her head as she made a small sound, like a balloon deflating. Eve moved quickly enough to break her fall, then left the APA sprawled unconscious in the hallway to continue the oral portion of her incident report.

"Entry to residence was gained through entry and search warrant. Single household droid was reactivated by automated security system. Crime scene shows no sign of forced entry, no sign of struggle."

Eve held her hand out for her field kit when Peabody came back. Her partner stepped over the APA. "What happened to her?"

"Fainted. Do what you can."

"I guess Southern types are delicate."

Eve sealed up, then carried her kit inside. For form, she checked for vitals, found none. "DOS, confirmed." She scanned his prints. "Identification confirmed. Peabody, do a sweep through the house, but secure the droid first."

"I already secured the droid. I'll do the sweep once I wake up Sleeping Beauty. He go out the same way as his father?"

"Looks that way." She took the body temperature, worked the gauge. "He's been dead less than two hours. Goddamn it."

Eve straightened, studied the angle of the body, the angle of the weapon. "In close again. He's lying down. He's deactivated the droid—leaving it and the house security programmed for do-not-disturb. But he's lying here and he doesn't worry about somebody coming in, leaning over him. Tranqs maybe. We'll check the tox screen. But I don't think so. I don't think so. He knew her. He wasn't afraid of her. He didn't fear for his life when she came into the room."

She stepped back to the doorway to see it in her head. Reo was sitting up now, her head in her hands. Peabody stood by, smirking.

"The sweep, Detective."

"Yes, sir. Simply making certain the civilian is all right."

"I'm okay, I'm okay. Just a little shaken up." She waved a hand in Peabody's direction. "Go ahead. I've never seen a body before," she said to Eve. "Images, photographs. But I've never walked in on a real one. It just took me by surprise."

"Go downstairs, wait for Crime Scene."

"I will, in a minute. I heard you say he'd only been dead a couple hours." Her eyes were still a little glassy, but they met Eve's straight on. "I couldn't get the warrant any faster. I did damn handsprings to get it at all. I couldn't move it faster."

"I'm not blaming you."

Reo leaned her head back against the wall. "Maybe not. But it's hard to convince myself not to. We sure as hell found something, didn't we? Did you expect this?"

"No. And it's hard to convince myself I shouldn't have. Go downstairs, Reo. I've got work here."

Reo got to her feet. "I can contact the next of kin."

"Do that. Don't tell her he's dead. Just tell her we need her back in the city, now. Do another handspring and get her into a police shuttle, and back here within the hour. Keep it under media radar, Reo. This is going to be one hell of a mess soon enough."

Eve lifted the thermal pot, sniffed. Coffee. She marked it, the cup, the plate of fruit and cheese for the lab.

Leaving the body, Eve crossed to the desk and began to check incoming and outgoing transmissions, recent data input or deleted. She bagged all discs, marked the unit itself for EDD transfer.

"House is empty," Peabody reported. "Domestic droids—three in full—were all deactivated. All doors and windows were fully secured. No sign of tampering. McNab told me that the current security disc—which, in order from the previous, would have run since nine hundred hours this morning—is missing two hours."

Eve glanced back, frowned. "Two hours."

"Affirmative. There's no record through the system of entry or exit of the premises during that time. The disc stops at eighteen-thirty, and picks up again at twenty hundred and forty-two hours.

It clearly shows us approaching, being verified, and admitted at twenty-one sixteen."

Minutes, Eve thought. Missed her by minutes. She gestured toward the desk 'link. "He had that on privacy mode. Set it at seventeen hundred. No transmissions in the holding area. Let's check the other 'links."

They headed down while the sweepers headed up.

"Icove's wife is being picked up now. She'll be here in about twenty minutes," Reo told them. "ME's on his way now. I got you Morris."

"Then you got me good. I need to check with my e-man. You can hold here, or go."

"Go?" Reo let out a short laugh. "Screw that. I've never been in on a homicide from the get. They're going to want to pull this out from under me when you close it down. I need ammo, to stay at the table. I'm here."

"Fine. Where's the security room?" she asked Peabody.

"Utility and security space, off the kitchen. Rear of the house."

"Start checking the 'links for transmissions. Bag any discs for review. Let's tag all the units. Wife's, kids', domestics'." She looked back at Reo. "Did you speak with the wife, personally?"

"Yes. At the connection the household droid gave me. Hamptons."

"Okay." Eve nodded, walked off to find McNab.

He may have looked like a victim of Fashion Trends R Us, but McNab could romance electronics. He sat, a skinny tube of neon, flipping through screens on a console and muttering commands into a handheld.

"What are you doing? What's the deal?"

He spared Eve the briefest glance, and shoved his long, loose golden hair out of his face. "You really want to know?"

"Bottom line it. In English."

"Checking the system for jams, glitches, bypasses. You got a top-line here. Multisource, full scan, motion, voice, and visual detection. Entry through code and voice print. All I got on me is my PPC, but it's prime. I'm not finding any holes."

"So how'd they get through?"

"That's the question." He swiveled on the stool, away from the security console, scratched the side of his jaw. "We'll take a closer look in-house, but it's looking like they came through on green."

"Meaning someone let them in, or they cleared security."

"I took a look at the door unit, and there's no sign of tampering. Mostly it's going to show. Mostly. We'll take a closer at that, too, and other entries, but if you want my own site, yeah. Bad guy waltzed through. Either cleared through or was aided by an inside source. Maybe the dead guy let him in."

"Then went upstairs, locked his office door, and stretched out on the couch and waited for a knife in the heart?"

He puffed out his cheeks, blew out air. Patting his pockets, he came up with a silver ring, then threaded his hair through it forming a tail. "Okay, maybe not. Anyway, whoever it was took the discs for the time frame he'd show on camera. Slid them right out. No sign of search or fumbling around in here. And I had to use my master to open the door. Locked up behind himself, nice and neat."

Eve studied the security room. It was about the size of her office at Central, and a hell of a lot slicker. A series of screens relayed images of various rooms and entryways. McNab had left them live, and she could see sweepers in their protective suits working the scene, Reo on the main level talking on her 'link, Peabody doing the tags on a data and communication center in the kitchen.

She stood another moment, watching the screens. "Okay," she said, then watched Morris come through the front door. He had a brief consult with Reo, who then directed him up the stairs.

"Okay," she said again, and left McNab to his e-work.

The domestic droid was standing in the kitchen on wait mode. Eve engaged it.

"Did Dr. Icove have any visitors after his wife left the house today."

"No, Lieutenant."

"Did Dr. Icove leave the house at any time after he returned from work today?"

"No, Lieutenant."

One thing about droids, Eve thought, they kept to the point.

"Who set the evening security? Who ordered the lockdown for the night?"

"Dr. Icove locked down personally at seventeen-thirty, just prior to deactivating me for the night."

"And the other droids?"

"Both deactivated before me. I was the last. Set on sleep mode at seventeen thirty-five, with do-not-disturb command."

"What did he have for dinner?"

"I was not asked to serve an evening meal. I served soup—chicken and rice—at thirteen-fifteen. However, Dr. Icove only consumed a small portion of the serving, along with a cup of ginseng tea and three wheat crackers."

"Did he eat alone?"

"Yes, Lieutenant."

"What time did his wife leave?"

"Mrs. Icove and the children left the house at twelve-thirty. Mrs. Icove gave instructions for me to serve Dr. Icove soup and tea. She expressed concern that he wasn't eating properly and would make himself ill."

"Did they have a conversation?"

"Conversations between family members and guests are private."

"This is a murder investigation. Your privacy functions are overridden. Did they have a conversation?"

The droid looked as uncomfortable as a droid could manage. "Mrs. Icove expressed the desire that Dr. Icove accompany them, or that he allow her to send the children with the nanny droid so that she could remain with him. Dr. Icove insisted that she go with the children, and told her he'd join them in a day or so. He communicated his desire to be private."

"Nothing else."

"They embraced. He embraced the children. He wished them a good trip. I prepared and served him the meal Mrs. Icove had ordered for him. Shortly thereafter, he left for the Center, informing me he would return by five, which he did."

"Alone."

"Yes, he returned alone, at which time he began deactivation of the domestics and lockdown."

"Did you serve fruit and cheese this evening?"

"No, Lieutenant."

"All right. That's all for now."

Upstairs, Morris was finishing his on-site. He wore a clear gown over a shimmery deep purple shirt and narrow black pants. His hair was pulled back in three stacked tails, perfectly aligned.

"Did you dude up just for me?" Eve asked him.

"Late date, with serious heat potential." He straightened. "But I'll get him started for you. What you got here is like father, like son. Same method, same weapon type, same cause of demise."

"Got it lying there."

"Yep." Morris leaned over the body. "Killer at this angle, and round about this distance. Up close and personal."

"Need a tox screen."

"Yeah." He straightened again, glanced at the tray. "None of that looks touched. Waste. That's some good-looking fruit."

"Domestic droid reports he ate a little chicken and rice soup, a couple of crackers, and tea about thirteen hundred. He shut the droids down just after seventeen hundred. None of them served this tray of stuff."

"So he got it himself. Or the killer brought it to him."

"Maybe it's tranq'd, maybe not. Either way, the guy just lies there and takes a knife in the heart."

"Knew his killer."

"Knew, and trusted. Comfortable enough to stretch out. Maybe he let the killer in himself, and was lured up here. But I don't see it." She shook her head. "Why bother bringing the vic upstairs, putting food on a tray? Why not just stick him downstairs, save the trouble? Maybe you want a conversation first, but hell, you can have that downstairs, too. Door's locked. Inside lock."

"Ah, a locked-door mystery. And you our Poirot—minus the mustache and accent."

She knew who Poirot was because she'd dug into some Agatha Christies after viewing *Witness for the Prosecution*—and the murder that had gone along with it.

"Not so mysterious," Eve corrected. "Killer knows the codes. Just does the job, sets the codes from inside, shuts the door, and walks away. Takes the security discs for the time elapsed. Even re-sets the security."

"Knew his way around the place."

"Her. I'm betting her. And she had to. You get him in, I need a close check for any other wounds, any pricks, pressure marks, anything. But I don't think you'll find them. Or the tranq. Like father, like son," she repeated. "Yeah, just like."

EVE TOOK TIME TO CONTACT ROARKE.

"Got into Icove's place, found him dead. Gonna be late."

"There's a pithy report, Lieutenant. Dead how?"

"Same as his father." She walked outside as she spoke, the better to keep an eye out for the new widow. "Wife and kids went to their weekend place earlier today. He was home alone, house locked up tight, domestics deactivated. And he's taking a little lie-down on his office sofa. With a scalpel in his heart. Room's locked, and there's a tray of healthy snacks on the table."

"Interesting," Roarke replied.

"Yeah. More interesting that EDD, at this point, hasn't found any holes or tampering in security, and the disc for the murder time is missing. Security was fully activated on our arrival, and in full DND mode as the domestic reports the doctor himself set it this evening. The killer entered approximately ninety minutes thereafter. This is slick business."

"Are you back to considering a professional?"

"All the earmarks, none of the vibes. Anyway. See you later."

"Anything I can do from here?"

"Find me the money," she said and ended transmission as she watched a sedan draw up behind one of the black-and-whites.

She walked down to meet Avril Icove herself.

Avril was dressed in dove gray, pants and sweater, with a dark red coat thrown stylishly over her shoulders. Soft, heeled boots matched the coat.

She leaped out of the car before her driver could make his way around to open her door. "What's happened? What's wrong? Will!"

Eve blocked her path, and with a hand on the woman's arm, felt the vibration of her body. "Mrs. Icove, I need you to come with me."

"What is it? What is it?" There was a jump in her voice, and her eyes stayed trained on the door of her home. "Was there an accident?"

"We're going to go inside and sit down."

"They called, they called and said I needed to come home right away. No one would tell me why. I tried to call Will, but he doesn't answer. Is he here?"

There were plenty of gawkers gathered behind the police barricades. Eve merely nudged them aside and steered Avril toward the house. "You left this afternoon."

"Yes, yes, with the children. Will wanted me and the children away from . . . everything. And he wanted some time alone. I didn't like to leave him. Where is he? Is he hurt?"

Eve got her inside, drew her away from the steps and into the living area. "Sit down, Mrs. Icove."

"I need to speak with Will."

Eve kept her gaze level. "I'm sorry, Mrs. Icove. Your husband's dead. He was killed."

Avril's mouth moved, but no sound came out as she lowered to a chair. Her hands fluttered once, then locked together in her lap. "Will." Tears shimmered, turning her eyes to liquid amethyst. "An accident."

"He was murdered."

"How can that be? But how can that be?" The tears slid down her cheeks now, slowly. "We were only . . . he was going to join us tomorrow. He only wanted some quiet."

Eve sat. "Mrs. Icove, I'd like to record this, for my report. Do you object?"

"No. No."

Eve switched on her recorder, fed the salient data into the record.

"Mrs. Icove, I'm going to need to verify your whereabouts from five-thirty this afternoon to nine this evening."

"What?"

"For the record, Mrs. Icove. Can you verify your whereabouts during that time frame?"

"I took the children. I took the children to our house. The Hamptons." She reached up absently, brushed the coat from her shoulders. It looked like a pool of blood against the quiet colors of the room. "We left . . . we left just after noon."

"How did you travel?"

"Shuttle. Our personal shuttle. I took them for a walk on the beach. We'd hoped to have a picnic, but it was chilly. We had a swim in the indoor pool, and some lunch. Lissy, our little girl, she loves the water. We went into town and had ice cream, and saw our neighbors up there. They came over. Don and Hester. They came over for drinks."

"What time was that?"

Her eyes had gone empty during the recital. She blinked now, like a woman coming out of a dream. "Excuse me?"

"What time did your neighbors come over?"

"At six, I think. At around six or a little before, and they stayed, they stayed for dinner. I wanted the company. Will likes to be alone when he's stressed or upset, but I like company. We had dinner, about seven, and the kids went to bed at nine. We played cards. Three-handed bridge. Don and Hester and myself. Then they called—the woman, I can't remember her name. She called and said I needed to come home. Hester stayed with the children for me. My children."

"What was your husband stressed about?"

"His father. His father was murdered. Oh God." Her arms crossed over her belly. "Oh God."

"Did your husband feel endangered? Threatened? Do you know if anyone made threats?"

"No. No. He was grieving. His father. Of course, he was grieving and upset." Avril cupped her elbows, rubbed her hands there as if chilled. "And he felt . . . I'm sorry, but he felt you weren't doing a

very good job. He was angry because he felt you were somehow trying to compromise his father's reputation."

"How was I doing that?"

"I can't say. I don't know. He was upset and wanted time alone."

"What do you know about his work?"

"His work? He's a surgeon, a very skilled and important surgeon. The facilities at the Center are among the finest in the
world."

"Did he discuss his work with you? Most specifically his private
project and research?"

"A man with such a high-powered and demanding profession
doesn't like to bring that work home night after night. He needs a
sanctuary."

"That doesn't answer my question."

"I don't understand the question."

"What do you know about projects your husband and father-in-
law kept off the books, so to speak?"

There were still tears but they were just glimmering now, blur-
ring the eyes, the voice. "I don't know what you mean."

"I'm interested in a long-term private project, one your husband
and your father-in-law have been pursuing, actively. One that
would require extensive facilities—in or outside the center. One
that involves treatment of young women."

Two tears spilled over, and for a moment, just an instant, those
lavender eyes were clear. Something was in them, something sharp
and cool. Then it was gone, wavering behind another shimmer of
tears.

"I'm sorry. I don't know anything about it. I wasn't involved in
Will's work. Are you saying you think his work is somehow responsible for his death?"

Eve changed tacks. "Who has the security code for this house?"

"Ah . . . Will and myself, of course. His father—his father did.
The domestics."

"Anyone else?"

"No. Will was very cautious about security. We changed the
codes every few weeks. A bother," she said with the barest hint of a
smile. "I'm not very good with numbers."

"How was your marriage, Mrs. Icove?"

"How was my marriage?"

"Any problems? Friction? Was your husband faithful?"

"Of course he was faithful." Avril turned her head away. "What a terrible thing to ask."

"Whoever killed your husband was either let into the house or knew the codes. A man, under stress, might send his wife and children out of town for a day or two in order to spend time with a lover."

"I was his only lover." Avril's voice dropped to a whisper. "I was what he wanted. He was devoted. A loving husband and father, a dedicated doctor. He would never hurt me or the children. He would never stain our marriage with infidelity."

"I'm sorry. I know this is difficult."

"It doesn't seem real. It doesn't seem possible. Is there something I should do now? I don't know what I should do."

"We'll need to take your husband's body in, for examination."

Avril winced at that. "Autopsy."

"Yes."

"I know you have to. I don't like the thought of it, of what will happen. One of the reasons we rarely discussed Will's work was because I don't like the thought of the . . . the cutting and lasering."

"Squeamish? A doctor's wife—and a woman who likes crime drama."

There was a hesitation before that ghost of a smile. "I guess I like the end results, but could do without the blood. Do I have to sign anything?"

"No. Not now. Is there anyone you'd like us to call for you? Anyone you want to contact?"

"No. There's no one. I have to get back to my children." Her hands came out of her lap, pressed to her lips as they trembled. "My babies. I have to tell my babies. I have to take care of them. How will I ever explain?"

"Do you want a grief counselor?"

Avril hesitated again, then shook her head. "No, not now. I think they'll need me. Just me, for now. Me, and time. I have to go to my children."

"I'll arrange to have you escorted back." Eve got to her feet. "I'm going to need you to stay available, Mrs. Icove."

"Of course. Of course I will. We'll stay in the Hamptons tonight. Away from the city. Away from this. The media, they won't leave us alone, but it'll be better there. I don't want the children exposed. Will would want me to shield the children."

"Do you need anything from here?"

"No. We have all we need."

Eve watched her go, drive away in the sedan, this time with a police escort.

When she was satisfied with her on-site, Eve gestured to Peabody. "My home office is closer. I'm going to write the report from there, and arrange for your transport home."

"You want me with you?"

"For the moment." She headed out to her car, handing Peabody the record of her interview with Avril Icove. "Listen to it, then give me your impressions."

"Sure."

Peabody settled into the car, switching the replay on as Eve drove.

Eve drove through her own gates, listening to Avril's voice, her own questions.

"Shaky," Peabody said. "Teary, but holding up."

"What's missing?"

"She never asked how he died."

"Never asked how, never asked where or why or who. And never asked to see him."

"Which is strange, I grant you. But shock can make for strange."

"What's the number-one question a shocked family member asks when informed?"

"Number one's probably: Are you sure?"

"She never asks, never insists on proof. She starts off with the 'Was there an accident?' routine, fumbles around to find her balance. Okay on that. She was shaking when I took her in, that works, too. But she never asks how he died."

"Because she knew? That's reaching, Dallas."

"Maybe. She never asked how we got in—how we found him.

Never said: 'Oh God, was there a break-in, a burglary?' Never asked if he went out and got himself mugged. I never told her he was killed in the house. But if you watch her face on the record, she looked through the doorway toward the stairs going up several times. She knew he was dead up there. I didn't have to tell her."

"We can verify whether or not she was where she said she was during the time frame."

"She'll have been there. She had that pat. She'll be alibied tight. But she's in this somewhere."

They sat in front of the house, Eve frowning through the windshield.

"Maybe he was catting around on her," Peabody suggested. "She uses what happened to his father as inspiration, and gets somebody to off him. Maybe she was doing the catting, and figured she could lap up more cream with him dead. Gets her lover the security code, clears his voice print prior. He sticks the husband, mimicking the MO from the first murder."

"Where'd the tray of fruit and cheese come from?"

"Shit, Dallas. Icove could've ordered himself a snack."

"Came from the kitchen unit. I checked."

"So."

"So why go downstairs, order a snack, haul it up. You want a snack, use the office AutoChef."

"Lee-Lee Ten," Peabody reminded her. "Maybe it's like that. Maybe he likes to putter in the kitchen when he's got something on his mind."

"He's no kitchen putterer. She might be, Avril, but not him. Not Dr. Will."

"He could've been downstairs, decided to go up. Ordered it to take up with him. Gets up there, decides, I'm not hungry right now, stretches out, falls asleep. Wife's handsome yet sleazy lover slips into the house, goes up, goes in, shoves the scalpel into his heart, takes the disc, resets security, and walks away."

Eve made a noncommittal sound. "We'll talk to friends and neighbors and associates, check her personal finances again, go through her routines."

"But you don't like my handsome-yet-sleazy-lover angle."

"I don't discount the handsome yet sleazy lover. But if so, they moved damn fast to have it this smooth. I'm betting this was planned as carefully, and as much in advance, as the old doc's. Same people, same motive behind both."

"Maybe Dolores is her handsome yet sleazy lover."

"Maybe. In any case, we look at Avril, and find the link."

Eve pushed open her door. "Take the vehicle. Come back at seven hundred. We'll put in a couple hours here before we go into Central."

Peabody checked her wrist unit. "Wow! Looks like I may get five hours' sleep."

"You want sleep? Sell shoes."

Eve wasn't surprised to find Summerset, still fully dressed, in the foyer. "Icove's son's now as dead as he is." She peeled off her coat, tossed it over the newel post. "You really want to help, turn up the soft glow of memory light and look back hard. He was into something."

"Must everyone you see carry stains?"

She glanced back as she walked upstairs. "Yeah. If you want to find out who killed him more than you want to canonize him, you'll look for them, too."

She kept going up, and straight into her office. Roarke came through the adjoining door.

"If I came home and a cop met me at the door," she began, "and told me you'd been murdered, what do you figure I'd do?"

"Fall into a pit of despair from which you would drown for the rest of your sad, empty life."

"Yeah, yeah, yeah. Get serious."

"I rather liked that one." He leaned on the doorjamb. "First, I imagine you would kick the unfortunate messenger—and anyone else stupid enough to get in your path—out of your way. To see for yourself. I would hope you'd weep an ocean of hot and bitter tears over my body. Then you'd find out everything that could be found out and hunt my killer down like a rabid dog to the ends of the earth."

"Okay." She sat on the edge of her desk and studied him. "What if I didn't love you anymore?"

"Then my life would no longer be worth living, and I'd have probably self-terminated or simply died of a broken, battered heart."

She had to grin at him, then sobered and shook her head. "She didn't love him. The widow. She put on a dignified show, but she didn't have all the lines, and she didn't— What's it when actors . . ." She threw out her arms, put a horrified expression on her face, slapped her arms crossways over her chest.

"Miming? Please don't do that again. It's rather frightening."

"Not miming. People should be allowed—no, they should be required to chase mimes down the street with bats. Emote, that's the word. Avril didn't emote believably. See there was a tone when she talked about him, and another when she talked about her kids. She loves the kids. She didn't love their father, or not anymore. Not through and through. Peabody figures she had some side action."

"Seems reasonable. You don't?"

"When do I have time for side action when you're nailing me every chance you get?"

He reached out, gave her hair a quick tug. "Quick tonight, aren't you?"

"Must be the buzz, because I've got one going on this. Maybe she had a side dish. And maybe she's that smart and that quick and calculating. Duplicating her father-in-law's murder to muddy the waters. But I'm thinking it is what it looks like. Connected murders by or on behalf of the same parties. And she's in it."

"Why? Money, sex, fear, power, rage, jealousy, revenge. Aren't those the headliners?"

"Power's in there. They were powerful men, killed with a tool of their own trade. If it's rage, it's ice cold. I don't see fear, and money doesn't give me the buzz. Jealousy's unlikely. Revenge—that's the unknown."

"The money's plentiful, and well channelled. I haven't, as yet, found any that's questionable. Their accounts are ordered, extremely well organized and maintained."

"There's more somewhere."

"Then I'll find it."

"Here's the gist."

Eve ran it through for him quickly. As she spoke, he came in, opened a recessed door, and took out brandy. He poured a snifter for himself, and knowing his wife, ordered her a cup of black coffee. He hoped it would be her last of a long day.

She didn't like them, her victims, he thought. It wouldn't stop her from pursuing whoever was responsible for their deaths, but it wasn't punishing her as murder often did.

It was the puzzle that gave her the buzz she'd spoken of, the buzz she'd use and burn through until she found the answers.

But the dead, this time, didn't haunt her. The girls she believed they'd used would. And for them, he knew, she'd burn through until she found those answers and exhausted herself.

"It's not impossible the system was compromised," he said when she'd finished. "Depends on the skill of your B-and-E man." He passed her the coffee. "But in that neighborhood, at that time of the evening, you'd have to have extreme skill. Particularly extreme if when EDD examines the system they still find no sign of tampering."

"It's more likely she had the codes, and a voice box or clearance. We've taken in the droids, too, and EDD will take them apart, see if any were compromised. If Icove's orders were countermanded by the wife at some point earlier today, one of the droids could have opened the door for the killer, then had its memory washed."

"It would show. Unless, again, you're extremely skilled."

"He wasn't eating—Icove. No appetite. So if his tummy rumbled, okay, he wants a little bite. But he's working in his office. Sequestered there. Wiping data, I'll bet your fine ass."

She paced now, walking it through. "He doesn't go downstairs to the kitchen to order a tray of food. It's not efficient. And you know what it is—a pretty tray with pretty fruit, artfully arranged cheese and whatnot. It's wifely."

"I wouldn't know," Roarke said dryly. "I don't believe my wife has ever artfully arranged cheese on a tray for me."

"Bite me. You know what I'm saying. It's female and fussy. The sort of thing fussy females do to cajole somebody to eat. But it wasn't the wife. She's in the Hamptons, eating ice cream with the kiddies, entertaining the neighbors. Making damn straight sure somebody can swear on a mountain of Bibles she was somewhere else when that scalpel went into Icove's heart. So maybe Icove was fooling around and somehow his side dish and his wife are in league."

"Back to sex."

"Yeah. Maybe he was cheating on both of them. Maybe his sainted father was a perv and diddled with all three. But that's not it." She shook her head. "It doesn't feel like sex. It's the project. It's the work. She lied to me about knowing about his work, knowing about any long-term private research. That was the missed beat in her routine. There was the rage, just a flicker. I saw it in her eyes."

She sipped her coffee. "She could've planted the weapon at the Center. Who's going to question Dr. Will's wife if she wanders around? Easy enough to palm a scalpel, conceal one. She's the main link between the two victims. Former ward of one, wife of the other. Maybe, if this project goes back far enough, she was part of it."

"It's a long time to wait to take your revenge," Roarke pointed out. "A lot of emotional ties during that time. She couldn't have been forced to marry and live with, have children with Will Icove, Eve. It had to be her choice. If she's involved, isn't it more likely she found out about this project—objected, was appalled or enraged?"

"Then she's still got a choice. If you're that appalled, you report it. Could do it anonymously. Give the authorities just enough to make them investigate. You don't kill the father of your children because you're upset about his side work. You leave him, or you fry him legally. You kill two men like this? It's a personal act, caused by a personal act."

She shrugged. "I think. I'm going to talk to Mira."

"It's late. Let's get some sleep."

"I want to write this up first, while it's fresh in my mind."

He crossed to her, kissed her brow. "Don't drink any more coffee."

Alone, she wrote the report, added some case notes. Then some questions.

Avril Icove—living relatives?

Exact date and circumstances of Icove's guardianship?

Daily, weekly routines? Times out of the house alone? Where? When?

Possible connection to woman known as Dolores Nocho-Alverez.

Any body or face work?

Last visit to the Center prior to father-in-law's death.

I'm what he wanted.

What, if anything, did she take to the Hamptons?

She sat back, let it circle through her mind another time or two. Wished for coffee.

She shut down and walked to the bedroom. He'd left the light on low, so she wouldn't come into the dark. Eve stripped, dragged on a nightshirt. When she slid into bed, he drew her into his arms to spoon.

"I wanted more coffee."

"Of course you did. Go to sleep."

"She didn't want them to suffer."

"All right."

She started to drift, warm in his arms. "She wanted them dead, but she didn't want them to suffer. Love. Hate. It's complicated."

"It certainly is."

"Love. Hate. But no passion." She yawned, hugely. "If I needed to kill you, I'd want you to suffer. A lot."

He smiled in the dark. "Thanks, darling."

She smiled along with him, and slipped into slumber.

10   AT SEVEN A.M., EVE WAS DRINKING HER SEC-
ond cup of coffee and studying the data she'd pulled
up on Avril Icove.

She noted Avril's date of birth, her parents' dates of death, and
that she'd become Icove's legal ward before her sixth birthday.

Eve read through Avril's educational data—Brookhollow Academy, Spencerville, New Hampshire, grades one through twelve,
with continuing education Brookhollow College.

So the kindly doctor had put his ward in a boarding school
straight off the bat. How had she felt about that? Eve wondered.
Loses her mother—and where had the kid been while Mommy was
off in . . . where had it been? Africa. Who'd kept the girl while the
mother was off saving lives, and losing her own in Africa?

Then she loses her mother and gets shipped off to school.

No living relatives. Really bad luck there, Eve thought. No sibs;
parents were both only children. Grandparents dead before she was
born. No records of aunts or uncles or fricking second cousins twice
removed.

Kinda weird, Eve thought. Most everyone had some relation
somewhere. However distant.

She didn't, but there were always some exceptions to the rules.

Jeez, look what had happened to Roarke. Go around all your life
thinking you're it, then bam! Got yourself enough relatives to
people a small city.

But Avril's records indicated no blood kin except her two children.

So, she's almost six years old, tragically orphaned, and Icove, her legal guardian, puts her in a swank school. Busy surgeon, busy becoming Icon Icove, raising his own kid, who'd have been, what, about seventeen.

Teenage boys had a habit of getting into trouble, causing trouble, being trouble. But her run of Dr. Will had shown her a record as spotless as his father's.

Meanwhile Avril's doing sixteen years at basically the same school, which struck her as close to a prison term. Of course, she considered as she sipped more coffee, school had been a kind of jail for her.

Marking time, she remembered, until she'd been of legal age and could escape the system that had gobbled her up after she'd been found in that alley in Dallas. Then straight to the Police Academy. Another system, she admitted. But her choice. Finally, her choice.

Had Avril had a choice?

Art major, Eve read, with minors in domestic sciences and theater. Married Wilfred B. Icove, Jr., the summer after she'd gotten her degrees—putting him in his middle thirties, with no blemish on his official data, no cohabs.

She'd have to nudge Nadine, see if the reporter could find any juice on serious relationships for the young, rich doctor in any old media records.

No employment for Avril. Professional mother status after the birth of her first child.

No criminal.

She heard the faint swish of airskids and took another hit of coffee as Peabody came in.

"Avril Icove," Eve began. "Personality assessment."

"Well, hell, I didn't know there was going to be a quiz first thing." Peabody dumped her bag, squinted her eyes.

"Elegant and contained," she surmised. "Well-bred and -mannered, and I want to say correct. Assuming the house is her territory—as it most likely would be considering she's a pro mom and he's a busy doctor—I'd say tasteful and discreet."

"She wore a red coat," Eve commented.

"Huh?"

"Nothing, maybe nothing. All that quiet elegance in the house, and she wears a bright red coat." Eve shrugged. "Anything else?"

"Well, she also strikes me as being subservient."

Eve's gaze whipped over. "Why?"

"Our first visit to the house, Icove told her what to do. It wasn't 'Hey, bitch, get your ass out in the kitchen.' It wasn't harsh, not even really direct, but the dynamic was there. He was in charge, he made the decisions. She's the WIFE, in big letters."

Peabody glanced hopefully at the coffee, but kept going. "Which is something I've been thinking about. She's used to him running the show, making the decisions. So it's not that off-base that she'd be kind of blank and out of it when you tell her he's dead. Nobody's giving her a playbook now."

"She's had sixteen years gilded private education, with honors."

"A lot of people are school smart and don't have any practical skills."

"Get coffee, you're starting to drool."

"Thanks."

"Her father took off, mother's a medical missionary type, off in the wilds. Dies there." Eve raised her voice as Peabody hotfooted it to the kitchen. "Only connection I find to Icove is the mother's professional association. Could be they were lovers, but I don't know that it matters."

Eve cocked her head, studied Avril's ID image on screen. Elegant, she thought. Stunning. And at first glance, she would've said soft. But she'd seen that flash, that one instant. And there'd been steel in those eyes.

"We're going back to the scene," she continued. "I want to go through the house, room by room. Talk to neighbors, other domestics. We'll need to verify her alibi. And I want to know the last time, prior to her father-in-law's death, she was in the Center."

"Going to be busy," Peabody said with her mouth full of glazed doughnut. "They were right there," she mumbled when Eve frowned at her.

"Where?"

"Under D on the menu." She swallowed hastily. "McNab went in with the electronics, so he got home after me. Way. He said he red-flagged them. He'll bring Feeney up to date this morning, save you the trouble."

"She wasn't worried about the electronics. She wasn't sweating the security, the transmissions, data." Eve shook her head. "Either she's ice, or there's nothing there to point at her."

"I'm still leaning toward the adultery angle. If Avril's in it, she had to have a partner. You don't kill for someone unless you love them, or they've got you by the short hairs on something."

"Or you pay them."

"Yeah, that. But I was rolling it around. I know it's high yuck factor, but what if the father-in-law had been up her skirt? We're looking at him to have an interest in young women with that project. She was his ward. So he could've been using her sexually. Then passes her to the son so he could, um, keep her handy. Maybe they were tag-teaming her."

"It's crossed my mind."

"Then how about this? She's been dominated and used by men. So she turns to a woman. Emotionally, maybe romantically. They hatch it up."

"Dolores."

"Yeah. Say they meet, become lovers." Peabody licked sugar off her fingers. "Between the two of them they figure out how to take out both Icoves, without implicating Avril. Dolores might have worked on Junior, hooked up, seduced him."

"He saw her picture after his father's murder. He didn't blink."

"Okay, that's cold. But it's not impossible. Or she might've looked different with him. Changed her hair, that kind of thing. We damn well know Dolores killed number one. The same method, same weapon used on number two. Probability is ninety-eight and change that she did both."

"Ninety-eight point seven. I ran it, too," Eve said. "Going by that and adding my conviction that Avril's in this, they know each other. Or Avril hired her. It also means Dolores was in town after the first murder. And may still be. I want to find her."

The door between the offices opened, and Roarke stepped

through. The charcoal suit that showed off that lithe body somehow deepened the already staggering blue of his eyes. His hair was swept back from that gorgeous face, and the slow easy smile did something almost obscene to a woman's belly.

"You're drooling again," Eve muttered to Peabody.

"So?"

"Ladies. Am I interrupting?"

"Running a few things," Eve told him. "We're going to head out shortly."

"Then my timing's good. How are you, Peabody?"

"Up, thanks. And I wanted to thank you for the invite to Thanksgiving. We're bummed we can't make it, but we're going to shuttle it to my parents' for a couple days."

"Well, it's about family, isn't it, and give them our best. We'll miss you. I like your necklace. What's the stone?"

It was somewhere between red and orange, and chunky. Eve's only thought on seeing it around her partner's neck was that in a chase it would probably swing up and put Peabody's eye out.

"Carnelian. My grandmother made it."

"Really?" He stepped forward, lifted the pendant. "Lovely work. Does she sell her jewelry?"

"Mostly through Free-Ager channels. Indie shops and fairs. It's kind of a hobby."

"Tick-tock," Eve grumbled, and had both of them glancing over at her, Peabody bemused, Roarke amused.

"It certainly suits you," he continued and let the pendant drop again. "But I have to confess, I rather miss your uniform."

"Oh, well." She pinked up as Eve rolled her eyes behind Peabody's back.

"I'll be out of your way in a minute, but I have a thing or two that might interest you." Roarke glanced down at the cup Peabody had forgotten, in a hormonal haze, she held. "I could use some of that coffee."

"Coffee?" Peabody all but sighed it, then snapped back. "Oh yeah, sure. I'll get it. I'll get it."

Roarke smiled after her. "She is a treasure," he stated.

"You got her stirred up. You did it on purpose."

His expression was all innocence. "I haven't any idea what you mean. In any case, I'm glad you'd asked her and McNab for dinner, and I'm sorry they won't make it. Meanwhile, I've done some poking around for you, after my morning meeting."

"You had a meeting? Already?"

"Holo-conference. Scotland. They're five hours ahead of us, and I accommodated them. I needed to speak with my aunt in Ireland as well."

Which explained, she thought, why he hadn't been in his usual spot in the sitting area of their room when she'd gotten up at six.

"You find me money?"

"In a sense." He paused, smiling over at Peabody again as she brought in a tray.

"I got fresh for you, Dallas."

"In the sense of what?" Eve demanded impatiently.

But Roarke took his time, personally pouring coffee all around. "In the sense of large bequests and annuities channeled through various arms of Icove's holdings. On the surface, extremely generous and philanthropic. But added up, pushed through the surface and carefully examined, questionable."

"How?"

"Nearly two hundred million—so far—over the last thirty-five years that I can't account for through his income. A man gives away that kind of green, it should put a bit of a dent here and there in his pockets. Not so." He drank coffee.

"Indicating another source of income. A hidden source."

"It would seem. I suspect there's more. I've only just started on this line. Interesting, isn't it, that a man with a questionable income would choose to donate it—quietly, even anonymously—to worthy causes. Most would buy themselves a nice little country."

"Anonymously."

"He's gone to considerable trouble to distance himself from the donations. A lot of layers between. Trusts, nonprofits, foundations, all crisscrossing, padded between with corporations and organizations." He shrugged. "I don't imagine you need or want a lesson in tax shelters or the like, Lieutenant. Let's just say he has excellent financial advice, and had elected to dump these funds without taking credit for them. Or the considerable write-off on his income. Then again, he isn't reporting the income."

"Tax evasion."

"In a sense. Difficult though, even for the Internal Revenue to squeeze anything out, since the money was shifted to charities. But surely there's an infraction."

"So we need to find the source of the income." Eve took her coffee, circled the office. "There's always a trail."

Roarke's lips curved, slyly. "There isn't, no. Not always."

She shot him a narrowed look. "Somebody who knows how to erase trails ought to be able to find one."

"Somebody should."

"Maybe start at the back end," Peabody suggested. "Places that got the money."

"Give me, say, the five biggest beneficiaries," Eve said to Roarke. "You can shoot it to my office at Central."

"I'll do that. The biggest, by far, is a small private school."

"Brookhollow?" Eve felt the sizzle.

"Gold star for you, Lieutenant. Brookhollow Academy, and its higher-education companion, Brookhollow College."

"Pop." Eve turned back to her wall screen with a thin, satisfied grin. "Guess who got her entire education at those institutions."

"It rings," Peabody agreed. "But it could be argued he sent his ward there because he believed in the school and put his money in it. Or he put his money in it because his ward went there."

"Check it out now. When was it established, by whom? Lists of faculty, directors, whatever the hell. Find me a list of the current students. And the names of female students who took the tour with Avril Hannson."

"Yes, sir." Peabody hurried to Eve's desk unit and set to work.

"This feels hot," Eve said, then looked over at Roarke. "It's a good lead."

"My pleasure." He tipped her chin up with his finger, touched his lips to hers before she could object. "On a personal front, would you like me to contact Mavis about Thanksgiving? We're getting close to the mark, and it appears your plate's more full than mine at the moment."

"That'd be good."

"Anyone else?"

"I don't know." She shifted, uncomfortable. "I guess Nadine, maybe. Feeney'll probably be doing a family deal, but I'll run it by him."

"What about Louise and Charles?"

"Sure. Fine. Are we really doing this?"

"Too late to turn back." He kissed her again. "Keep in touch, will you? I'm caught up now." He strolled back into his office, shut the door.

"I love McNab."

Even as she turned toward Peabody, Eve could feel the muscle under her right eye vibrating toward a twitch. "Oh man. Do you have to do this?"

"Yeah. I love McNab," Peabody repeated. "It took me a while to realize it, or get there, however it works. But he's the one. If you were to drop down dead, and Roarke decided I could comfort him with wild sex, I probably wouldn't do it. Probably. But even if I did, I'd still love McNab."

"At least I'm dead in your sexual fantasy."

"It's only fair. I wouldn't cheat on my partner. So I probably wouldn't have sex with Roarke, should the opportunity arise, unless both you and McNab were killed in a freak accident."

"Thanks, Peabody. I feel a lot better now."

"And we'd probably wait a decent interval. Like two weeks. If we could control ourselves."

"It just gets better and better," Eve remarked.

"In a way, we'd really be celebrating your lives, and our love for you both."

"Maybe you're the ones who die in a freak accident," Eve tossed back. "Then me and McNab . . . No, Jesus. No." She visibly shuddered. "I don't love you that much."

"Aw, that's not very nice. Too bad for you, because McNab's an airjack in the sack."

"Shut up now. Save yourself."

"Brookhollow Academy," Peabody said in dignified tones. "Established 2022."

"Just a couple years before Avril was born? Who's the founder? Put the data on-screen."

"On screen one."

"Private educational institution," Eve read, scanning. "For girls. Just girls. Founded by Jonah Delecourt Wilson—secondary run on him, Peabody."

"On that."

"Grades one through twelve, full boarding. Accredited by the International Association of Independent Schools. Ranked third in U.S., fifteenth worldwide. An eighty-acre campus. That's a lot of ground. Six-to-one student-to-instructor ratio."

"Serious individual attention."

"College preparatory, full housing for students and staff. An Intentional Community. Huh, some phrase. A challenging, yet supportive, environment. Blah, blah. Foundation for Brookhollow College, and blah about that. Tuition . . . Holy Mother of God."

"Wowzer!" Peabody's eyes widened. "That's a semester. That's a semester for a *six*-year-old."

"Get me a comparison to another top-level boarding school."

"Coming up. What are we chasing here, Dallas?"

"I don't know. But we're gaining. Double," she replied. "Brookhollow's priced double a comparative facility."

"Got the founder. Jonah Delecourt Wilson, born August 12, 1964. Died May 6, 2056. That's Dr. Wilson," Peabody added. "M.D. as well as Ph.D. Known for his research and work with genetics."

"Really? Hmm."

"Married Eva Hannson Samuels, June of 1999. No children. Samuels also doctor—predeceased her husband by three years. Private shuttle crash."

"Hannson. Avril's maiden name. Gotta be related."

"Wilson founded the school, served as its first president for five years, then his wife took the helm. She remained in that position until her death. Current president is an Evelyn Samuels—listed here as her predecessor's niece—and one of the first graduates of Brookhollow College."

"All in the family. Bet when you pump money into an institution like this, you get all sorts of perks. I bet you could have your own lab. Maybe send some of your subjects in as students. Get them a fine education, while you were monitoring them. A geneticist, a reconstructive surgeon, and a private all-girls' boarding school. Mix well, what might you get?"

"Um. Really, really major fees?"

"Perfect females. Gene manipulation, surgical enhancements, specified educational programs."

"Jesus, Dallas."

"Yeah, pretty fucked up. Screwed squared if you take it a step further and speculate that the grads might be 'placed' for a stinging fee with interested parties. She said—last night during her statement—Avril said she was what Will Icove wanted. Just like that. Wouldn't a doting daddy want to give his only son what he wanted?"

"It's a little science fiction, Dallas."

"DNA."

"And?"

"Dolores Nocho-Alverez. DNA. I bet that alias is a little private joke." She picked up her 'link when it beeped. "Dallas."

"Got a freaking tome so far on Senior. Due to the recent events, am working on one for Junior. What's going on, Dallas?" Nadine demanded.

"Is there anything in that tome regarding an association with a Dr. Jonah D. Wilson?"

"Funny you should ask." Nadine's eyes sharpened. "They both gave their time and skill during the Urbans. Became friends, and associates. Helped found rehabilitation centers for children during and after the wars. There's more on that, and other things, but I need to dig more. I'm getting a whiff of something—maybe a censure from the AMA, internal inquiries, but it's buried deep."

"Mine it out, and if I'm on the right track, you might just have the story of your career."

"Don't toy with me, Dallas."

"Send me everything you've got. Get more."

"Give me something to air. I need a—"

"Can't. Gotta go. Oh hey, if Roarke contacts you, it's about an invite for Thanksgiving."

"Oh yeah? Frosty. Can I bring a date?"

"I guess. Later."

She clicked off. "Let's go take another look at Icove's house."

Peabody saved data, jumped up. "Are we going to New Hampshire on this?"

"I wouldn't be surprised."

In a palatial house overlooking the sea, the privacy screens on the walls of glass protected those inside from intrusion. Through them, the water was a soft blue-gray stretching toward the horizon.

She would paint it that way, she thought. Empty and quiet and wide, with only birds strutting along the surf.

She would paint again, and paint vividly. No more of the soft and pretty portraits, but the wild and the dark, the bright and the bold.

She would live—soon—she would live the same way. Freedom, she imagined, was all of those things.

"I wish we could live here. I'd be happy if we could live here. We could live here with the children and just be who we are."

"Maybe someday, somewhere like it." Her name wasn't Dolores, but Deena. Her hair was dark red now, and her eyes a vivid green. She'd killed, would kill again, and her conscience was clear. "When it's finished, when we've done all we can do, it'll have to be sold. But there are other beaches."

"I know. I'm just feeling blue." She turned, contained elegance, then smiled. "No point in feeling blue. We're free. At least as close to it as we've ever been."

Deena walked over, took the hands of the woman she considered a sister. "Scared?"

"Some. But excited, too. And sad. How can we help it? There was love, Deena. Even if it was twisted at its root, there was love."

"Yeah. I looked in his eyes when I killed him, and there was love in them. Sick and selfish and wrong, but love. I couldn't think about it, couldn't let myself." She breathed deep. "Well, they trained me how to do just that, shut out feelings and do the job. But after . . ."

She closed her eyes. "I want peace, Avril. Peace and quiet and days with nothing but both. It's been so long. Do you know what I dream of?"

She squeezed Deena's fingers. "Tell me."

"A little house, a cottage really. With a garden. Flowers and trees, and birds singing. A big silly dog. And someone to love me, a man to love me. Days of that, quiet days of that with no hiding, no war, no death."

"You'll have it."

But Deena could look back, year by year. There was nothing but hiding, nothing but death. "I made you a killer."

"No. No." Avril leaned close, kissed Deena's cheek. "Freedom. That was your gift." She walked back to the wall of glass. "I'm going to paint again. Really paint. I'll feel better. I'll comfort the children, poor little things. We'll take them away from all this as soon as we can. Out of the country, at least for a while. Somewhere they can grow up free. As we never were."

"The police. They're going to want to talk again. More questions."

"It's all right. We know what to do, what to say. And nearly all of it's the truth, so it isn't hard. Wilfred would have respected her mind, this Lieutenant Dallas. It's so fluid, and somehow straightforward. She's someone we'd like, if we could."

"She's someone to be careful with."

"Yes. Very. How foolish of Wilfred, how egocentric of him to have kept personal records in his home. If Will had known—poor Will. Still, I wonder if it's to the good that she knows about the project. Or knows something. We could wait, see if she's able to follow it through. She might end it for us."

"We can't take that chance. Not after we've come this far."

"I suppose we can't. I'll miss you," she said. "I wish you could stay. I'll be lonely."

"You're never alone." Deena went to her, held her. "We'll talk every day. It won't be much longer."

She nodded. "It's horrible, isn't it, to wish for more death. To want it to come quickly. In an awful way, she's one of us."

"Not anymore—if she ever was." Deena eased back, then kissed her sister's cheeks. "Be strong."

"Be safe."

She watched while Deena put a blue bucket hat over her hair, dark glasses over her eyes, then picked up a bag to sling over her shoulder.

Deena slipped out the glass door, jogged quickly over the terrace, down the steps to the sand. She walked away, just a woman taking a stroll on a November beach.

No one would know what she was part of, where she'd come from. Or what she had done.

For a long time, there was only the water and sand and birds. The knock on Avril's door was soft, as was her voice command to release the lock.

The little girl stood there, blonde and delicate like her mother, rubbing her eyes. "Mommy."

"Here, sweetie, here, my baby." With love bursting inside her, she hurried over to lift the child into her arms.

"Daddy."

"I know. I know." She stroked her child's hair, kissed her damp cheek. "I know. I miss him, too."

And in a strange way, one she couldn't understand herself, she spoke the pure truth.

EVE CLEARED HER MIND AND LET HERSELF see. The quiet house. Familiar. Through the door, alone.

She'd gone to the Center alone. Killed alone.

Back to the kitchen. Why the tray? she asked herself as she took the route she imagined the killer had used. To comfort and distract.

Someone he knew. Had he known his father's killer, hidden that?

In the kitchen, she stood a moment, gauging the ground.

"The domestic didn't put the food on a tray. It's unlikely Icove did it for himself."

"Maybe he was expecting her all along," Peabody suggested. "So he shut down the droids."

"Possible. But why lock down for the night? You're expecting company, why set full night security? Could have set it, shut down the droids, then been contacted by her. Came down, let her in himself. Hey, let's have a snack."

But she didn't like it.

"The way he was positioned on the couch up in the office. It's not entertaining company. It's 'I just want to lie down awhile.' Let's try it this way for now. She comes in, knows the code or has clearance. She comes back here, puts the food together. She knows he's upstairs."

"How does she know?"

"Because she knows him. She *knows*. Could easily verify by the house scanner if she's not a hundred percent. Probably used it, yeah, I would have. Confirm not only his location, but that he was alone in the house. Checks the droids, too, makes sure they're shut down. Carries the tray up."

She turned, walked the way she'd come.

Was she nervous? Eve wondered. Did the plate rattle on the tray, or was she calm as a sea of ice?

Outside the office door, Eve mimed holding a tray, cocked her head. "If he's locked in, she'd use voice command to unlock and open. Why put the tray down to free her hands? Let's have EDD take a look, see what they see."

"Check."

Eve walked in, studied the angle. "He wouldn't have seen her, not at first. He'd have heard her if he'd been awake, but he was facing away from the door. Crosses over, sets the tray down. Did they talk? I brought you a little something. You need to eat, take care of yourself. See, that's wifely. She shouldn't have bothered with the tray. That's a mistake."

Eve eased a hip down near the outside center of the sofa. There'd been room for that, she thought, bringing the image of Icove's body position into her mind. "If she sat like this, it blocks him from getting up, and it's wifely again. It's nonthreatening. Then all she has to do is . . ."

Eve leaned forward, fisting her hand as if holding the handle of a blade, pressed it down.

"Cold."

"Yeah, but not entirely. The tray's the thing. Maybe the contents were tranq'd, and it was backup. Otherwise it was, I don't know, maybe guilt. Give the guy a last meal. There was nothing like that the first time. Go in, do it, walk out. No frills."

She got up again. "Everything else is efficient. Lock the door behind you, take the discs, reset security. This tray keeps shouting at me."

She blew out a breath. "Roarke does stuff like that. Pushes food on me. It's an instinct with him. If I'm feeling off or upset, he's going to be shoving a bowl or plate under my nose."

"He loves you."

"That's right. Whoever did this had feelings for him. A relationship of some sort."

She took a turn around the room. "Let's go back to him. Why does he lock himself in here?"

"To work."

"Yeah. But he lies down. Tired, off, maybe he thinks better on his back. Whatever." She poked into the adjoining bath as she thought it through. "Kinda dinky bathroom for a swank house like this."

"It's off the office, inaccessible from the rest. He wouldn't need plush."

"Yes, he does," Eve responded. "Look at the rest of the space. Oversized, fancy furniture, art. His private bath at the center was bigger than this, and this is his home."

Curious now, she stepped all the way in. "Dimension's aren't right, Peabody."

She hurried out, Peabody behind her, and went to Avril's office on the other side of the bath. She stared at the wall, covered with art, the small table, two chairs precisely centered.

"There's something between. Something between this wall and the bath." Walking back over, she studied the small linen and supply closet, pulled the doors open.

She rapped the back with a fist. "Hear that?"

"Solid. Heavy. Probably reinforced. Hot doggies! We got us a secret room, Dallas."

They searched for a mechanism, running hands over the walls, the shelves. Finally, Eve sat back on her heels, muttered a curse, and pulled out her 'link.

"Can you squeeze out any time between formulating plans for world domination and buying all the turkey in all the land?"

"Possibly. If there was incentive."

"I've got a hidden room. Can't find entry. It's probably electronically activated. I can call in EDD, but since you're still home, you're closer."

"Address."

She gave it to him.

"Ten minutes."

Eve sat more comfortably on the floor. "I'll wait for him, contact the alibi while I do. You want to have chats with some of the neighbors?"

"No problem."

Eve made the call from where she sat, and wasn't surprised when Avril's Hamptons alibi checked out precisely. For the hell of it, she contacted the ice-cream parlor where Avril stated she'd taken the children. And was again unsurprised when the statement held up to the letter.

"You were damn well prepared," she muttered, and rising, walked back downstairs.

She tagged Morris.

"Just about to buzz you, Dallas. Stomach contents confirm the reported last meal. Tox shows a blocker. Standard stuff. And a mild tranq. Both ingested under an hour prior to death."

"How mild?"

"He'd have been relaxed, a little sleepy. He had a standard dose in him of both meds. A cocktail you might take if you had a nasty headache and wanted to rest."

"Fits." She thought of his position on the sofa. "Yeah, it fits. Got anything else?"

"No other trauma. Healthy male, superior face and body work. He'd have been conscious at time of death, but groggy. Identical weapon, single wound to the heart."

The door opened, and Roarke strolled in. "All right. Appreciate the speed. Later. You didn't have to pick the locks," she said to Roarke.

"Practice. Lovely home." He studied the decor of the foyer and living area. "A bit overly traditional, not particularly creative, but lovely of its kind."

"I'll be sure to put that in my report." She jerked a thumb toward the stairs, then started up.

"It's good security, by the way," he said conversationally. "It would have taken me longer if EDD hadn't already fiddled with it. As it was, a couple of neighbors gave me the eye. I believe they took me for a cop. Amazing."

She glanced over at him, the god of eye candy in his ten-thousand-dollar suit. "No, they didn't. It's in here."

He looked around the office. He could see the trace dust left by the sweepers, noted the lack of electronics. Already in EDD, he assumed. "The paintings are the best part of the decor."

He walked to a chalk sketch, an informal family portrait. Icove sitting on the floor, one foot planted, his wife sitting beside him, head tipped toward his arm, her legs swept to the side. And the children snuggled in front of them.

"Lovely, loving work. Pretty family. The young widow is talented."

"I'll say." But Eve took time out to stand beside him, study the portrait. "Loving work?"

"The pose, the light, the body language, her lines and curves. It strikes me as a happy moment."

"Why do you kill what you love?"

"We couldn't count the reasons."

"You're right on that," Eve agreed, and turned toward the bathroom.

"You believe she did it."

"I know she was part of it. Can't prove dick at this point, but I know." She hooked her thumbs in her front pockets, nodded. "It's behind there, other side of that closet."

Like she had, he took scope of the room. "It would be." From his pocket, he took a handheld. It shot out a thin red beam when he engaged it. Roarke ran the beam over the wall and shelves.

"What does that do?"

"Sssh."

She heard it, barely. A low hum emitting from the gadget he held.

"You've got steel behind the wall," he said, glancing at the readout.

"I figured that out without the toy."

He merely lifted an eyebrow at her. Moving closer, he keyed something into the handheld. The hum became a slow, rhythmic beep. He played the beam of light, centimeter by centimeter, until she could hear her own teeth grinding.

"What if you—"

"Sssh," he ordered again.

Eve gave up and walked out to meet Peabody when she heard the front door open.

"Snagged a couple neighbors. Nobody noticed any activity. Lots of shock and dismay over Icove. Nice, happy family, according to next-door. Caught the woman—Maude Jacobs—before she headed out to work. Belongs to the same health club as Avril Icove, and they'd work out together sometimes. Have a veggie juice after. Describes her as a nice woman, good mother, happy. Families did the dinner party thing every couple months. She never noticed any friction."

Peabody glanced upstairs. "I figured I'd come back since I saw Roarke was here. Check out the room before we hit more neighbors."

"He's working on it. We'll call EDD," she continued as they headed back to the office. "Have them bring down— Never mind."

The back wall was open. The door, more accurately, Eve corrected. It was a good six inches thick, and she could see a complex series of locks on the inside now.

"Frr-osty," Peabody said as she moved toward the opening.

From inside, Roarke turned, shot her a grin. "It's an old panic room converted to a high-security office. Once you're inside, door shut, engaged, there's no getting in from the outside. All the electronics are independent." He gestured to a short wall of screens. "You've got full surveillance of the house, inside and out. Stock provisions, you could hold out against home invasion, possibly a nuclear attack."

"Records." Eve looked at the blank computer screen.

"Unit's passcoded and fail-safed. I could bypass, but— "

"We'll take it in," she interrupted. "Keep the chain of evidence clear."

"Well, you can, but I can tell you it's likely been wiped. And there's not a single disc in the room."

"He destroyed them first, or she took them. If it's the latter, she knew about the room. The wife would've known. Even if Icove didn't tell her about it, she'd have known. She's an artist for one thing. She'd understand symmetry, dimensions, balance, and the proportions are off in the bathroom."

She took a hard look at the room, walked back out, took another study of the office.

"He's not going to destroy the discs," she decided. "He's too organized, too like his father. And you know what, this project is their life's work. It's their mission. He didn't think he was going to die, and he's got that vault in there. He feels secure about that. He feels secure except I'm asking questions, and he realizes his father kept records—coded, sure, but a little too accessible. So maybe he checks the room, just reassures himself. And it's under his skin."

"If he knew the woman who killed his father, wouldn't he worry she'd come for him?" Peabody stepped out with Eve. "Could be why he sent his wife and kids away. For their safety."

"A guy thinks there's a knife at his heart, he's going to shed some sweat. He didn't. He was pissy because I poked at his father. Concerned, even afraid that his father's death was a result of their work and we might screw that up. But you're afraid for your life, you run and hide. You don't hunker down in your house and take a sedative. Standard, mild. Morris," Eve said before Peabody could ask.

"If there were records," she added, "the killer has them. Question is, What was on them? And why does she want them?"

She turned to Roarke. "Let's look at it this way. You want to eliminate an organization, a company. Destroy it or take it over, whatever. What do you do?"

"A variety of things. But the quickest, most ruthless would be to cut off its head. Detach the brain, the body falls."

"Yeah, like that." Her lips curved, grimly. "The Icoves were pretty brainy guys. Even then, you'd want all the data, all the intel you can gather. Especially inside stuff. They didn't run it alone. You'd want to know the other players. Even if you know them, or some of them, you'd want the data. And to cover your tracks."

"You think the killer will pick off others involved in this project?"

She nodded at Roarke. "I'm thinking hey, why stop now. Let's get the sweepers in here, Peabody. Then we're at Central. We've got a lot of reading to do."

She started downstairs while Peabody called it in. "Oh, and Nadine's on for Thanksgiving," she said to Roarke. "With maybe a date."

"Good. I spoke with Mavis. She said she and Leonardo will be there, ringing."

"Ringing what?"

"With bells on, I assume."

"What does that mean, anyway? Why would people come to your house wearing bells. It would just be annoying."

"Mmm. Oh, and Peabody, she said if I spoke with you before she . . . No, let me get this just right. If I tagged on you before she made the beep, I should tell you that she and Trina are jacked, and if it chills you, they'll group it tonight at Dallas's."

Eve went dead white. "Dallas's what? Trina? No."

"There, there," Roarke soothed, and patted her hand. "Be brave, my little soldier."

Instead, she rounded on Peabody like a panther. "What have you done?"

"I was . . . it was just I was thinking about maybe doing something with my hair, and I was talking to Mavis."

"Oh. Oh. You bitch. I'll kill you. Rip out your internal organs with my bare hands then strangle you with your own large intestine."

"Can I get my hair extensions first?" Peabody tried a game smile.

"I'll give you hair extensions." She might have leaped, but Roarke wrapped his arms around her from the back, held her in place. "Better run," he warned Peabody, but she was already heading out the door at a trot.

"You could always kill Trina," Roarke suggested.

"I don't think she can be killed." Eve thought of the hair and skin specialist, and possibly the only entity on or off planet that terrified her. "Let go. I won't murder Peabody—yet—because I need her."

He turned her around, gave her a squeeze. "Anything else I can do for you, Lieutenant?"

"I'll let you know."

On the street there was no sign of Peabody. Waving Roarke off, she sat down on the steps to wait for the sweepers. Since her day was already ruined with the prospect of an evening beauty treatment, she called the lab and had a round with the chief tech, Dick Berenski, not-so-affectionately known as Dickhead.

"Fruit was clean—and delicious." His skinny face oiled onto her screen. "Cheese, crackers, tea, the whole shot. Cheese from cows and goats. Prime stuff. Too bad for his bad luck on dying before he ate."

"Did you consume my evidence?"

"Sampled. Ain't evidence as it ain't tampered with. Got a couple strands of blond hair—natural blond. One off his sweater, two off the sofa. Nada on the murder weapon. Sealed tight. No prints on the snack tray either. Nothing on the food, plate, napkin, utensils. Nothing nowhere."

No prints, she thought after she broke connection. If Icove had gotten the tray, odds are he'd have left prints on something. So that added weight to her theory.

"Uh, sir?"

Peabody stood a safe distance away on the sidewalk. She rolled to the balls of her feet like a woman prepared to run. "I spoke with another neighbor. Same tone. I did verify the domestic's statement regarding family routine and schedule."

"Dandy. Why don't you come over here and sit down, Peabody."

"No, thanks. Stretching my legs."

"Coward."

"No question about it." Her face worked itself into an expression of mournful apology. "I didn't really do anything. It's not really my fault. I just ran into Mavis and said how I was thinking about new hair, and she grabbed that ball and sprinted for the touchdown."

"You couldn't intercept from a pregnant woman?"

"She's fat, but she's spry. Don't kill me."

"I've got too much on my mind right now to plan your murder. You'd better hope I stay busy."

Back at Central, she set Peabody up with the masses of data Nadine had unearthed. Let her read until her eyes bleed, Eve thought, nearly satisfied.

She whipped around from Peabody's desk and grabbed Baxter by the collar. "You sniffing at me?"

"The coat. I was sniffing at the coat."

"Cut it out." She released him. "Sick bastard."

"Jenkinson is Sick Bastard."

"Yo," Jenkinson called from across the room.

"If you can't keep your squad straight, Dallas, I worry about your command abilities."

She angled her head at Baxter's winning smile. "You ever had face or body work, Baxter?"

"My intense good looks are a product of exceptional genes. Why? Something wrong with my face and body?"

"I want you to go through the Wilfred B. Icove Center. Soft clothes. You want a consult with their top face guy."

"What's wrong with my face? Women melt when I use the power of my smile upon them."

"The top face guy," Eve repeated. "I want to know exactly what process you go through for the consult. I want the fee schedule, the vibe. I want to know what kind of shape they're in with both Icoves in the morgue."

"Happy to help, Dallas, but let's consider this. Who'd believe I'd want something done to this face." He turned his head, lifted his chin. "Check the profile, if you dare. It's a killer."

"Use it to snuggle up to some of the female staff. Get me the what. You want a tour of the place before you put your face in their hands, and like that. Got it?"

"Sure. What about my boy?"

Eve looked over where Officer Troy Trueheart, Baxter's aide, sat in his cube doing paperwork. He was still as fresh as spring grass, but Baxter was fertilizing. "How's his lying coming along?"

"Better."

Maybe, but he was young, built, and pretty. Better to send in a seasoned cop—self-described killer profile or not. "Give him a pass on this. It should only take you a couple hours."

She tagged Feeney, offered to buy him what passed for lunch at Central's eatery.

They squeezed into a booth and both ordered fake pastrami on marginally fresh rye. Eve disguised hers by drowning it in mustard the unfortunate color of infected urine.

"First Icove," Feeney began, slopping a soy fry through a puddle of anemic ketchup. "No transmissions in or out the night before the murder on his desk 'link, home office. Got copies of transmissions in and out on his office 'link, his pocket. Nothing to, from, or pertaining to the suspect."

He chewed, swallowed, tried the stringy substance masquerading as pastrami. "Took a look at Dr. Will's 'links. Wife tagged him from her personal from the Hamptons about fifteen hundred the day of."

"She didn't mention that."

"Quick check-in. Kids're fine, had ice cream, friends coming over for drinks later. Wanted to know if he'd eaten anything, if he was getting any rest. Domestic stuff."

"I bet he told her he was going home, locking down."

"Yeah." Feeney drowned another fry. "Told her he was going to try to get some work done, then close it down. He was tired, had a headache, and he'd had another round with you. Nothing on there anybody could call wonky."

"But she knew his plans for the rest of the day. What else you get on Senior?"

"Patient records and charts are pretty extensive. I've got one of my boys with some med training weeding through those. But here's the thing." He washed down the sandwich with truly horrible fake coffee. "Got a memo book, separate from the appointment calendar his admin turned over. Personal reminder stuff—grandkid's playdate, flowers for daughter-in-law, consult with one of the doctors on his staff, board meeting. He had the appointment with her in there. Just her first initial, just D, the time, the date. Every other, if he was meeting another doctor, talking to a patient, he used first and last name, the time, the date, and a little buzzword pertaining to the purpose. Every single time, except for this one. And there's another ping."

"What?"

"Memo book holds a year. We're in November, so that's eleven months. For eleven months, except when he's out of town on business or pleasure, he's got Monday and Thursday evenings and Wednesday afternoons clear. Not one booking. No dates, no appointments, nothing."

"I saw that in his other book, but it didn't go back the full year." Yeah, that was a ping, all right. "Regular activity he doesn't note down."

"Regular like you never miss your daily portion of fiber." Feeney wagged a soy chip. "Maybe you're into something, and you're organized, you manage to keep a night open regular. But two nights and an afternoon, every week for eleven months? That's pretty damned focused."

"I'm going to need you to spread it out, go back further. Do the same on Icove Two. See if they took any of the same nights off. And I'm interested in any mention of Brookhollow Academy and/or College. Any mention of Jonah D. Wilson or Eva Hannson Samuels."

Feeney took out his own memo book to key in the names. "Going to tell me why?"

She filled him in while they worked their way through lunch.

"How bad could the pie be?" he wondered, and punched a selection into the table menu, along with requests for two more coffees.

"Okay, Dr. Will," he said. "Anybody tampered with locks or security, they had invisible hands. Nothing shows."

"They had to pass the voice print. Can you pull out the voice?"

"Can't." He shook his head. "System doesn't hold it. Security. Doesn't leave room for somebody to pull it out, record it, clone it. I gotta say whoever came in was let in or was authorized, or is a freaking genius."

"She's smart, but not a genius. Smart enough not to make it look like a break-in. More confusing," she said when Feeney raised his brows. "The wife's solid in the Hamptons. According to her, to the domestics, nobody outside the household had the codes or was authorized. So that leaves us with a ghost. We gotta look at the wife. Look again, but she's got several independent witnesses who put her miles away while her husband was getting his heart cut open. We're looking for an accomplice, for a connect between her and Dolores. And so far, there's zip.

"Except there's this project."

"And the school."

Eve nodded. "Yeah. I think I'm going to have to take a trip to New Hampshire. What do people do in New Hampshire?"

"Beats the hell out of me." Feeney frowned at the plate that slid out of the order slot. On it was a mushy triangle on the brown side of orange.

"Is that supposed to be pumpkin pie?" Eve asked. "It looks more like a slice of—"

"Don't say it." Gamely, Feeney grabbed his fork. "I'm eating it."

Figuring Peabody would be at it hours yet, Eve went from lunch to Whitney's office to update him.

"You think a school with a reputation like Brookhollow is a front for what, sex slavery?"

"I think it pertains."

Whitney dragged his fingers through his short crop of hair. "If memory serves, it was on my wife's list of potential colleges for our daughter."

"Did you apply?"

"Most of that process is, thankfully, a blur. Mrs. Whitney would remember."

"Sir, speaking of Mrs. Whitney . . ." Touchy, touchy. "I've sent Baxter in on an informal recon, under, as a potential client. Get him in, tour the facilities, check out the system. However, I wondered, should it become necessary, would Mrs. Whitney agree to talk with me about her, um, experience?"

He looked, for a moment, as pained as Eve felt. "She won't care for it, but she's a cop's wife. If you need a statement, she'll give you one."

"Thank you, Commander. I doubt I will. I hope I won't."

"So, Lieutenant, do I. More than you know."

From there, she went to Mira's office, wheedled her way past the admin between patients. She didn't sit, though Mira gestured to a chair.

"You okay?" Eve asked her.

"A bit dented, actually. Both of them gone. I knew Will, enjoyed him and his family on the occasions we got together."

"How would you characterize his relationship with his wife?"

"Affectionate, a bit old-fashioned, happy."

"Old-fashioned in what sense?"

"My impression is that he very much headed the house. That it ran around his needs and routine, but my impression is also that the dynamic suited them. She's a very loving and devoted mother, and enjoyed being a doctor's wife. She has talent, but seemed happy to dabble with her art rather than passionately pursue it."

"And if I told you she had a part in the murders?"

Mira's eyes blinked, then widened. "On the basis of my professional evaluation of her character, I would disagree."

"You saw them socially—now and then. You saw them as they wanted to be seen. Would you agree?"

"Yes, but . . . Eve, my profile of the killer indicates a cool-headed, efficient, highly controlled individual. My impressions of Avril Icove—and these come over years—is of a soft-hearted, mild-tempered woman who was not only content with her life but enjoyed living it."

"He raised her for his son."

"What?"

"I *know* it. Icove molded her, educated her, trained her, he all but fucking created her as the perfect mate for his son. He wasn't a man to settle for less than perfect."

She sat now, leaned forward. "He sent her to school—small, exclusive, private, where he had control. He, and his friend and associate, Jonah Wilson. A geneticist."

"Wait." Mira held up both hands. "Wait. Are you talking about gene manipulation? She was five or more when Wilfred took over her guardianship."

"Maybe, or maybe there was an interest in her long before. There's a relationship between her and Wilson's wife. They share a family name, yet there's no data on the connection. There had to be a relationship between her mother and Icove, who became her guardian. Wilson and his wife founded the school—Icove sent Avril there."

"There may very well be some connection, which might very well be why he chose the school. The simple fact that he knew or had an association with a geneticist—"

"There are bans on gene manipulations that veer outside of disease and defect control. Put there because people, and science, always want more. If you can cure or fix an embryo, why not make it to order? I'll have a girl, thanks, blonde, blue eyes, and give her a pert little nose while you're at it. People pay a hell of a lot for perfection."

"These are huge leaps, Eve."

"Maybe. But you've got a geneticist, a reconstruct surgeon, a tony private school. With those building blocks I don't have to leap too far to wonder. I know what it's like to be trained." She sat back now, gripped the arms of her chair.

"You can't imagine that a man like Wilfred would physically, sexually abuse a child."

"Cruelty is only one training method. You can do it with kindness. Sometimes he brought me candy. Sometimes he gave me a present after he raped me. Like you give a dog a treat for doing a trick."

"She was fond of him. Eve, I saw it. Avril thought of Wilfred as a father. She wasn't locked away. If she'd wanted to leave, she could have done so."

"You know better," Eve replied. "The world's full of people who are locked away without any bars. I'm asking you if he could have done something like this. Could the pull of it, the *science,* the thrill of perfecting have pushed him into manipulating a child, turning her into a wife for his son, a mother for his grandchildren."

Mira closed her eyes a moment. "The science of it would, certainly, have intrigued him. Coupled with his perfectionist tendencies, it may have seduced him. If you're right on any level, on any level at all, he would have seen what he was doing as being for the greater good."

Yeah, Eve thought. Self-made gods always did.

12 WHEN EVE JUMPED ON THE GLIDE, BAXTER clomped on just behind her.

"That place is a racket."

"Why? What have you got?"

"What I don't have is an asymmetrical nose that unbalances the proportions of my jaw, chin, brow ratio. That's crap."

Frowning, she studied him. "I don't see anything wrong with your nose."

"There isn't."

"It's right in the middle of your face where it belongs." She got off the glide on their level, pointed to the soft drink machine, then passed him credits.

"Get me a tube of Pepsi."

"You're going to have to interact with the vending machines again sooner or later."

"Why? Did they give you a hard sell?" she asked. "Pressure you, push you to sign a contract."

"Depends on your point of view. I figured you wanted me to play some rich asshole, so I sprang for the electro-imaging analysis. Five bills, and I'm putting in for it."

"Five? Five? Shit, Baxter." She thought of her budget, grabbed her tube and the spare credits she'd given him. "Buy your own drink."

"You wanted me in, getting a good look at the client areas and routine." He pouted over the credits, then just plugged in his code and came up with a cream soda. "You're lucky I didn't go for phase two, and the full-body imaging program. That's a grand. They put you up on-screen, magnified. My pores looked like moon craters, for crissake. And they're drawing these lines over me, showing how my nose is off, and my ears should be closer to my head. My ears are *fine*. And talking about derma resurfacing. Nobody's resurfacing my derma."

Eve just leaned against the wall and let him go.

"And after they're done destroying your self-esteem, they show you how you'd look after. I played like: Wow, I gotta have that, even though there was no difference. Hardly. Barely noticeable. It was a tribute to my prevarication skills. I sweet-talked the tech into showing me around, and the place is plush. Ought to be, for what they charge. The quote on the work they want to do on me? Twenty large. Two-oh, and look at me." He threw out his arms. "I'm a damn good-looking son of a bitch."

"Get over yourself, Baxter. Did you feel anything off?"

"Place was like a tomb. Penthouse of tombs if you get me. All the staff—everyone—wearing a black armband. I asked the tech what was up, and she got teary. Sincerely. She told me about the murders, at which time I pulled out my thespian skills. She thinks it's a failed medical student turned serial killer targeting doctors out of professional jealousy."

"I'll be sure to put that one in the hat. Did you speak to one of the surgeons?"

"Being charming as well as a damned handsome son of a bitch, I got her to squeeze me into a Dr. Janis Petrie's consult schedule. Or as I call her, Dr. Bombshell. She's a walking ad for her trade, and touted to be one of their best. I got the murders into the conversation again, making like I was nervous to be there, or to consider treatment there, with what was going on."

He took a slug of cream soda. "Damp eyes again. She assured me that the Icove Center was the finest reconstructive and sculpting facility in the country, and that even with the tragedies, the center was in good hands. My continued nerves got me a tour through security with two guards. It's solid. Couldn't talk my way into any of the staff or med areas. Absolutely no patients, clients or potentials, allowed."

"Good enough for now. I'll let you know if there's more." She stepped away, then narrowed her eyes at him. "Nothing wrong with your nose."

"Fucking A."

"But maybe the ears are a little off, now that I think about it."

She left him frantically trying to see his reflection in the vending machine.

When she turned into the bull pen, Peabody sprang up from her desk and hotfooted after her. The minute they were in Eve's office, Peabody tried the hangdog look.

"Have I been punished enough?"

"There is no punishment great enough for your crimes."

"How about if I tell you I think I've found a supporting link between Wilson and Icove for your theory on their partnership in questionable medical procedures?"

"You may, should the information warrant, be eligible for parole."

"I think it's good. Nadine is so thorough I think my brains started leaking out my ears sometime during hour three, but she saved us a lot of time we'd have spent generating the same information."

Then Peabody folded her hands as if in prayer. "Please, sir, may I have coffee."

Eve jerked a thumb at the AutoChef.

"I waded through Icove, the early years," Peabody continued as she programmed. "Education, his research into reconstructive areas, his innovations therein. He did a lot of work with kids. Good work, Dallas. He earned degrees up the wazoo, awards, grants, fellowships. Married a wealthy socialite whose family was known for their philanthropic philosophies. Had a son."

She stopped to drink a little coffee and make a long *ahhhh* sound. "So along come the Urban Wars. Chaos, strife, rebellion, and he volunteers his time, skill, and considerable funds to hospitals."

"You're not telling me anything I don't know."

"Wait. I have to put it in context. Icove and Wilson were instrumental in forming Unilab—which provided and provides mobile research and laboratory facilities for groups like Doctors Without Borders and Right to Health. Unilab won a Nobel Peace Prize for its work. That was right after Icove's wife was killed in an explosion in London, where she was volunteering in a children's shelter. Over fifty casualties, mostly kids. Icove's wife was five months pregnant."

"Pregnant." Eve's eyes narrowed. "Did they have the sex of the fetus?"

"Female."

"Mother, wife, daughter. He lost three females we assume were important to him. Very rough."

"Extreme. Lots written about the wife's tragic and heroic death, and them as a couple. Big love story, shitty ending. Apparently, he went reclusive awhile after that, working in or for Unilab or cloistered with his son. Wilson, on the other hand, traveled around the world campaigning for the lifting of bans against less mainstream applications of eugenics."

"I knew it," Eve said quietly. "I'd've made book."

"Wilson gave speeches, lectures, wrote papers, threw money at it. One of his platforms was the war itself. With gene modification and manipulation, children would be born with higher intelligence, lower violent tendencies. We're using it to cure or prevent birth defects, so why not to create a more peaceful, more intelligent race? A superior race.

"It's an old argument," Peabody continued. "One that's been on the pro side of the debate for decades. He made some converts, powerful ones, in what was a war-weary atmosphere. But there's the whole issue of who decides what's intelligent enough, or what violence is acceptable, even necessary for self-preservation and defense. And while we're at this master-race crap, should we only breed white kids, black kids? Blondes? And where are the lines between nature and science? Who will pay? And he's pushing the line about how mankind has an innate right, even duty, to perfect itself, to eliminate death and disease and end war, to take the next evolutionary leap. Through technology we'd create a superior race, improve our physical and intellectual abilities."

"Wasn't there another guy who talked a similar game, back in the twentieth century?"

"Yeah, and his opposition didn't hesitate to play the Hitler card. But Icove comes out of his cave, adds his weight. He's got images of babies and kids he's operated on and starts asking if there's any difference in preventing these genetic defects before birth or fixing them after. And since law and science and ethics have allowed the research and gene manipulation on what they've deemed right and acceptable, wasn't it time to expand? His voice went a long way to loosening some ties on the bounds, opening the areas of genetic modification to prevent genetic defects. But rumors started to spread that Unilab was experimenting in forbidden and illegal areas. Designer babies, for one, selection, genetic programming, and even reproductive cloning."

Eve had slumped in her chair. Now she straightened. "Rumors or fact?"

"Never substantiated. I got bits—Nadine highlighted—that both men were investigated. But there wasn't a lot of media or data on that. My guess would be that nobody wanted to blacken a couple of Nobel Prize winners, one of whom was a war hero, a widower raising a child alone. Add big vats of money to that, and the grumbles died down.

"And when the tide began to turn—the whole natural era of postwar, where, by the way, Free-Ageism enjoyed its highest popularity—Icove and Wilson backed off. Wilson and his wife had already founded their school, and Icove moved forward in his field of reconstructive surgery, adding his cosmetic sculpting. He built a clinic and shelter in London in his wife's name, continued to construct his medical empire, and began work on building his landmark center here in New York."

"And about the time Brookhollow's getting off the ground and Icove's designing clinics and centers, he becomes the guardian of an associate's five-year-old daughter. The timing makes it pretty handy for her to be enrolled. Unilab's got facilities worldwide."

"And two off planet. One of them's in the Icove Center here in New York."

"Be convenient to have your work that handy," Eve mused.

"Risky, but convenient." Two evenings and one afternoon blank, every week. What better way to use them than to work on your pet project? "He'd have been more apt to keep it segregated, but we'll have to look. What the hell are we looking for?"

"Beats the living crap out of me. I flunked biology, and barely got a skim through chemistry."

Eve sat, staring into space for so long Peabody finally snapped her fingers. "You in there?"

"I've got it. Get ahold of Louise. See if she's interested in getting her skin slathered or her hair fried, whatever's on tonight's menu. Push it."

"Sure. But what—"

"Just do it." She swiveled to her desk, engaged the 'link. Rather than go through channels and Roarke's admin, she used his private code and left a voice mail.

"Get back to me when you can. I have an underhanded assignment that's right up your alley. I'm heading home shortly, so if you're tied up awhile, I'll just fill you in when you get there."

Two blocks from home she spotted him in her rearview. It amused her enough to have her use the dash 'link.

"I can spot a tail, pal."

"I'm always delighted to see yours. Your message didn't sound urgent, but it did sound intriguing."

"I'll fill you in in a few. Just in case, you got a full dish tomorrow?"

"A bit of this, a bit of that. All portions in my endless feast of world domination and turkey hoarding."

"Kick free for a couple hours?"

"Will it involve sweaty and possibly illegal sex acts?"

"No."

"In that case, I'll just have to check my schedule."

"If the time you put in helps me close this case, you get the sweaty and illegal sex act of your choice."

"Well, fancy that. As luck would have it, I believe I have a couple hours free tomorrow."

She laughed, and led the way through the gates toward home.

"I don't think we've ever done this before," she said when they both stepped out of their vehicles. "Gotten home at the same time."

"Then let's do something we rarely do, and take a walk."

"It's getting dark."

"Plenty of light yet," he disagreed, and slung a friendly arm around her shoulders.

She fell into step with him. "What do you know about Unilab?"

"A multipronged organization, roots in the Urban Wars. Humanitarian prong provides permanent and mobile laboratories for volunteer medical groups. UNICEF, DWB, Peace Corps, and so on. Its medical research prong, with its main base here in New York, is considered one of the top in the country. It also has clinics in urban and rural areas worldwide to provide care for the financially challenged. Your first victim was one of the founders."

"And with him dead, his cofounder dead, his son dead, Unilab might be interested in an outside source with plenty of moolah."

"Most are interested in moolah, but why do you suppose the board of directors of Unilab would be interested in mine, particularly."

"Because it goes along with your brain, your contacts, your savvy. Seems to me if you made interested noises they'd agree to a meet, and a grand tour."

"More likely to get a warm welcome if there was the carrot of a substantial donation or endowment."

"If you took that angle, would it look wrong for you to take along your medical expert?"

"No. It would look wrong if I didn't have an entourage." As they walked, soft lights winked on at ground level, triggered by motion. He wondered if he should plan any outdoor activities on the grounds for the children. Perhaps he should have some playground equipment installed.

Perhaps he was making himself crazy.

"What are we looking for?" he asked Eve.

"Anything. The place is huge. I'd never get a warrant to go through the whole facility. If I tried they'd get a TRO, tie me up for months. If there's anything to find it'd be gone if I ever broke that down. If they're doing illegal gene engineering or manipulation, it's likely they're doing the serious work elsewhere. Private property."

"Like the school."

"Yeah. Or some underground bunker in Eastern Europe. Or off planet. It's a great big freaking universe. But it strikes me that Icove, both Icoves, would want somewhere to work close by. The Center's the likely candidate."

She gave him a thumbnail progress report as they strolled around the house. Twilight softened and cooled toward dark.

"Perfect children," Roarke declared. "That's where you're headed."

"I think that's what drove him. He worked with children in his early career. He had a child. He lost one along with his wife. A female child. He has the ability through surgery not only to rebuild or repair, but to change—improve. Perfect. His close friend and associate is a geneticist, with radical leanings. I bet he learned a lot about gene research and treatment. I bet the good doctors had a lot of intense conversations."

"Then another child falls into his hands."

"Yeah. With a connection to Samuels. Funny Wilson and his wife weren't named guardians—and I have to dig there. But they control her. Adults control children, especially if they isolate them."

Roarke turned his head, brushed a kiss over her hair. A silent message of understanding and comfort.

"Wilson could have screwed around with Avril even before she was born." The idea made Eve's stomach roll. "I'm damn sure they experimented on her in one way or another after. Maybe her kids were part of the project, too. That could be what snapped her. Having her kids under the microscope."

By the time they'd circled the house—the equivalent, Eve thought, of hiking four crosstown blocks—she caught the glint of headlights turning through the gates.

"Damn. I guess the circus is coming to town after all."

A circus, he thought. Maybe he could . . . stop the madness.

"I love a parade."

She might've tried to bolt up the steps, hide out at least for a bit. But Summerset merely stood like a statue at the base.

"Hors d'oeuvres are in the parlor. Your first guests are arriving."

Even as Eve curled her lips into a snarl, Roarke was nudging her away. "Come on, darling. I'll pour you a nice glass of wine."

"How about a couple of double Zingers?" She rolled her eyes when he merely chuckled. "Yeah, yeah, a nice civilized glass of wine before the torture."

He poured, leaned down to buss her lips with his as he handed her the glass. "You're still wearing your weapon."

She brightened immediately. "Yeah, I am."

But the brightness dimmed as she heard Trina's voice riding along with Mavis's chirpy tones as Summerset let them in. "Might as well take it off," Eve grumbled. "She doesn't have a nervous system to compromise."

She wasn't sure how she'd ended up with a gang of females, or why all of them seemed so thrilled with the prospect of getting their faces, bodies, hair slathered with goo. They really didn't have that much in common, to Eve's mind. The dedicated doctor with blue blood, the ambitious and savvy on-air reporter, the stalwart cop with a Free-Ager background. Add in Mavis Freestone, the former street thief and current music vid sensation and the terrifying Trina with her bottomless case of glops and goos, and it was a strange mix.

But they sat, stood, sprawled around Roarke's lush and elegant parlor, happy as a pack of puppies.

They chattered. She'd never understood why women chattered, and seemed to have an endless supply of *stuff* to talk about. Food, men, men, each other, clothes, men, hair. Even shoes. She'd never known there was so much to say about shoes, and that none of it actually correlated to walking in them.

And since Mavis was knocked up, babies were high on the chatter list.

"I feel completely mag." Mavis gobbled up fancy cheese, crackers, stuffed veggies, and whatever else was in reach as if food were about to be declared illegal. "We're going into week thirty-three, and they say he/she can, like, hear stuff, and even see in there, and its head's down now—assuming the position. Sometimes you can feel his/her foot poking."

Poking what? Eve wondered. The kidneys, the liver? The very idea had her avoiding the pâté.

"How's Leonardo handling it?" Nadine asked.

"He's aces. We're taking classes now. Hey, Dallas, you and Roarke need to sign up for your coaching class."

Eve made some sound, but found it impossible to express the full terror.

"That's right, you're coaching." Louise beamed. "That's wonderful. It's so good for the mom to have people she loves and trusts with her during labor and delivery."

Eve was saved from coming up with a comment when Louise began to ask Mavis what method she planned to use, where she intended to give birth.

But she did manage a muttered "Coward" under her breath when she spotted Roarke slipping out of the room.

So she poured a second glass of wine.

Despite her strange and expanding shape, Mavis never stopped moving. She had traded her usual heels or platforms for gel-soles, but even they were what Eve assumed was the height of fashion. The boots were some sort of abstract pattern of pink on green and rose to the knees.

With them Mavis wore a sparkly green skirt with a snug green top that highlighted her protruding belly rather than disguising it. The sleeves of the shirt carried the same pattern as the boots and ended in a lot of pink and green feathers.

Her hair was wound high, pink and green ropes. There were feathers hanging from her ears. And a sparkly miniature heart at the corner of one eye.

"We should get started." Trina, who'd transformed her own hair into a waterfall down her back, in blinding white, smiled—evilly, Eve thought. "Lots to do. Where we going for it?"

"Roarke had the pool house set up," Mavis said and popped something else in her mouth. "I asked if we could play there. Swimming's good for me and the belly."

"I need to talk with Nadine and Louise. Separately," Eve added. "Official."

"That's chilly. We can split off down there. We can take the food, right?" Mavis grabbed a tray, just in case.

It was no way to conduct official business, Eve thought, sitting in the steam room with Louise.

"I'm in," Louise said, and chugged from a bottle of water. "I'll set up the time with Roarke. If I see anything suspicious, I'll let you know. It's doubtful—if there is illegal genetic manipulation or engineering going on—that they'd be in accessible areas, but I might get a sense of something."

"You agreed pretty fast."

"Adds a little excitement to my day. Plus, there are lines, or should be in medicine and science. This is one of them for me. I don't have a problem with the illegality, frankly. Hell, birth control for women was illegal right here in the U.S. of A. less than two hundred years ago. Without research and underground movements, we might still be having kids every year and burning our bodies out by forty. No, thanks."

"So what's the problem with tidying up genes until everything's just perfect?"

Louise shook her head. "Have you looked at Mavis?"

"Hard not to."

With a laugh, Louise took another drink. "What's happening to her is a miracle. Anatomy and biological process aside, creating life is a miracle, and should stay that way. Yes, we can—and we should—use our knowledge and our technology to insure the health and safety of the mother and child. Eliminate birth defects and disease whenever possible. But crossing that line into designing babies? Manipulating emotions, physical appearance, mental capacity, even personality traits? That's no miracle. It's ego."

The door to the steam room opened, and Peabody, her face covered in blue gunk, stuck her head in. "You're up, Dallas."

"No, I'm not. I have to brief Nadine."

"I'll go now." With what Eve considered sick enthusiasm, Louise sprang up.

"Send Nadine into my office," Eve ordered Peabody.

"Can't. She's in stage one of detoxification. Wrapped up like a mummy," Peabody explained. "In a seaweed deal."

"That's revolting."

Eve pulled on a robe. The pool area, always lush with plants and tropical trees, had become a horrifying treatment center. Padded tables with bodies stretched on them. Weird smells, weirder music. Trina had decked herself out in a lab coat. The splatters on it were a rainbow. Eve might have preferred blood. At least she understood blood.

Mavis lay, her colorful hair covered with a clear, protective cap, the rest of her coated with various hues of substances Eve didn't want to identify.

The belly was . . . prodigious.

"Check out the tits." Mavis lifted her arms, waggled her fingers toward her breasts. "They're, like, mongo now. It's a total side benny of being pregs."

"Great." She patted Mavis on the head and moved on toward Nadine.

"I'm in heaven," Nadine murmured.

"No, you're naked in a bunch of seaweed. Pay attention."

"The toxins are oozing out of my pores, even as we speak. Which means, yay, more wine for me when I'm done."

"Pay attention," Eve repeated. "Off the record until I give you the go-ahead."

"Off the record," Nadine mimicked, eyes still closed. "I'm going to pay Trina a thousand bucks to tattoo that on your ass."

"I believe the Icoves headed, or at least actively participated in, a project with its roots in gene manipulation, and a good portion of the funding for said project may have come from selling females who had been engineered and then trained to suit the needs of prospective clients."

Nadine's eyes popped open, sharp green against skin painted pale yellow. "You are shitting me."

"No, and you look like a fish. Smell like one, too. It's bad. I believe Avril Icove might have been part of this experimentation, and that she was an accessory in the deaths of her father-in-law and husband."

"Get me out of this thing." Nadine tried to sit up, but the thin warming blanket was strapped around the table.

"I don't know how, and I'm not touching it anyway. Just listen. I'm hitting this from a lot of angles. I may be off on some of it, but I know I've got the gist. I want you on Avril Icove."

"Try to keep me off her."

"Wheedle an interview, you're good at it. Get her to talk about the work both these guys are known for. Circle around the genetic stuff. You found the connection to Jonah Wilson, so you can touch on that. But you've got to keep it sympathetic, play up what they did for humanity and all that crap."

"I know how to do my job."

"You know how to get the story," Eve agreed. "I want you to get data. And if I'm right, and she's been part of two murders, if she thinks you're digging close to that mine, why would she hesitate to eliminate you? You're research, Nadine. I don't have anything on her, nothing I can use to pull her into Interview."

"But she may say something to a sympathetic female reporter that could point you."

"You're smart. That's why I'm asking you to do this, even though you're lying there looking like some sort of mutant trout."

"I'll get you something. And when I break this story, the fucking sky's the limit for me."

"It doesn't break until the case is closed. The Icoves couldn't have been the only ones involved in this. I don't know if she's going to be satisfied with taking only them out. So you're looking for the human angle. Her father figure and her husband, father of her kids, both lost to inexplicable violence. Ask her about her education, her art. You want the woman, the daughter, the widow, the mother."

Nadine pursed her yellow lips. "The many facets of her, appealing to her individuality. So she leads me into her relationships with the men, rather than them leading me into her. She's the spotlight. That's good. And it'll keep my producer very happy in the meantime."

There was a soft triple ding. "I'm done," Nadine announced.

"I'll get the tarter sauce."

There was no getting around it. With Mavis sitting beside her, hands and feet in frothy blue water, and Peabody snoring lightly nearby under relaxation VR, Eve stoically endured a facial. The cumlike substance Trina swore by was already slicked through her hair.

"What we're gonna do is a full-body facial while your hair soaks up the joy juice."

"That doesn't make any sense. The body is not the face."

"Some people'd be better off if their ass *was* their face."

Eve snorted out a laugh before she could stop herself.

"Everybody but Mavis is getting hair. Did hers this morning. You want something different with yours?"

"No." Defensively, Eve reached for her hair, and got her hand covered in slime. "Oh man."

"Could give you a temp tint, or try extensions. Just for fun."

"My world can't take any more fun. I don't want different."

"Can't blame you."

Eve opened one eye, suspiciously. "For?"

"Keeping it as is. It's working for you. But you don't take care of it, or your skin, like you should. Doesn't take that long for basic maintenance, you know."

"I maintain," Eve said, but under her breath.

"Your body, yeah. You got a prime one. Mag muscle tone. Some of my clients? They got shit under the sculpting."

Eve's eyes blinked open. Fear, she thought in disgust, had blinded her to an excellent source.

"You work on anybody who's used the Icove Center?"

"Shit." Trina sniffed as she worked. "Probably fifty percent of my base. You don't need them, take my word."

"Ever worked on Icove's wife? Avril?"

"She uses Utopia. I worked there about three years ago. She had Lolette, but I filled in on her body care one appointment 'cause Lolette was out with a black eye. Boyfriend was an asshole, which I told her, but would she listen. No, not until he—"

"Avril Icove," Eve interrupted. "Could you tell if she'd had any work done? Sculpting, reconstruction, surgical enhancements."

"You get a body naked under the scanners, you know all the dish. Sure, she had some. Little face work, little boob job. Top work, but you'd expect that."

Her husband had claimed she was just blessed, Eve remembered. "You're sure about that?"

"Hey, you know your job, I know mine. Why?"

"Just curious." Eve closed her eyes again. Thinking about murder made a facial almost bearable.

**AFTER AN ENDLESS EVENING, AND MORE**
wine than was probably wise—but extremely neces-
sary—Eve trudged up to her office. Maybe a couple
hits of strong coffee would counteract the alcohol, and she could
squeeze in an hour of work.

First on the list was a check of Avril's standard medicals. She'd
be interested to see just what sort of elective surgery she'd find.

Then she wanted a closer look at Brookhollow Academy.

She was taking the first slug of coffee when Roarke walked in
from his office.

"Yellow belly," she said.

"Excuse me?"

"Your belly's as yellow as Nadine's was a couple hours ago."

"I don't even want to know what that means."

"You skipped out, left me alone."

He gave her a look that would have passed for innocence on anyone else. "It seemed obvious that tonight's festivities were for
women only. Respecting female ritual, I discreetly got lost."

"To quote you, Yellow Belly, 'Bollocks.' You slithered out as soon
as Mavis started yapping about coaching classes."

"Guilty as charged, and I'm not ashamed. Lot of good it did me,
for all that." He took her coffee, drank. "She hunted me down."

"Oh yeah?"

"Oh aye, look smug—for you're in it, my friend, as deep as me.

Sometime between the body scrub and polish, she scouted me out and gave me the contact information and schedule for the instruction we're going to be forced to take in order to participate in the birthing. There's no escape for us."

"I know. We're doomed."

"Doomed," he repeated. "Eve, there are vids."

"Oh God."

"And simulations."

"Stop. Stop now." She grabbed her coffee mug and chugged. "It's still months away."

"Weeks," he corrected.

"That's like months. It takes weeks to make a month. It's not now, that's the important thing. I have to think of something else. I have to work. And you know," she added as she walked to her desk, "things could happen. Like . . . we could get abducted by terrorists right before she goes into labor."

"Oh, if only."

She had to grin as she called up the Icoves' client and patient lists. "It turns out Trina slopped cream on Avril Icove once, and claims she found sculpting when she was under the scan. Now, it's most likely that one of the Icoves would've done the work, or at least consulted."

"Consulted, most likely. I'd think working on a family member might be tricky, ethically."

"If one or both of them consulted, she'd be listed. That's legal standard. Computer, search for Avril Icove, medical consult and/or procedures."

Working . . . Avril Icove is not listed in selected files.

"You see, that just doesn't jibe for me. You're in a medical family—top of the line—and you don't use them for any of your elective work? You don't have your beloved husband consult on a procedure, one in which he's a leading expert?" She drummed her fingertips. "If I had a cargo ship of money I wanted to invest, I'd go to you, not to some stranger. If I wanted to break into the National Treasury—"

"Now, wouldn't that be fun?"

"I'd go to you."

"Thank you, darling. They might have examined and consulted off record."

"Why? See that's the thing. I can get Dr. Will claiming his wife's perfect face and body is God-given—privacy. And hey, nosy cop, none of your business. But I don't get this kind of secrecy for some fine-tuning or whatever. If she had the procedures, on record, and used the Icove Center—which is logical—why not document the consult? It's covering your legal ass, for one thing."

"So she might have had the procedures off record, at another of their facilities."

"That's my thought, which leads to another why. I need images of her. Old images, for comparison. Then there's Brookhollow. The most logical place for Avril and Dolores to have met—if they've worked together on the murders—is the school. But there's no Dolores listed on their registry, not as a graduate anyway. So I'm going to generate ID images of everyone who attended during Avril's time there, then do a match search with the image I have of Dolores."

"Which is again logical. It'll take a bit, and you smell delicious."

"It's the stuff."

"I'm a helpless victim of cosmetic merchandising." To prove it he slipped behind her and nipped the nape of her neck.

She gave him an elbow nudge back. "I need to get started on this."

"Me, too. Computer. Access registry for Brookhollow Academy and College—"

"Hey, this is *my* machine."

Ignoring her, he wrapped his arms around her waist. "Search and mark ID photos of students, staff—"

"Female spouses and offspring of staff and any female employees, female spouses, and offspring of employees."

"Very thorough," Roarke commented.

"Let's keep being thorough."

"Doing my best," he said and slid his hands under her sweatshirt.

"Not that way. I'm going to let it run for the whole time. Maybe she met Dolores at some alumni function. Computer, search for a match with— Jeez, Roarke, hold on a minute."

His hands were very busy. "What did Trina put on you this time? Let's buy a vat of it."

"I don't know. I'm losing my track. Match the generated images with the ID photo and security image on file for Nocho-Alverez, Dolores."

Multiple commands acknowledged. Working . . .

"Or she met her off-site, at the center, at the fricking salon. Hired her. Dozens of options."

"Have to start with one." Roarke turned Eve around to face him. "Your hair smells like autumn leaves."

"Dead?"

"Burnished. And you taste like . . . let me see." He nibbled his way down her temple, over her cheekbone, to her mouth. "Sugar and cinnamon, warmed together." He flipped open the button of her pants as he deepened the kiss.

"Now I have to do a search of my own, see if Trina's left any surprises for me."

"I told her I'd twist her arms into knots if she put any temp tattoos on me this time."

He cruised his hands up, over her breasts, and her heart began to shudder.

"You know that only challenges her. Nothing here," he said as he drew her sweatshirt up, off. "Just my wife's lovely, unadorned breasts."

"Mavis's are mongo." Eve let her head fall back as his lips skimmed over her.

"Yes, I noticed."

"She had Trina paint one nipple blue and the other pink."

He lifted his head slightly. "That may be just a bit too much information. Why don't I just say I prefer yours."

Her stomach tightened, pleasurably, as he closed his mouth over hers. "You could say that. I had too much wine. Otherwise, I wouldn't be making this so easy for you."

He flipped open the next button, and her pants slid down her hips. "Step out," he murmured.

"You're still dressed." And her head was spinning.

"Step out," he repeated, sliding those hands over her as she did. "You're all naked and soft, and I like the idea of riding my tongue over you, top to bottom, bottom to top until you . . . Well, well. What have we?"

Her brain had gone dull on her, so she only blinked at first when she followed Roarke's gaze down her own body.

There, low on either side of her belly, were three small, sparkling red hearts, with a long silver arrow piercing through each trio. Pointing, she realized, at the goal.

"For crap's sake. What if somebody sees them?"

"If someone other than me sees them, you're in serious trouble." He traced a finger down one trio, made her shudder. "And they're very pretty."

"They're sparkly hearts pointing at my crotch."

"They are, yes. And while I appreciate the directional assistance, I believe I could find my way all on my own." To prove it, he slid his fingers down her. Into her.

Her breath gasped out as she gripped his shoulders for balance.

God, the heat of her. The quick, wet heat. That alone seduced him. "I love to watch your face when it goes through you. When I go through you. Love to watch when it takes you over. Eve."

Her knees had dissolved, and everything above them throbbed with sensation. Liquid excitement, pouring through her as his hands, his lips, tongue, teeth explored. To hear him say her name as he took her over, the music of his voice enticed her even as his hands teased, tormented.

She let herself ride the wave, then let herself melt into it.

Her pliancy, such a contrast to her strength and will, was arousing. Outrageously. Her absolute involvement in him, in them, while everything else around them washed away in pleasure and passion, in love and lust. When he pulled her with him to the floor, she slid down, slid under him like silk. There he had her mouth, warm and generous. Her skin, smooth and fragrant.

Then he was inside her, where there was nothing else. And he let her yielding take him with her.

She could have curled up to sleep on the floor without a word of complaint. Every cell in her body was relaxed and satisfied. But when she felt herself starting to drift off, she shook it off, sat up. And let out a startled yelp when she saw the cat perched on her desk, staring unblinkingly with different-colored eyes.

Roarke studied the cat while he ran a hand lightly down Eve's back. "Does he approve or disapprove, do you think? He never lets on."

"I don't give a rat's ass, but I don't think he should be watching us while we're having sex. It can't be right."

"Maybe we should get him a girlfriend."

"He's been fixed."

"He still might enjoy the companionship."

"Not enough to share his salmon fixes." Because it was just weird to have the cat staring, especially when she was wearing little sparkly red hearts, she grabbed her pants, pulled them on.

As she raked her fingers through her hair, her computer beeped. Galahad jumped a little, then immediately shot up a leg and began to lick his backside.

Tasks complete . . .

"Hey, there's timing." She leaped up now, grabbing her sweatshirt. "Plus I think the sex burned the alcohol out of my system."

"You're welcome."

He said it with a laugh, but she'd learned a few things in over a year of marriage. "The way you touched me? It counteracted the trauma that is Trina. This is great power."

His eyes warmed for her as he got to his feet.

"But the hearts have got to go. Computer, display matches, on wall screen."

Singular match displayed . . .

"Score," Eve bellowed when the images flashed on, side by side. "Hello, Deena."

Flavia, Deena, DOB June 8, 2027, Rome, Italy. Father, Dimitri, doctor, specializing in pediatrics. Mother, Anna Trevani, doctor, psychiatry. No siblings. No marriage, cohabitation on record. No offspring on record. No criminal on record. Last known address, Brookhollow College. No data on record after May 19–20, 2047. Image displayed is of official ID taken June 2046.

"Lovely young woman," Roarke stated. "Extremely lovely."

"And she poofs. Early graduation. Computer, search for any missing persons report on Flavia, Deena. International search."

Working . . .

"Side task. Are her parents still living? If so, where, and under what employment?"

Acknowledged. Working . . .

"Her address was listed at the college, not a residence. No criminal, no marriage, no cohab, and she goes into the wind before her twentieth birthday."

"And surfaces," Roarke put in, "a dozen years later to kill the Icoves."

"Couple years younger than Avril, but they'd have been at school at the same time. Exclusive boarding school, they'd have brushed up against each other."

"A long way from school chums to partners in crime."

"Yeah, but it connects them. She saw the image from the center, and didn't say, 'Hey, that's Deena from Brookhollow. Haven't seen her in years.' And yeah," she said, holding up a hand, "a defense attorney's going to say Avril's not required to remember everyone she went to school with. That it's been a dozen years since she got out of college, which coincidentally coincides with Deena's vanishing act. But it puts her in the same place, at the same time, with the suspect."

Secondary task complete. Flavia, Dimitri, and Trevani, Anna, reside in Rome, Italy. Both are employed on staff at The Children's Institute in that city . . .

"Cross-check the Children's Institute for association with Icove, Wilfred B., Sr. and/or Wilfred B., Jr., also association with Wilson, Jonah Delecourt."

Added task. Working . . .

"I can save you the time," Roarke told her. "I've contributed to that institution through my Italian companies. I know that, at least at one time, Icove Sr. served on the advisory board."

"Better and better. So he connects with the Flavias, who connect with Deena, aka Dolores, who connects with Avril, who connects with Brookhollow. I've got me a fucking diagram."

Primary task complete. No missing person's report was filed to any known authority on Flavia, Deena . . .

"They don't file because either they know where she is or because they don't want the cops nosing around. If it's the second, they hired private. Either way she's under data radar for a decade. And—"

Additional task complete. Icove, Wilfred B., Sr., served on advisory board and as guest surgeon, guest lecturer, for the Children's Institute from its creation in 2025 to his death. Wilson, Jonah Delecourt, served on advisory board from 2025 to 2048.

"Okay, now we've got—"

Question . . .

"What," Eve snapped.

Do you wish to end task involving images from Brookhollow at this time?

"What other images are there?"

Secondary match, current enrollment Brookhollow Academy correlating to Flavia, Deena.

"You said singular match. Display, damn it."

Affirmative . . .

The image that came on was rounder, softer than Deena Flavia. And it was a child.

Eve's heart fluttered into her throat. "Identify current image."

Rodriguez, Diana, DOB March 17, 2047, Argentina. Parents, Hector, laboratory technician, and Cruz, Magdalene, physical therapist.

"Places of employment."

Working . . . Rodriguez, Hector, employed Genedyne Research. Cruz, Magdalene, employed St. Catherine's Reconstructive and Rehabilitation Center.

"Association of both places of employment to Icove, Wilfred B., Sr.; Icove, Wilfred B., Jr.; Wilson, Jonah; and Samuels, Eva or Evelyn."

"She's not their child," Roarke put in. "Not biologically. She's the image of Deena Flavia."

"Breed them and sell them. Breed and sell. Sons of bitches. Manipulate the genes—make them perfect, made to order. Train, educate, program them. Then sell them."

He reached out, instinctively rubbing her shoulders. "Would she have wanted the child, do you think? Or just revenge."

"I don't know. Depends on what drives her harder. Maybe she figures on getting both."

The computer came back, listing all four names with connections to the locations in Argentina.

"Computer, start search and match images. Any graduate of Brookhollow Academy or College with current students. List all data on all results."

Working . . .

"Let it task," Roarke said softly. "Let's get some sleep. You'll need a clear head tomorrow. I assume you're going to New Hampshire."

"Damn right I am."

She was up at dawn, and still Roarke was up and dressed ahead of her. With a grunted greeting she trudged into the shower, ordered jets on full at one-oh-one degrees, and boiled herself awake. She hit the drying tube, gulped down the first cup of coffee, and felt nearly human.

"Eat something," Roarke ordered, and switched from the financial reports on-screen to the morning media cast.

"Something," she repeated from inside her closet.

When she stepped out, he glanced at the clothes she'd grabbed and said, "No."

"No, what?"

"Not that outfit."

If the term *aggrieved* had an image beside its definition, it would have been her face. "Oh, come on."

"You plan to pay an official visit to an exclusive boarding school. You want to look authoritative."

She tapped the weapon holster she'd hung over the back of the chair. "Here's my authority, Ace."

"A suit."

"A what?"

He sighed, rose. "You do know the concept, and you happen to own several. You want power, prestige, simplicity. You want to look important."

"I want to cover my naked ass."

"Which is a shame, I grant you, but you may as well cover it well. This. Clean lines, and the dull copper color adds punch. Wear it with this." He added a scooped-neck top in a kind of muddy blue. And go crazy, Eve. Wear a bit of jewelry."

"It's not a fricking party." But she pulled on the pants. "You know what you need? You need a droid, a dress-up droid. Maybe I'll buy you one for Christmas."

"Why settle when I already have the real thing?" He opened the jewelry vault in her closet and selected etched gold hoops for her ears and a sapphire cabochon pendant.

To save time and aggravation, she dressed as ordered. But she balked when Roarke made a little circle in the air with his finger.

"Pushing your luck, pal."

"It was worth a try. You still look like a cop, Lieutenant. Just a very well tailored one."

"Yeah, the bad guys will be awed by my fashion sense."

"You'd be surprised," he replied.

"I've got work."

"You can call up the search results right here and eat some breakfast. If a machine can multitask, so can you."

It didn't feel quite right, but then neither did the suit. But since he was already giving the order, she programmed a bagel from the AutoChef.

"You can do better than that."

"I'm stoked." Her office wasn't the only place she could pace, she reminded herself, and began to do so while biting into the bagel. "Something's going to come."

"Data on-screen then."

Acknowledged. Match one of fifty-six . . .

"Fifty-six?" Eve stopped pacing. "That can't be right. Even figuring the amount of time, number of students, you wouldn't have so many visual matches. You can't . . . wait."

She stared at match one.

Delaney, Brianne, DOB February 16, 2024, Boston, Massachusetts. Parents Brian and Myra Delaney née Copley. No siblings. Married Alistar, George, June 18, 2046. Offspring: Peter, September 12, 2048; Laura, March 14, 2050. Resides Athens, Greece.

Matched with O'Brian, Bridget, DOB August 9, 2039, Ennis, Ireland. Parents Seamus and Margaret O'Brian née Ryan. Both deceased. No siblings. Legal guardianship to Samuels, Eva, and upon her death Samuels, Evelyn. Currently enrolled and residing Brookhollow College, New Hampshire.

"Computer, pause. She had a kid at twelve?" Eve asked.

"It happens," Roarke said, "but—"

"Yeah, but. Computer images only, split screen, magnify fifty percent."

Working . . .

As they came on, Eve stepped closer. "Same coloring, that's fine. The red hair, the white skin, freckles, green eyes. I'd say the odds are reasonable for those inherited traits. Same nose, same mouth, same shape of the eyes, the face. I bet you could count the fricking freckles and get the same number for each. Kid's like a miniature of the woman. Like a . . ."

"Clone," Roarke finished quietly. "Christ Jesus."

Eve took a breath, then another. "Computer, run the next match."

It took an hour, and the sickness came into the center of her belly and lay there like a tumor.

"They've been cloning girls. Not just messing with DNA to boost intellect or appearance. Not just designing babies or tuning them up physically, intellectually, to enhance. But creating them. Flipping off international law and creating them. Selling them. Some into marriage," Eve continued, staring at the screen. "Some into the marketplace. Some created to continue to work. Doctors, teachers, lab techs. I thought they were designing babies, training LCs. But it's worse, worse than both."

"There are rumbles now and then about underground reproductive cloning research, even the occasional claim of success. But the laws are so strict, so onerous and universal, no one's come out and proved it."

"How does it work? Do you know?"

"Not precisely. Not remotely, actually. We do some research cloning—well within the parameters of the law. For tissue, organs. A cell implanted in a simulated female egg, triggered electrically. If it's privatized, as ours would be, the cells are donated by the clients, who pay handsomely for the generated replacement tissues, which would have no risk of being rejected after transplant. I'd have to gather that in reproductive cloning, you'd have cells, and actual eggs—once merged—would be implanted in a womb."

"Whose?"

"Well, that's a question."

"I've got to get this to the commander, get the go-ahead and get to the school. You can fill Louise in on this."

"I can."

"He'd have made billions on this," Eve added.

"Grossed."

"I'll say it's gross."

"No, no." It was a relief to laugh. "Gross income. It would cost—has to cost enormously to run the labs, develop the technology, the school, the network. The net income would be substantial, I'd think, but Eve, the cost, the risk? I think you're looking at a labor of love."

"You think?" She shook her head. "We've got nearly sixty on record now attending the Academy. There must be hundreds more, already graduated. What happened to the ones that didn't come out exactly right? How much do you think he loved the ones that weren't perfect?"

"That's a hideous thought."

"Yeah. I've got a million of them."

She took time to put it together into a report, to contact Whitney and request an early briefing. She tagged Peabody on the way to Central and arranged to pick up her partner.

Peabody hopped into the car, tossed her hair. It was longer by a good four inches and did a kind of flip at the tips.

"McNab truly spiked on my hair. I've got to remember to shake things up more often."

Eve gave her a cautious sidelong glance. "It makes you look girly."

"I know!" Obviously pleased with the comment, Peabody snuggled back in her seat. "And it was great being a girl after I got home last night. He went ape shit over the papaya boob cream."

"Stop now, save us both. We've got a situation."

"Figured you didn't offer to pick me up to save me a fight with the subway."

"I'm going to brief you on the way, then the commander. We'll have a full briefing—EDD included—at ten hundred."

Peabody said nothing as Eve ran through the data she'd gathered overnight. Her silence carried through into the garage at Central.

"No questions, no observations?"

"I'm just . . . absorbing, I guess. It's so contrary to my makeup. My DNA, I guess you could say. The way I was raised, taught. Creating life is the job of a higher power. It's our job, our duty and our joy, to nurture life, protect and respect it. I know that sounds Free-Agey, but—"

"It's not so far off from what I think. But personal sensibilities aside, human reproductive cloning is illegal under the laws of New York, the laws of the country, and the laws governing science and commerce on and off planet. Evidence indicates the Icoves broke those laws. And their murders, which is our domain, were a direct result of that."

"Are we going to have to turn this over to the— Who handles this kind of thing? The FBI? Global? Interplanetary?"

Eve's face was set as she slammed out of the vehicle. "Not if I can help it. I want you to hit research mode. Get everything you can on human cloning. Technical areas, legal areas, equipment, techniques, debates, claims, histories, myths. We want to know what we're talking about when we get to Brookhollow."

"Dallas, with what you found out, we're going to find them up there. Some of them are just kids. They're just kids."

"We'll deal with it when we come to it."

Whitney wasn't as reticent as Peabody, and peppered Eve with questions throughout her report.

"This is a Nobel Prize winner, Lieutenant, whose memorial service, scheduled for fourteen hundred this afternoon, will be attended by heads of state, worldwide. His son, whose reputation and acclaim were rising to match his father's, will be similarly honored next week. New York will hold both these events, and the security, the media—the fucking traffic details are already a nightmare. If a whiff of this leaks, it could go beyond nightmare into the realm of international clusterfuck."

"It won't leak."

"You better be damn sure of that, and damn sure of your facts."

"Fifty-six matches, sir, through Brookhollow Academy alone. I believe many if not all of these correspond to the coded files Icove Sr. kept in his apartment—his currents, so to speak. He worked closely with a geneticist, and was, at one time, a vocal proponent of genetic manipulation."

"Genetic manipulation is a thorny area. Human cloning is a dark, dank forest. The ramifications—"

"Commander, the ramifications already involve two deaths."

"The ramifications will echo beyond your two homicides. Political, moral, religious, medical. If your allegations are fact, there are existing clones, many of them minor. For some, they'll become the monster, for others the victims." He rubbed his eyes. "We'll need some expert legal opinions on this. Every agency from Global to Homeland is going to jump on this."

"If you notify them of the recent findings, they'll take it from us. They'll shut down the investigation."

"They will. What's your objection?"

"They're my homicides, Commander."

He was silent a moment, watching her face. "What's your objection, Lieutenant?"

"Beyond that, and that is my primary objection, sir. It's . . . It needs to be stopped. Government—any government puts their finger in this pie, they're going to want to pull out a plum. More hidden research, more experimentation. They'll sweep all this under the rug, and put everything we've found under the microscope. They'll Code Blue it, and block the media, block the information. The Icoves will be memorialized with all honors, and the work they did in the dark will never come to light. The . . . the subjects," she said for lack of a better term, "created will be rounded up and examined, debriefed, confined, and questioned. They were manufactured, sir, but they're blood and bone, like the rest of us. They won't be treated like the rest of us. Maybe there's no stopping that, no way to prevent that from happening, but I want to follow this through. Until I've got nowhere else to go."

He laid his palms on the desk. "I'll need to bring Tibble into this."

Eve nodded. "Yes, sir." They could hardly circumvent channels without the knowledge of the chief of police. "I think APA Reo could be useful, in the legal areas. She's smart, and ambitious enough to keep the lid on until it's time to take it off. I've used both Dr. Mira and Dr. Dimatto as medical experts thus far in the investigation. Their input could also be useful. I'll need a warrant for records at the school and would like to take Feeney or his pick with me to go through data on-site."

He nodded. "Consider this investigation as Code Blue status. Need-to-know only, full media block. Put your team together." He glanced at his wrist unit. "Brief in twenty."

14 SHE'D ALTERED HER APPEARANCE. SHE WAS good at it. Over the past twelve years she'd been many peo-ple. And no one. Her credentials were impeccable—meticulously generated, flawlessly forged. They had to be.

Brookhollow Academy was red brick and ivy—no contemporary glass domes or steel towers, but dignity and blue-blooded tradition. It was expansive grounds, sturdy trees, lovely gardens, thriving orchards. There were tennis courts and an equestrian center, two of the sports deemed suitable for Brookhollow students. One of her classmates had won Olympic gold in dressage at the tender age of sixteen. Three years before she'd been sent away to marry a young British aristocrat as keen on horses as she.

They were created for a purpose, and they served that purpose. Still she'd been happy to go, Deena remembered. Most of them were.

Deena didn't begrudge them their happiness, and would do all she could to protect the lives those like her had built.

But every war had its cost, and some might be exposed. Still more would finally, finally taste the freedom that had forever been denied them.

What of those who had resisted, or failed, or questioned?

What of them?

For them, and the others to come, she'd risk anything.

Here at the Academy, there were three swimming pools—two indoors—three science labs, a holo-room, two grand auditoriums, a theater complex that rivaled any on Broadway. It boasted a dojo and three fitness centers as well as a fully staffed clinic for healing and for teaching. Inside its walls was a media center where students earmarked for media careers trained, and yet another studio for music and dance.

Twenty classrooms with live and automated instructors.

There was a single dining hall, where the food was well-balanced, tasty, and served three times a day, precisely at seven A.M., twelve-thirty and seven P.M.

Midmorning and afternoon snacks were available in the solarium at ten and four.

She'd loved the scones. She had good memories of the scones.

The living quarters for the students were spacious and well decorated. If, at the age of five, you passed all the tests, you were moved into those quarters. Your memory of those first five years was . . . adjusted.

In time, it was possible to forget—or nearly—the experience of being a mouse in a maze.

You were given uniforms, and a suitable wardrobe. One that was designed to suit your personality type and background.

You had a background, somewhere. You'd come from something, though it was not what they gave you. It was never what they gave you.

Instruction was rigorous. A Brookhollow student was expected to excel, then to move on to the college, and continue. Until Placement.

She herself could speak four languages fluently. That had been handy. She could solve complex math theorems, identify and date archaeological artifacts, execute a perfect double-gainer, and organize a state dinner for two hundred.

Electronics were like toys to her. And she could kill with efficiency, using a variety of methods. She knew how to pleasure a man in bed and could discuss interplanetary politics with him in the morning.

She had been intended not for marriage or mating, but for covert ops. In that, she supposed, her education had succeeded.

She was beautiful, had no genetic flaws. Her estimated life span was one hundred and fifty years. Which might be considerably extended through continued advancement in medical technology.

She had run at twenty, and had lived a dozen years in hiding, forging her way underground, honing the skills she'd been given. The thought of living another century as she had to this point in her life was her constant nightmare.

She did not kill coldly, however efficiently. She killed in desperation, and with the fervor of a warrior defending the innocent.

For this death, she wore a stark black suit custom-tailored for her in Italy. Money was no problem. She'd stolen half a million before she'd run. Since then, she'd accessed more. She could have lived well, avoided any detection. But she had a mission. In all of her life, she had only one.

And was well on the way to accomplishing it.

The starkness of the suit only made her look more feminine, and it set off the bright red of her hair, the deep green of her eyes. She'd spent an hour that morning subtly changing the contours of her face. A slightly rounder chin, a fuller nose.

She'd added a few pounds to her body, all of them curves.

The changes would be enough, or they wouldn't.

She wasn't afraid to die, but she was terrified of being taken. So she had what she needed in a capsule should she be identified and captured.

The father had allowed her to come in, had granted her audience, had believed her claim of loneliness and regret. He hadn't seen his death in her eyes.

But here, in this prison, they would know what she'd done. If they recognized her, her part was over. But there were others who would step forward if she fell. Too many others.

If there was fear in the back of her throat, her face was calm and serene. She'd learned that, too. Show them nothing. Give them nothing.

Her eyes met the driver's in the rearview mirror. She worked up a smile, nodded.

They paused at the gates for the security scan. Her heart tripped now. If it was a trap, she'd never go out those gates again. Dead or alive.

Then she was inside, winding through the lovely grounds. The trees, the gardens, the sculptures.

The main building loomed in front of her, five stories. Soft, soft red brick bedecked with ivy. Sparkling windows and gleaming columns.

The girls, she thought, and wanted to weep. Young and fresh and lovely, walking alone or in pairs, in groups, to other buildings. For instruction, for recreation.

For tests. For improvements. For evaluation.

She waited for the driver to park, to come around and open her door. Offer a hand. And hers was cool and dry.

She showed no reaction other than a small, polite smile when Evelyn Samuels stepped out of the great front door to greet her.

"Mrs. Frost, welcome to Brookhollow. I'm Evelyn Samuels, the head of the Academy."

"A pleasure to meet you at last." She offered a hand. "Your grounds and buildings are even more impressive in person."

"We'll give you the full tour, but please come inside for tea."

"That would be lovely." She passed through the doors, and her stomach curdled. But she glanced around, as a prospective parent might when visiting a school she considered for her daughter.

"I'd hoped you'd bring Angel, so we could get acquainted."

"Not yet. As you know, my husband has doubts about sending our daughter so far away to school. I prefer coming alone, this time."

"I have no doubt that between us we can convince him that Angel will not only be happy here, but benefit from a superlative education and community experience. Our great hall." She gestured. "The plantings were developed and nurtured through our horticultural programs, as are all our gardens. The art you see was created by the students themselves over the years. In this building, on this level, we have our administrative offices, our dining hall, solarium, one of our six libraries, the kitchens and culinary science areas. My day quarters are here, as well. I'd be happy to show you through now, if you like."

Her mind was screaming to get out, to run, escape, hide. She turned, smiled. "If you don't mind, I'd love that tea."

"Absolutely. One moment." She took out a pocket 'link. "Abigail, would you see that tea is set up in my quarters here for Mrs. Frost? Right away."

As Evelyn guided her, she gestured, explained.

How much the same she was, Deena thought. Starched and handsome, boasting of her school in her cultured voice. Moving efficiently, always efficiently. She wore her hair short and soft now, and in a quiet brown. Her eyes were dark and sharp. The eyes were the same. Ms. Samuels's eyes.

Eva Samuels's eyes.

Deena let the words buzz in her ears. She'd heard all of it before, when she was a prisoner. She saw girls, neat as dolls in their blue and white uniforms, speaking in undertones as was expected in the great hall.

Then she saw herself, so slim, so sweet, coming gracefully down the steps from the east wing. She trembled once—only once was allowed—and deliberately looked away.

She had to pass the child, so close she could smell her skin. She had to hear her voice as she spoke: "Good morning, Ms. Samuels. Good morning, ma'am."

"Good morning, Diana. How was your cooking class?"

"Very good, thank you. We made soufflés."

"Excellent. Mrs. Frost is visiting us today. She has a daughter who may join us at Brookhollow."

She made herself look, made herself look into the deep brown eyes that were her own. Was there calculation there, as there had been in hers? Was there the rage and the determination, bubbling, boiling under that serene surface? Or had they found a way to smother it?

"I'm sure your daughter would love Brookhollow, Mrs. Frost. We all do."

My daughter, she thought. Oh God. "Thank you, Diana."

There was a slow, easy smile, and their eyes held one more instant before the child said her good-byes and walked away.

Her heart bounded. They'd known each other. How could they not? How could you look into your own eyes and not see?

As Evelyn led her away, she glanced over her shoulder. So did the child. Their eyes locked again, and there was another smile, a full one, a fierce one.

We'll get out, Deena thought. They won't keep us here.

"Diana is one of our treasures," Evelyn said. "Bright and questing. Quite athletic, too. While we focus on giving all our students the most well-rounded of educations, we do comprehensive testing and evaluations so we're able to showcase their strengths and main areas of interests."

Diana, was all she could think with emotions cartwheeling through her. But she said the right things, made the right moves, and was shown into Samuels's quarters.

Students were only admitted to this sanctuary when they were particularly good, or had committed some major infraction. She'd never been through the door.

She'd been very careful to blend.

But she'd been told what to expect, had been given the precise layout and specifications. So she concentrated on it now, on what needed to be done now, and forced all thought of the child away.

The suite was decorated in the school colors—blue and white. White walls, blue fabrics. White floor, blue rugs. Two windows west, one double window south.

It was soundproofed, contained no cameras.

There was security, of course, windows and door. And Samuels wore a wrist unit that held a communicator. There were two 'links, one for the school, one private.

A wall screen, and behind the screen a vault that held files on all students.

Tea was spread on a white table. Blue dishes, white cookies.

She took the chair she was offered, waited until Samuels poured tea.

"Why don't you tell me more about Angel?"

Despite her efforts, she thought of Diana. "She's my heart."

Evelyn smiled. "Of course. You mentioned she shows artistic abilities."

"Yes, she enjoys drawing. It gives her great pleasure. I want her happy, more than anything."

"Naturally. Now—"

"What an interesting necklace." Now, she thought, do it now, before you sicken. "May I?"

Even as Evelyn glanced down at the pendant, Diana was rising from her chair, leaning forward as if studying the stone. The scalpel was in her hand.

And into Evelyn's heart.

"You didn't recognize me. Evelyn," she added as Samuels gaped at her. Blood trickled onto her crisp white blouse. "You only saw what you expected to see, just as we thought. You perpetuate this obscenity. But then, you were created for that, so maybe you can't be blamed. I'm sorry," she said as she watched Evelyn die. "But it has to end."

She rose, sealing her hands quickly, moving to the screen. She found the control where she'd been told it would be, opened it, then used the decoder she'd tucked in her purse to unlock the vault.

She took every disc. She wasn't surprised or displeased to find a substantial amount of cash as well. Though she preferred electronic funds, paper would always do.

She relocked the vault, swung the screen back in place, secured it.

She left the room without a backward glance, set the privacy mode.

Unhurriedly, pulse galloping, she walked out of the building to where the car and driver waited.

She breathed, just breathed as they drove toward the gates. When they opened, the pressure on her chest lifted a fraction.

"You were quick," the driver said softly.

"It's best to be quick. She never knew me. But . . . I saw Diana, and she did. She knew."

"I should have done this part."

"No. The cameras. Even with an alibi, you couldn't beat the cameras. I'm smoke. Desiree Frost is already gone. But Avril

Icove." She leaned up in the seat, squeezed Avril's shoulder. "She still has work to do."

The push of his name, and the considerable billions behind it, bagged Roarke a ten o'clock meeting with the acting CEO of the Icove Center.

"It'll be informal, and very preliminary," he told Louise as they were driven through ugly traffic. "But it gets us in the door."

"If Dallas is on the right track, the repercussions are going to be staggering. Not only the technology that's been developed underground, the explosion of the Icoves' reputation, and of this facility and all the others involved, but for God's sake, Roarke, the ethical, legal, moral dilemma of dealing with the clones themselves. Medical, legislative, political, religious wars are inevitable. Unless it can be buttoned up, covered up."

He shifted to face her, lifted a brow. "Is that what you'd choose?"

"I don't know. I admit, I'm torn. As a doctor, the science of it fascinates. Even bad science is seductive."

"Often more so."

"Yes, often more so. The debate on artificial twinning crops up from time to time, and while I'm opposed to it on a basic level, it's powerful stuff. In the end, too powerful. And too fraught. Replicating human beings in a lab, selecting traits, eliminating others. Who decides what are the parameters? What of the failures, as there must be in any sort of experimentation of procedures. And again, if she's on track, what of the temptation a man as reputable as Icove allegedly gave in to—to use those clones as commodities?"

"And if, and when, it gets out," he added, "people will be horrified and fascinated. Is my next-door neighbor one of them? And if he is, and pisses me off, don't I have the right to destroy him? Governments will vie for the technology. And yet, should those responsible go into history untainted? There has to be payment, balances. Justice. That's what Eve will think."

"First things first, I suppose. We're nearly there."

"Will you know what to look for?"

She moved her shoulders. "I guess we'll find out if I see it."

"Would you want it?"

She glanced over at him. "What?"

"To re-create yourself."

"Oh God, no. You?"

"Not in a million. We tend to . . . reinvent ourselves, don't we? We're in constant evolution, or should be. And that's more than enough. We change, we're meant to. People and circumstances, experiences change us. Better or worse."

"My background, my blood, upbringing, early environment, all of that was supposed to—according to my family—predispose me for a certain kind of life and work." She lifted a shoulder. "I didn't choose it, and those choices and experiences I had changed me. Meeting Dallas changed me again—and it's given me the opportunity to work at Duchas. Meeting the two of you put Charles in my path, and our relationship has changed me. Opened me. Whatever our DNA, it's living and being that make us. We have to love, I think—as frothy as that sounds—we have to love to be fully alive, fully human."

"It was death that brought me and Eve together. And as frothy as it sounds, there are times I feel as though that was when I took my first breath."

"I think that sounds gorgeous."

He laughed a little. "Now we have a life, a complicated one. We're hunting killers and mad science—and planning Thanksgiving dinner."

"To which Charles and I are delighted to be invited. We're both looking forward to it."

"It's the first we've done something this . . . familial. You'll meet my relations from Ireland."

"Can't wait."

"My mother was a twin," he said, half to himself.

"Really? I didn't know that. Fraternal or identical?"

"Identical, apparently. With all this going on, it makes you wonder a bit. How much does my aunt share with her, besides the physical traits?"

"Family relationships are like any other. It takes time to find out. And here we are."

She flipped out a mirror, checked her face, fluffed at her hair as the car veered to the curb.

They were met by three suits, expressed through security, then escorted to a private elevator. Roarke gauged the lone female, thirtyish, brunette, sharp eyes, sharp suit, was in charge.

His impression was verified when she took the reins.

"We're pleased with your interest in the Wilfred B. Icove Center," she began. "As you know, we've suffered from a double tragedy in recent days. The memorial service for Dr. Icove will be held today, here in the chapel. Our administrative and research-and-development facilities will close today at noon, out of respect."

"Understandable. I appreciate you fitting us in, on such short notice, and at such a difficult time."

"I'll be available throughout your visit, to answer any questions—or find the answers to them," she added with a brilliant smile. "To assist you in any way."

He found himself thinking what he'd predicted others would: Was she one of them? "And your function here, Ms. Poole?"

"I'm chief operating officer."

"Young," Roarke commented, "for the position."

"True." Her smile never dimmed. "I came to the Center directly from college."

"Where did you go to university?"

"I attended Brookhollow College, taking an accelerated course." The doors opened, and she gestured. "Please, after you. I'll escort you directly to Mrs. Icove."

"Mrs. Icove?"

"Yes." Poole gestured again, leading the way through the reception area, through the glass doors. "Dr. Icove served as CEO, with Dr. Will Icove retaining that position upon the death of his father. Now . . . Mrs. Icove is acting CEO until such time as a permanent successor can be named. Even through tragedy, the Center will run efficiently, and serve the needs of its clients and patients. Their care and satisfaction is our highest priority."

The doors to what had been Icove's office were open. Poole stepped inside. "Mrs. Icove?"

Her back was to the room as she faced the wide windows looking out on New York and a sulky sky. She turned. Her blond hair was swept back from her face, rolled under at the nape. She wore black, and her lavender eyes seemed weary and sad.

"Oh yes, Carla." Mustering a smile, she moved forward, extended her hand to Roarke, then Louise. "I'm very pleased to meet you both."

"Our condolences, Mrs. Icove, on your recent losses."

"Thank you."

"My father was acquainted with your father-in-law," Louise put in. "And I myself attended a series of lectures he gave while I was in medical school. He'll be missed."

"Yes, he will. Carla, could we have a moment, please?"

Surprise flickered briefly over Poole's face, and was quickly masked. "Of course. I'll be outside when you need me."

She went out, closed the doors.

"Shall we sit? My father-in-law's office. Intimidating, I find. Would you like coffee? Anything?"

"No, don't trouble."

They settled in the sitting area, and Avril laid her hands in her lap. "I'm not a businesswoman, and have no aspirations in that area. Far from it. My function here is—and will continue to be—that of a figurehead. The Icove name."

She looked down at her hands, and Roarke saw her run a thumb over her wedding ring.

"But I felt it was important that I meet with you personally when you expressed interest in Unilab and the Center. I need to be frank."

"Please do."

"Carla—Ms. Poole—believes you have intentions of acquiring majority shares in Unilab. At least that this visit is a kind of scouting expedition toward that end. Is it?"

"Would you object to that?"

"At this moment, I feel it's important that we evaluate and reconstruct, as it were, the Center, and all its facilities and functions. That I, as the head of the family, be involved in that process as much as it's feasible. In the future, possibly the near future, I would like to think that someone with your reputation and skill, your instincts, could be a leading hand in the work done here. I'd like time for that evaluation and reconstruction. As you know, probably with more comprehension than I, the center is a complex, multifaceted facility. Both my husband and his father were very hands-on, on every level. It's going to be a laborious restructuring."

Forthright, Roarke thought. Logically so, and very well prepared for this meeting. "You have no desire to take a permanent, active part in running Unilab or the Center?"

She smiled. Contained, polite, nothing more. "None whatsoever. But I want time to do my duty, and the option of then putting it in capable hands." She rose. "I'll leave you to Carla. She'll be able to give you a much more comprehensive tour than I, and answer your questions more intelligently."

"She seems very capable. She mentioned she went to Brookhollow College. I'm sure you understand I had some research done before this meeting. You also graduated from Brookhollow, correct?"

"Yes." Her gaze stayed steady and level. "Though she's younger than I, Carla actually graduated ahead of me. She was on an accelerated course."

A t Central, Eve conducted the briefing in a conference room. Attending included the chief of police, her commander, APA Reo, Mira, Adam Quincy—chief legal counsel for the NYPSD—as well as her partner, Feeney, and McNab.

Quincy, as was typical in Eve's—thankfully rare—dealings with him, played devil's advocate.

"You're seriously alleging that the Icoves, the Icove Center, Unilab, Brookhollow Academy and College, and potentially all or some of the other facilities with which these two lauded doctors were associated are involved in illegal medical practices that include human cloning, physiological imprinting, and the merchandising of women."

"Thanks for rounding it up for me, Quincy."

"Lieutenant." Tibble was a tall man, lean, with a dark face that could set like stone. "As chief counsel points out, these are stunning and serious accusations."

"Yes, sir, they are. They aren't made lightly. Through the investigation of the homicides we have ascertained that Wilfred Icove, Sr., was acquainted with and worked with Dr. Jonah D. Wilson—a noted geneticist who supported the lifting of bans on areas of genetic manipulation and reproductive cloning. After the death of his wife, Wilfred Icove came out publicly in support of his associate's stand. While Icove ceased his public support, he never retracted his statements, and together these men built facilities—"

"Medical clinics," Quincy put in. "Laboratories. The respected Unilab, for which they won the Nobel Prize."

"Undisputed," Eve snapped back. "Both these men were also instrumental in founding Brookhollow. Wilson served as its president, succeeded by his wife, then his wife's niece."

"Another respected institution."

"Avril Icove, Senior's ward, who subsequently became Junior's wife, attended that institution. Avril's mother was an associate of Icove Sr.'s."

"Which correlates logically to being named her guardian."

"The woman suspected of killing Icove Sr., and visually identified as Deena Flavia, also attended Brookhollow."

"First, visually identified." Quincy lifted a hand, tapped one finger. "Second—"

"Will you just wait?"

"Quincy," Tibble said mildly, "save the rebuttal. Continue, Lieutenant. Lay it out."

Somebody, somewhere, claimed a picture was worth a thousand words. She figured Quincy had a couple of billion words. But she had plenty of pictures. "Peabody, first images, please."

"Yes, sir." Peabody keyed them in, as previously discussed.

"This is the image generated by the security cameras of the woman calling herself Dolores Nocho-Alverez exiting Icove Sr.'s office moments after what has been confirmed as time of death. Sharing the screen is the ID image of Deena Flavia, taken thirteen years ago, shortly before her disappearance. A disappearance that was not reported to any authority."

"Look the same to me," Reo commented and cocked an eyebrow

at Quincy. "Granted there are ways to duplicate images, or to change your own appearance—temporarily or permanently. But, it could be argued, why? If Dolores accessed Deena's ID image, it could also be argued she would have known or assumed either her cooperation or her death. Which ties them together again."

"Feeney?" Eve asked.

"The data listed for Dolores Nocho-Alverez is fabricated. Right down the line: name, DOB, POB, parents, residence. It's what we call a sleeve—just a quick, temporary cover, with nothing inside it."

"Next image, Peabody," Eve said before Quincy could interrupt. "This is a student ID image, from Brookhollow. Age twelve."

"We've established the woman known as Deena Flavia attended the Academy," Quincy began.

"Yes, we have. But this isn't Deena Flavia. This is Diana Rodriguez, currently age twelve, currently a student at Brookhollow Academy, and identified through computer verification of image matching and aging programs as Deena Flavia."

"Could be her kid," Quincy murmured.

"Computer puts them as the same person. But if this is her offspring, it still leaves the question of false identification and data records on this minor female. It still leaves the question of how a minor was allowed to become impregnated and give birth—off the records—at a respected institution. There are no records of adoption or guardianship. There are fifty-five more matches, just like this, of former students of Brookhollow and current minor females attending same. What do you figure the odds might be for fifty-six students giving birth to fifty-six female offsprings who so perfectly replicate their physical appearance?"

Eve waited a beat, and was met with silence. "All one hundred and twelve of them educated or being educated at the same institution, none of the data on the offspring indicating adoption, guardianship, or fostering that included their true biological parents."

"I wouldn't put money on it," Tibble murmured. "You've bottled some lightning here, Lieutenant. We're going to have to figure out how to keep it from frying our asses. Quincy."

He was rubbing his fingers down the bridge of his nose. "We

need to see them all." He lifted his hand up before Eve could speak. "We have to verify every one if we're going to the wall on this."

"All right." She felt time dribbling away from her. "Next images, Peabody."

15 AT THE CENTER, ROARKE ALLOWED THE EFFI-
cient Carla Poole to guide them through elaborate
imaging and simulations labs, into state-of-the-art
examination and procedure areas.

He noted the cameras, particularly the ones that were promi-
nently displayed. And the security at every egress. He made comments, asked the occasional question, but let Louise take the lead.

"Your patient analysis facilities are superb." Louise stood, looking around a large room equipped with a contour exam chair, medical and imaging computers, body and face scanners.

"We have twelve rooms for this purpose, each of which is individually controlled and can be adjusted to meet patient or client
needs or demands. The subject's vital signs, brain wave patterns,
and so on are monitored, analyzed, and documented throughout
the examination or consult."

"And the VR options?"

"As you know, Doctor, any procedure, however minor, causes
stress in the client or patient. We find offering a selection of VR
programs helps the client relax during the examination. We can
also personalize a program to allow the client to see and feel how he
or she will appear post-treatment."

"You're also associated with the adjoining hospital and emergency facilities."

"Yes. In case of injury, if reconstruction is necessary or desired, the patient might be brought here after stabilization in our emergency sector. A full medical and technical team is assigned to each patient, chosen by an analysis of that patient's needs. The same is provided for clients."

"But a patient or client can certainly select his or her primary doctor."

"Of course," Poole said smoothly. "If, after our recommendation, the subject wishes alternate medical personnel, we bow to their wishes."

"Observation privileges?"

"Limited due to our privacy policies. But we do permit, with the subject's consent, some observation for teaching purposes."

"But the procedures are recorded."

"As the law demands," Poole said smoothly. "Those records are then sealed, to be opened only at patient request or due to litigation. Now I believe you'd be very interested in seeing one of our surgical rooms."

"I would," Louise agreed. "But I'm so interested in your research areas. What the Icoves and this center accomplished, well, it's legendary. I'd love to have a look at the labs."

"Of course." She didn't miss a beat. "Some of those areas are restricted, due to the sensitivity of the research, contamination or security. But there are several levels I believe you'll find interesting."

She did, and found the sheer volume of space, personnel, equipment astonishing. The lab area they were shown was fashioned like a sunburst, with individual rays spreading out from a hub where six people worked at screens, facing out along their channel. High walls framed each ray, and counters, workstations, screens. The walls in each sector were color coded, and the techs within wore lab coats of the same hue.

There was no access, Roarke noted, between rays.

She led them to a clear door at the wide end of the blue ray, and used her security card and palm print for access.

"Each section here is specific to its own research area and team. I'm not able to explain all the work being done, but we have clearance for this. As you see, several medical droids are undergoing treatment or analysis. The droids here have been programmed not only to feed data into the core center, headed by each section's chief, but to internally access response and reaction on human patients. It was through this process that the technology for what is commonly called *derma* was developed. Its use on burn victims, as you know, Dr. Dimatto, was revolutionary."

Roarke tuned them out, all the while portraying absolute attention. He had labs of his own, and recognized some of the sims and tests under way. He was more interested, just now, in the structure, the setup, the security.

And the fact that he recognized the chief tech of the blue ray from the alumni data of Brookhollow College.

Fifty-six perfect matches," Eve concluded. "In addition to this substantial evidence, we add that thirty-eight percent of Brookhollow graduates are now employed in some capacity at one of Icove's facilities. Another fifty-three percent are married or cohabitating, and have been so engaged from the year of their departure from the college."

"Pretty high ratio of marriages or cohabbing," Reo commented.

"Well over the national average," Eve agreed, "and off the probability scale. The remaining nine percent of students, like Deena Flavia, fell off the radar."

"No data?" Whitney asked.

"None. Captain Feeney and Detective McNab will run search matches through imaging. Though there is no relation listed, on official data, both Avril Icove and Eva Samuels carried the same family name of Hannson. It's the conclusion of this investigative team, and all probabilities run, that entrance to the Icove residence on the night of Icove's murder was gained through inside assistance, and that Icove himself knew his killer with some degree of intimacy."

"He knew Deena Flavia." Reo nodded. "It makes sense."

"No, I don't think so. I don't think Deena Flavia killed Wilfred Icove, Jr. I think his wife did."

"She wasn't in the city at the designated time," Reo pointed out. "Her alibi is solid."

"Seems to be. But what if there's more of her?"

"Oh." Reo's jaw dropped. "Holy, please pardon me, shit."

"You think Icove cloned his own daughter-in-law?" Whitney sat back until his chair creaked. "Even if he went that far, the clone would be a child."

"Not if he cloned an infant. His early work, his predominant interest, was in children. He set up facilities, specifically for children during the wars. A lot of injured children then. A lot of orphaned children. She was his ward, since childhood, which separates her from the rest of the field. Something about her was special to him, or remarkable. Could he then resist creating her, replicating her? Dr. Mira."

"Given what we know and suspect, no. She was, in a very real sense, his child. He had the skill, the knowledge, the ego, and the affection. And she would know," she continued before Eve could ask. "His affection would also demand she knew. She would have been trained, programmed if you will, to accept this, perhaps even to celebrate it."

"And if that programming broke down?" Eve asked. "If she no longer accepted?"

"She may have been compelled to eliminate what bound her to that secret, that training, that life. If she was no longer able to accept what had been done to her as a child, by the man she should have been able to trust most, she may have killed."

Quincy held up a hand. "Why aren't there—if this data is correct—more of her at the school?"

"If this data is correct," Mira repeated, and seemed to Eve to be holding on to the hope that it was flawed, "she married his son, gave him grandchildren. His son may have requested there be no further artificial twinning on his wife—or either or both of them may have her cells preserved for a future procedure. A kind of insurance. A kind of immortality."

"Dr. Mira." Tibble folded his hands, tapped them on his bottom lip. "In your professional opinion, does Lieutenant Dallas's theory have weight?"

"Given the data, the evidence, the circumstances, the personalities of those involved, I would come to the same conclusions as the lieutenant."

Tibble got to his feet. "Quincy, let's go get Lieutenant Dallas her warrant. Lieutenant, arrange for transportation for your team and APA Reo. Jack, you're with me. Let's see what we can do about keeping this mess from exploding in our faces."

He blew out a breath. "I'm not yet calling any federal agency. At this time, this continues to be a homicide investigation. Any criminal activity discovered through that investigation falls, until we're boxed, within the aegis of the NYPSD. If you find what you're looking for, Dallas, if it becomes necessary to shut those schools down, to take minors into protective custody, we're going to have to alert Federal."

"Understood, sir. Thank you."

She waited until Tibble, Whitney, and Quincy left the room. "He bought us some time, so let's use it. Peabody, field kits. Feeney, we need portable electronics—scanners, keys, data analyzers and retrievers—whatever you've got in your bag of tricks. The best you've got. We've taken a lot of time here, so I'm tapping my source. We'll meet up on the main helipad, twenty minutes."

"Already on the way. Kid." Feeney jerked a thumb toward the door for McNab.

McNab headed out, then stopped and turned back. "I know this is inappropriate, but I gotta say, this is freaking arctic."

He zipped out before Eve could dress him down, but she figured she could leave that to Feeney.

"I'm not part of your on-site team," Mira began. "I'm consult, and I know those limitations. But it would be a great favor to me if I could go with you. I may be able to help. And if not . . . it would be a great favor to me."

"You're in. Twenty minutes."

She pulled out her 'link, contacted Roarke on his personal.

"Just got me," he said. "We've only just left the Center."

"You can fill me in later, I'm going to New Hampshire. I need fast transpo, big enough to carry six people and portable electronics. And I need it here."

"I'll have a jet-copter to you within thirty."

"Main helipad, Central. Thanks."

She was buzzed when she pushed open the door to the roof and the primary helipad. On other towers and flats, the traffic copters or emergency air vehicles were a constant hum and clatter. She hoped to Christ they didn't shake their way to New Hampshire.

Wind tugged at her hair and sent Peabody's new 'do into wild waves. "Give me what you've got on cloning."

"I got a lot," Peabody shouted back. "Organized discs into history, debates, medical theory and procedure—"

"Just give me some basics. I want to know what I'm looking for."

"Lab work, probably a lot like what you'd see in infertility centers and surrogate facilities. Refrigeration and preservation systems for cells and eggs. Scanning equipment to test for viability. See, when you just bang and breed, the kid gets half its genes from the egg, half from the sperm."

"I know how banging and breeding work."

"Yeah, yeah. But see, in clonal reproduction, all the genes come from one person. You have a cell from the subject, and you remove the nucleus and implant it in a fertilized egg that's had its nucleus removed."

"Who *thinks* of this stuff?"

"Wacky scientists. Anyway, then they have to get the egg going. It can be triggered by chemicals or electricity so it develops into an embryo, which, if successful and viable, can be implanted in a female womb."

"You know, that's just gross."

"If you leave out the single-cell bit, it's not that different from in vitro conception. But the thing is, if the embryo is successfully brought to term, the result is an exact dupe of the subject who donated the original cell nucleus."

"Where do they keep the women?"

"Sir?"

"Where do they keep the women who get implanted? They can't all be students. It had to *start* somewhere. And not all students are clones. You can't have a bunch of women with Mavis bellies walking around campus. Have to be housing, wouldn't there? They'd have to monitor them throughout gestation. They'd have to have facilities for labor and delivery, for whatever you call it after the kid comes out."

"Neonatal. And pediatrics. Yeah, they would."

"And security, to ensure nobody changes their mind or blabs. Like, 'Hey, guess what? I gave birth to myself yesterday.'"

"That *is* gross."

"And data fixers, crunchers, hackers. Techs who have the skill to generate IDs that'll pass the system checks. That doesn't even touch on the network for moving clones out of the facility and into the mainstream. And where's the damn money? Roarke's got them donating big fat chunks. Where's the operating money?"

She turned as Feeney and McNab came through the door. Each carried a large EDD field bag.

"Got the works," Feeney told her. "Any on-site contingency. Warrant come through?"

"Not yet." Eve looked at the moody sky. It was going to be a nasty ride.

Feeney pulled a bag of cashews out of his pocket, offered them around. "You gotta wonder why, when there's so many fricking people in the world anyway, some asshole would make a bunch more just because he can."

Eve bit into a nut and grinned.

"Takes the fun out of it, too." McNab opted for a square of gum over cashews. "You eliminate the good part right off. There's no 'Oh, Harry, look at our beautiful, bouncing baby. Remember that night we both got shit-faced and said to hell with contraception?' I mean, hey, if you're going to be wiping some kid's butt for a couple years, you ought to get the bang at the start."

"And there's no sentiment," Peabody added, and popped a cashew. "None of the 'Honey, he's got your eyes, and my chin.'"

"And oddly," Eve added, "your admin's nose."

Feeney spewed out cashew crumbs.

They all sobered when Mira came through the door with Reo.

She looked worn, Eve thought. Shadowed and tired. Taking her was probably a mistake, shoving the whole thing in her face.

"My boss, Quincy, your bosses, working on a judge now," Reo told Eve. "Hope to have it signed and sealed while we're in transit."

"Good." Eve nodded toward the east. "I hope that's ours." She shifted, stepped over, and spoke quietly to Mira. "You don't have to do this."

"I do. I think I do. Truth isn't always comfortable, but we have to live with it. I need to know what that truth is. Since I was younger than you are now, Wilfred was a kind of standard for me. His skill and accomplishments, his devotion to healing, to improving lives. He was a friend, and today I'm doing this rather than attending his memorial."

She looked directly into Eve's eyes. "And I have to live with it."

"Okay. But if you need to take a step back, any time, nobody's going to think less."

"Stepping back isn't an option for people like you and me, is it, Eve? We step forward because that's what we've promised to do." She patted Eve's arm. "I'll be fine."

The copter was big, black, sleek as a panther. It stirred the air— and Eve smelled rain in it—then set down on the pad. It didn't surprise her to see Roarke at the controls. It barely irritated.

He flashed a smile as she climbed aboard. "Hello, Lieutenant."

"What a ride!" Louise was already unstrapping from the copilot's seat to move rear. "I'm inappropriately excited about this whole business."

"Then sit with McNab," Eve ordered. "And the two of you can giggle all the way. Just why are you and Louise included in this?"

"Because it's my copter—and," he added, "we can give you a rundown on our trip to the center on the way."

"Something definitely off there," Louise called up as Feeney and McNab stowed equipment.

"Mmm, plush." Reo rubbed a hand over the arms of her chair, then shrugged at Eve's narrowed look. "If she can be inappropriate, so can I. Cher Reo, APA," she said and offered Louise her hand.

"Louise Dimatto, M.D."

"Eve Dallas, AK. Ass-kicker. Strap in," Eve ordered. "Let's move."

"Ladies, gentlemen, the air's a bit rough so you'll want to keep your seats until it smooths out." Roarke tapped controls, waited for his screen to show him air clearance. Then he boosted the copter into a straight vertical that had Eve's stomach rolling over and pitching toward Ninth Avenue.

"Shit, shit, shit." She muttered it under her breath, then sucked in air and braced. The copter punched forward, slapping her back. The first drops of rain splattered the windshield, and she prayed, sincerely, that she wouldn't boot her morning bagel.

She heard McNab's delighted "Yee-haw!" as they streaked, shook, and scooped through the sky. She imagined choking the life out of him to take her mind off what she was doing.

"Peabody, before we get official, let me say your hair is charming."

"Oh." She colored a little as she lifted a hand to the new, flippy ends. "Really?"

"Absolutely." Roarke heard Eve's low growl beside him. "Avril Icove, as acting CEO, met us in her father-in-law's office."

"What?" Eve's eyes—she didn't remember squeezing them shut—popped open. "What?"

He'd known that would distract her from her fear and queasiness. "She's acting CEO, until the board designates a successor, and arranged to meet with us privately. She claims not to be a business-woman, nor to have any desire to become one. I believed her. She also asked that if I had any plans to buy up a controlling interest in Unilab or the Center, that I give the facility a window of time to re-cover from the loss of its two main spearheads."

"She seemed sincere." Louise leaned forward against her safety straps. "The controlled grief seemed equally sincere. She also, diplomatically, spoke of believing the Center would benefit from someone with Roarke's skills and vision."

"You figured she'd be willing to see you take over?"

"I do." Roarke adjusted for the turbulence. "She has no medical or business training. But I doubt her board would be as amenable, which is why she met us privately. Develop a relationship, a foundation, with the general before the coup."

"But she needs time so she can get what she needs out of it, or cover it up, or break it down. What the hell *does* she want?"

"That I can't tell you, but the COO, a Brookhollow alumni, was very careful about the areas we toured."

"If you're taking it at face value, the privacy obsession might not make you blink," Louise explained. "But if you're looking for undercurrents, it leads to all manner of questions."

"Particularly the hidden cameras in exam and procedure areas."

Eve measured Roarke. "If they were hidden, how do you know they're there?"

He gave her a look caught between smug and pitying. "Because, Lieutenant, I happened to have a sensor with me."

"How'd you get it through security?"

"Perhaps because this particular canny device looks like, and reads like, a simple memo book. In any case, every area we toured had them, and they were active during our visit. You're going to find, at the center, a substantial subsecurity and data sector."

"Then there was the lab," Louise put in. "Architecturally interesting, elaborate, superbly equipped. And remarkably inefficient."

"How?"

Louise explained the setup while rain slapped the windscreen. "You might have different security levels," she continued. "You might have separate floors or tiers for specific areas of research and testing. You would certainly, on sensitive work, require high clearance. But this setup had no logical flow."

"Separate clearance required for every ray," Eve repeated.

"Exactly. And a separate chief, each completely isolated from the other lines."

"Standard security cams in view," Roarke added. "An equal number hidden for area scans. And, most interesting, every station fed data into its hub. Not results, but every step, every byte of data."

Eve thought of the police lab. The chief tech could access any sector, review and/or study any test in progress. But the place was like a hive, a maze of rooms, glass walls. While some sectors required high clearance, most areas connected with the busy bees buzzing not only in their own chambers but in others as well.

"Keep each line focused on its work. Limit or eliminate fraternizing and shop talk. Deny access to all but the top level. Not inefficient if you want to keep dicey stuff wrapped."

She rolled it around in her head, then peered through the rain. "There'd be room there to close off a sector from the rest. Room for . . . what do you call the having-a-baby area of medicine."

"Obstetrics," Louise answered.

"The patient room I saw was like a high-end hotel suite. So maybe you keep your human incubators in-house, in style, segregated from the general population. Peabody, run a list. See what graduates got themselves medical degrees—highlight obstetrics and pediatrics."

"Warrant's coming through." Reo had a small, bulky briefcase unit in her lap. As it started to hum, her face brightened. "We're good to go."

"Need to practice, though," Eve mumbled. "Practice makes perfect. School's all about practice. Gotta have something going there."

"Hopefully, we'll soon see." Roarke tapped controls. "Starting descent."

She saw it shimmer out through the damp mists and splattering rain. Red brick and domes and sky walks. Stone walls and denuded trees. The dull blue of a swimming pool covered for the season, the bright green and white of tennis courts. Paths snaked through the gardens and grounds, for scooters, she thought, for walks or bikes or mini shuttles. She saw horses, and to her shock what she recognized as cows in an outdoor enclosure.

"Cows. Why are there cows?"

"Animal husbandry, I imagine," Roarke commented.

The term gave her a horror flash of humans marrying bovines. She shook it off.

"Cops. We've got cops. Three units, and an ME van. Goddamn it."

Not state, she decided, trying to get a bead on the vehicles and uniforms as Roarke angled toward the helipad. County, she decided. Probably county. She yanked out her PPC and did a quick search for the local police.

"James Hyer, sheriff. Age fifty-three, born and bred this county. Did four years regular army, right out of school. Had the badge twenty years, current status the last twelve. Married eighteen years, one offspring, male—a Junior—age fifteen."

She studied his ID image as well as his basic data to try to get a bead on him as well. Fleshy face, ruddy. Maybe liked the outdoors and the local brew. Military haircut, light brown. Eyes light blue, plenty of crow's-feet. So he didn't go in for the face treatments, looked his age and maybe a few extra.

She was already yanking off her safety strap as Roarke touched down. She was out, striding toward the school before the two uniforms were able to reach the pad.

"This is a secured area," one of them began. "You're going to need to—"

"Lieutenant Dallas." Eve flipped up her badge. "NYPSD. I need to speak with Sheriff Hyer. Is he on-scene?"

"This isn't New York." The second uniform stepped forward—leading, Eve thought dryly, with his balls. "The sheriff's busy."

"That's funny, so am I. APA Reo?"

"We have a warrant to enter any and all of these facilities," Reo began, and held up the copy she'd printed out. "To search same for evidence pertaining to two homicides in the State of New York, borough of Manhattan."

"We have a secured scene," the second uniform repeated, and planted his feet.

"Name and rank," Eve snapped.

"Gaitor, Deputy, James County Sheriff's Department."

He sneered when he said it, and Eve allowed him to keep his skin, due to the possibility that he was just dirt stupid.

"You're going to want to check with your superior, Deputy Gaitor, or I will detain you and charge you with obstruction of justice."

"You don't have any authority here."

"This warrant gives me authority to fill out its terms and requirements, which were agreed to by the State of New Hampshire. So you're going to contact your boss, Gaitor, within the next ten seconds, or I'm going to take you down, cuff you, and toss your idiotic, puffed-up ass in the nearest confinement facility."

She saw it in his eyes, saw the twitch of his hand. "You reach for that weapon, Deputy, and you won't have use of your hand for a week. But you won't need it as I'll have twisted your undersized dick into a pretzel so even the thought of jerking off will cause you unspeakable pain."

"Jesus, Max, ease back." The first deputy took his fellow by the arm. "I contacted the sheriff, Lieutenant. He's coming out. We can walk over and meet him."

"Appreciate it."

"I love watching her work," Roarke commented to Feeney.

"Was kind of hoping that asshole would reach for his weapon. Better show that way."

"Maybe next time."

Gaitor strode ahead, intercepting a man Eve recognized as Hyer. Hyer listened, shook his head. Then he pulled off his hat, rubbed his hand over his head before jabbing a finger toward one of the patrol cars.

Gaitor peeled off, stiff-legged. Hyer walked toward Eve.

"What's New York doing dropping out of the sky in that big, black son of a bitch?"

"Search warrant, relating to two homicides on my turf. Lieutenant Dallas," she added, offering a hand. "Homicide, NYPSD."

"Jim Hyer, sheriff. And ain't this a kick in the gonads? You threaten to manhandle and detain my deputy, New York City?"

"I did."

"I'm betting he earned it. Got us a hell of a thing here. School president found dead as a split trout inside her private quarters."

"That would be Samuels, Evelyn?"

"It would."

"And would cause of death be stabbing? Single wound, medical scalpel, to the heart."

His eyes leveled, considered hers. "That would be one hundred percent correct. Gonna have to get you a stuffed ladybird as your prize this afternoon. We going to do some tit for tat here, New York City?"

"No problem for me. Peabody? My partner, Detective Peabody. I have with me the captain of our EDD sector and an EDD detective, two doctors, an APA, and an expert consultant, civilian. We'll be at your disposal on your homicide, Sheriff, and will share the data that will link yours to ours."

"Can't ask for better than that. You want to see the body, I expect."

"I do. If the rest of my team can be shown where to wait, my partner and I will take a look at your scene."

"Freddie, take care of these nice tourists. It's the damnedest thing," he continued as they walked toward the main building of the Academy. "Victim had an appointment with some rich woman from out of state. Witness statements—those we've taken so far— and security cameras show them doing a quick tour, then going into the victim's quarters. Refreshments were ordered prior and already in place. Eleven minutes later, the woman walks out, shuts the door, strolls out of the building and into the car she came with. Driver heads out, and they're gone."

He snapped a finger. "We got the vehicle, make, model, and its plates from the cameras. Duly registered in the name of the woman. We got her cold on the discs. Name of Desiree Frost."

"It'll be bogus," Eve told him.

"Is that a fact?"

Schools never failed to give Eve the jitters, but she walked with Hyer across the great hall. It was silent as a tomb.

"Where do you have the students, the staff?"

"Moved the whole kit and caboodle to the theater in another building. They're secure."

They walked up the wide steps, stopped at the doorway of the scene. Eve saw, with some relief, that the body had not yet been moved. Inside were three people, two still wearing the protective suits of crime scene and the third examining the body.

"What we got here is Dr. Richards, our local ME, and Joe and Billy—they're forensics."

Eve nodded to them as she and Peabody sealed up. "Any problem if we record this?"

"Not for me," Hyer said.

"Record on. Let's get started."

16 WHEN EVE COMPLETED HER EXAMINATION OF the scene and the body, she stepped back out. "I'd like my EDD team to run the electronics. And I'd like my civilian consultant to take a look at the scene."

"You going to tell me why?"

"I have two victims, male, who were killed by the same method. Those victims have an association with this institution."

"You're talking about the Icoves."

Impatience rippled through her. "If you know, why are you wasting my time?"

"Just want to hear your angle. I see a body get that way by the same method used to kill two prominent doctors in New York, it gets me thinking. And I recall the picture flashed on of the suspect, and she's a pretty young thing. I got a pretty young thing as my prime, too. Don't look like the same pretty young thing, so maybe there's more than one. Or maybe if I run those two images through the computer for a match, they will. So why does some woman—or women—who wants two city doctors dead come all the way out here to kill the head of a girls' school?"

"We have reason to believe the killer or killers attended this institution."

Hyer glanced back inside. "Must've been damn unhappy with her grade point average."

"School's a bitch. You've been sheriff a number of years. How many times have you been called out here?"

He had a thin mouth, but there was considerable charm in it when it curved up slow. "This would make one. Been out off duty plenty of times. The theater puts on plays three, four times a year. Open to the public. My wife likes that kind of thing. And they have a garden tour every spring. She usually drags me to that."

"Does it seem odd to you that in all this time, you never got a call about some homesick kid climbing over the wall. Or a theft, an unattended death, vandalism."

"Maybe it has. But I can't come out and complain they're not making trouble."

"You ever know of one of the girls hooking up with a local boy, or going into town and getting into trouble?"

"Nope. They don't go in, and yeah, I figured it odd. Enough that when my wife dragged me out here, I poked around a little, asked some questions. Nothing to go on," he said with another glance around. "Nothing but a gut thing, you get me?"

"Yeah, I get you."

"But it's a snooty school and we're small change, so there's nothing I can pin that gut thing on. Now, there's been a few times some of the young boys tried to get in, over the wall, over the gate. That's natural enough. Security picks them up before they get on the grounds. I'm giving, New York," he added. "I don't feel like I'm getting."

"I'm sorry. I can't tell you much. I'm under Code Blue."

Now his eyes widened. "That's higher than I expected."

"I can tell you we have strong reasons to believe that there's more going on here than education. Your gut's not wrong, Sheriff. I need to let my team loose. I need to see the security discs and the student records. I need to interview witnesses."

"Give me something more. Show of faith."

"Wilfred Icove was murdered by a woman who attended this institution and subsequently vanished. There are no records of her after that date, and no missing persons was filed. We believe her official data was fabricated, by or with the knowledge of her victim. We believe she killed, or had a part in killing Wilfred Icove, Jr. And that she and an accomplice just dumped this homicide in your lap. This school is the breeding ground for that. I don't think she's finished. I think there's data here that will help us both. I'll give you everything I'm authorized to give. And when I'm able to give you more, you'll get that, too."

"You think this place is some sort of cult?"

"Not that simple. I've got two doctors with me. They could examine some of the students. One is a licensed counselor. She could help them with the trauma of the situation."

"They got doctors and counselors on staff."

"I'd like ours to handle it."

"All right."

"Thanks. Peabody, brief the team. You can help Sheriff Hyer with the ID match shortly. Have Roarke meet me at the scene in ten."

She studied the security vid. It was a good alteration, Eve decided. The hair was so bold, it drew the eye, and the face was fuller. Softer. Cooler skin tone, different eye color. Shape of the mouth, too. Must've used an appliance for that.

"It's her," Eve said. "If you weren't expecting her, if you weren't looking, you wouldn't make her. She's good. You'll want to run the program to be sure—and you've got her hands, her ears—but that's her."

Or maybe one of her, Eve thought. How could she be sure?

"Vic doesn't make her," Eve added. "It's all . . ."

She trailed off, staring as Diana Rodriguez came down the stairs on the vid.

What was it like, she wondered, to see yourself walking toward you. The child you were.

She thought of herself at that age. A loner, marking time, with so many wounds under the mask it was a wonder she hadn't bled to death.

She'd been nothing like this beautiful young girl who stopped and appeared to speak politely to the older women. Nothing near as poised, nothing near as confident.

Eve swallowed the exclamation when she saw Deena's and Diana's eyes meet.

She knows. The kid knows.

And she watched them each glance back as they walked in oppo-site directions and thought: *Not just knows. Understands. Approves.*

Well, why wouldn't she? They're the same person.

"Want me to run it forward?" Hyer asked her when Samuels and Deena walked into the sitting room.

"Huh? Yeah, please."

"Nobody came near the door during the elapsed time," he con-tinued. "No transmissions in or out, either." He stopped the disc, re-sumed at real time. "Here she comes."

"Cool. The same as with Icove. She doesn't hurry, she just . . . She took something from the room."

"How you figure?"

"Her bag. Her purse, it's heavier. Look how she's got her body angled to adjust for the weight. Run it back, run it back to when she went inside, freeze and split the screen with her exit."

He obliged, pulled on his bottom lip as they both studied. "Could be, could be. Missed it. Bag's not big, so she couldn't have taken anything bigger than—"

"Discs. What do you bet she took discs or records. She doesn't kill to steal, not for profit. Vic had good jewelry on. It'd be informa-tion— that slides right in."

She took Roarke to the murder scene. "What do you see?" she demanded.

"A nicely appointed sitting room. Female, but not overly fussy. Very neat, very upscale."

"What don't you see?"

"No security cameras, as there are in other areas. But," he contin-ued as he took out what appeared to be a memo book, "that's what makes it private. And it is. No eyes in here."

"Okay. So we have private. No eyes, soundproofed. She'd have an office, and maybe more than one. She'd have living quarters, and we'll get to all that. But this is her little sanctuary, in the main build-ing. She might secret data, journals, records, and so on elsewhere. But why have a little sanctuary if you don't use it? Deena took something out of here, something she put in her handbag. But . . . what do you see?"

He took another, longer measure of the room. "Everything in its place. Very ordered and tasteful. Balanced. Much like, though in smaller scale, the Icove home. No signs it's been searched or anything taken. How long did she have in here?"

"Eleven minutes."

"Then, particularly considering she killed in that time frame, whatever she took was in plain view, or she knew just where to find it."

"I'm going with door number two, because she wouldn't have been after a damn vase, or a souvenir. And our vic isn't going to have any incriminating data in the open. This isn't thrill killing, it's purposeful. She knew the routine."

Knew it, Eve thought. Practiced her way through it.

"Samuels met with parents or guardians of potential students in here. Not that they took in many from the outside, just enough to add income and diversity. Keep up a strong public rep. She interviewed potential staff in one of her offices. Deena could've gone that route, but she chose this one. She wanted in here. She wanted something in here in addition to terminating Samuels. Let's find the hole."

She went to a small desk first. It was obvious, but sometimes things were obvious for a reason.

"I'm going to have to convince Hyer to let me transport the body to New York."

Roarke ran his fingers delicately over walls, around art. "Because?"

"I want Morris on it. Just Morris. I want to know if she had face and/or body work. I want to run a match program on her with images of Wilson's wife, Eva Samuels."

He stopped long enough to look back at her. "You think she was a clone. Eva Samuels's clone."

"Yeah, I do." She hunkered down to search under a table. "And when I was examining the body, I learned something."

"What?"

"They bleed and die like anybody else."

"If you're right about Deena, they kill, like their naturally conceived counterparts. Ah, there we are."

"Found it?"

"Seems I have." He drew out the wall screen as she rose and crossed to him. "Now this is a beauty," he murmured, dancing his fingers over the face of the wall vault. "Titanium core with a duraplast shell. Triple combination including voice code. Incorrect sequence will automatically reset it to an alternate combination and code, while triggering silent alarms in all or any of five selected locations."

"And you know that by looking at it."

"As I'd recognize a Renoir, darling Eve. Art is art, after all. I'll need some time with it."

"Take it, tag me when you're in. I need to check in with the rest of the team and get some statements."

She contacted Mira and met her outside the theater. "What's your take?"

"They're children, Eve. Young girls. Frightened, confused, excited."

"Dr. Mira—"

"They're children," she repeated, and the strain showed in her voice. "However they came to be. They need to be comforted, protected, reassured."

"What the hell do you think I'm going to do, round them up for mass extermination?"

"Some will want just that. They're not us, they're artificial. Abominations. Others will want to examine them, study them, as they would a mouse in a lab."

"What do you think *he* did? I'm sorry it hurts you, but what do you think he did with them, all these years, but examine and study them, test and train them."

"I think he loved them."

"Oh, *fuck* that." Eve spun around, strode a few paces away in an attempt to cool her blood.

"Was he right, was he moral?" Mira lifted her hands, as if to reach out. "No, not on any level. But I can't believe they were nothing but experiments to him. Means to an end. They're beautiful girls. Bright, healthy. They—"

"He made damn sure of that." Eve whirled back. "Damn sure they met and maintained his specifications. Where are the ones who didn't? And these?" She swung her arm toward the theater doors. "What are their choices. None. *His* choices, his vision, his standards, every one. What makes him different, at the core, than a man like my father? Breeding me, locking me up like a rat in a cage, training me. Icove had more brains, and we'll assume his training methods didn't include beatings, starvation, rape. But he created, imprisoned, and sold his creations."

"Eve—"

"No! You listen to me. Deena might have been a reasoned adult when she killed him. She may not have been in fear for her life. But I *know* what she felt. I know why she drove that knife into his heart. Until he was dead, she was still in the cage. It won't stop me from tracking her down, from doing my job to the best of my capabilities. But she didn't kill an innocent. She didn't assassinate a saint. If you're not capable of putting aside your image of him as one, I can't use you."

"How objective are you, when you see him as a monster?"

"The evidence portrays him as a monster," Eve snapped back. "But I'll use that evidence in my attempts to identify, apprehend, and incarcerate his killer or killers. Right now I've got nearly eighty minor females in there—and this doesn't speak to the nearly two hundred at the college—who may or may not have legitimate legal guardianship. They have to be accessed and interviewed, and yes, fucking A, they have to be protected. Because none of this is their fault. It's his. While I'm dealing with them, I want you to go back, wait in the transpo until such time as I can arrange to have you taken back to New York."

"Don't you speak to me that way. And don't treat me like one of the screwups you enjoy slapping back."

"I'll speak to you any way I damn well please, and you *will* obey my orders. I'm primary on the homicide investigations of both Wilfred B. Icoves. You're here under my authority. And you are screwing up. You either go back to the transpo on your own, or I'll have you escorted."

She may have looked tired, but Mira went toe-to-toe. "You can't interview those children without me. I'm a licensed counselor. You can't interview minors without the presence of a licensed counselor without the express permission of said minor's parents or legal guardians."

"I'll use Louise."

"Louise isn't NYPSD-authorized in this capacity. So to borrow a phrase, Lieutenant, bite me."

Mira turned on her heel and stormed back inside.

Eve kicked the door behind her. When her 'link beeped, she yanked it out. "What, goddamn it."

"I'm in," Roarke told her. "And have a look."

She scowled at her screen as he turned his 'link so she could view the empty vault. "Great. Terrific. Hit her offices next, pass anything you find to Feeney."

"Happy to oblige. Oh, Lieutenant, you might want to yank out whatever foreign entity's crawled up your ass before it ruins the line of your suit."

"I'm too busy to be amused." She snapped off the 'link, then marched into the theater. "I want Diana Rodriguez," she told Mira, "in a private area."

"There's a small lounge one level down."

"Fine. Bring her." As she walked away, Eve took out her communicator. "Peabody. Report."

"Computer match on Flavia and Frost. No result, as yet, on the APB out on her or the vehicle. I'm checking all transpo stations within a hundred-mile radius."

Eve took a moment, cleared her mind. "Check on any flights leaving any local stations for New York City and the Hamptons. You have the list of other properties under the Icove name?"

"Yes, sir."

"Add them. Whatever you find, we need passenger lists. We need all private transpos to all or any of those locations."

"On that."

Eve broke off, beeped Feeney. "Give me something."

"Working on it. School's units have layers, more shields than the frigging Pentagon. But we're knocking them out. Might have something for you on the exterior cams. Maybe a partial on the driver."

"I'll take it. Send it to me."

"Let me play with it a little first. See if I can clean it up and enhance."

"ASAP, then."

She was calmer, Eve decided. That was good. The go-round with Mira had stirred her up. And had stirred up emotions and memories she'd worked viciously to suppress throughout the investigation. Couldn't afford them, she reminded herself as she hunted up the lounge. Couldn't afford to think about what she'd been, where she'd been, what had been done to her.

The lounge was bright, cheerful, equipped with choice vending machines, three AutoChefs, long, clean counters, colorful tables and comfortable chairs. There was an entertainment unit, and she noted a prime selection of vids.

She'd been kept in dirty rooms, often in the dark. Denied food. Denied companionship.

But a silk-lined cage, she thought, was still a cage.

She eyed one of the vending machines. She needed a hit, but there was no one around to run interference between her and the evil machine. She studied it, jingling loose credits in her pocket.

She'd nearly cracked when she heard footsteps. Instead, she settled at one of the colorful tables and waited.

The kid was a beauty. Gleaming dark hair, deep, dark eyes. Her face would fine down more, Eve supposed, lose some of the roundless of youth. She wasn't quite gangly, but was closing in on that stage.

"Diana, this is Lieutenant Dallas."

"Good afternoon, Lieutenant."

Eve dug out the credits. "Hey, kid, why don't you get us something to drink. Whatever you want. I'll have a Pepsi. Doctor?"

"I'm fine, thank you."

At least someone else had a foreign entity up her butt, Eve thought.

"I have academic and athletic credit," Diana said as she approached Vending. "I'm happy to use them for our drinks. Diana Rodriguez," she said to the machine. "Blue Level 505. One Pepsi and one orange fizzy, please. I have a guest."

Good afternoon, Diana. Request granted. Your credits will be deducted.

"Would you like a glass and ice, Lieutenant Dallas?"

"No, just the tube, thanks."

Diana brought both tubes to the table, sat, her movements neat and efficient. "Dr. Mira said you needed to speak to me about what happened to Ms. Samuels."

"That's right. Do you know what happened to Ms. Samuels?"

"She was killed." Her voice remained polite, without a single tremor of upset or excitement. "Her personal assistant, Abigail, found her dead in her private quarters at about eleven-thirty this morning. Abigail was very upset, and she screamed. I was on the stairs, and I saw her run out and scream. Everything was very confused for a while, then the police came."

"What were you doing on the stairs?"

"We'd made soufflés earlier today in culinary science. I had a question I wanted to ask my instructor."

"You were nearby earlier that morning, and spoke with Ms. Samuels."

"Yes, that was when I was leaving culinary science for my next class, Philosophy. Ms. Samuels was greeting a guest in the great hall."

"Did you know the guest?"

"I'd never met her before." Diana paused, took a small, tidy sip of her drink. "Ms. Samuels introduced her as Mrs. Frost, and said that Mrs. Frost was interested in sending her daughter to Brookhollow."

"Did Mrs. Frost speak to you?"

"Yes, Lieutenant. I said that I was sure her daughter would enjoy attending Brookhollow. She said thank you."

"That's it?"

"Yes, ma'am."

"I was looking at the security discs, and it seemed to me that there was more. Both you and Ms. Frost looked back at each other as you walked away."

"Yes, ma'am," Diana said without hesitation, her dark eyes level and clear. "I was a little embarrassed that she caught me looking. It isn't polite. But I thought she was pretty, and I liked her hair."

"Did you know her?"

"I'd never met her before today."

"That's not what I asked. Did you know her, Diana?"

"I don't know Mrs. Frost."

Eve sat back. "You're smart."

"I have an intelligence quotient of one hundred eighty-eight, with a nine point six on the practical application scale and a ten-point comprehension. My problem-solving scale rate is also ten."

"I just bet. If I told you I know this school isn't what it pretends to be, what would you say?"

"What is it pretending to be?"

"Innocent."

Something flickered over Diana's face. "When a human trait or emotion is applied to an inanimate object, it poses an interesting query. Is it the human element that expresses that trait or emotion, or can an object itself hold that trait or emotion?"

"Yeah, you're smart. Has anyone hurt you?"

"No, Lieutenant."

"Do you know of anyone else here at Brookhollow who's been hurt?"

There was the slightest sparkle in those careful eyes. "Ms. Samuels. She was killed, and I assume it hurt."

"How do you feel about that? About Ms. Samuels being murdered."

"Murder is illegal and immoral. And I wonder who will run Brookhollow now."

"Where are your parents?"

"They live in Argentina."

"Do you want to call them?"

"No, ma'am. If it's necessary, someone from the school will contact them."

"Do you want to leave Brookhollow?"

For the first time, Diana hesitated. "I think my . . . mother will decide if I'm to stay or go."

"Do you want to leave?"

"I'd like to be with her, when she thinks it's right."

Eve leaned forward. "Do you understand I'm here to help you?"

"I believe you're here to do your sworn duty."

"I'll help you get out."

"Eve," Mira interrupted.

"I *will* help her get out. Look at me, Diana. Look at me. You're smart, and you know if I say I'll do it, I'll find a way. If you're straight with me, you'll walk out of here with me today, and never have to come back."

There were tears, just a glimmer of them, but they never fell. Then her eyes were dry. "My mother will tell me when it's time for me to leave."

"Do you know Deena Flavia?"

"I don't know anyone by that name."

"Icove."

"Dr. Wilfred B. Icove was one of the founders of Brookhollow. The Icove family is one of our biggest benefactors."

"You know what happened to them?"

"Yes, Lieutenant. We had a small service in our chapel yesterday to honor them. It's a terrible tragedy."

"Do you know why it happened to them?"

"It would be impossible for me to know the reason they were killed."

"I know why. I want to make it stop. The person who killed the Icoves and Ms. Samuels wants to make it stop, too. But her way is wrong. Killing is wrong."

"In wartime killing is necessary and encouraged. In some cases it's considered heroic."

"Don't play games with me," Eve said impatiently. "Even if she considers it a war, she can't get them all. But I can stop it. I can make it stop. Where do they make you?"

"I don't know. Will you destroy us?"

"No. Jesus." Eve reached over, gripped Diana's hands. "No. Do they tell you that? Is that one of the ways to keep you here, keep you in line?"

"No one will believe you. No one will believe me. I'm just a little girl." She smiled when she said it, and looked ageless.

"I believe you. Dr. Mira believes you."

"Others—higher authorities, or smaller minds—if they believe, they'll destroy or lock away. Life's important; I want to keep mine. I want to go now, back with the other girls. Please."

"I'll stop the tests, the training."

"I believe you. But I can't help you. May I be excused?"

"All right. Go on."

Diana rose. "I don't know where I began," she said. "I don't remember anything before the age of five."

"Could it be here?"

"I don't know. I hope she does. Thank you, Lieutenant."

"I'll take her back." Mira got to her feet. "Would you like me to bring in another student?"

"No. I want whoever's next in line of authority. Vice president."

"Ms. Sisler," Diana told Eve. "Or Ms. Montega."

Eve nodded, had gestured Mira to take Diana out, when her communicator beeped. "Dallas, what've you got?"

"You alone?" Feeney asked.

"Yeah, for the moment."

"I got enough of a match on the driver's ear, left hand, profile to just squeak by getting a warrant on Avril Icove."

"Son of a bitch. Avril Icove was seen by numerous people, including Louise and Roarke, at the same time. Going to be an interesting interview. Wrap it up, haul it in. We're going to organize a full search, cooperating with the locals. I need you heading that. We'll get droids from our house to maintain the security of the operation. I'll leave you McNab, but I need Peabody. Tag Reo, give her what you've got and have her arrange the warrant. I'm going to pick up our suspect."

17

IT TOOK TIME, AND SHE CHAFED AT IT. TIME
to requisition, receive, and program a team of
search droids that Feeney could oversee. Time to do
the diplomacy dance with the locals. Time to wait while Reo argued her way into a warrant.

"Questioning as possible witness to a crime," Reo said. "That's the
best you're going to get with Feeney's partial match. Particularly
given that Avril Icove gave a live screen interview at the WBI Center
at eleven this morning to Nadine Furst, as part of a three-part series of
one-on-ones. Furst sure as hell ropes them in. You can pull Avril Icove
in for questioning, but you're not going to get an arrest warrant."

"I'll take what I can get."

Peabody came up at a half-jog. "No progress on the suspect or
the vehicle. No name match on any of the known names she's used
on any transport, public or private. I had a number of privates, and
was able to eliminate all but three. None to New York, city or state,
but we've got privates to Buenos Aires, Argentina, Chicago, and
Rome, Italy. Icove property or facilities in each location."

"Argentina. Shit." Eve yanked out her communicator, keyed in
her notes, and contacted Whitney. "Sir, I need International Relations. I believe Rodriguez, Hector, and Cruz, Magdalene, listed as
Diana Rodriguez's parents, may be in immediate danger. The probability is high that Deena is there, or en route. I need the locals to
put them in protective custody."

"This widens to international, we won't be able to keep our grip on it for long."

"I don't think I'll need long. I'm bringing Avril Icove in for questioning."

It was after eight P.M. when Eve approached the Icove residence. The house was dark but for the security lights.

"Maybe she's at the beach house. Or she's grabbed the kids and gone rabbit."

"I don't think so." Eve pressed the bell, produced her badge for the security plate. The same do-not-disturb message relayed, and she countermanded.

The household droid answered. "Lieutenant Dallas, Detective Peabody. Mrs. Icove and the children are in seclusion and don't wish to be disturbed. I'm to ask if your business can wait until morning."

"It can't. Tell Mrs. Icove to come down."

"As you wish. Will you step into the living room?"

"Not this time. Just get her."

The droid started up the stairs, and Avril started down. Household security cameras, Eve thought. She'd watched and heard.

"Lieutenant, Detective. You have some news on the investigation?"

"I have a legal writ requiring you to accompany me to Central for questioning."

"I don't understand."

"We have reason to believe you were a witness to a homicide this morning at Brookhollow Academy."

"I've been in New York all day. My father-in-law's memorial."

"Yeah, interesting how that works. We've identified Deena Flavia. I spoke with Diana Rodriguez personally. Yeah, that gives you a little jolt," Eve observed when Avril visibly jerked back. "I've got enough to start blowing the schools, the Center, and several other facilities wide open. And when I do, I'm going to find more, enough to arrest you and Flavia on multiple counts of conspiracy to murder. But for now, Mrs. Icove, you're a witness. We're going downtown to talk about it."

"My children. They're resting. It's been a hideous day for them."

"I bet it has. If you're not comfortable leaving them with their care droid, I can arrange for a representative from Child Protection—"

"No! No," she said more calmly. "I'll leave instructions with the household. I'm entitled to contact someone, aren't I?"

"You're entitled to ask for and receive a lawyer or representative or to contact the representative of your choosing. That party can demand to verify the writ, and be present during interview."

"I'll need a moment to contact someone, to see to my children's welfare."

She went to the 'link first, ordered privacy mode, turned her back. Her voice remained at a murmur throughout. When she clicked off, turned, the fear on her face was gone.

She brought all three droids in, giving specific and detailed instructions on what to do should either or both of the children wake, what they were to be told. The do-not-disturb was to go on and remain on until she countermanded.

"It's important that my representatives meet me here, and that we all go in together. Can you indulge me an hour?"

"Why is that?"

"I'll answer your questions. You have my word." Avril linked her fingers together, seemed to dig for calm. "You think you know, but you don't. An hour isn't so long to wait, and it may be less than that. In any case, I'd very much like to change, then to look in on the children before we go."

"All right. Peabody."

"I'll go with you, Mrs. Icove."

Alone, Eve used the time to check in with Feeney.

"In a lab now, attached to a kind of clinic. They're billing it as an in-house treatment, evaluation, and teaching center. How they monitor the kids' health, well-being, nutritional index, and give instruction on medical shit. Treat minor injuries here, have sims for students. Got six medical staff, rotating, and two med-droids on, twenty-four/seven. Place is equipped with all the latest. So much latest I've never seen some of it before. I'm working on the data centers and scanners. It's early yet, but it's looking like students are required to have weekly exams."

"Extreme, but not illegal."

"Give me time," Feeney promised.

She moved from him to Roarke, who had made it home. "I'm going to be really late."

"I suspected as much. With my absolute confidence in you, I'm wagering you'll close this by morning, then be entitled to—and willing to—take at least a few hours personal."

"For what?"

"Mad sex would be nice, but as some of my relations will be here tomorrow afternoon—"

"Tomorrow. It's not Thanksgiving tomorrow." Was it?

"No, but it's the Wednesday before Thanksgiving, and they'll be staying a few days. As we discussed."

"Yeah, but we didn't discuss Wednesday, specifically, right?"

"You didn't even know tomorrow was Wednesday."

"Beside the point. I'll shake some time loose if I can. Right now, I've got a big, fat mess waiting to crap all over me."

"You've had the shittiest imagery going lately. Still, it might perk you up to know I've got a line on more of the money."

"Why didn't you say so in the first place? Where—"

"Darling, of course, you're welcome. Don't think a thing about the fact I've been wracking my brain over this little chore."

"Jeez. Okay, thanks. Kiss, kiss. Gimme."

"I adore you. There are times I don't comprehend why, but still, I adore you. There's what you could call a funnel leading out of Brookhollow, and—"

"Out of the school? They used the schools to disburse funds? Forget kiss, kiss. This plays out, I'll screw you blind and deaf, first op."

"That sounds lovely, I'll check my schedule. Meanwhile, yes, they've used the school to wash the funds, then funnel it out to various accounts, under various nonprofit organizations—including Unilab—set up—"

"Nonprofit?" She did a little victory dance. "I'll wear costumes, your choice."

"Well now, that *is* interesting. I've always had a little yen for—"

"We'll talk about it later. Document it, get me every little detail you can manage. If I can show they used the school for laundering unreported income, channeling it into nonprofits, I can use RICO, tax fraud, all manner of juicy stuff, and have those schools shut down whether or not we find anything wonky on premises."

"You'll have to hand it to Federal."

"I won't give a rat's ass. You know how long it would take to ferret out every facility where they might be doing this work, aspects of this work, moving girls out? But you cut off the funding, you cut off the work. I gotta go, somebody's coming to the door. Might be Avril's rep. I'll get back to you."

She started toward the door with a little spring in her step. She could see how it could work, nearly all the way through.

Then she heard the security green light go on. She drew her weapon as the front door opened.

And held it steady even as her heart gave a little thud.

Two women stood just beyond the threshold. They were identical—face, hair, body. Even down to clothes and jewelry.

Both gave her a slow, sober smile. "Lieutenant Dallas, we're Avril Icove," they said together.

"Hands behind your heads, turn and face the wall."

"We're unarmed," they said.

"Hands behind your heads," Eve repeated levelly. "Turn and face the wall."

They obeyed, their movements in synch. Eve took out her communicator. "Peabody, secure the witness. Bring her down now."

"On our way."

Eve patted each of them down. Weird, she thought, to feel exactly the same shape, the same textures.

"We've come to answer your questions," the one on the right told her.

"We'll waive the right to an attorney at this time." Both glanced over their shoulders. "We'll give you full cooperation."

"That'll be peachy."

They glanced up, toward the stairs, and each smiled.

"Oh wow." Peabody's voice had a kick that was both shock and excitement. "Surreal Town."

Eve waited while the woman with Peabody took her place with the others. "Which one of you is Avril Icove of this address?"

"We are Avril Icove. We're the same."

"Yeah." Eve cocked her head. "This is going to be some party. In." She gestured to the living area. "Sit. Quiet."

They moved the same, she noted. She couldn't detect the slightest difference in rhythm or stride.

"What do we do now?" Peabody spoke in undertones, her eyes locked on the three women.

"Change of venue, for one. We can't take them into Central, not on Code Blue. We take them out quickly, discreetly, to my place. We'll set up there. Contact Whitney. He's going to want to be in on this." She pulled out her 'link, called home.

"Moving to Plan B here," she told Roarke.

"Which is?"

"Working on that. I'm going to need a contained interview area, and a secondary area for observation. I'm bringing in . . . Better just show you."

She turned her 'link, panned the three women who sat together on the sofa.

"Ah. That's interesting."

"Yeah, I'm riveted. We're coming now."

She pocketed her 'link, holstered her weapon. "Here's how it's going to work. The three of you are going out, getting directly into the rear of my vehicle. Any one of you tries to resist or run, you're all going to spend the night in a cage. You'll be taken to a secure location where the interview will be conducted. You're not under arrest at this point, but you are under obligation to attend this interview. You each have the right to remain silent."

They did so as she recited the Revised Miranda.

"Do you understand your rights and obligations?"

"We do." Their voices blended like one.

"Peabody, let's move it out."

There was no resistance. Each slid gracefully into the waiting car, linked hands. And spoke not a word.

Did they communicate telepathically? Eve wondered as she got behind the wheel. Or did they have to communicate at all? Were their thoughts simply the same thoughts?

That didn't work for her, but it was a hell of a puzzle.

Clever of them, she decided, to have coordinated the outfits. Gave the observer a bigger jolt and merged them into a unit. It'd be wise to remember they were smart women.

Intelligence had been one of Icove's prerequisites in his work. Maybe if he hadn't insisted his creations be so smart, he'd still be alive.

She signalled Peabody to remain silent as well and began to outline her strategies.

"You have a remarkable home," one of them said when Eve drove through the gates.

The next smiled. "We've always wanted to see the inside."

"Even," the third finished, "under such unusual circumstances."

Rather than respond, Eve continued up the drive, then parked in front of the house. She and Peabody flanked the trio and escorted them to the door.

Roarke opened it himself. "Ladies," he said, smooth as ever.

"Secured?"

He glanced at Eve. "Yes. If you'd come this way."

He took them to the foyer elevator, a snug fit for six. "Level-three meeting room," he ordered.

Eve wasn't sure she knew they had a level-three meeting room, but kept that information to herself as the elevator began to glide.

When the doors opened she recognized the area, vaguely, as one Roarke used on occasions when he had live or holo-meetings too large to suit his office space.

There was a glossy conference table in the center of the room, with two seating areas on either end. A long, gleaming bar rode one wall, backed with sparkling mirrors. On its opposite was a data and communication center.

"Sit," Eve ordered. "And wait. Peabody, stand for the moment." She gestured to Roarke and walked out with him into the hall.

"Observation behind the mirrors?"

"There, yes. Also the room is under full video and audio. Your observers can sit comfortably in the adjoining lounge. Why aren't you fascinated?"

"I am, but I have to think. They're tricky. They've been waiting for this, on some level, all their lives. They're prepared."

"What they are is unified."

"Yeah. Maybe they don't have a choice on the unification. I don't know. How can we know? They're not sweating this. She was— the first one. But as soon as she made the call, she smoothed out. Show me observation."

She went with him into a spacious sitting room, all muted colors and relaxation. Glass doors opened onto one of the many terraces, and an entertainment screen spread out on the connecting wall.

"Screen on," Roarke instructed. "Observation mode. Engage audio."

It seemed as though the wall melted. She could see the whole of the meeting room. Peabody stood by the door, her face schooled in professional blankness. The three women sat at one end of the table. Their hands remained linked.

Eve slid her hands into the pockets of the coat she'd forgotten she had on. "They don't say 'I,' they say 'we.' Is that smart or is it honest?"

"Maybe it's both. But smart's a factor. Dress, hairstyle identical. That's calculated."

"Yeah." She nodded. She took out her communicator, buzzed Peabody. "Privacy mode," she ordered, waited. "Leave them there for now, come out, turn right, come in through the first door."

"Yes, sir."

"They'll know you're watching," Roarke pointed out. "They're used to being watched."

"Hey," Peabody said as she came in, saw the observation window. "More frost in a series of frosty events and happenings. Is it just me, or does that have a very high creepy factor?"

"Imagine how it is for them," Eve countered. "Whitney?"

"He's coming in, as is Chief Tibble. He's requested Dr. Mira attend."

Eve felt her back tighten. "Why?"

"I don't make a habit of questioning the commander." She said it piously. "I like being a detective."

Eve paced the length of the glass. There wasn't so much as a murmur from inside. And the women sat, relaxed. "We ID them through prints first, request they voluntarily provide DNA samples, test those. We're going to make damn sure what we're dealing with. We can start that before the observation team arrives."

Putting it into order in her head, Eve shrugged out of her coat. "Let's separate them while we're running the ID. They won't like that."

As she expected, she saw the first crack in composure when she returned and ordered Peabody to escort one of the women from the room.

"We want to stay together."

"Routine. You'll need to be identified and questioned separately at this time." She tapped one of the two remaining on the shoulder. "If you'll come with me."

"We're here to cooperate. But we want to stay together."

"This won't take long." She took her Avril out and into a small parlor where she'd placed an ID kit. "I can't question you until I verify your identification. I'm going to ask you to submit to print scan, and to give me a DNA sample."

"You know who we are. You know what we are."

"For the record. Do you agree?"

"Yes."

"Are you the Avril Icove I spoke with after Wilfred Icove Jr.'s murder?"

"We're the same. We're one."

"Right. But one of you was there. One was at the beach. Where was the third?"

"We can't be together physically often. But we're always together."

"That's starting to sound like Free-Ager pap. Prints verified as Icove, Avril. DNA. Hair or spit?" she asked.

"Wait." Avril closed her eyes, drew a breath. When she opened her eyes again there were tears. She picked up a swab, coated it with her own tears, handed it to Eve.

"Neat trick." Eve inserted the swab into her portable scanner. "Are all your emotions manufactured?"

"We feel. We love and hate, laugh and cry. But we're well trained."

"I bet. We broke Icove's code on his personal logs. This is going to take a few minutes." She let the scanner hum, studied Avril. "What about your children? Did he create them?"

"No. They're only children." Everything about her softened. "Conceived in our body. They're innocent, and have to be protected. If you give us your word you'll protect our children, we'll believe you."

"I'll do everything I can to protect the children." She read the scanner. "Avril."

All three were tested. According to scanners and readouts, all three were the same person.

Eve joined the observation team, which included Reo. Once again, she had Peabody remain in the room with the reunited women.

"DNA matches. No question to the ID. What we've got in there are all legally, biologically Avril Icove."

"It should be unbelievable," Tibble commented.

"What it is, is fraught with legal minefields," Reo put in. "How do you question a witness and/or suspect when you have three who are the same?"

"By using the fact they're coming here as a single unit," Eve said to Reo. "That's their stand, so we use it."

"Physiologically that may be true. But emotionally . . ." Mira shook her head. "They haven't had the same experiences, they haven't lived the same lives. There will be differences between them."

"DNA samples. One gave me a tear. Rolled it out on command. The other two went with saliva. Number one was showing off. But all three made identical requests that the children be protected."

"The relationship between mother and child is one of the most primal. While only one gave birth . . ."

"Two kids," Eve interrupted. "We don't know, unless they agree to an exam, if two of the three gave birth."

A fresh flicker of horror ran over Mira's face. "Yes, you're right. If . . . in any case, with the intimate connection between these women, their primal instinct toward the children could very well be just as intimate."

"Could they communicate telepathically?"

"I can't say." Mira lifted her hands. "Genetically, they're identical. It's likely their early environment was as well. But at some point they were separated. Identical siblings are known to have a unique bond, to sense each other's thoughts. Even those separated by years of time or miles of distance have proved to have this connection. It's also possible they might be sensitives. That this quality was either inherent in the cell used to create them or evolved due to their extraordinary circumstance."

"I need to get started."

They looked up, as one, as Eve entered the room. For form she walked to a recorder, engaged.

"Interview with Avril Icove regarding the unlawful deaths of Wilfred B. Icove, Sr., and Wilfred B. Icove, Jr. Mrs. Icove, have you been informed of your rights and obligations?"

"Yes."

"Do you understand these rights and obligations?"

"Yes."

"It would make it easier, for the purposes of this interview, if you would speak one at a time."

They glanced at each other. "It's difficult to know what you expect from us."

"Let's shoot for the truth. You." She pointed to the woman at the corner of the table. "For now, you can answer. Which one of you lived at the location where Wilfred Icove, Jr., was murdered?"

"We've all lived there, at one time or another."

"Through your choice or because you were directed into this situation by your husband or father-in-law?"

"It was the arrangement our father dictated. Always. Choice? It isn't always an option."

"You call him your father."

"He was the father. We're his children."

"Biologically?"

"No. But he made us."

"As he did Deena Flavia."

"She's our sister. Not biologically," Avril added. "But emotionally. She's like us. Not us, but like us."

"He created you, and others like you, through illegal procedures."

"He called it Quiet Birth. Should we explain?"

"Yeah." Eve sat, kicked back in the chair. "Why don't you?"

"During the wars, the father became friends with Jonah Wilson, the noted geneticist, and his wife, Eva Samuels."

"First, what's your relationship to Eva Samuels? You have the same maiden name."

"There's no relation. We're not of her. The name was a convenience for them."

"Were your biological parents those listed as such on your official data?"

"We don't know who our parents were. But it's doubtful."

"Okay, go on. Icove, Wilson, and Samuels hooked up."

"They were very interested in each other's work. Though the father was, initially, skeptical and wary of Dr. Wilson's more radical theories and experiments—"

"Even then, you see," the second Avril continued, "there were experiments. Though he was skeptical, he couldn't deny his fascination. When his wife was killed, grief took him. She was carrying their daughter, and both were lost. He tried to reach them in time, to get to her body. But nothing was viable. He was too late."

"Too late to attempt to preserve her DNA, and potentially recreate her."

"Yes." The third Avril smiled. "You understand. He couldn't save his wife and the baby she carried. For all of his skill and knowledge, he was helpless, as he'd been to save his own mother. But he began to see what could be done. How many loved ones might be saved."

"By cloning."

"Quiet Birth." The first took over again. "There were so many dead, so many lost. So many in pain. So many children, orphaned, injured. He intended to save them. Was driven to."

"By extraordinary means."

"They, the father and Wilson, worked in secret. The children, after all, so many of the children would never have real lives. They'd give them better. They'd give them the future."

"They used children they found in the wars?" Peabody demanded. "They took kids?"

"This appalls you."

"Shouldn't it?"

"We were a child in the war. Dying. Our DNA was preserved, our cells taken. Should we have died then?"

"Yes."

They looked back at Eve. And each nodded. "Yes. It's the natural order. We should have been allowed to die, to stop being. But we weren't. There were failures. And the failures were destroyed, or used for further study. Again and again, day after day, year after year, until there were five who were viable."

"There are two more of you?" Eve asked.

"There were. We were born in April."

"Back up a minute. Where did he get the women who were implanted?"

"There weren't any. We weren't developed in a human womb. We weren't given even that gift. The wombs are artificial, a great achievement." Now her voice hardened, and the anger simmering under it flashed into her eyes. "Every moment of development can be monitored. Every developing cell can be engineered, adjusted, manipulated. We have no mother."

"Where? Where is it done?"

"We don't know. We don't remember the first years. It was erased. Drugs, treatments, hypnosis."

"Then how do you know what you're telling me?"

"Will. He shared some of this. He loved us, was proud of what we are. Was proud of his father and the achievements. Some we know from Deena, and some we learned when we began to question."

"Where are the other two?"

"One died at six months. We were not able to sustain. The other . . ."

They paused, linked hands. "We learned the other lived for five years. We lived five years. But we weren't strong enough, and our intellect wasn't developing according to the required levels. He killed us. He injected us as you might a terminally ill pet. We went to sleep, and never woke. And so, we're three."

"There's documentation of this?"

"Yes. Deena obtained it. He made her very smart and resourceful. Maybe he miscalculated the range of her curiosity, her . . . humanity. She learned she'd been two, but one hadn't been allowed to develop past the age of three. When she told us, we couldn't believe it. Didn't want to believe it. She ran away, she wanted us to come, but . . ."

"We loved Will. We loved the father. We didn't know how to be without them."

"She contacted you again."

"We were always in contact. We loved her, too. We kept her secret. We married Will. It was so important to make him happy, and we did. When we got pregnant, we asked only one thing of him and the father. One thing. Our child—any children we would have together—would never be re-created. They'd never be used this way. They gave their word."

"One of us had a son."

"Another a daughter."

"And a third carries a daughter."

"You're pregnant?"

"The child was conceived three weeks ago. He didn't know. We didn't want him to know. He broke his word. The one sacred thing. Eleven months ago, he and the father took cells from the children. It has to be stopped. Our children must be protected. We've done—and will do—whatever it takes to stop it."

18

EVE ROSE, WALKED TO THE BAR, PROGRAMMED coffee for herself and Peabody. They were speaking one at a time now, but with the same unity. One picking up the recitation where the other left off. "Want anything?" she asked them.

"We'd like water. Thank you."

"How'd you find out they'd broken their promise?"

"We knew our husband, and knew something was wrong. While he was out of the house, we checked the logs in his private office, and found the records on the children. We wanted to take them, take our babies and run."

"But it wouldn't protect the ones they'd create. Create, then alter and perfect. Test and evaluate."

"They grew inside us, warm inside us, and they'd take that and make replicas in the cold lab. In his notes Will said it was a precaution only, in case something happened to the children. But they aren't *things* to be replaced. In all our years, it was the only thing we asked, and he couldn't honor his promise."

"We told Deena, and we knew it had to be stopped. They'd never stop, as long as they lived. We'd never learn all we needed to learn until they were dead and we had more control."

"So you killed them both. You and Deena."

"Yes. We planted the weapon for her. We believed she wouldn't be identified. Or if she was, we'd get to all the records first; we'd be able to shut down the project. And we took the children away, safely away, then came back for Will."

Eve worked with their rhythm, and in a strange way found it efficient. "You drove Deena to the school to kill Samuels."

"She was like us, taken from Eva Samuels's DNA, and designed to continue the work. She's Eva, replicated. You know that."

"Eva helped kill us and Deena when we weren't perfect enough. She terminated others. Many others. Do you see us? We're not allowed a flaw, no physical or biological flaw. This is the father's directive. Our children have flaws, as any child does, should. We knew they would take what they were and alter it."

"They gave us no choice, not from the moment they made us. There are hundreds who had no choice, who were trained every day for up to twenty-two years to become. Our children will have a choice."

"Which one of you killed Wilfred Icove, Jr.?"

"We're the same. We killed our husband."

"It was one hand that held the knife."

Each held up an identical right hand. "We're one."

"Bullshit. You've each got a set of lungs, a heart, kidneys." Eve tipped a water glass so drops fell on the left hand on the one nearest her. "Only one of you has a wet hand. One of you walked into that house, into the kitchen, prepared a nice, healthy snack for the man you intended to kill. One of you sat down beside him where he lay on the sofa. Then stuck a knife in his heart."

"We were one to them. One of us would live in the house, mother to our children, wife to our husband. One would live in Italy, in the Tuscan countryside. The villa's large, the estate beautiful. As is the château in France where one of us would live. Every year, on the day of our becoming, we would be switched. And the other of us would be given a year with our children. We thought we had no choice."

Tears glimmered now in three pairs of eyes. "We did what we were told to do. Always, always. One year of every three to be who we were made to be. Two years to wait. Because we were what Will wanted, and what the father deemed he could have. He made us to love, and we loved. But if we can love, we can hate."

"Where's Deena?"

"We don't know. We contacted her when we agreed to cooperate with you. We told her what we intended, what had to be done, and that she should disappear again. She's good at it."

"The school has a second generation."

"Of many. Not us. This was what Will requested of his father. But we know there are more of our cells preserved somewhere. In case."

"Some have been sold."

"Placement. He called it placement, yes. Made-to-order generated a great deal of money. It required a great deal of money to continue the project."

"Were all the . . . the *base* for the project . . . all from the wars?" Eve asked.

"Children, some adults who were mortally injured. Other doctors, scientists, technicians, LCs, teachers."

"All female."

"That we know of."

"Did you ever ask to leave? The school?"

"To go where, and to what? We were taught and trained and tested every day, all of our lives. We were given a purpose. Every minute was regimented and monitored. Even what was called our free time. We're imprinted to be, to do, to know, to act, to think."

"If so, how do you kill that which made you?"

"Because we were imprinted to love our children. We would have lived as they'd wanted us to live, if they'd left our children alone. Do you want a sacrifice, Lieutenant Dallas? Choose any one of us, and that one will confess to it all."

They linked hands again. "That one will go to prison for the rest of our lives, if the other two are free to go, to take the children away where they'll never be touched or *observed*. Where they'll never have to be stared at, pointed out. Be objects of fear or fascination. Aren't you afraid of us, of what we are?"

"No." Eve got to her feet. "And I'm not looking for sacrifices, either. We're breaking from interview at this time. Please remain here. Peabody, with me."

She went through the door, secured it, then went straight into the observation area. Reo was already on the 'link, having an avid conversation in undertones.

"They'd know Deena Flavia's location," Whitney said.

"Yes, sir. They know where she is, or how to find her. Certainly they have contact information. I can separate them again, go at them individually. With the confession on record, I can get a warrant to have them tested, find out which, if any, is pregnant. If so, that one would be the most vulnerable. Peabody could soft-pedal with them, one on one. She's good at it. Next hit is to push on locations for the labs specifically used for the project, where they've put whatever data they've already taken, and who, if anyone, is on Deena's termination list. They're not done. They haven't accomplished everything they were after, and they're oriented to succeed."

She glanced at Mira for confirmation.

"I agree. At this point they're giving you what they want you to have. They want your help in shutting this down, and your sympathy. They want you to know why they did what they did, and why they're willing to sacrifice themselves for it. You won't break them."

Eve lifted her eyebrows. "Want to put money on it?"

"It has nothing to do with your interview skills. They *are* the same person. Their life experiences are so minutely different it barely registers. They were created to be the same, then trained and given a routine that ensured they would *be* the same."

"One hand held the knife."

"You're being literal," Mira said impatiently. "In a very real sense, that one hand belonged to all of them."

"They can all be charged," Tibble pointed out. "Conspiracy to murder. First degree."

"Never get to trial." Reo shut her 'link. "My boss and I are in agreement on this. With what we just heard in there, what we know, we'd never get this to stick. Any defense would whoop our asses long before we got to a murder trail. Frankly, I'd like to defend them myself. Not only a slam dunk, but I'd be rich and famous by the end of it."

"So they walk?" Eve demanded.

"You try to charge them, the media's going to chew it bloody. Human rights groups are going to get in on it, and in five short minutes, we'll have the newly formed Clone Rights organizations.

You get them to lead you to Deena, that's chummy, Dallas. I'd like to hear her story. And maybe, if there's only one of her, we manage to cut some deal. But with these?"

She gestured toward the glass, and the three women at the table. "You've got enforced imprisonment, brainwashing, diminished capacity, child endangerment. And if I were going to bat for them, pure old self-defense. I'd make it work, too. There's no way to win this."

"Three people are dead."

"Three people," Reo reminded her, "who conspired to break international laws, and who broke said laws for decades. Who, if you're getting the truth in there, created life, then terminated those lives if they didn't meet certain standards. Who created that which killed them. They're smart."

She walked closer to the glass. "Did you hear what they said? 'We were imprinted to be, do, feel,' and so on. That's a strong, impenetrable line of defense. Because they *were* created and engineered and imprinted. They acted as they'd been programmed to react. They defended their children against what many will see as a nightmare."

"Get what you can out of them," Tibble ordered. "Get Deena Flavia, get locations. Get details."

"And then?" Eve asked.

"House arrest. We'll keep them under wraps until we get this closed down. They wear bracelets. Guards—droids—twenty-four/seven. We're going to have to pass this up, Jack."

"Yes, sir, we are."

"Get details," Tibble repeated. "We're going to verify every one of them, cross every T. Twenty-four hours, max, and we're passing this ball. Let's make sure it doesn't bounce up and smash into our faces."

"I've got to head in, start strategizing what we do when and if we do it." Reo picked up her briefcase. "You get anything I can use, I need to know. Day or night."

"I'll show you all out." Roarke stepped to the door.

"I need to speak with the lieutenant." Mira stayed where she was. "Privately, if you don't mind."

"Peabody, go in. Give them each a bathroom break, offer them food, drink. Then pick one. Take her out and start working her. Soft sell."

When she was alone with Mira, Eve walked to the large coffeepot Roarke must have put on a table. She poured a cup.

"I'm not going to apologize for my comments and reactions of earlier today," Mira began.

"Fine. Me, neither. If that's it—"

"Sometimes you seem so hard it's difficult to believe anything gets through. I know that's not true, and still . . . If Wilfred and his son did the things they—she—claims, it's reprehensible."

"Look through the glass. See them? I think that goes a long way toward corroboration of the statements given."

"I know what I see." Her voice trembled a little, then strengthened. "That he used children—not consenting, informed adult volunteers, but innocents, minors, the injured, the dying. Whatever his motives, whatever his goals, that alone condemns him. It's difficult, Eve, to condemn someone you considered a hero."

"We've been around that lap already."

"Damn it, have some respect."

"For who? Him? Forget it. For you, okay, fine. I do, which is why you're pissing me off. You got any dregs of respect left for him, then—"

"I don't. What he did was against every code. Maybe, maybe I could forgive what he started to do, out of grief. But he didn't stop. He perpetuated it. He played God with lives, not just in the creating of them, but in the manipulation of them. Of her, and all the rest. He gave her to his son as if she were a prize."

"That's right, he did."

"His grandchildren." Mira pressed her lips together. "He would have used his own grandchildren."

"And himself."

Mira let out a long, unsteady breath. "Yes. I wondered if you'd realized that yet."

"A man has the power to create life, why bow to mortality? He's got cells preserved somewhere, with orders to activate on his death. Or he's already got a younger version of himself working somewhere."

"If so, you have to find him. Stop him."

"She's already thought of that." Eve gestured toward the glass. "She and Deena. And they've got a big jump on me. She'd like the trial."

Eve moved to the glass, studied the two women still in the meeting room. "Yeah, if the kids were away, protected, she'd fucking love to face trial, and spill all this out. She'd spend her life in prison without batting an eye to make sure what was done is in the open. She knows she'll never spend a day in a cage, but she'd do it if she had to."

"You admire her."

"I give her an A for balls. I admire balls. He put her in a mold, and imprint or no, she broke it. She broke him."

She knew what it took to kill your jailer. Your father. "You should go home. You're going to have to spend time with them tomorrow if we're going to cross all Tibble's T's. It's too late to start that tonight."

"All right." Mira started for the door, paused. "I'm entitled to some degree of upset," she said. "To my irrational outbursts earlier, to anger and hurt feelings."

"I'm entitled to expect you to be perfect, because that's how I see you. So if you go around acting flawed and human like the rest of us lower beings, it's going to throw me off."

"That's so completely unfair. And touching. Do you know there's no one in this world who can annoy me so much as you, other than Dennis and my own children?"

Eve slid her hands into her pockets. "I guess that's supposed to be touching, too, but it sounds like a slap."

A smile whispered around Mira's lips. "That's a mother's trick, and one of my favorites. Good night, Eve."

Eve stood at the glass, watched the two women. They nibbled on what looked to her like a grilled chicken salad, sipped water.

They spoke little, then only about the innocuous. The food, the weather, the house. Eve continued to study them when the door opened and Roarke stepped in.

"Does having a conversation with your clone constitute talking to yourself?"

"One of the many questions and satirical remarks that will be made if and when this becomes public knowledge." He moved to her, behind her, laid his hands on her shoulders. And found exactly the spot where the worst of the tension knotted.

"Relax a bit, Lieutenant."

"Gotta stay up. I'm giving it about ten more minutes, then we'll juggle them around again."

"I take it you and Mira have made up."

"I don't know what we did. I guess we're down to irritated rather than supremely pissed."

"Progress. Did you discuss the fact that Reo told you what you'd hoped to hear?"

She let out a sigh. "No. I guess she was irritated enough that one got by her." She glanced over her shoulder, met his eyes. "Not you, though."

"I'm not irritated with you, which is approaching a term record, I believe. You don't want them punished. Charged and tried and judged."

"No. I don't want them punished. Not my call, but it's not what I want. It's not justice to lock them up. They've been locked up all their lives. It has to stop. What's being done, what they're doing."

He leaned over, kissed the top of her head.

"They've got a place to go already. Got a place to run already set up. Deena would have that nailed down. I could probably find it, sooner or later."

"Given enough time, I imagine so." Now he stroked her hair. "Is that what you want?"

"No." She reached back to take his hand. "Once they get sprung, I don't want to know where they are. Then I don't have to lie about it. I've got to get back to this."

He turned her, kissed her. "Let me know if you need me."

She worked them. Took them as a group, separated them. She tag-teamed them with Peabody. She let them sit alone, then hit them once more.

She was going by the book, right down the line. No one studying the record of the interview could claim it wasn't thorough or correct.

They never demanded a lawyer, not even when she fit them with homing bracelets. When she took them back to the Icove residence in the early hours of the morning, they showed considerable fatigue, but that same unruffled calm.

"Peabody, wait for the droids, will you? Get that set up." She left her partner in the foyer, moved the three women into the living area.

"You're not permitted to leave the premises. If you attempt to do so, your bracelets will send out a signal, and you'll be picked up and—due to the violation—brought into Central holding. Believe me, you'll be more comfortable here."

"How long do we have to stay?"

"Until such time as you're released from this restriction by the NYPSD or another authority." She glanced back to make certain Peabody was out of earshot, and still kept her voice low. "The record's off. Tell me where Deena is. If she kills again, it's not going to help anyone. You want this stopped, and I can help stop it. You want this public, and I've got a line on that."

"Your superiors, and any government authority that gets involved, won't want this public."

"I'm telling you I've got a line on it, but you're squeezing me. They'll block me out. They'll block me and my team and the department out. They'll scoop you up like hamsters, you and anyone else like you they can find, and put you in a fucking habitrail so they can study you. You'll be back to where you started."

"Why would you care what happens to us? We've killed."

So had she, Eve thought. To save herself, to escape the life someone else planned for her. To live her own.

"And you could've gotten out of this without taking lives. You could've gotten your kids and poofed. But you chose this way."

"It wasn't revenge." The one who spoke closed those strange and lovely lavender eyes. "It was liberty. For us, for our children, for all the others."

"They would never have stopped. They'd have made us again, replicated the children."

"I know. It's not my job to say whether or not you were justified, and I'm already going outside the lines. If you won't give me Deena, find a way to contact her. Tell her to stop, tell her to run. You're going to get most of what you're after. You've got my word."

"What of all the others, the students, the babies?"

Eve's eyes went flat and blank. "I can't save them all. Neither can you. But you can save more if you tell me where she is. If you tell me where the Icoves have their base of operations."

"We don't know. But . . ." The one who spoke looked at her twins, waited for their nod. "We'll find a way to contact her, and do what we can."

"You don't have much time," Eve told them, and left them alone.

Outside, the air was cold on her face, her hands. It made her think of winter, the long, dark months coming.

"I'll drive you home."

Peabody's tired face brightened. "Really? All the way downtown?"

"I need to think anyway."

"Think all you want." Peabody climbed into the car. "Gotta get ahold of my parents in the morning. Let them know we'll be delayed if we make it out there at all."

"When were you going?"

"Tomorrow afternoon." Peabody yawned, enormously. "Maybe beat the most insane of the holiday shuttle traffic."

"Go."

"Go where?"

"Go as planned."

Peabody stopped rubbing her exhausted eyes to blink. "Dallas, I can't just take off to go eat pie at this point of the investigation."

"I'm telling you that you can." Traffic was blissfully light. She avoided Broadway and its endless party, and drove through the canyons of her city nearly as alone as a lunar tech on the far side of the moon. "You've got plans, you're entitled to keep them. I'm stalling this," she said when Peabody opened her mouth again.

Peabody shut it, smiled smugly. "Yeah, I know. Just wanted you to say it. How much time you figure we can buy?"

"Not that much. But my partner's off with her face in the family pie. I got Roarke's relations zeroing in on us. People start scattering with turkey on the brain, they're harder to get in touch with, get balls rolling."

"Most federal offices are closed tomorrow, and through to Monday. Tibble knew that."

"Yeah. So maybe it slows things another few hours, maybe another day if God is good. He wants the same thing, so he'll make noises, but he'll stall, too."

"What about the school, the kids, the staff?"

"I'm still thinking."

"I asked Avril, well one of them, what they were going to do about the kids. How they were going to explain that there were three mommies. She said they'd be told they were sisters who'd found each other after a long separation. They don't want them to know, not about them. Not about what their father was doing. They're going to go under, Dallas, first opportunity."

"No question."

"We're going to give them one."

Eve kept her eyes straight ahead. "As police officers we won't, in any way, facilitate the escape of material witnesses."

"Right. I want to talk to my parents. Funny how when something really twists up your thinking—the order of things for you—you want to talk to Mom and Dad."

"Wouldn't know."

Peabody winced. "Sorry. Shit, I get stupid when I'm this tired."

"No problem. I'm saying I wouldn't know because I didn't have any—not normal ones. Neither did they. If that's what makes them artificial, then so am I."

"I want to talk to my parents," Peabody repeated after a long moment. "I know I'm lucky to have them, and my brothers, my sisters, all the rest. I know they'll listen, that's the thing. But not having that, having to make yourself out of what gets dumped on you, creating your life out of that . . . it's not artificial. It's as real as it gets."

The streets and sky were nearly empty. Occasionally an animated board bloomed out color and light. Dreams of pleasure and beauty and happiness. Bargain prices.

"Do you know why I came to New York?" Eve said.

"No, not really."

"Because it's a place where you can be alone. You can step out on the street with thousands of other people and be completely alone. Besides being a cop, that's what I thought I wanted most."

"Was it?"

"For a while, yeah. For a long while it was what I wanted. I'd gone from being anonymous to being monitored constantly through the foster program and state schools. I wanted to be anonymous again, on my terms. To be a badge, period. I don't know, if I'd caught this case ten years ago—five years ago—if I'd have handled it the way I'm doing now. Maybe I'd just have taken them down. Black and white. It's not just the job, the years on it that bring in all the gray. It's the people, dead and alive, you end up connected to who paint it in."

"I go with the last part. But no matter when you'd caught this, you'd go this way. Because it's right. And that's what counts, that's what you do. Avril Icove's a victim. Somebody needs to be on her side."

Eve smiled a little. "She has each other."

"Good one. A little bit of a cheap shot, but good nonetheless."

"Get some sleep." Eve pulled up in front of Peabody's building. "I'll tag you if I need you to come in, but for now plan to catch some sleep, pack, and go."

"Thanks for the lift." Peabody yawned again as she got out. "Happy Thanksgiving, if I don't see you before."

Eve eased from the curve, and saw in the rearview that McNab had left a light on in the apartment for Peabody.

There'd be a light on for her, too, she thought. And someone who'd listen.

But not yet.

She put her vehicle on autopilot, pulled out her personal 'link.

"Blah," Nadine said, and Eve could see the faintest of silhouettes on-screen.

"Meet me at the Down and Dirty."

"Huh? What? *Now*?"

"Now. Bring a notebook—paper not electronic. No recorders, Nadine, no cams. Just you, old-fashioned paper and pencils. I'll be waiting."

"But—"

Eve just clicked off, and kept driving.

The bouncer on the door of the sex club was big as a sequoia, black as onyx. He wore gold. A skin-shirt stretched across his massive chest, boots molded their way up the leather pants that coated his legs, and the trio of chains around his neck she imagined could be used as a weapon.

There was a tattoo of a snake slithering over his left cheek.

He was rousting two mopes as she walked up. One white, maybe two-fifty of hard fat, the other mixed race, heavy on the Asian, who looked like a contender for the sumo arena.

He had them both by the scruff of the neck and was quick-stepping them toward the curb.

"Next time you try to stiff one of my em-ploy-ees, I'm gonna twist your cocks clean off before you get a chance to use 'em."

He knocked their heads together—a technically illegal action—then let them fall in the gutter.

He turned, spotted Eve. "Hey there, white girl."

"Hey, Crack, how's it going?"

"Oh, can't bitch much." He slapped his palms together in a dry-ing motion, twice. "What you doing down here? Somebody dead I ain't heard about?"

"I need a privacy room. I've got a meet," she said when his eye-brows rose up into his wide forehead. "Nadine's on her way. We were never here."

"Since I figure you two don't want one of my rooms so you can roll around naked together—and ain't that a shame—this must be official. I don't know nothing about official. Come on in."

She stepped into the blast of noise, of smells that included stale brew, Zoner—and a variety of illegals that could be smoked or otherwise ingested—fresh sex, sweat, and other bodily fluids she didn't choose to identify.

The stage at the front was jammed with naked dancers and a live band outfitted in neon loincloths. Table dancers wearing feathers, glitter, or nothing at all jiggled or wiggled to the obvious delight of the paying patrons.

The bar was jammed, most of the occupants well drunk or stoned.

It was perfect.

"Business is good," she said at a conversational shout as he blazed a path through the packs of people.

"Holiday time. We be slammed from now 'til January, then we be slammed 'cause it's too fucking cold to party outside. Life's good. How 'bout you, skinny white cop girl."

"Good enough."

He led the way upstairs to the privacy rooms. "Your man treating you right?"

"Yeah. Yeah, he mostly has that down cold."

They backed up when a couple stumbled out of one of the rooms, half-dressed, laughing wildly, and smelling very ripe.

"I don't want their room."

Crack just grinned, uncoded another. "This here is our deluxe accommodations. Crowd tonight, mostly they're going for economy. She be clean. Make yourself at home, sweet buns, and I'll bring that sexy Nadine right on up when she shows.

"Don't you think about paying me," he said when Eve dug into her pocket. "I went to the park this morning, had a talk with my baby girl by the tree you and your man had planted for her. Don't ever think about paying me for a favor."

"Okay." She thought about Crack's younger sister, and how he'd wept in Eve's arms beside her body in the morgue. "Ah, you got any plans for Thursday?"

She'd been his family. His only family.

"Gobble Day. I got me a fine-looking female. Figure we might fit some turkey-eating in between other festivities."

"Well, if you want the full spread, without certain areas of festivities, we're having a dinner thing. You can bring your fine-looking female."

His eyes softened, and the street jive vanished from his voice. "I appreciate that. I'd be pleased to come and bring my lady friend." He laid the slab of his hand on Eve's shoulder. "I'll go keep watch for Nadine, even though I haven't seen either of you."

"Thanks."

She stepped into the room, gave it a quick study. Apparently "deluxe" meant the room had an actual bed rather than a cot or pallet. The ceiling was mirrored, which was a little intimidating. But there was a menu screen and an order slot, along with a very small table and two chairs.

She looked at the bed, and a long, liquid longing rose up in her. She'd have given up food for the next forty-eight hours for twenty minutes horizontal. Rather than risk it, she went to the menu screen and ordered a pot of coffee, two cups.

It would be hideous. Soy products and chemicals married together to, inexplicably, resemble rancid tar. But there'd be enough caffeine juiced through it to keep her awake.

She sat, tried to focus her mind on the business at hand while she waited. Her eyes drooped, her head nodded. She felt the dream crawling into her, a monster with sharp, slick claws that snatched and bit at her mind.

A white room, blazing white. Dozens upon dozens of glass coffins. She was in all of them, the child she'd been, bloody and bruised from the last beating, weeping and pleading as she tried to fight her way out.

And he stood there, the man who'd made her, grinning.

Made to order, he said, and laughed. Laughed. *One doesn't work right, you just throw it away and try the next. Never going to be done with you, little girl. Never going to be finished.*

She jolted out, fumbled for her weapon. And saw the pot and cups on the table, with the menu slot still closing.

For a moment, she put her head in her hands, just to get her breath back. It was okay, she'd pulled out. She'd keep pulling out.

She wondered what dreams bit at Avril's mind when they were too tired to beat them off.

When the door opened, she was pouring coffee.

"Thanks, Crack."

"Anytime, sugar tits." He winked, shut the door.

"Lock it," Eve ordered. "Engage privacy mode."

"This better be good." Nadine complied, then dropped into the second chair. "It's past three in the morning."

"And yet you look lovely, and apparently your tits are sugar."

"Give me some of that poison."

"Empty your bag on the bed," Eve said as she poured a second cup.

"Up yours, Dallas."

"I mean it. Empty the bag, then I'm going to scan you for electronics. This is the majors, Nadine."

"You should be able to trust me."

"You wouldn't be here if I didn't. But I've got to go the route."

With obvious ill humor, Nadine opened her enormous handbag, stomped to the bed, and upended it.

Eve rose, passed her a cup of coffee, and began going through the contents. Wallet, ID, credits and debits, two herbal cigarettes in a protective case, two notepads—paper—six pencils, sharpened. One electronic notepad—disengaged—two 'links, one PPC—also disengaged. Two small mirrors, three packs of breath fresheners, a little silver box holding blockers, four tubes of lip dye, brushes—face and hair—and eleven other tubes, pots, sticks, and cakes of facial enhancers.

"Jesus. You carry all this gunk and put it on your face? Is it worth it?"

"I'll point out that it's three in the morning, and I look lovely. You, on the other hand, have shadows under your eyes a pack of psychotic killers could hide in."

"NYPSD. We never sleep."

"Neither do the defenders of the Fourth Estate, apparently. Did you catch my interview with Avril Icove today?"

"No, heard about it."

"Exclusive."

"What did you think of her?"

"Quiet, dignified elegance. Lovely in grief. A devoted mother. I liked her. Couldn't get much going on her personally as she insisted this interview deal with her father-in-law and husband, out of respect. But I'll dig down the next layers. I've got a three-part deal."

The last two of which she would never collect, Eve thought. But there would be compensation. Big-time.

She ran a scanner over Nadine. "Believe it or not, I did all that to protect you as much as me. I'm about to break Code Blue."

"Icove."

"You're going to want to sit while I outline my conditions—nonnegotiable. First, we never had this conversation. You're going to go home and get rid of the 'link you used to take my transmission. You never received the transmission."

"I know how to protect myself and a source."

"Just listen. You've already done extensive research on the Icoves—and connected them, independently, to Jonah Wilson and Eva Hannson Samuels, and from there to Brookhollow. Your police sources would not confirm or deny any of your research. You're going to make a trip to Brookhollow. You'll need that on your logs. You're going to connect the murder of Evelyn Samuels to those of the Icoves."

Nadine started scribbling. "That's the Academy's president. When was she murdered?"

"Find out. You're going to be curious and smart enough to run ID checks on the students and cross them with same on former students. In fact, you've already done that." Eve drew a sealed disc out of her pocket. "Get this in your log. Get your prints, *only* your prints on the disc."

"What's on it?"

"More than fifty student IDs that match—*exactly* match—former students' IDs. Falsified data. Make another copy, put it wherever you put data you want to protect from confiscation."

"What were the Icoves doing that required falsifying data on students?"

"Cloning them."

Nadine broke the tip of her pencil as her head snapped up. "You're serious."

"Since the Urban Wars."

"Sweet little Baby Jesus. Tell me you have proof."

"I not only have proof, I have three clones known as Avril Icove under house restriction."

Nadine goggled. "Well, fuck me sideways."

"I've had a long day, I'm too tired for sex games. Start writing, Nadine. When we're finished you go home, you make an electronic trail that'll verify you found this information. You burn those notes and make new ones. Get to Brookhollow and dig. You can contact me, and probably should, demanding confirmation or denial. I'll give you neither, and that's on record. I'll go to my superiors with the fact that you're sniffing this out. I have to. So sniff fast."

"I've already done a lot of the legwork, put some of this together. I didn't jump this far. I figured gene manipulation, designer babies, black-market fees."

"That's in there, too. Get it all. I've got a day, maybe a few hours more, before the whistle's blown and the government steps in. They'll cover it. Spin what they can't bury. So get it all, get it fast. I'm going to give you everything I can, then I'm walking out. I won't give you any more. I'm not doing you a favor," Eve added. "If you go out with this, you're going to take a lot of heat."

"I know how to handle heat." Nadine's eyes were razor sharp as she continued to write. "I'll be soaking in the rays while I blow this open."

It took an hour, another pot of the vicious coffee, and both of Nadine's notebooks.

When she left, Eve didn't trust her reflexes and put her vehicle back on auto. But she didn't sleep, didn't close her eyes. Once home, she moved from the car to the house like a sleepwalker.

Summerset was waiting for her. "God. Even vampires sleep sometime."

"There's been no sanctioned or unsanctioned hit on either Icove."

"Yeah, fine."

"But you knew that. Are you also aware there is purportedly a fee-based operation that offers young women, educated through Brookhollow College in New Hampshire, to clients for purposes of marriage, employment, or sexual demands?"

She struggled to focus her exhausted brain. "How did you get that?"

"There are sources still available to me that aren't available to you, and due to his relationship with you, that are less forthcoming with Roarke."

"And did these sources give proof of these purported activities?"

"No, but I consider them to be very reliable. Icove was associated with Brookhollow. One of Roarke Enterprises' jet-copters logged a route to that location today, where, it seems, the president of the institution was murdered. In the same manner both Icoves were murdered."

"You're a fount of information."

"I know how to do my job. I believe you know how to do yours. People aren't commodities. To use education as a mask, to use them as such is despicable. Your pursuit of the woman who, in all likelihood, struck back at that, is wrongheaded."

"Thanks for the tip."

"You of all people should know." His words stopped her as she turned for the stairs. "You know what it is to be a child, trapped in a box, made to perform. You know what it is to be driven to strike back."

Her hand tightened on the newel post. She looked back at him. "You think that's all this is? As vicious and ugly as that is, it doesn't even scratch it. Yeah, I know how to do my job. And I know murder doesn't stop the vicious and the ugly. It just keeps re-forming, and coming back at you."

"Then what stops it? A badge?"

"The badge slows it down. Nothing stops it. Not a damn thing."

She turned away, drifted up the stairs feeling as insubstantial as a ghost.

The light in the bedroom was on dim. It was that simple thing that broke her enough to have tired tears sliding down her cheeks.

She shrugged off her weapon, took out her badge, and laid both on her dresser. Roarke had once called them her symbols. He was right, yes, he was right, but those symbols had helped save her. Helped make her real, given her purpose.

They slowed it down, she thought again. That was all that could be done. It was never quite enough.

She undressed, climbed the platform, and slid into bed beside him.

She wrapped herself around him, and because she could, with him, let the tears fall on his shoulder.

"You're so tired," he murmured. "Baby, you're so tired."

"I'm afraid to sleep. The dreams are right there."

"I'm here. I'll be right here."

"Not close enough." She lifted her head, found his mouth with hers. "I need you closer. I need to feel who I am."

"Eve." He said her name quietly, repeatedly, while he touched her in the dark.

Gentle, he thought, gentle now that she was fragile and needed him to remind her of all that she was. Needed him to show her she was loved, for all that she was.

Warm, he thought, warm because he knew how cold she could get inside. Her tears were damp on her cheeks, her eyes still gleaming with them.

He'd known she would suffer, and still her pain, wrapped so tight in courage, tore at his heart.

"I love you," he told her. "I love everything you are."

She sighed under him. Yes, this was what she needed. His weight on her, his scent, his flesh. His knowledge of her, mind and body and heart.

No one knew her as he did. No one loved her as he did. For all of her life before him, there'd been no one who could touch her, not all the way down to the tormented child who still lived in her.

When he slid inside her, all those shadows were pushed back. She had light in the dark.

When morning was blooming through the night, she could close her eyes. She could rest her mind. His arm came around her, and anchored her home.

The light was still dim when she woke. It confused her, as she felt reasonably rested. A little hungover from overworking her brain and body, but better than she should have with just a snatch of predawn sleep.

Obviously, she'd underrated the restorative powers of sex.

It made her feel sentimental, and grateful. But when she slid her hand across the sheet, just to touch him, she found him gone.

She started to sulk, then called for time.

The time is nine thirty-six A.M.

That news had her bolting straight up in bed. He'd darkened the windows, and the skylight.

"Disengage sleep mode, all windows. Shit!" She had to slap her hands over her eyes as the sudden blast of sun blinded her.

She cursed and squinted her way out of bed and into the shower.

Five minutes later, she let out a muffled scream when she blinked water out of her eyes and saw Roarke. He stood, wearing a casual white shirt and dark jeans—and held an oversized mug in his hand.

"Bet you'd like this."

She peered avariciously at the coffee. "You can't set the bedroom on sleep mode without telling me."

"We were sleeping."

"We never set it on sleep mode."

"Seemed like the perfect time to change our habits."

She shoved her wet hair back, and walked, dripping, to the drying tube. She glared at him while warm air swirled around her.

"I've got stuff to do, people to see."

"Just a suggestion, but you'll probably want to dress first."

"Why aren't you?"

"Aren't I?"

"Why aren't you wearing one of your six million suits?"

"I'm sure I have no more than five million, three hundred suits. And I'm not wearing one of them because it seemed overly formal considering we have people arriving today."

"You're not working." She stepped out, grabbed the coffee. "Has the stock market obliterated overnight?"

"On the contrary, it's up. I can afford to buy another suit. Here you are." He handed her a robe. "You can wear that while you have some breakfast. I'll have another cup of coffee myself."

"I have to contact Feeney, the commander, and check in with the droids on Avril. I have to write a report, check the forensics on Samuels."

"Busy, busy, busy." He strolled out and toward the AutoChef. And back, he thought with some relief. The exhausted woman had regenerated into the cop. "What you want's a nice bowl of oatmeal."

"No sane person wants a bowl of oatmeal."

"Fortified."

She wouldn't laugh. "Let's go back to the beginning. You can't set sleep mode without telling me."

"When my wife comes home weeping from exhaustion and stress, I'm going to see that she gets some rest." He glanced back, and there was that steel in his eyes. The kind that warned her arguing would end in a fight. "And she's lucky I did nothing more than darken the room to see she got some." He crossed to the seating area with a bowl, set it down on the table.

"Now, you'd better sit down and eat that, or we're going to start the day with one hell of a fight."

"Figured that already," she grumbled.

"And your schedule's already so full."

She came as close as she ever did to pouting when she studied the oatmeal. "It's got disgusting lumps."

"It certainly doesn't. What it's got is apples and blueberries."

"Blueberries?"

"Sit down and eat them like a good girl."

"Soon as there's room in my schedule, I'm going to punch you for that." But she sat, contemplated the bowl. It looked to her as if perfectly good fruit had been buried in mush. "Technically, I've been on shift since eight. But I'm entitled by regs, unless requested otherwise by a superior, to take eight hours between duty. It was after two when I left the Icove place."

"Have you decided to become a clock watcher?"

"Peabody and McNab had put in for vacation time, starting today. I told her to go."

"Depleting your team by two." He nodded, sat. "All within the confines of regulations, all perfectly aboveboard. The pace will slow. Add the holiday and it slows more. What do you intend to do with the time?"

"I already started doing it. I broke Code Blue. I met with Nadine and gave her everything." She poked a spoon into the oatmeal, lifted it, let the goop dribble out again. "I disobeyed a direct order, a priority order, and am prepared to lie through my teeth about it. I'm dragging my heels to give Avril Icove time to figure out how to disengage the bracelets, get the kids, and poof. And hoping they'll give me Deena's location, or at least the location or locations of operations."

"If you continue to beat yourself up over it, we're going to start the day with a fight after all."

"I've got no right to make decisions based on emotion, to circumvent orders, ignore my duty."

"You're wrong, Eve, on so many counts. First, you're not making this decision based on emotion, or not solely. You're basing it on instinct, experience, and your bone-deep sense of justice."

"Cops don't make the rules."

"Bollocks. You may not write them, but you edit them every day, to suit the situation. You have to because if the law, the rules, the spirit of them doesn't adjust and flex, it dies."

She'd told herself essentially the same a dozen times already. "I didn't tell Peabody all of this, but some. And I said I didn't think I'd have been able to play this the way I am, even five years ago. She said I would have."

"Our Peabody is astute. Do you remember the day I met you?" He reached in his pocket, took out the gray button that had come off the only suit she'd owned before he'd blasted into her life. He rubbed it between his fingers as he watched her.

"You struggled then, with procedure, the book of it. But you had then, and always had, I think, a clear sense of justice. Those two things will always be true. You'll struggle, and you'll see. It's what makes you as much as that badge makes you. Never in my life have I known anyone who has such a basic dislike of people, yet has such unstinting and bottomless compassion for them. Eat your oatmeal."

She took a bite. "It could be worse."

"I've got a 'link conference shortly, and there's a list of messages on your desk."

"Messages?"

"Three from Nadine, with increasing impatience. She demands you contact her regarding confirmation of information she had on Icove—plural—his connection with Brookhollow, and a further connection to Evelyn Samuels's murder in New Hampshire."

"She's right on schedule."

"There's another from Feeney. He's back from New Hampshire and has a report for you. He was circumspect, as I assume your Code Blue demands."

"Good."

"Commander Whitney wants your report, oral and written, by noon."

"You in the market to make admin?"

He smiled, rose. "Some of Ireland will be arriving around two, which, I'm annoyed to admit, makes me nervous. If you're delayed, I'll explain."

She ate, she dressed. Then she picked up her badge and got to work.

She met with Feeney first. In her office, with the door shut. She filled him in on everything, excluding her meeting with Nadine. Should she get busted for that, she'd go down alone.

"Three of them. Doesn't even seem that weird anymore." Feeney munched nuts. "Plays right in with what we found at the schools. Got the records."

He tapped the discs he'd already dumped on Eve's desk. "They ran two systems. One neat and tidy for your audits and checks. Had it fronting the second. Every student given a code number, and the code labeling the testing, the adjustments—"

"Adjustments? Such as?"

"Surgeries. Sculpting. They did some of that crap on eight-year-olds. Sons of bitches. Your basic eye fixes, hearing checks, disease control, that's all on the front, but you got the other on the coded. 'Enhanced intelligence training,' they called some of it. Subliminal instruction, visual and audio. Students earmarked for LC status or what they called 'partnerships' got their advanced sex education. And here's a kicker."

He paused to slurp down coffee. "Deena isn't the only one who ran."

"There are others who got out, the ones who dropped off the data screens?"

"Yeah. Files on their rogues. Got more than a dozen who poofed, after graduation, after 'placement.' She's the only one who got out of the school, but she's not the only one they lost track of. They started implanting the new ones, at birth, with an internal homer. That's after Deena slipped the knot. They've implanted all the current students, too. That was Samuels's brainstorm, and from her notes and records, it was an addition she didn't share with the Icoves."

"Why?"

"She figured they were too close—having one in the family, allowing her too much freedom. They'd lost their objective distance to the project, and to its mission statement. Which was to create a race of Superiors—their term—taking the next logical evolutionary leap through technology: eliminate imperfections and genetic flaws, and eventually mortality. Natural conception, with its inherent risks and questionable success rate, could, and should, be replaced by Quiet Birth."

"Just cut out the middleman, or -woman, so to speak. Then you do made-to-order in a lab. But to pull it off, you need more than technology, you need political punch. You'd have to get laws changed, bans overturned. You have to seed legislatures, state rooms."

"They're working on it. They've got some graduates in key government positions already. In the medical field, in research, in the media."

"That blond bitch on *Straight Scoop*? I bet, I just bet she's one of them. She's got those teeth, you know what I'm saying? Those really big, really white teeth." She caught herself at Feeney's bland stare. "Anyway."

"The estimate was another fifteen years, outside, to have the bans rescinded internationally. Another century to implement others that would ban natural conception."

"They wanted to outlaw sex?"

"No, just conception outside 'controlled environments.' Natural conception means natural flaws. Quiet Birth, they never refer to it as artificial, or cloning—"

"Already got a spin started."

"You got that." He took another hit of coffee. "Quiet Birth ensures human perfection, eliminates defects. It also ensures those who are deemed acceptable parents—"

"Yeah, acceptable. Had to go there."

"Right. Acceptable parents are guaranteed the child will meet their specific requirements."

Eve pursed her lips. "How long does the warranty hold up? What's the return policy?"

He grinned despite himself. "That's a kicker, isn't it? Women will no longer be subjected to the indignities of gestation or child birth."

"Maybe they're on to something."

"Their projections indicate sterilization laws will be in place in another seventy-five years."

Enforced sterilization, Quiet Birth, humanity created and tuned in labs. It was like one of Roarke's science fiction vids. "They think ahead."

"Yeah, but you know, time isn't a real problem for them."

"I can see the hype." She scooped up some nuts. "Want a kid without the hassle? Pick from our designer selection. Meet a sudden and tragic death? Sign up now for our second chance program. We'll preserve your cells and get you going again. Long for a mate who'll fulfill your every fantasy? Have we got a girl for you—restricted to adults only."

"Why be one when you can be three?" Feeney added. "Watch yourself grow up, in triplicate. Gives a whole new meaning to the term 'You're just like your mother.'"

Eve let out a half-laugh. "But no line on the base?"

"Lots of references to the 'nurseries,' but no location or locations given. I've got a lot to go through yet."

"I've got to meet with Whitney, take him what we've got. The schools are secure?"

"Droids on that. Droids guarding clones. It's a fucked-up world. We got legal guardians starting to push. We're not going to be able to keep a net over it for long."

"Oh yeah, we are." She picked up the discs. "Holidays just bog everything up. By the time they get debogged, international law's coming into it. Those 'legal guardians' are in for a world of hurt."

"You got that. Thing is, you got close to two hundred minors between the two schools. So far, only six guardians have made contact. Most are going to turn out to be ghosts."

Eve nodded, added her report disc to the carry file. "How are they going to mix in the mainstream, Feeney? Who's going to take them?"

"That's a problem for a bigger brain than mine."

"You got plans for tomorrow?" she asked him when he rose.

"Whole family's heading over to my son's new house. Did I tell you he upped and moved to New Jersey?" Feeney shook his head. "What're you gonna do. You gotta let them live their lives."

She hit Whitney's office at precisely noon. Her carefully written report was put into his hands, and she gave her oral rundown standing.

"The information on the schools, and all updates pertaining to them, were just given to me by Captain Feeney and are not included in my written, to date. I have his report, sir, and copies of discs containing the data he extracted from Brookhollow's records."

She laid those on his desk.

"There's no progress on locating Deena?"

"None, sir. With the records Feeney located, we'll be able to identify and locate all graduates, excluding those who've left their positions."

"And these nurseries referred to are not, to our knowledge, located on Brookhollow's ground."

"There was no evidence of artificial twinning areas, cell preservation, or the equipment needed found in that location. Sir, by law, the implants carried inside any minor must be removed."

He sat back, folded his hands. "Getting ahead of yourself, Lieutenant."

"I don't think so, Commander." And she'd thought it through very carefully. "Internal implants are in direct violation of privacy laws. In addition, with the evidence in our hands, the law demands that any and all legal guardians or any and all students be investigated and verified. We cannot, legally, turn over any minor to what evidence clearly indicates are individuals who are—or have participated in—falsifying identification records in order to claim false guardianship over said minor or minors."

"You've thought this through."

"They're entitled to protection. Brookhollow can be shut down. Evidence that purports violations of RICO and tax evasion gives local authorities this right until such time as federal authorities review. Sir, when that happens some of those involved in this are going to scatter, and some are going to circle the wagons. Those students are caught in the cross fire, particularly when the government moves into it."

"The government is going to want this handled quietly. The students will be debriefed, and . . ."

And, Eve thought. It was the *and* that worried her. "Quiet may not be an option, sir. I've had multiple contacts from Nadine Furst. She's asking me to confirm or deny several aspects of this investigation, which include the connection of the school, the murder of Evelyn Samuels. To this point, I've refused, given her the standard line about compromising an ongoing investigation, but she's got her ear to the ground."

Whitney kept his eyes level on hers. "How much does she have?"

"Sir, she's already looked hard at the school, from what I can ascertain. She's accessed student records. She's putting it together. Previously, she had done extensive research on Wilfred Icove, Sr., as part of her assignment to cover his death and memorial. At that time she made the connection to Jonah Wilson and Eva Samuels. In fact, sir, she made it before I did. She has resources, and she's got her teeth into this."

He steepled his fingers, tapped them together. "We know that circumspectly leaking information to media sources can and does aid an investigation, preserve public relations, and has its rewards."

"Yes, sir. But Code Blue expressly forbids any and all such leaks."

"Yes, it does. And if any member of this department should violate Code Blue status, for any reason, I would have to assume this individual would be smart enough to cover his or her ass."

"I couldn't say, sir."

"Best you don't. I note, Lieutenant, you did not elect to rescind Detective Peabody's holiday leave."

"No, sir, I did not. Nor did Captain Feeney elect to rescind Detective McNab's. We have Avril Icove on house restriction. The trail is currently cold as pertains to Deena Flavia. Brookhollow is secured, and this investigation is on the point of being passed to federal jurisdiction. It may not be feasible to make that pass comprehensively before Monday. What can be done from this point to that, sir, I can handle myself. It seemed unnecessary and unfair to cancel Peabody's leave."

She waited a moment, but he didn't speak. "Do you want me to have her and McNab called in, Commander?"

"No. As you point out, the government's damn near shut down for the holiday already. We're moving to a skeleton staff administratively this afternoon at Central. You've identified the perpetrators of the homicides under your investigation, and have ascertained the method and the motive. The PA has chosen not to charge one of these perpetrators. And in all likelihood will choose the same if and when Deena Flavia is apprehended. Essentially, Lieutenant, your case is closed."

"Yes, sir."

"I suggest you go home, enjoy the holiday."

"Thank you, sir."

"Dallas," he said as she started out. "If you had to take a wild guess, off the record, just a guess, when would you say Nadine Furst is going to break the story?"

"If I had to guess, sir, off the record, I'd say that Channel 75's going to have a hotter story than the Macy's Thanksgiving Day Parade."

"That would be my guess, too. Dismissed."

THE TRAFFIC WAS MEAN AS A CONSTIPATED
lion. New Yorkers, sprung from work early, were
out to battle their way home to prepare for the holiday, where they'd give thanks for not having to battle their way to
work. Tourists foolish enough to come to the city to see the parade—when, Eve thought, they should stay the hell home and
watch it on-screen—thronged the streets, sidewalks, and air.

Street thieves were rolling in the easy pickings.

Tour blimps were doing extra duty, blasting out the highlights
and landmarks as they lumbered along, bloating the sky and blocking the commuter trams. And thereby, Eve thought, stalling and in-
conveniencing the people who actually lived here who wanted to
get home to prepare for the holiday, and blah blah.

Billboards flashed and sparkled and sang brightly of the sales
that would lure the certifiably insane into the hell-world of the city
stores and outlying malls before their turkey dinners had been fully
digested.

Crosswalks, people glides, sidewalks, and maxibuses were so
mobbed she wondered if there was anyone left outside the borough.

The number of kids on airskates, airboards, zip bikes, and city
scoots told her school was out, too.

There ought to be a law.

The street hawkers were doing brisk business selling their designer knockoff everything, their gray-market electronics, their

wrist units that would keep time just long enough for the hawker to complete the sale, change location, and melt into the city fabric.

Let the buyer damn well beware, Eve thought.

She was stopped at a red when a Rapid Cab in the next lane attempted a maneuver and clipped the rental sedan behind Eve.

She let out a sigh, pulled out her communicator to inform Traffic. Her intention to let her involvement end there was quashed when the sedan's driver leaped out, began to screech and pound her fists on the cab's hood.

That brought the cabbie out, and just her luck, another woman. That had the pushy-shovey starting immediately.

Horns blasted, shouts raged, and a number of sidewalk onlookers began to cheer and choose sides.

She actually saw a glide-cart operator start making book. What a town.

"Hold it, hold it, hold it!"

Both women swung around at Eve's shout, and the driver of the sedan grabbed what Eve identified as a panic button, worn on an ornamental chain around her neck.

"Wait!" Eve snapped, but was blasted by the ear-splitting scream.

"I know what this is, I know what you're doing!" The woman blasted the button again and had Eve's eyes watering. "I know the kind of scams you run in this godforsaken city. You think because we're from Minnesota we don't know what's what? Police! Police!"

"I am the—"

She carried a handbag the size of her home state and swung it like a batter aiming for the fences. It caught Eve full in the face, and considering the stars that exploded in her head, must have been filled with rocks from her home state.

"Jesus Christ!"

The woman used her momentum to spin a full circle and swung at the cabbie. Forewarned, the cabbie nimbly leaped out of range.

"Police! Police! I'm being mugged right on the street in broad daylight. Where are the damn police!"

"You're going to be unconscious on the street in broad daylight," Eve warned, and ducked the next swing as she dug out her badge.

"I *am* the damn police in this godforsaken city, and what the hell are you doing in my world?"

"That's a fake! You think I don't know a fake badge just because I'm from Minnesota?"

When she hefted her purse for another swing, Eve drew her weapon. "You want to bet this is fake, you Minnesota moron?"

The woman, a good one-seventy, stared. Then her eyes rolled back. On the way down, she toppled over on the cabbie, who might have weighed in at one-twenty, fully dressed.

Beside her, as Eve glared down at the tangle of limbs at her feet, the sedan's window opened.

"My mom! She killed my mom!"

She glanced in, saw the sedan was packed with kids. She didn't care to count the number. They were all screaming or crying at a decibel that put the panic button in the shade.

"Oh, bloody, buggering hell." It was one of Roarke's favorites, and seemed most appropriate. "I didn't kill anybody. She fainted. I'm the police. Look." She held her badge to the window.

Inside the weeping and wailing continued unabated. On the ground, the cabbie, obviously dazed, struggled to pull herself from under her opponent.

"I barely tapped her." New York was so thick in her voice an airjack wouldn't have dented it. Eve felt immediate kinship. "And you saw, you saw, she started beating on my ride. And she shoved me first. You saw."

"Yeah, yeah, yeah."

"She clocked you good. You're coming up a bruise there. Damn tourists. Hey, you kids, button it. Your old lady's fine. Slam the lid down, *now*!"

The screams subsided to wet whimpers.

"Nice job," Eve commented.

"Got two of my own." The cabbie rubbed her bruised ass, shrugged. "You just gotta know how to handle them."

They stood a moment, studying the now moaning woman, as the hysteria of horns and voices raged around them. Two uniforms hotfooted it through people, through vehicles. Eve held up her badge.

"Fender bump. Cab against rental. No visible vehicular damage."

"What's with her?" one of the uniforms asked, nodding toward the woman who attempted to sit up.

"Got herself worked up, took a swing at me, passed out."

"You want we should take her in for assaulting an officer?"

"Hell, no. Just haul her up, load her in, and get her the hell out of here. She makes any noises about the bump, or pressing charges, then you tell her she pushes it, she's going to spend Thanksgiving in a cage. Assault with a damn purse."

She crouched down, shoved her badge in the woman's face again. "You hear any of that? You take any of that in? Do us all a favor. Get in that heap you rented and keep driving." Eve rose. "Welcome to godforsaken New York."

She glanced at the cabbie. "You sustain any injuries in the fall?"

"Shit, ain't the first time my ass hit the street. She lets it go, I let it go. I got better things to do."

"Good. Officers, it's your party now."

She got back in her car, checked her face in the mirror as she waited out the next red. The bruise was blooming from the tip of her nose right up her cheekbone to the corner of her eye.

People were a hazard to the damn human race.

Though her face throbbed, she swung by the Icove residence. She wanted another shot at Avril.

One of the police droids opened the door after verifying her ID.

"Where are they?"

"Two are on the second level with the minors and my counterpart. One is in the kitchen. They've made no attempt to leave, and have made no outside contact."

"Stand by," she ordered, and walked through the house to the kitchen.

Avril was at the stove pulling a tray of cookies out of the oven. She was dressed casually in a blue sweater and black pants, and her hair was pulled back in a shining tail.

"Ms. Icove."

"Oh, you startled us." She set the tray down on the stovetop. "We enjoy baking on occasion, and the children love when we have fresh cookies."

"There's only one of you in here, so why don't you drop the trio bit? Why didn't you tell me about the surgeries, the subliminal control programs performed on minors routinely at Brookhollow."

"They're all part of the process, the training. We assumed you already knew." She began to move the cookies from baking tray to cooling rack. "Is this an official, recorded interview?"

"No. No record. I'm off duty."

Avril turned fully, and concern moved into her eyes. "Your face is bruised."

Eve poked a tongue at the inside of her cheek, relieved she didn't taste blood. "It's a jungle out there."

"I'll get the med kit."

"Don't worry about it. When's Deena due to contact you, Avril?"

"We thought she would by now. We're starting to worry. Lieutenant, she's our sister. That relationship is as true for us as if we were blood. We don't want anything to happen to her because of something we did."

"What about something you didn't do? Like telling me where to find her?"

"We can't, unless she tells us."

"Is she working with the others? The others who got away?"

Avril carefully removed her apron. "There are some who formed an underground. There are some who simply wanted to disappear, to live a normal life. Deena's had help, but what she's done—what *we've* done," she corrected, "is what she, and you, I imagine, would call unsanctioned. Deena felt something had to be done, now. Something strong and permanent. We felt, because of what we'd learned about our children, that she was right."

"By this time tomorrow, Quiet Birth will be all over the media. You want it stopped? Public outrage is going to go a long way to making sure it is. Help me clean up the rest of it. Where are the nurseries, Avril?"

"What will happen to the children, the babies, the yet born?"

"I don't know. But I suspect there'll be a lot of loud voices calling for their rights, their protection. That's part of human makeup, too, isn't it? Protecting and defending the innocent and the defenseless."

"Not everyone will see it that way."

"Enough will. I can give you my word I know how this story'll be broken, the tone that's going to be set. The odds of Deena going to prison for her crimes to date are slim to none. Those odds start climbing if she continues her mission now that we've taken steps to stop the project, to shut down the training area."

"We'll tell her, as soon as we can."

"What about the data removed from the private office upstairs?"

"She has it. We gave it to her."

"And the data she removed from Samuels's quarters?"

Surprise flickered. "You're very good at your work."

"That's right, I am. What was in the files she took from Samuels?"

"We don't know. There wasn't time for her to share it with us."

"You tell her if she gets me the data, the locations, I can slam the door on this. She doesn't have to do any more."

"We will, when we can. We're grateful." She lifted a platter already loaded with cookies. "Would you like a cookie?"

"Why not?" Eve said, and took one for the road.

There were kids in the yard. It gave Eve a jolt, especially when one dropped out of a tree like a monkey. He seemed to be of the male variety, and let out war whoops as he raced her car to the house.

"Afternoon!" he said, with an accent much broader and somehow greener than Roarke's. "We're in New York City."

"Okay." He didn't appear to consider it godforsaken.

"We've never been before, but we're having an American holiday. I'm Sean, and we've come to visit our cousin, Roarke. This is his grand house here. Me da said it's big enough to have its own postal code. If you're after seeing Roarke, he's inside. I can show you the way."

"I know the way. I'm Dallas. I live here, too."

The boy cocked his head. She was bad with ages when it came to the underaged, but she figured maybe eight. He had a lot of hair the color of the syrup she liked to drown pancakes in, and enormous green eyes. His face exploded with freckles.

"I thought the lady who lived in the grand house with cousin Roarke was Eve. She's with the garda, and wears a weapon."

"Dallas, Lieutenant Eve." She shoved back her coat so he could see her sidearm.

"Oh, brilliant! Can I—"

"No." She flapped the coat back before his reaching fingers made contact with her weapon.

"Well, that's all right, then. Have you blasted many people with it?"

"Only my share."

He fell into step with her. "Were you in a fight, then?"

"No. Not exactly."

"It looks like someone planted a right one on you. Will you be going with us on the city tour?"

Did the kid do anything but ask questions? "I don't know." Did she have to? "Probably not. I've got . . . things."

"We're after going skating at the place, the outside place. Have you done that already?"

"No." She glanced down, and with hopes of discouraging his inexplicable attachment to her, gave him her flat-eyed cop stare. "There was a murder there last year."

Instead of shock and terror, his face registered delicious excitement. "A *murder*? Who was it? Who killed him? Did the body freeze onto the ice so it had to be scraped off? Was there blood? I bet that froze so it was like red ice."

His questions slapped at her ears like gnats as she quickened her pace to, hopefully, escape into the house.

She opened the door to voices, a great many voices.

And there was a small, human creature of undetermined sex crawling over the foyer tiles. It moved like lightning, and it was heading her way.

"Oh my God."

"That's my cousin Cassie. Quick as a snake, she is. Best close the door."

Eve not only closed it, but backed up against it as the crawling thing made a series of unintelligible noises, quickened the pace, and cornered her.

"What does it want?"

"Oh, just to say hello. You can pick her up. She's the sociable sort. Aren't you, Cassie darling?"

It grinned, showing a couple of little white teeth, then to Eve's horror, got a grip on the bottom of her coat and hauled itself up on its chubby legs. It said: "Da!"

"What does that mean?"

"It means most anything."

A man dashed out of the parlor. He was tall, beanpole thin, with a messy thatch of dense brown hair. He grinned and in other circumstances Eve might have found him charming.

"There she is. I'm on watch, and I take my eyes off the monkey for a split second and she's off to the races. No need to mention this to your aunt Recnic," he said to Sean. Then to Eve's vast relief, scooped the baby up to bounce her casually on his hip.

"You'd be Eve. I'm your cousin Eemon, Sinead's son. It's lovely meeting you at last."

Before she could speak, he'd wrapped his free arm around her, pulled her into a hug, and into intimate proximity with what was on his hip. Tiny fingers shot out, grabbed her hair.

Eemon laughed. "She's a fascination with hair, as she has so little of it yet herself." Competently, he tugged the fingers free.

"Um" was all Eve could think of, but Eemon flashed that smile once more.

"And here you are, barely in your own door and we've got you surrounded. We're already scattered about the place, and sure a beauty of a place it is. Roarke and some of us are in the parlor there. Can I help you with your coat?"

"Coat? No. Thanks." She was able to ease away, peel it off, toss it over the newel post.

"Gran!" Sean raced forward, and some of Eve's tension faded when she saw Sinead step into the foyer. At least this was someone she'd already met.

"You'll never guess it." Brimming with excitement, Sean danced in a circle. "Cousin Eve said there was a *murder* at the skating place. A dead body."

"Murder usually involves a dead body."

It occurred to Eve, quite suddenly, that murder probably hadn't been an appropriate point of conversation. "It was last year. It's okay now."

"I'm relieved to hear it, as there's a considerable horde who's looking forward to taking a spin on the ice." She grinned, stepped forward.

She was slim and lovely. Delicate white skin and fine features, golden red hair and sea green eyes. The same face, Eve thought, her twin—Roarke's mother—would have had if she'd lived.

She kissed Eve's cheek. "Thank you for having us in your home."

"Oh. Sure, but it's Roarke's—"

"Whatever he built, it's the home you've made together. How is it you manage such a place?" She hooked an arm through Eve's as she walked back toward the parlor. "Sure I'd be lost half the time."

"I don't, really. Manage it. Summerset."

"Competent, he looks it. A bit intimidating as well."

"I'll say."

But she'd have handled him better than the sight in the parlor. There were so many of them. Had he said there were so many? They were all talking and eating. More kids—the couple others she'd seen outside. They must have come around the side, she thought. Or just whizzed through, invisibly.

Roarke was in the process of serving an older woman a cup of something. She sat in one of the high-backed chairs, her head crowned with white hair, her eyes strong and blue.

There was another man standing by the fireplace having a conversation with yet another who might have been his twin if you carved away the twenty-odd years she judged came between them. They appeared to have no problem ignoring the two kids who sat at their feet and poked viciously at each other.

Another woman, early twenties, sat in the windowseat, looking dreamily out while a baby of some kind sucked heroically at her breast.

Jeez.

"Our Eve's home," Sinead announced, and conversation trailed off. "Meet the family, won't you?" Sinead's arm tightened like a shackle, and moved Eve forward. "My brother Ned, and his oldest Connor."

"Ah, nice to meet you." She started to extend a hand, and was enveloped in a bear hug by the older, passed to the younger for the same treatment.

"Thanks for having us."

"That's Connor's Maggie there, nursing their young Devin."

"Pleasure." Maggie sent Eve a slow, shy smile.

"Scattered about on the floor would be Celia and Tom."

"She's got a blaster." Since it was the girl who made the whispered observation, Eve assumed it was Celia.

"Police-issue combo." Instinctively Eve laid her hand over it. "It's on stun. Lowest setting. I . . . I'll go up and put it away."

"Somebody punched her face." Tom didn't bother to whisper.

"Not exactly. I should go up, and . . ." Hide.

"My mother." Sinead tugged Eve forward another step. "Alise Brody."

"Ma'am. I'm just going to—"

But the woman got to her feet. "Let's have a good look at you. Don't you feed her, boy?" she demanded of Roarke.

"I try."

"Good face, strong jaw. Good thing if you're going to have to take a punch here and there. So you're a cop, are you now? Running about after murderers and the like. Good at it?"

"Yes. I'm good at it."

"No point in doing something and not doing it well. And your family? Your kin?"

"I don't have any family."

She laughed, hard and long. "God sake, child, like it or no, you've got one now. Give us a kiss here, then." She tapped her cheek. "And you can call me Granny."

She wasn't much of a cheek kisser, but there didn't seem to be any choice.

"I really need to just . . ." Eve gestured vaguely toward the doorway.

"Roarke's told us you're in the middle of an investigation." Sinead gave her an easy pat. "Don't mind us if you need to be doing something."

"I just—a couple of things. For a minute."

She started out, started to take her first easy breath. Roarke caught up with her at the stairs. "How'd you get the bruise this time?"

"Minnesota backhand. I should've done something about it before I got here. I should've locked my weapon in my vehicle." The fact Roarke looked so ridiculously happy only flustered her more. "And I shouldn't have tried to get the kid—the Sean kid—to stop hammering me with questions by telling him there'd been a murder in Rockefeller Center last year."

"Certainly not to the last, as you say murder to a young boy, you've only enticed him." He slid an arm around her waist, rubbed his hand up and down her torso. "You don't have to be what you're not with them. That, at least, I've learned. I appreciate you tolerating this, Eve. I know it's not entirely comfortable for you, and the timing turned out poor."

"It's okay. It's the number of them that threw me off, especially since so many of them are kids."

He leaned in, just to brush his lips over her hair. "Would this be the best time to tell you there are several more having a swim?"

She stopped dead. "More?"

"Several. One of the uncles stayed back, along with a scatter of cousins and my grandfather. They're minding the family farm. But that leaves a number of other cousins, and their children."

Children. More. She wasn't going to panic; what was the point. "We're going to need a turkey the size of Pluto."

He turned her, drew her in, pressed his lips to the side of her neck.

"How you holding up?" she asked him.

"There are so many feelings coming and going inside me." He rubbed her arms, stepped back.

Touching her, she realized, keeping contact maybe because both of them needed it.

"I'm so pleased they're here. I never thought to have any blood of mine under my roof." He gave a quick, baffled laugh. "Never thought I had any I'd care to welcome. And still, I can't catch up with them. I don't know what to make of them, that's God's truth."

"Well, Jesus, there's so many it'd take you a couple years just to sort through and assign names to faces."

"No." But he laughed again, more easily. "That's not what I meant. I'm happy they've come, but at the same time, I can't get used to having them. They . . . I can't think of the word. Flummox is closest. They flummox me, Eve, with their acceptance, their affection. And there's part of me, part that's still the Dublin street rat, that's waiting for one of them to say: 'Roarke, darling, how about a little of the ready, since you've so much to spare.' It's uncalled for, and unfair."

"It's natural. And it'd be easier for you if they did. You'd understand that. So would I." She angled her head. "Am I really supposed to call her Granny? I don't think I can get my mouth around it."

He brushed a kiss on her brow. "It'd be a great favor to me if you'd try. Just think of it as a kind of nickname, that's what I'm doing yet. Now if you need to work, I'll make your excuses."

"Nothing much left for me to do but wait. Mostly waiting now for the media to hit, and the feds to scramble. Departmentally, the case is essentially closed. Except, I was going to ask you to get me schematics, blueprints on the Center. If the base isn't at the school, I'm betting it's there. Maybe auxiliaries scattered. But there's got to be an operation center."

"I can do that. I can get a search started, and check in on it by remote."

"That'd be good. And maybe we could run another search and match on Deena. Use the image from the discs from Brookhollow. Possibly she's got more ID with that basic appearance. Could get lucky."

"But the case is essentially closed," he said dryly.

"Departmentally. But I'm damned if this is getting away from me until I've tried every avenue."

There were more of them. Eve let names and faces buzz through her brain. It seemed there was at least one of every specimen, from seventy years to less than that many days. Every one of them was inclined to talk.

As Sean seemed determined to shadow her every move, she concluded that young boys were much like cats. They insisted on giving their company to those who most feared or distrusted them.

As for her cat, Galahad made an appearance, regally ignored everyone under four feet until he clued in that this variety of human was more likely to drop food on the floor, or sneak him handouts. He ended in a gluttonous coma, tubby belly up under a table.

She escaped the party Roarke escorted out for what Sean called the city tour, and with her head ringing from endless conversation, slipped up to her office.

The case wasn't closed, she thought, until it was closed.

She sat at her desk, ordered the data from Roarke's unit, and studied the blueprints on record for the Icove Center.

There could be others, and Roarke agreed. His computer would continue to search for unrecordeds. For now, she'd work with these.

God knew it was enough.

"Computer, delete all public areas."

She crossed back and forth in front of the screens, studying the accesses, the floor space.

Because it was there. She was sure of it now. It was ego as well as convenience. He'd have based his most personal project in the enormous center that bore his name.

That's where he spent his free time. Those days and evenings never booked. Just a quick walk or drive from home.

"Delete patient areas. Hell of a lot of space yet, for labs, for staff sectors, for administration. Wasting my time, probably wasting my time," she muttered. "Feds'll run through the place like ants in another day, two at the most."

The NYPSD couldn't lock it down. There were civilian patients to consider, privacy laws to wrestle, and the sheer size of the place would make a reasonable search all but impossible.

But the feds would have the juice for it, and the enhanced equipment. Probably should leave this end to them. Let them wrap it up.

"Screw that. Computer, give me lab areas, one at a time, beginning with highest security. Unilab's got some research on this site, some of the mobiles must have pieces of the project," she said quietly when the new image came up. "But how do you find which ones without slapping a lock on all of them?"

Which meant legal wrangles from every country where they had facilities. Civil suits, undoubtedly, from staff and patients.

"They're mobile. Good networking tool, so maybe one of the ways they move graduates from school to placement. Maybe. Nobel Prize, my ass—they're going to be shut down before this is over."

She swung around at the sound in her doorway. Sinead stopped, backing out.

"I'm sorry. I've got myself turned around, and when I heard you talking I came this way. Then when I saw you were working, I tried to slip out again."

"I was just thinking out loud."

"Well now, I do the same all the time myself."

"You didn't go with the others."

"I didn't, no. I stayed back to help my daughter and daughter-in-law with their babies. The lot of them are sound asleep now. And I thought to myself I'd find that beautiful library Roarke showed us earlier, have a book and a little lie down. But I got lost as Gretel in the woods."

"Gretel who?"

"Hansel's sister. It's a fairy tale."

"Right. I knew that. I can show you the library."

"Don't trouble yourself, no. I'll come upon it. You're working."

"Not getting anywhere anyway."

"Could I see, do you think, just for a moment?"

"See what?"

"The police part of things . . . well, I'm not as bloodthirsty as our Sean, but I can't help wondering. And it looks more like a little flat than a cop's office."

It took Eve a moment to translate flat into apartment. "Actually, Roarke kind of replicated my old apartment. It was one of his ways of luring me in, getting me to move in here."

Sinead's smile was very warm. "Clever, and sweet. I find him to be both, though you can see the fierceness in him, the power all over him. Do you wish us all back to Clare, Eve? I won't be offended."

"I don't. Really. He's—" She wasn't sure how to put it. "He's so happy that you've come. He isn't unsure about much, but he's unsure about you—all of you. Especially you. He's still, I guess, grieving, for Siobhan, still guilty on some level about what happened to her."

"The grief's natural enough, and probably good for him. But the guilt is useless, and it's aimed wrong. He was just a baby."

"She died for him. That's how he sees it, and always will. So having you here . . . Especially having *you* here, it means a lot. I wish I knew more how to handle it all. That's all."

"I wanted to come, so much. I'll never forget the day he came, the day he sat in my kitchen. Siobhan's boy. I wanted . . . Oh, look at me, going foolish."

"What's wrong?" The sudden sheen of tears had Eve's stomach knotting. "What is it?"

"I'm here. And there's part of me can't stop thinking how much Siobhan would have loved to be. How proud she'd be of everything her son's accomplished. What he has, what he's become. I wish I could give her even an hour of my life that she could stand here and talk to his wife in their beautiful home. And I can't."

"I don't know much about it, but I'd guess she'd be glad you're here. I guess she'd be grateful you've, well, you've taken him in."

"Just the right thing to say. Thanks for that. I'm happy to stand in as his mother, and sad that my sister had so little time with her child. He has our eyes. Not the color, the shape of them. It comforts me to look in them, and see that part of us. Of her. I hope it comforts him to see her in me. I'll let you get back to work."

"Wait. Wait." Eve held up a hand, let the thoughts circle. "Your brother, the one who's here."

"Ned."

"He went to Dublin looking for your sister and her baby."

"He did." Her mouth set. "And was nearly beaten to death for it. Patrick Roarke." She all but spat it. "The police were no help. We knew she was gone, our Siobhan. We knew but had no proof of it. We tried to find him for her, and nearly lost Ned."

"Hypothetical. If you'd known where to find Roarke when he was a kid, how to get to him, what was happening to him, when he'd been a boy, what would you have done?"

Those lovely eyes went hot and hard. "If I'd known where that bastard had my sister's child, my blood and bone, my heart that he'd murdered? That he was treating that child worse than you'd treat a stray dog, trying to train him to be what he himself was? I swear before God, I'd have moved heaven and earth to get to that boy, to get him away, to get him safe. He was mine, wasn't he? He was, is, part of me."

"Son of a bitch! Sorry," she said when Sinead's eyebrows shot up. "Son of a bitch." And she leaped to her desk 'link. "Lieutenant Dallas. Get me the lead officer on duty," she barked. "Now."

"This is Officer Otts, Lieutenant."

"Determine location of student Diana Rodriguez, age twelve. Immediately. Security check, full parameter. I'm staying linked until you report affirmation on both. Move your ass!"

Sinead's eyes were wide, and for a moment resembled her grandson's. "Well now, you're formidable, aren't you?"

"Stupid, stupid, stupid!" Eve kicked her desk as Sinead looked on. "Her mother. Waiting for her mother. Well, who the hell's her mother? Not that bogus data listing, that's for damn sure. Deena. She meant Deena."

"I'm sure she did," Sinead replied softly.

"Lieutenant, Diana Rodriguez can't be located. I've ordered a full search of the facilities and the grounds. There's been an unreported breach in the southwest wall. I'm checking on that."

"You're checking on it."

Sinead stood, fascinated, as Eve verbally chewed Officer Otts down to bare bone.

20 "I SHOULD'VE THOUGHT OF IT. I SHOULD'VE known." She had to calm down, Eve told herself. Feeney was on his way. They'd use the homer implant. They'd track the kid.

"You have thought of it," Roarke reminded her.

"After it was too late to stop it. To use it. You got a top security facility, you've got seasoned cops, and still she walks in, gets the kid, walks out."

"She'd studied the system, Eve. She'd gotten through it once before. And her motivation was very strong."

"Which makes me more of an idiot for not realizing the kid was key. She wants to stop it. Will kill to stop it. That's what I focused on. But the kid, more than a replica of her. She's *from* her."

"Her child," Roarke agreed. "Obviously knowing Diana existed was one thing. Seeing her, face to face, pushed getting her out to priority."

"She wasn't trained the same as Avril," Eve pointed out. "Look at her records. Languages, electronics, comp sciences, martial arts training, international law and global studies, weaponry, explosives. Light on domestic sciences."

"Training her to be a soldier."

"No, a spook." Furious with herself, she shoved at her hair. "I'm betting spook. Infiltrate covert ops, move up the ranks. But she used her training to get out, stay gone. The murders looked professional because they were. They looked personal because they were."

"They . . . encoded her . . ." Roarke said, for lack of a better term, ". . . to do exactly what she did."

"That's the point, and the point Legal will use if and when she goes to trial. See here? They shifted training with Diana somewhat. Trying to prevent her from repeating the same pattern. Add in more of the domestic sciences, push art appreciation, theater, music. Blah, blah. Maybe, maybe it would've worked. But here comes the intangible. She sees the person she considers her mother."

He was working on the center, manually now, his sleeves rolled up, his hair tied back. "If they've based anything here, they've covered themselves brilliantly. Every area is fully accounted for."

"Okay, forget that, forget it." She pressed her fingers to her temples as if to clear her brain. "This is your place, your base. Where do you put it?"

He pushed back, considered. "Well, you go under. This isn't the sort of thing you can run cleverly in plain sight. That's the most fun, of course, but you can't mix this—or not all of it, not the core of it—in with the work-a-day. Some of the lab business, yes. With the setup they've got, you've plenty of checkpoints there. Certainly you could do alterations, sculpting, the subliminals, whatever you liked in any number of locations. But for the creating, the—for lack of a better word—the gestating. You'd need maximum cover."

"Sublevel, then." She leaned over him, studied the screen. "How do we get in?"

"Are we breaking and entering, darling? You'll get me stirred up."

"Cut it out. Nobody's stirring anything with a houseful of relatives. It's too distracting."

"I'd point out they're all tucked up neatly in bed now, but the idea of breaking into the Center has *me* distracted. First you walk in."

"One of the public areas. Emergency care, maybe. Most vulnerable to security, right?"

"Most likely. And as good as any. Let's have a look."

"You look. I have to think. Would she take her along? Take the kid?"

Because she felt a certain kinship with Deena, she asked herself what she'd do.

"Doesn't seem to follow. You pull her out of what you consider a dangerous situation, you don't dump her into another. But she'd keep her close. She'd put her where she feels it's safe. With Avril, or where Avril can get to her. If so, she has to contact Avril. Already has," she said, nodding to herself. "No move on Diana's legal guardians in Argentina. I'm betting Avril got word to her, and Deena caught another flight back, or aborted the flight she was on."

"Or never went at all," Roarke suggested. "Tossed you a red herring."

"Maybe, yeah, maybe. If she's had contact with Avril, she knows or will know that this whole thing's about to go public. What does she do?"

She paced. "She's got her mission. Most of what she wants is going to come down. But . . ." Case is basically closed, she thought, but was that stopping her from pursuing it, from doing what she could to finish it out herself?

"She'll try to finish it. Hell, they trained her for this kind of work. They imprinted her to succeed. She's already gone rogue from her own underground. She's been in the Center once already that we know of. To kill Icove. But she doesn't attempt to do anything else there."

"She's focused."

"So far," Eve agreed. "Icove to Icove to Samuels. Because even if she does get in, compromises their database, their equipment . . . Hell, even if she blows the place up, key members are still around to put it back together. Take out the human factor first, then the system."

She paced some more. "Don't take the chance on the government getting the system, covertly continuing the program. I put the clock on her with Nadine. She's got to move on it tonight."

She stopped when Feeney came in. He was, if possible, more rumpled than usual.

"I need that tracking."

"I got the data from Samuels's records on the type of implant."

He looked at Roarke. "You got anything in here that'll track an internal?"

"I've got a few things we can put together in the computer lab. There's—"

"Go do that," Eve interrupted, sensing a compu-geek mode coming on. "I'm going to outline the op."

"What op?" Feeney wanted to know.

"I'll catch you up." Roarke started out with him. "Have you ever worked with an Alpha-5? The XDX version?"

"Only in my dreams."

"Your dream's about to come true."

Eve gave them twenty minutes. It was all she believed they could spare.

"Got her?"

"Got something," Feeney told her. "It's being jammed, and it's weak, but it matches the codes of the implant listed for Diana Rodriguez. We wouldn't be getting anything, I can tell you, if we weren't working with the Alpha, 'cause the jam is choice. Might not even get what we got with the Alpha, except the implant's within a mile of our location."

"Where?"

"Moving north. West of here. Got that map ready?" he asked Roarke.

"Just coming. And on."

A city map flashed under the fuzzy blip on-screen. "The Center." Eve set her jaw. "She's less than a block from the Center. She's taking the kid and going in. Feeney, don't lose her. Contact Whitney. You're going to have to convince him to let you break Code Blue on communications. Then you've got to convince him to get us a warrant and a team. Use the kid. Minor civilian, suspected abduction, imminent jeopardy. With or without, I'm going in. I'm changing to Delta frequency on my communicator. Use it only if you get affirmative."

She spun to Roarke. "Let's gear up."

She yanked on her weapon, strapped on a clutch piece. She opted against body armor as it was too bulky and annoying, but hooked on a combat knife.

When Roarke joined her he wore a knee-length leather coat. She had no idea what sort of weaponry and illegal electronics might be under and/or in it.

She'd leave it to him.

"Some couples," he said, "go out to a club for an evening."

Her smile was thin and sharp. "Let's dance."

Diana slipped into the Emergency Room. She knew how to look innocent, and better, knew how to move so that she was all but invisible to most adults. She kept her gaze down, away from their faces as she passed by those waiting to be treated, and those who would treat them.

It was late, everyone was tired or angry or hurt. No one wanted to bother with a young girl who appeared to know where she was going.

She knew because she'd heard Deena tell Avril.

She'd known Deena would come for her. And she'd prepared for it. She'd taken only what she was sure she'd need and put it in her backpack. Food she'd squirreled away for emergencies, her journal discs, the laser scalpel she'd stolen from Medical.

They thought they knew everything, but they hadn't known about the food, the journal, the things she'd stolen over the years.

She was a very good thief.

Deena hadn't had to explain when she'd climbed in the window. She hadn't had to tell her to be quiet, to be quick. Diana had simply taken the backpack out of her hiding place and climbed out with her.

There'd been something she'd scented in the air when they'd gone over the wall. Something she'd never scented before. It was freedom.

They'd talked all the way to New York. That was a first time, too. To talk to someone without having to pretend *anything*.

They would go to Avril's first. Avril would disengage the security, then Deena would go in and disengage the two police droids. It would be fast, she'd promised. Then she would take her and Avril and their children to a safe location where they would wait until she'd finished what she'd set out to do.

Quiet Birth would be shut down. No one would ever be forced to become again.

She'd watched Deena go into the pretty house, watched her come out again only minutes later. And it was righteous.

The safe house was only minutes away, and that was smart. To hide so close. They could stay there, undetected, until it was safe to go somewhere else.

She pretended to go to bed.

She heard Deena and Avril arguing, in low voices. It would be done, Avril said, all they could expect to be done would be done in a day.

But it wasn't enough. Deena said it wasn't enough until she'd killed the root. Until she had, they'd never be free. They'd never be safe. It would never, never stop. She was going tonight, to finish it.

Then she told Avril exactly what she intended to do.

So she waited, and when Deena switched security to yellow to go out the front door, she went out the back.

She'd never been in a city before—that she remembered. Never been completely alone. And it was exhilarating. She had no fear, none. She reveled in the sound of her footsteps on the sidewalk, at the sensation of cool air on her face.

She worked out her route and her movements by treating the whole business like a logic puzzle she was required to solve. If Deena was going to the Center, she was going to the Center.

It wasn't far. Though she was on foot, she could run well, and run long. And Deena would have to park some distance from the target, then take the last two blocks on foot as well. If she timed it right they'd get there simultaneously, then she could follow Deena through the street-level emergency area.

By the time she was discovered, it would be too late—and too illogical—to take her back.

Simple was usually the most successful.

Because she knew where to look, she spotted Deena quickly. She looked ordinary, everything about her from the light brown hair, the jeans, the hooded jacket. The bag she carried looked like one anybody might carry—just a lightweight shoulder sack.

Simple is successful.

She was waiting, but didn't wait long. When an emergency vehicle raced up, Deena used someone's misfortune to slide into the confusion and into the center.

Diana counted to ten and bounded after. But she slowed, cast her gaze down, and moved with what she considered casual purpose once she was inside.

No one bothered her. No one asked what she was doing, and there was another burst of freedom in that.

She cut away toward Ambulatory, then watched from the corner as Deena casually dropped something in a recycler. Deena kept walking, even stopped a harried-looking intern to ask directions. Simple and smart.

When she reached a fork, alarms began to peal. Deena quickened her pace, still not obviously hurrying, and split off to the left. Diana risked a quick look back, saw smoke rolling into the corridor. And for the first time allowed herself a grin.

Deena came to a set of double doors marked STAFF ONLY. She swiped a code card in the slot, and the doors parted. Diana forced herself to wait until they'd started to close, then sprinted forward and nipped inside.

Medical supplies, Diana noted. A lot of them. Some portable diagnostic equipment, secured drug cabinets. Why here? she wondered, then heard the faint swish of a bag being opened. She eased forward, and found herself against the wall with a stunner at her throat.

"Diana!" Deena hissed as she jerked the stunner away. "What the hell are you doing?"

"Going with you."

"You can't. For God's sake. Avril must be out of her mind by now."

"Then we'd better hurry, get done, get back."

"I have to get you out of here."

"You've come too far to turn back now. Someone might come looking soon."

"No, they won't, not where I'm going. And where I'm going, what I'm going to do, you can't have any part of that. Listen to me." She took Diana's shoulders. "There's nothing more important than your safety, than your freedom."

"Yes, there is." Diana's eyes were clear and dark. "Ending it."

Alarms were shrilling when Eve strode into the ER. So were a lot of people, she noted. But then, they would. Panic was as natural to some as breathing.

Health care workers, security guards were trying to restore order.

"This will be her work." Eve badged an ER nurse who barely gave her a glance. "Emergency entrance has to be the weakest point. Add some disorder to the natural disorder an area like this has, and go about your work." She glanced at Roarke. "Let's take a page out of her book."

He looked down at the scanner he'd palmed. "Beacon is a hundred meters northwest. No current movement."

They followed the trail, came to a dense cloud of smoke.

"Sulphur cube," Roarke said when Eve cursed at the stench. "Kids tend to make them up. I did myself. Messy, smelly, and harmless."

Eve sucked in a breath, moved into the stench at a jog. A maintenance worker wearing a safety mask waved her back. She shoved her badge into his visor, then kept going.

"Harmless?" she said on the other side. "How about the hour we're going to have to spend in fumigation?"

"The fact it reeks to heaven and back is part of the fun." He coughed, winced. "When you're twelve. Forty-six meters, east." He adjusted his earpiece. "We've still got her," he told Feeney on the other end. "Got that. He says the commander's authorized backup. Feeney'll be guiding them in using the beacon. As long as he can hold it."

"Just so it's long enough. She couldn't pull this off alone. I don't care how smart she is. She's got to be with Deena."

"Smart timing. Make your sortie not only through the weak spot, but at the weak point in time. Late night, holiday eve. A lot of the sectors would be shut down, skeleton staff. People's minds are on their holiday plans, or they're aggravated they have to work while others are sitting about eating turkey or watching the game on-screen.

"Through there." He nodded toward the secured doors. "Wait. She's heading down."

Eve tried her master through the security slot, and was rejected. "Get us through."

He pulled a device out of his pocket, attached it to the head of the slot, then tapped keys. "Try now."

The second swipe opened the doors.

"Just a different kind of cloning," Roarke told her. "She must've done something similar herself, blocking out any code but her own. Target's still descending."

"From where?" Eve demanded, and Roarke tilted the scanner, aimed it at a floor-to-ceiling drug box. "There's your point. Elevator, has to be."

"How the hell does it open?"

"I doubt it's 'open sesame.'" He ran his fingers over one side while she searched the other. "It can't be manual. Too easy to trigger it accidentally."

Eve gave it a vicious shove and earned a pitying glance from Roarke.

"It's fused to the wall."

"Not on this side," he mused. "Switch."

He worked the opposite side while Eve bellied down to search the floor for any signs. "It's got glides. It's on a glide."

"I'm getting it," he muttered. "I'm getting it."

He pried open a small panel, studied the controls with satisfaction. "Now I've got you."

"Where is she? Where's the kid?"

Rather than respond, he handed her the scanner and got to work on the controls. "Code slot has to be around here somewhere, but this should be quicker than hunting it up."

"She's stopped descending, moving west. I think. We're losing the signal. Hurry."

"There's a certain amount of delicacy required to—"

"Screw delicacy." She whipped off her coat, tossed it aside.

"Pipe down for two bloody seconds," he snapped. Then sat back on his haunches as the cabinet and wall slid left. "You're welcome."

"Sarcasm later, hunt down lair of mad scientists now."

Authorization required,

the security panel announced when they stepped in.

Red sector only.

"Try your master," Roarke suggested.

Incorrect code. Please insert correct code, and stand for retinal scan within thirty seconds . . .

Eve pulled back a fist. Roarke cupped his hand over it. "Don't be hasty, darling." Once again, he affixed his scanner to the panel, tapped keys. "Now."

Incorrect code. You have twenty-two seconds to comply . . .

"Or what?" Eve snarled as Roarke reconfigured.

"Again."

Code accepted. Please step to the rear of the unit for retinal scanning.

"How the hell do we get by that?" Eve demanded.

"She did. I'll wager she's done the work for us."

The scan beam shot out of the panel, but it wavered, then pulsed twice.

Welcome, Doctors Icove. Which level do you require?

"That's good." Roarke's voice held quiet admiration. "That's bloody good. I wonder if this Deena would like a job."

"Return to previous level," Eve ordered.

Level One is requested.

The doors slid shut.

"Fast work on compromising the scan," Roarke commented. "Smarter than disengaging. Bound to be an alarm trigger for that. This way you skip some steps and add the irony. I could find quite the happy position for Deena."

"Damn it, damn it, the signal's gone. Make sure Feeney has the last coordinates."

She drew her weapon as the computer announced arrival at Level One.

She came out low, with Roarke taking high, into a wide, white corridor. The walls were tiled and glossy, the floors gleaming. The only color was from the large red "1" directly across from the elevator, and from the black eyes of the security cams.

"A bit like the morgue," Roarke commented, but she shook her head.

There was no smell of death here. No smell of human. Just empty air pumped and recycled. They headed west.

There were archways right and left, with codes posted, again in red, on the walls.

"Lost Feeney. We're deep." Roarke looked up. The ceiling was white, too, and curved like a tunnel. "And there's probably security plates to block unauthorized communications."

"Have to know we're here." She lifted her chin toward another camera. "Maybe security's automated."

She strained to hear. Voices, footsteps. But there was nothing but the quiet hum of the air system. The tunnel curved, and she saw the remains of a droid scattered over the white floor.

"I'd say we're on the right track." He crouched to study the pieces. "Bug, equipped with stunners and signals."

Because they looked like mutant spiders, they disgusted her on an innate level. And where there was one, there were bound to be more.

Her theory proved out when she heard the scuttle behind her. She turned, fired, as the bug droid rounded the curve. Three more came behind it.

She dropped to avoid the beam, clipped one, and was rolling to her feet when Roarke obliterated the third. The injured one let out a high-pitched signal before she kicked it, full force, and set it smashing against the wall.

"Damn insects."

"That may be. But in a place like this, I'd say they're the first wave." Anticipating, Roarke drew a second blaster. "We can expect worse."

They hadn't made it another ten feet when they got worse.

They came, front and rear, and at quick march, in perfect formation. Eve counted more than a dozen before her back slapped against Roarke's.

Droids, she hoped they were droids. They were identical: stony faces, hard eyes, bulky muscle under what were outdated military uniforms.

But young, oh Christ, no more than sixteen. Children. Just children.

"This is the police," she shouted out. "This is a sanctioned NYPSD operation. Stop where you are."

They kept coming, and as one entity, drew weapons.

"Take them down!"

She'd barely gotten the words out when the explosion rocked her. She flipped her weapon to full stun, fired first in a sweep, then in quick, focused bursts.

Something seared her left arm, brought a quick shock of pain. Even as she fired into one of the oncoming's face, the one behind him fell on her.

She nearly lost her weapon as the force slammed her to the floor. She smelled blood, ripe and fresh, saw the human in his eyes. And without remorse, jammed her weapon against his throat, and fired on full.

His body jerked, convulsed, and was dead before she shoved him aside. She avoided, narrowly, the combat boot that kicked toward her face. Yanking her knife free she drove it up, into the hard belly.

Chips of tile flew, sliced at her exposed skin as she rolled. There was another jolt of pain, a pinch at her hip. She caught sight of Roarke battling two, hand to hand. And more were coming.

She clamped her knife between her teeth, thumbed to maximum blast, and flipped her clutch piece out of its holster. She somersaulted back, took one of Roarke's opponents out, cursed when she couldn't get a clear shot of the other, then began to fire two-handed, like a mad thing, at what remained standing.

Then Roarke was beside her, kneeling beside her. "Fire in the hole," he said, dead calm, and heaved the miniboomer in his hand.

He grabbed her, shoved her back, and threw his body over hers.

The blast punched at her eardrums. She heard, dimly, shards of tile raining down. Then only her own labored breaths.

"Get off, get off!" If there was panic now, it was for him, so she pushed, shoved, rolled him away, then snatched at him again. He was breathing hard now, and he was bleeding.

A gash at the temple, a slice that had gone through the leather of his coat just above the elbow.

"How bad? How bad?"

"Don't know." He shook his head to clear it. "You? Aw, fuck them," he said, viciously, when he saw the blood running down her arm, seeping through her pants at the hip.

"Dings mostly. Mostly dings. Backup's coming. Help's coming."

He looked her dead in the eyes, and he smiled. "And we're just going to sit here and wait for the cavalry, are we?"

The smile loosened the sweaty fist around her heart. "Hell, no."

She pushed herself up, offered him her hand. What she saw around them made her stomach pitch and her heart shrivel. They'd been flesh, blood, bone. They'd been boys. Now they were pieces of meat.

She shut herself down, began to gather weapons. "We don't know what else we've got coming. Take all you can carry."

"Bred for war, that's what they were," Roarke said softly. "They had no choice. They gave us no choice."

"I know that." She shouldered on two combat rifles. "And we're going to exterminate, destroy, decimate what bred them."

Roarke hefted one of the weapons. "Urban War era. If they'd been better equipped and more experienced, we'd be dead."

"You had boomers. You had illegal explosives."

"Well, be prepared, I say." He aimed the rifle at one of the cameras, blasted it. "You've only used one of these a couple of times in sims down in the target gallery."

"I can handle it." She aimed, took out a second camera.

"No doubt."

From their position, Diana looked over her shoulder. "It sounds like a war."

"Whatever it is, it's keeping it off our backs." For now, she thought. She'd estimated she'd had a fifty-fifty chance of coming out of tonight alive. Now she *had* to survive. She had to get it done and get Diana to safety.

But her palms were sweating, and that only lowered the odds. Avril had been the only person she'd ever loved. Now even that strong current was tame beside the tidal wave of emotion that swept her. Diana was *hers*.

Nothing was ever going to touch her child again.

So she prayed that the data she and Avril had accessed was still valid. Prayed that whatever was behind them would wait until she got through the doors marked GESTATION.

Prayed that her courage wouldn't fail.

At last the light glowed green. She heard the swish of air as the doors opened into an airlock. What she saw through it, through the glass, drained the heart out of her.

She made herself go in, made herself look.

While her vision blurred with tears, the monster, dead for a decade, stepped into the white stream of light.

Jonah Delecourt Wilson was fit and handsome and no more than thirty. In his arms he carried a sleeping infant. One hand held a stunner and was pressed to the child's throat.

At his feet was the body of a young Wilfred Icove.

"Welcome home, Deena. It's a testament to both of us that you got this far."

Instinctively Deena pushed Diana behind her.

"Saving yourself?" He laughed, and turned the baby to the light. "Which one of yourself will you sacrifice? Infant, child, woman? Fascinating conundrum, isn't it? I need you to come with me now. We don't have much time."

"You killed your partner?"

"Despite all the work, all the adjustment, all the improvement, he proved to be inherently flawed. He objected to some of our most recent advances."

"Let her go. Give the baby to Diana, and let them go. I'll go with you."

"Deena, understand I've terminated my closest associate, the man—well, men, as there are two more of him equally dead—who shared my vision for decades. Do you think I'd hesitate to kill any of you?"

"No. But it's wasteful to kill the children. It's wasteful to terminate me, when you can take me, use me. Study me."

"But you're flawed, you see. As Wilfred proved to be in the end. And you've cost me beyond measure. All this, about to be destroyed. Two generations of progress. Fortunately, I have countless generations to rebuild it, improve it, then see it flourish. You'll all come with us, and be a part of that. Or you'll all die here."

Another stepped out of the opposite door, and had a sleepy toddler by the hand. "Keep your hands up," he ordered her, and stepped forward.

"Transportation's waiting for those selected," the first told her.

"What of the rest?"

"Once we're clear? Fail-safe. A difficult sacrifice. But we understand difficult choices, don't we? We have all the records we need, and the funds, the time to rebuild. Move forward."

As she did, Diana pulled the laser scalpel out of her pocket and aimed it at the eyes of the one holding the toddler.

The little girl screamed, and began to wail when the man holding her hand convulsed and fell. Equipment exploded as Diana swung the beam. Even as Wilson returned fire, Deena shoved Diana to the ground, then dove toward the younger child. As she scooped the toddler up, spun, she saw Wilson, and the infant, were gone.

"Take her." She pushed the screaming child—her child—into Diana's arms. "You've got to take her. I've got to go after him. Don't argue! Just listen. Someone must be trying to get through—all the fire we heard."

"You're hurt."

"It's nothing." Deena dismissed the burn on her shoulder, and pushed past the pain. "You get her to safety. I know you can. I know you will." She pulled Diana into her arms, kissed her, kissed the little girl. "I have to stop him. Now go!"

She sprang up, ran out of the nightmare, and into hell. Diana struggled to her feet under the weight of the child. She had the laser still, she thought, and would use it again if she had to.

21 THEY SHOULD SPLIT UP. TIME-SAVING, MORE efficient, but the risks were too many. Her hip was a low, continual scream, but Eve kept moving, kept moving.

At every fork, every turn, every doorway, she braced for the next assault.

"There may be little else in direct defense. You'd assume with the level of security above, and the defense here, no one would get through."

Rather than finesse, he blasted the locks on a door marked EX-PERIMENTAL STUDIES.

"Mother of Christ," he whispered as they saw what was in the room.

Medical trays, preservation drawers, tanks filled with clear liquid. In them were fetuses at various stages of development. All were deformed.

"Defects," Eve managed while her blood ran cold. "Failures or defective results, stopped when defects were observed." She studied the electronic charts. Something worse than sickness was clogged in her throat.

"Or they were allowed to develop further, even created this way, so they could be studied. Experimented on," she said, swallowing bile. "Kept viable until they were no longer useful."

There was nothing viable there now. No hearts beat in the room but hers and Roarke's.

"Someone's turned off the life systems here, all of them."

"There have to be more."

"Eve." Roarke kept his back turned to what couldn't be changed, couldn't be saved, and studied the equipment. "They haven't just been turned off. It's on a Yellow Alert."

"Meaning?"

"Might be a level for the security breach, automated as you suggested. Or it could be a holding pattern before Red, and self-destruct."

She spun back. "Deena couldn't have gotten that far ahead of us. She's not that damn good. If . . . Someone else set it."

"Bury it," Roarke said. "Bury all this and everything in it rather than have it taken."

"Can you abort?"

He was working, manually, through his scanner. And shook his head. "Not from here at any rate. This isn't the source."

"Then we find it, and whoever's running this show, before it goes to Red."

She turned, pushed through the doors.

In the white tunnel outside, she saw Diana standing with her hand gripped on a younger, smaller version of herself. In her other hand was a laser scalpel.

"I know how to use it," Diana said.

"Bet." And Eve knew exactly what it felt like to have the beam slice through flesh. "But that would be pretty damn stupid as we've come to get you the hell out of here. Where's Deena? Has she set for self-destruct?"

"He did. She went after him. He had a baby." She glanced at the sniffling toddler. "Our baby sister."

"Who did she go after?"

"Wilson. He had her." She lifted the toddler's hand a fraction. "Her name's Darby. I killed him, one of him, with this. I set it on full and aimed at his eyes. I killed him."

"Good for you. Show me where they went."

"She's tired." Diana looked down at Darby. "I think they gave her something to make her sleepy. She can't run."

"Here." Roarke stepped forward. "I'll take her. I won't hurt her."

Diana studied his face. "I'll have to kill you if you try."

"That's a deal. More help's coming." He hoisted the child.

"They better get here soon. This way. Hurry."

She went off in a sprint.

Eve loped behind her, shoving her back at splits and turns until she'd checked for the all-clear.

The Gestation area was still unsecured. Diana bounded right in, and for the second time Eve had shock slap her back.

The room was full of chambers, interlocked and stacked like the inside of a hive. In each chamber a fetus floated, in thick, clear liquid. A tube—she supposed to replicate an umbilical cord—attached each one to a mass she assumed was artificial placenta. Each chamber held an electronic chart and monitor, recording respiration, heartbeat, brain waves, listing the date of conception, the donor, and the date listed for Quiet Birth.

She jolted back when one of the occupants turned, like an alien fish swimming in strange waters.

There was a record as well of stimuli. Music played, voices, languages, and the continual beat of a heart.

There were dozens of them.

"He killed Icove." Diana gestured to the bodies on the floor. "This Icove anyway. He's going to destroy it."

"What?"

"He's going to take what he wants, the ones he's picked, and destroy everything else. Deena was going to destroy it, but she couldn't." Diana looked around. "We came in here, and we knew she couldn't. She went that way, after him. One of them. There may be more than two."

"Get them out of here." She swung to Roarke. "Get them up and out."

"Eve."

"I can't do both. I need you to do this. I need you to get them to safety. Fast."

"Don't ask me to leave you here."

"You're the only one I can ask." She gave him a long last look. Then she rushed in the direction Deena had taken.

She passed into a lab, what she realized was a conception area. Life was being created in clear dishes in smaller chambers than the ones in Gestation. Electrodes hummed bloodlessly.

Beyond that was a preservation area. Refrigeration units, every one labeled. Names, dates, codes. There were operating rooms, examination cubes.

She came to a door, saw another corridor, another tunnel beyond. Stepping into it, she swept her weapon, and spun back inside as a laser stream blasted the wall.

She swung the rifle off her shoulder—braced it so she could fire it with one hand—and gripped her blaster in the other. She sent out a stream of fire, right, left, right, then dove out, firing right again.

She saw the man fall, white lab coat spreading up like wings. As she rolled, she caught a secondary movement and fired blindly left.

There was a howl, more of rage than pain. She saw she'd winged him, that he was down, crawling, dragging his useless leg behind him.

She let some of her fury free when she reached him, and kicked him hard over on his back.

"Doctor fucking Wilson, I presume."

"You can't stop it, it's inevitable. Hyperevolution, man's right to immortality."

"Save the hype, 'cause it's done. And you're getting mortal all over the place. Where's Deena?"

He grinned, young, handsome. And, Eve thought, completely mad. "Which one of her?"

She heard the scream, desperate and terrified. *"No!"* To save time, she used the butt of her stunner and knocked him unconscious. She yanked off the security card he wore around his neck.

She sprinted toward the sound and caught just a flicker of Deena rushing a doorway.

It was marked STAGE ONE NURSERY, and through the glass Eve could see clear bins holding infants.

When she saw Wilson inside, a weapon jammed under the soft jaw of an infant, she pulled up short. If she blasted inside, he'd kill. Deena possibly, the infant almost certainly.

She scanned the corridor, looking for options. She saw doors marked STAGE TWO NURSERY, and beside them STAGE THREE, and felt her blood curdle.

The kid was tireless, Roarke thought. She'd run, full out, down nearly a mile of corridor. He was only able to keep pace with sheer grit. Blood dripped into his eyes, seeped from his arm, and the little girl he carried weighed like lead by the time they'd reached the elevator.

So did the fear at the base of his stomach.

"I know how to get out. It'll take too long for you to take us all the way, try to get back. Nobody tried to stop us. Nobody's going to bother with us now."

He made his decision fast. "Straight up and out. I have a car outside, ER lot. It's a black ZX-5000."

For an instant, she looked like what she was. A near-teenage girl. "Iced."

"Take her, take the code." He pulled a key card out of his pocket. "Swear to me, Diana, on your mother's life, that you'll go to the car, get in the car, lock it. You'll stay there, both of you, inside it until we come."

"You're bleeding a lot. You're bleeding because you tried to stop it, you tried to help. And she sent you with us, like Deena sent me with Darby." She reached out for the child. "So I swear, on Deena's life, my mother's life, I'll lock us in the car and wait."

"Take this." He gave her the earpiece. "When you're safely outside, you put this on, and tell the man on the other side where we are, how to get where we are."

He hesitated, then gave her a stunner. "Don't use that unless you have no choice."

"Nobody's trusted me before." She jammed the stunner in her pocket. "Thank you."

When the door shut, he began to run.

Eve bellied over to Stage Two, used the card she'd taken to open the doors.

Inside were five cribs. The children in them—hell, what did she know? A few months, a year. Even in sleep they were monitored.

As were the children she could see beyond—Stage Three—who slept on narrow cots in a kind of dormitory style. Fifteen, Eve counted.

The doors connecting the sections required no card. At least not from the Stage Two area. She could see Deena inside One, her hands in the air. Her mouth was moving. Eve didn't need to hear the words to know they were pleas. It was all over her face.

Get him to put the kid down, Eve thought. Get him to lower the stunner, one damn inch for one damn instant. It's all I need.

She nearly took her chances, but saw the speaker system by the door. Engaging it, she listened.

"There's no point. There's no point. Please, give her to me."

"There's every point. Over forty years of work and progress, and hundreds of Superiors. You were a great hope, Deena. One of our finest accomplishments, and you threw it away. For what?"

"For choice, of living, of dying. I'm not the only, I'm not the first. How many of us have self-terminated because we couldn't go on existing, knowing what you'd made of us."

"Do you know what you *were*? Street garbage, a nit, nothing more. Already in pieces when they brought you to us. Even Wilfred couldn't put you back together. We saved you. Again and again and again. We improved you. Perfected you. You exist because I *permitted* it. That can end now."

"No!" She jerked forward when he jammed the stunner harder under the baby's jaw. "It won't gain you anything. It's over, you know it's over. You can still get away. You can still live."

"Over?" His face was bright with excitement. A fever. "Barely begun. In another century what I've created will *be* existence for the human race. I'll be there to see it. Death is no longer an obstacle for me. But for you . . ."

He swung the stunner up, and Eve was through the door. Before she could fire, he swung the baby up like a shield, and dove with it.

She hit the floor, rolled to avoid a stream that blasted the doors behind her. The air burst with the wails of infants, the shriek of alarms.

"This is the police." She shouted it over the din, and bellied to cover. "This facility is shut down. Throw out your weapon, put the kid down."

The comp unit just over her head shattered with another blast.

"Well, that didn't work," she muttered.

She couldn't return fire, not when he had the infant. But she could draw it, she decided, and gauged the distance to the doors leading to the corridor.

She saw a movement outside the glass, wasn't sure whether to curse or cheer when she saw Roarke position himself.

"You're surrounded, Wilson. You're done. I've already taken out two of you personally. You want to make it three, that's up to you."

He let out a scream, and as she gathered herself to charge the far doors, she saw the child he'd held fly up. She had an instant to jerk her body around, but Deena was already leaping into the open.

Wilson's blast hit her in midair, just as her arms snatched the child.

"You'll die! And suffer and sicken and stumble your way through what pathetic lives you have. I would have made men gods. Remember who ended it, remember who damned you to mortality. Initiate fail-safe!"

He rose, his face alive with a mad fervor. When he aimed at Eve, she fired even as Roarke slammed through the doors. Wilson went down between their blasts.

Fresh alarms shrilled, and a passionless computerized voice began to drone.

Warning, warning, fail-safe has been initiated. You have ten minutes to safely evacuate these facilities. Warning, warning, these facilities will self-terminate in ten minutes.

"Perfect. Can you stop it?" she demanded of Roarke.

He scooped up a small device beside Wilson's body. "This is just a trigger. Single mode. I'd need to find the source before I could begin to override."

"Can't."

Eve rushed to where Deena lay on the floor, still holding the screaming baby. "We'll get you out."

"Get her out. Get the children out. Can't override. Multiple sources and levels. Not enough time. Please get them out. I'm already gone."

"Police and medical assistance is on the way." Eve glanced back toward Roarke. "I hear them coming. Kids in the adjoining rooms. Get them out."

"Take her, please take her." Deena struggled to pass the baby to Eve.

She fumbled to hitch the infant under one arm. And saw Deena was right. She was gone. Where her clothes had been singed by the blast, burned skin was exposed, some to the bone. Blood was already seeping out of her ears, her mouth. She'd never make it out the doors.

"Diana, and the little one?"

"Safe." Eve looked at Roarke for confirmation. "They got out."

"Give them to Avril." Deena clamped a hand on Eve's arm. "Please. Please, God, give them to Avril, let them go. Deathbed confession. I'm giving you a deathbed confession."

"No time. Roarke."

She pushed the baby at him. "Get those kids out. Now."

Warning, warning, all personnel must evacuate. This facility will self-destruct in eight minutes.

"I killed them all. Avril knew nothing about it. I killed Wilfred Icove, Sr. Wilfred Icove, Jr. Evelyn Samuels. I intended . . . Oh God!"

"Save it. You're right, you're gone. I can't help you." She heard children crying, screaming, feet pounding, and kept her eyes on Deena's face. "We'll get everyone out."

"Gestation." Deena gritted her teeth, hissed against the pain. "If you take them out of the tanks, unhook the tanks, tamper . . . they'll die. They can't . . ." Blood slid out of her eyes like tears. "They can't be saved. I was going to do what Wilson did, knowing that. But I couldn't. You have to leave them, save the rest. Please let them go. Avril . . . She'll take care of them. She—"

"Are there any others, in this facility?"

"No. I pray no. Just care-droids this time of night. Wilson . . . Wilson must've shut them down. Killed Icove replicas. Son of a bitch. I'm going to die where I was born. I guess that's okay. Tell Diana. Well, she'll know. The little one . . ."

"Darby. Her name's Darby."

"Darby." She smiled even as her eyes began to film over.

Her hand slid off Eve's arm.

Warning, warning, this facility will self-destruct in seven minutes. All personnel must evacuate immediately.

"Eve, the nurseries are cleared out. The response team's taking the children up. We have to move. Now."

Eve got to her feet, turned. She saw Roarke still had the infant. "The Gestation area. She said it couldn't be tampered with or they'd die. Prove her wrong."

"I can't." He gripped her arm, pulled her out. "The life support, the artificial wombs, are integral to the system. If it's disengaged, the oxygen's cut off."

"How can you—"

"I looked. I've already checked. If there was time, there might be a way to bypass. There isn't. We couldn't get them out, Eve, we couldn't get the chambers out and up in time, even if we could bypass. We can't save them."

She saw the horror of it in his eyes, the same cold horror that was balled in her gut. "We just leave them here?"

"We save her." He shifted the baby awkwardly, and with his hand gripping Eve's began to run. "We move now, or we're all buried here."

She ran, past the husks of what she'd killed, through the shattered bodies of boys who'd been created to kill. She smelled death, and her own blood, Roarke's blood.

They'd shed it, and still it hadn't been enough.

Nothing stops the vicious and the ugly, she remembered. She'd said it herself.

Warning, warning, red line for safe evacuation has been reached. All remaining personnel must evacuate immediately. This facility will terminate in four minutes.

"I wish she'd shut the fuck up."

She kept up the limping run. Her hip was now an insane symphony of pain. A glance at Roarke showed her his face was bone-white and clammy under the smears of blood.

She saw the elevator ahead, its doors shut.

"Can't leave them unsecured." Roarke's voice was labored, and Eve was nearly as horrified when he shoved the baby at her as she was with the countdown. "Wasn't time to augment the security and keep them open." Instead he swiped a card, once, twice.

"Buggering hell. Gotten sweaty, bloody, too. Won't read." He dug out a handkerchief and began to polish it off while under his breath he cursed in Gaelic.

Hooked in her arm, the baby screamed as if she were pounding it with a hammer.

Red line plus sixty seconds. This facility will terminate in three minutes.

He swiped the card a third time, and they leaped inside. "Street level," he shouted, then cursed again when Eve pushed the baby at him. "What? You've got her."

"No, you've got her. I'm in charge of this op."

"Screw that. I'm a bloody civilian."

Eve tapped a hand on her weapon. "You even try to give it back to me, I'm stunning you. Self-defense."

Red line plus ninety seconds. All personnel should be at maximum safe distance.

"Cutting it close," Eve mumbled as sweat rolled down her back. "Is there any other way?"

"This thing could go faster. This son-of-a-bitching thing could really go faster." She gritted her teeth when the warning announced red line plus two minutes. "We're still in this when it blows, it'll take us out, too, right?"

"Likely."

She stared at the controls as if her wrath could speed things up. "We couldn't have gotten them out. No matter what we'd done."

"We couldn't, no." He rested his free hand on her shoulder.

"You brought that one so I'd have to leave the rest. So I'd have to go, get her out. So I'd have something tangible to make me move my ass."

"I also figured you'd be the one holding her on the way out, while she's screaming my eardrums ragged."

Terminate in thirty seconds.

"If we don't make it, I love you and blah, blah, blah."

He laughed, and shifted so his arm wrapped around her shoulders. "I'll say the same. It's been a hell of a ride so far."

When the final countdown commenced, she reached up, gripped his hand.

Terminate in ten seconds, nine, eight, seven . . .

The doors opened. They flew through them together. She heard the count go down to three as the doors secured behind them.

She snatched her coat from where she'd tossed it, and bolted through the room with him.

There was a rumble under her feet, a wave of vibration. She thought of what was below her, in tanks, in hives. Then pushed it away, shoved it back. Her nightmares would begin soon enough to go back there now.

She shrugged back into her coat. If her hands shook, he was the only one who knew it. "This is going to take me a while."

He glanced toward the line of cops.

"Take your time. I'll be outside."

"You can pass that one onto one of the uniforms. We'll have CP here shortly to deal with the minors."

"I'll be outside," he repeated.

"Go get treated," she called after him.

"In this place? I don't think so."

"Got a point," she replied, then moved forward to do the job.

Outside, Roarke went directly to his car. Only more relief washed over him when he saw Diana lying on the backseat with the younger girl curled against her.

He opened the door, crouched down when Diana's eyes opened. "You kept your word," he said.

"Deena's dead. I know."

"I'm very sorry. She died saving . . . saving your sister." He held out the baby when Diana opened her arms. "She helped save the children."

"Is Wilson dead?"

"Yes."

"All of him."

"All we found, yes. The facilities are gone. Destroyed. The equipment in them, the records, the technology."

Her eyes were clear, level. "What are you going to do with us now?"

"I'll take you to Avril."

"No, you can't. Then you'll know where we are. She won't stay if you know, and we need time before we go again."

She was a child, he thought, with two other children. Yet in some ways, she was older than he. All of them, older than he. "Can you get to her, with them, on your own?"

"Yes. Will you let us go?"

"It was all your mother asked, the last thing she asked. She thought of you, of what would be best for you." As his own mother had, he thought. His mother had died doing what she'd thought best for him. How could he not honor that?

She got out, her hand gripping the younger child's, the baby in the crook of her arm. "We won't forget you."

"Nor I you. Be safe."

He watched them until they were out of sight. "Well, God-speed," he whispered, then took out his 'link and contacted Louise.

It was nearly two hours before Eve joined him. She took one look at the mobile clinic beside his car and hissed. "Look, I'm tired. I want to go home."

"Soon as I do a little triage, you're off." Louise pointed toward the mobile. "Unfortunately I don't have fumigation facilities on board. The pair of you reek."

It was coming onto dawn. Rather than waste more time, she sat in the mobile. "No tranqs, no blockers. It's bad enough without me getting goofy." She gave Roarke a hard look, but he merely smiled.

"I don't mind the tranq myself. Smooths out nasty edges."

"He zoned?" she asked Louise, and hissed as the wand rolled over her arm wound.

"A little bit. Mostly just exhausted. Lost considerable blood, too. Bad gash in his arm, and with that and the head wound, I don't know how he managed to stay upright this long. Same for you. I'd rather take you both into the clinic."

"I'd rather be in Paris drinking champagne."

"We'll go tomorrow." Roarke stirred himself enough to sit beside her.

"You've got a houseful of Irish relatives."

"Right you are. We'll stay home and get drunk instead. My Irish relatives should appreciate a good drunk. If not, well, they're no true relations of mine, are they?"

"Wonder what they're going to think when we get home, stink-ing, bloody, and beat to shit. God damn it, Louise!"

"Easier on you with a tranq. You called it."

Eve blew air out her nose, then sucked it in to brace for the next medical onslaught. "I'll tell you what they'll think. That we lead full and interesting lives."

"I love you, darling Eve." Roarke nuzzled a kiss at her throat. "And blah, blah, blah."

"More than a little zoned," was Eve's opinion.

"Go home and get some sleep." Louise sat back. "Charles and I will come early. I'll give you another treatment."

"The fun never ends." She hopped out, didn't quite disguise the wince at the jar on her injured hip.

"Thank you, Louise." Roarke took her hand, kissed it.

"All in a day's work. I live a full and interesting life, too."

Eve waited until the mobile pulled out. "Where's Diana, and the other two?"

He looked toward the sky, noted the stars were going out. "I couldn't say."

"You let them go."

His eyes were tired, but perfectly clear when they met hers. "Did you intend to do differently?"

She didn't speak for a moment. "I contacted Feeney to request he shut down the tracker. No need. When the place blew, the homers disengaged. Officially, Diana Rodriguez is dead. Lost in the explosion that took place in the Quiet Birth facilities. There's no record of the other two minors. There won't be."

"And no one exists, officially, without records."

"There's technology for you. Avril Icove is missing. I have a deathbed confession that clears her of all involvement with the homicides under my jurisdiction. Even without it, the PA doesn't intend to charge. It would be an inefficient use of departmental time and funds to attempt to locate her, at this time. Federal authorities may think different."

"But they won't find her."

"Unlikely."

"How much heat will you take over this?"

"Minimal. Nadine's going to blast this out of the water in a couple hours. What was in there, belowground?" She turned to study the center. "It's gone. Governmental authorities may be able to identify and track some of the clones, but most of them will blend into the mainstream. They're smart, after all. Far as I can see, it ends here."

"Then let's go home." He cupped her face, kissed her brow, her nose, her lips. "You and I, we've a lot to be thankful for."

"Yeah. Yeah, we do." She gripped his hand once, hard, as she had when death had been seconds behind them.

Then she let it go to walk around the car, slide in beside him.

The world wasn't a perfect place, and never would be. But just now, watching dawn come over her godforsaken city, it seemed like a damn good deal.